THE LOEB CLASSICAL LIBRARY

EDITED BY

T. E. PAGE, LITT.D.

E. CAPPS, PH.D., LL.D.   W. H. D. ROUSE, LITT.D.

HORACE
SATIRES, EPISTLES, ARS POETICA

HORACE
SATIRES, EPISTLES
AND ARS POETICA

WITH AN ENGLISH TRANSLATION BY
H. RUSHTON FAIRCLOUGH
PROFESSOR OF CLASSICAL LITERATURE IN STANFORD UNIVERSITY
CALIFORNIA

293

LONDON: WILLIAM HEINEMANN LTD
NEW YORK: G. P. PUTNAM'S SONS
MCMXXIX

First printed 1926
Revised and reprinted 1929

ALFREDO BAKER
TORONTONENSI
PROFESSORI EMERITO
AMICITIAE GRATIA

PREFACE

As is the case with many other volumes in the Loeb
Classical Library, it has been found necessary to
make this book something more than a mere trans-
lation — something approaching a new edition of
the poet.

Each of the *Satires* and *Epistles* has been provided
with its own Introduction, and, inasmuch as the
poet's transitions are not seldom rather abrupt, and
often it is no easy matter to re-establish the con-
nexion, a careful effort has been made to indicate
the sequence of thought. Numerous allusions have
been explained in the notes or Index; many dubious
passages have been discussed, however briefly, and
the Latin text itself has been scrutinized in every
detail. All important variant readings have been
duly registered and considered, and the results of
both old and recent scholarship have been utilized
in translation or interpretation.

Acknowledgements are due to the general editors
of the series, one of whom, Dr. T. E. Page, has read
my manuscript carefully and offered many a timely

and wise suggestion. Some explanations given of puzzling passages are due to him.

H. R. F.

Harvard University,
  December 15, 1925.

In preparing for a reprint of this volume, I take the opportunity of thanking all who have offered me helpful criticism, especially Professor Charles N. Smiley of Carleton College, and Professor B. O. Foster of Stanford University.

H. R. F.

February 4, 1929.

CONTENTS

CONTENTS

x

INTRODUCTION

A. Chronology of the Poems

THE First Book of the *Satires* is the first work which
Horace published, though it is possible that some of
the *Epodes* were composed before any of the *Satires*.
In *Sat.* i. 10. 45 Horace refers to Virgil's *Eclogues*,
which were published in 37 B.C., while the introduc-
tion to Maecenas (*Sat.* i. 6. 54 ff.) is commonly
assigned to 38 B.C. Allowing some time for the
friendship between the poet and statesman to mature,
and for the general interest, referred to in *Sat.*
i. 6. 47, to be aroused, and keeping in view certain
passages in *Satires* ii. (*e.g.* 6. 40), we may claim
35 B.C. as the probable date of the publication of
Book I. At this time the poet was in his thirtieth
year.

In 33 B.C. Horace received from Maecenas the gift
of his Sabine farm, which figures so prominently in
Book II. The Sixth Satire of this book makes several
allusions to political events. In l. 53 mention is
made of the Dacians, who in the struggle between
Octavian and Antony offered themselves first to one
leader and then to the other. At this time Octavian
was necessarily absent from Rome, and in l. 38
Horace speaks of the administration of home affairs
as being in the hands of Maecenas. After the battle

of Actium (31 B.C.) public lands were assigned to the disbanded soldiers (l. 55). On the other hand the absence of any allusion to the closing of the temple of Janus or to the celebration of a triple triumph shows that Book II. appeared before 29 B.C. We may therefore claim 30 B.C. as the year of its publication.

In the interval between the appearance of the *Satires* and that of the *Epistles*, Horace published the *Epodes* (29 B.C.) and Books I.-III. of the *Odes* (23 B.C.). The next work to appear was Book I. of the *Epistles*, the last verse of which (*Epist.* i. 20. 28) gives the consulship of Lollius as the date of writing. This would naturally imply that the book was finished in 21 B.C., but allusions to later events, such as the close of Agrippa's Cantabrian campaign, the restoration of the standards taken from Crassus (*Epist.* i. 12. 26 ff.), and the triumphal progress of Tiberius through the East (*ib.* i. 3. 144), show that the book was not published before the following year (20 B.C.).

The three *Literary Epistles* which remain are often classed together as the three *Epistles* of Book II., but the MSS. and Scholia recognize only two *Epistles* in that Book, giving the third an independent position and a special name as *Ars Poetica*. Of the two the Second undoubtedly precedes the first in point of composition. It is addressed to Florus, to whom *Epist.* i. 3 had been sent, and who is still absent from Rome in the suite of Tiberius. The occasion for this absence need not be the same as for the earlier letter, yet in view of Horace's renunciation of lyric poetry (*Epist.* ii. 2. 65 ff.), this Epistle can hardly have been written in the years when the *Carmen Saeculare* and *Odes* iv. were produced (17–13

INTRODUCTION

B.C.). It was therefore, in all probability, written about 19–18 B.C.

The introduction to *Epist.* ii. 1 gives the main reason for believing that the *Epistle to Augustus* was written after both the *Epistle to Florus* and the *Ars Poetica*. Moreover, there are several passages in it which indicate a connexion between it and Horace's later lyrics. Thus ll. 132–137 refer unmistakably to the *Carmen Saeculare* of 17 B.C., and ll. 252–256, as Wickham has pointed out, show certain correspondences with the political *Odes* of Book IV., which was published in 13 B.C.

In the MSS. the *Ars Poetica* appears after either the *Carmen Saeculare* or *Odes* iv. Its present position is due to sixteenth-century editors, and Cruquius (1578) first called it the Third Epistle of Book II. It was perhaps published by Horace independently, while Augustus was absent in Gaul, 16–13 B.C., but the fact that it reflects so much of the influence of Lucilius would indicate a still earlier date of composition.[a] It is not certain who the Pisones (a father and two sons) addressed in it are. According to Porphyrio, the father was L. Calpurnius Piso, *praefectus urbi* in A.D. 14. He was born in 49 B.C. and became consul 15 B.C., but could hardly have had grown-up sons several years before Horace's death. It is more likely that Piso *pater* was Cn. Calpurnius Piso, who, like Horace, fought under Brutus at Philippi and was afterwards consul in 23 B.C. He had a son, Gnaeus, who was consul 7 B.C., and another, Lucius, who was consul 1 B.C.

---

[a] See Fiske, *Lucilius and Horace*, pp. 446–475. According to Professor A. Y. Campbell, " the *Ars Poetica* was written at some time between 23–20 B.C. inclusive " (*Horace*, p. 235).

INTRODUCTION

B. Earlier History of Satire

The great literary critic Quintilian proudly claims Satire as a purely Roman creation, *satira quidem tota nostra est* (x. 1. 93). This kind of literature had originated in a sort of rustic farce, the mixed character of which had given it its name. As *lanx satura* was a dish filled with various kinds of fruit offered to the gods, and *lex satura* was a law which included a variety of provisions, so, in the literary sphere, *satura (sc. fabula)* was a miscellaneous story, which was originally presented as a dramatic entertainment.[a] After the introduction of the regular drama from Greece, the dramatic *saturae*, like the mimes and the *Atellanae*, survived as afterplays (*exodia*),[b] but the *saturae* of Livius Andronicus and Naevius were probably of the earlier, dramatic type.

Different from these were the *saturae* of Ennius and Pacuvius. These, to be sure, were miscellaneous both in subjects and in metrical forms, but they were composed for reading, not for acting. The *Saturae* of Ennius included the *Epicharmus*, a philosophic poem ; the *Euhemerus*, a rationalistic treatment of mythology ; the *Heduphagetica*, a mock heroic poem on gastronomy ; the *Sota*, in the Sotadean metre ; and the *Scipio* and the *Ambracia*, which dealt with contemporary persons and events. Of the Satires of Pacuvius we know nothing, and

---

[a] It is here assumed that the account given of the origin of the drama in Rome by the historian Livy (vii. 2), though somewhat confused, is essentially correct. Certain writers, however, notably Leo and Hendrickson, have regarded Livy's account as pure fiction.

[b] *i.e.* comic scenes performed separately after tragedies.

those of Ennius were quite overshadowed by his epic
and dramatic poems.

The writer uniformly recognized as the founder of
literary Satire (*inventor*, Horace, *Sat.* i. 10. 48) was
Gaius Lucilius, who lived from 180 to 103 B.C. He
was of equestrian rank and a man of wealth, the
maternal uncle of Pompey the Great and a member
of the Scipionic circle. His thirty books of *Saturae*,[a]
written partly in trochaics, elegiacs and iambics, but
mostly in hexameters, handled a great variety of
topics. Fragments, numbering over 1300 verses,
have been preserved, and are accessible in the splen-
did edition by F. Marx (2 vols., 1904, 1905), which
has supplanted all earlier collections. A study of
these throws a flood of light upon the important
question of the relation of Horace to his model in
the satiric field, and we are fortunate in having a
very thorough survey of the subject in *Lucilius and
Horace, a study in the Classical Theory of Imitation*,
by Professor George Converse Fiske,[b] to which every
future editor of Horace will be much indebted, and to
which, therefore, we must often refer.

The Satires of Lucilius were largely autobio-
graphical,

> . . . quo fit ut omnis
> votiva pateat veluti descripta tabella
> vita senis.
>
> (Horace, *Sat.* ii. 1. 32 ff.),

and if they had survived intact we should to-day have

---

[a] Cited thus by grammarians but called by Lucilius him-
self *ludus ac sermones* (fr. 1039). Note that the latter term
sermones (or " Talks ") was adopted by Horace in his turn
as the title of his *Satires*.

[b] Published in University of Wisconsin Studies in Lan-
guage and Literature, Madison, 1920.

as complete a picture of the poet's life and times as any modern diarist has given of his. Lucilius portrayed not only himself but also his friends and foes, and at the same time discoursed upon the follies and vices of his day, as well as upon philosophy, religion, literature, and grammar ; upon travels and adventures ; upon eating and drinking, and the many incidents of daily life.

In his criticism of others Lucilius was unrestrained, and it is because of this παρρησία or freedom of speech that Horace makes him dependent upon the Old Comedy of Athens (*Sat.* i. 4. 1 ff.). Lucilius does indeed show an inexhaustible power of invective, but in this he harks back, not so much to Aristophanes, as to " the vivid and impromptu utterances of the Cynic and Stoic popular preachers." [a] He was, it is true, familiar with the whole range of Greek literature, and makes citations from Homer, Aristophanes, Euripides, Menander, and Plato. He alludes to Socrates and Aristippus, and draws freely upon the Academy and later exponents of Greek philosophy. Fiske aims at showing that " Lucilian satire is the product of a highly sophisticated Hellenistic environment combined with the Italian *penchant* for frank, vigorous, dramatic expression." In his diction, Lucilius was quite unlike Terence, that *puri sermonis amator*, for " Gallic words, Etruscan words, Syrian words, and words from the Italic dialects, Oscan, Pelignian, Praenestine, Sardinian, and Umbrian, even bits of Greek dialect slang, are found in his pages." [b]

We must remember both the plebeian origin of satire, and the chief characteristics of Lucilius, as well as the ancient mode of adhering closely to

[a] Fiske, p. 128.   [b] Fiske, p. 116.

literary types, if we are to understand some of the features of later satire. Thus its excessive coarseness, especially in Juvenal, is largely a survival from early days, and this element in Horace's *Satires*, strictly limited to Book I., is due to our poet's following here too closely in the footsteps of Lucilius. So, too, the fierce invective, which Juvenal has taught us to regard as the main feature of satire, is a distinct inheritance from Lucilius.

C. Relation of Horace to Lucilius

In the *Satires* and *Epistles* of Horace, it is easy to trace an interesting development in tone and character from the more peculiarly Lucilian compositions to those that are more distinctly independent and Horatian. Thus in the First Book of *Satires*, the Seventh, which sketches a trial scene before the court of Brutus, is to be closely associated with a satire in Book II. of Lucilius, where Scaevola is accused by Albucius of peculation in the province of Asia. In the Second, dealing with a repulsive subject, not only " the satiric moulding of the material," but even the vocabulary is " distinctly Lucilian." [a] Both of these poems, as well as the Eighth, were probably composed before Horace's introduction to Maecenas. The Eighth, however, is the only one of this First Book which shows no obvious connexion with Lucilius. It is a Priapeum—a late *genre* in Roman literature—but treated in satirical fashion.

The famous Fifth and Ninth Satires, though giving personal experiences of the writer, are nevertheless modelled somewhat closely upon Lucilius. Of the

[a] Fiske, pp. 271, 272.

Fifth Porphyrio says, "Lucilio hac satyra aemulatur Horatius," and Horace's encounter with the bore will lose none of its interest, even when we learn that the Sixth Book of Lucilius contained a similar satire, which was his direct model.[a] The First Satire handles two themes which were much discussed in the popular philosophy of the Stoics, viz., discontent with one's lot and the love of riches. Both of these figured in more than one satire of Lucilius, the scanty fragments of whose Nineteenth Book furnish sufficient material to enable Fiske to reconstruct the particular Satire which was Horace's model here.[b]

In the remaining Satires of Horace's First Book, viz., the Third, Fourth, Sixth and Tenth, Horace is on his defence against hostile criticism. He makes a plea for satire as a literary form and tries to prove that it should not be disliked because of its subject matter. It is therefore not without reason that he places the Third next to the Second in the collection, so as to stand in direct contrast with it, for while the Second is coarse, brutal, and extremely personal,[c] the Third, dropping all abuse and invective, shows a kindly and genial tone which must tend to disarm all criticism. The Fourth and Tenth Satires still further show that the poet is casting off the spell of Lucilius. He is ready to criticize the very founder of the satiric *genus scribendi* and to set up standards of his own. "In fact," as Fiske says,[d] "Horace's Fourth satire may be regarded as an aesthetic and

---

[a] Fiske, p. 335.   [b] Fiske, pp. 246, 247.

[c] "From no other Satire, as the commentators point out, do we have such an extensive portrait gallery of contemporaries" (Fiske, p. 270).

[d] Fiske, p. 278.

INTRODUCTION

ethical analysis of the Lucilian theory of satire,"
while the Tenth, composed under the smart of
hostile criticism, is a vigorous polemic directed, not
so much against Lucilius himself, as against those
critics of Horace's own day, who upheld the standards
or lack of standards illustrated by the Satires of
Lucilius. It is "only in the general recognition of his
predecessor as the originator of the poetical form, and
in acknowledgement of his skill in the employment of
the harshest weapons of satire," that Horace here
" treats Lucilius with consideration." [a] And as the
Fourth and Tenth Satires are a defence of his art, so
the Sixth is a defence of the poet himself, as well as
of his noble patron and the circle of friends to which
Horace has been admitted. The fragments show
that in the Thirtieth Book Lucilius had discussed
his own relations to some patron, and had placed
the poet's calling above the lure of wealth, as Horace
places it above political ambition.[b] If we had the
whole poem, we should doubtless find that Horace
had drawn a contrast between his own lowly birth,
and the aristocratic origin of Lucilius.[c]

In the Second Book of the *Satires*, published as
we have seen in 30 B.C., Horace finds it no longer
necessary to make a serious defence of his satire.
His position as a writer is now well established, and
the controversies underlying Book I. have been
settled in his favour. Yet the poet is not wholly

[a] Hendrickson, *Horace and Lucilius*, in *Studies in Honor
of B. L. Gildersleeve*, p. 162 (Baltimore, 1902).

[b] Fiske, p. 318.

[c] See *Sat.* i. 6. 58, 59, where *claro natum patre* probably
refers to Lucilius, who, according to Cichorius, had estates
near Tarentum. *Cf.* Fiske, p. 320.

INTRODUCTION

free from anxiety, for there were certain legal restrictions that might prove embarrassing to the writer of satire.[a] Horace, therefore, in the First Satire of this book, asserts his right to freedom of speech, and makes an attack, however disguised in its humorous form, upon the libel laws of Rome, proclaiming at the same time that, as a satirist, he is armed for defence not offence, and that he must have the same privilege as Lucilius enjoyed, that of writing down his inmost thoughts and his personal comments upon the world.

The Second Satire of Book II. corresponds in theme, as well as position, with the Second of Book I. It applies the philosophic doctrine of " the mean " to daily living, eating and drinking, just as the earlier one applied it to sexual morality. It is strongly under the influence of Lucilius, though, like *Sat.* i. 2, it abounds in ideas which were common in the sermons of philosophers.

Closely connected with the Second are the Fourth and Eighth, which belong to a *genre* whose history is outlined in the introduction to the Fourth. The satiric δεῖπνον, of which the *Cena Trimalchionis* of Petronius is the most famous example, was represented in Lucilius by at least five satires.

The influence of Lucilius is still strong in the lengthy Third Satire, which deals with the Stoic paradox, ὅτι πᾶς ἄφρων μαίνεται, a theme which it would seem Lucilius had handled at least twice.[b] It is interesting to find that even the scene reproduced

---

[a] See Lejay, pp. 289-292. In Book I. twenty-four contemporaries are criticized ; in II. only four. So Filbey, cited by Fiske, p. 416.

[b] Fiske, pp. 390 ff.

INTRODUCTION

by Horace (ll. 259-271) from the *Eunuchus* of Terence, was also utilized by Lucilius.[a]

In the remaining Satires of Book II., the Fifth, Sixth and Seventh, the influence of Lucilius seems to be very slight. The Sixth, it is true, illustrates the autobiographical element so conspicuous in Lucilius, and epic parody, exemplified in the Fifth, was doubtless employed by Lucilius, even as it had figured in the Middle and New Attic Comedy, but Horace is no longer under his sway, and when in the Seventh we find the poet professing to make *himself* a target for the shafts of satire, we realize that now at least he can be independent of his model.

The *Epistles* belong essentially to the same literary class as the *Satires*. Both kinds are conversational:[b] *epistulis ad absentes loquimur, sermone cum praesentibus*, says Acron. In subject matter the *Epistles* cover much the same field as the *Satires*. They deal with human foibles and frailties, discuss philosophic principles, open windows upon the poet's domestic circle, and give us incidents and scenes from daily life.

Lucilius had used the epistolary form in a satire of his Fifth Book, and Horace came to realize that this was the most satisfactory mould for him to adopt, when expressing his personal feelings and when passing judgement upon the literary and social problems of his time. As to thought and contents, however, the influence of Lucilius upon the *Epistles* is relatively very slight.[c] These poems, indeed, are the offspring of Horace's maturity, and themes

---

[a] Fiske, pp. 394 ff.

[b] Hendrickson, "Are the Letters of Horace Satires?" *American Journal of Philology*, xviii. pp. 312-324.

[c] See Fiske, pp. 427-440.

already handled in the *Satires* are now presented in more systematic fashion, the writer disclosing a riper judgement and a more subtle refinement of mind. " Good sense, good feeling, good taste," says Mackail, " these qualities, latent from the first in Horace, had obtained a final mastery over the coarser strain with which they had at first been mingled." [a] The *Epistles*, indeed, with their criticism of life and literature, are the best expression of that " urbanity," which has ever been recognized as the most outstanding feature of Horace.

The two Epistles of the Second Book are devoted to literary criticism, which is an important element in the First Book of the *Satires*, and which, we may well believe, was first suggested to Horace by his relation to Lucilius. Even in these late productions, therefore, may be found traces of Lucilian influence,[b] but Horace writes with a free spirit, and in his literary, as in his philosophic, life, he is

nullius addictus iurare in verba magistri.[c]

As to the puzzling *Ars Poetica*, it is evident from the researches of Cichorius[d] and Fiske that it is quite largely indebted to Lucilius, who had a theory of literary criticism " formulated according to the same rhetorical σχήματα, and under substantially the same rhetorical influences . . . as Horace's *Ars Poetica*." [e] Moreover, a detailed comparison of the fragments of Lucilius with the *Ars Poetica* show numerous and striking similarities. To the present

[a] *Latin Literature*, p. 111.
[b] Fiske, pp. 441-446.   [c] *Epist.* ii. 1. 14.
[d] *Untersuchungen zu Lucilius*, pp. 109-127.
[e] Fiske, p. 468.

writer it would seem to be an obvious inference from these facts that the *Ars Poetica* was largely composed some years before it was published. It may have been written originally in the regular satiric form, and afterwards adjusted, for publication, to the epistolary mould.

D. MANUSCRIPTS AND COMMENTARIES

The text of Horace does not rest on as firm a foundation as that of Virgil. Whereas the great epic writer is represented to-day by as many as seven manuscripts written in uncial or capital letters, all of the extant Horatian manuscripts are of the cursive type, and not one can claim to be older than the ninth century. Yet, putting Virgil aside, Horace, in comparison with the other Augustan poets, has fared very well, and his text has suffered comparatively little in the process of transmission.

The MSS. number about two hundred and fifty, and have given rise to endless discussion as to their mutual relations, their classification, their line of descent from a common original, and their comparative value. Such questions have been rendered more uncertain by the incomplete knowledge which we possess of the four Blandinian MSS. which were destroyed in 1566, when the Benedictine abbey of St. Peter, at Blankenberg near Ghent, was sacked by a mob. These MSS. had, however, been rather carelessly collated a few years earlier by Cruquius, who, beginning with 1565, edited separate portions of Horace, and finally in 1578 published a complete edition of the poet at Antwerp. Of these lost Blandinian MSS. Cruquius valued most highly the one which he calls *vetustissimus*, and which Bentley, Lachmann, and other later editors have regarded as the soundest foundation for the establishment of a correct Horatian text. Unfortunately, doubt has been cast upon the accuracy of the statements of Cruquius, and Keller and Holder depreciate the value of this lost MS.

The two scholars just named, the most painstaking editors of the Horatian text, have adopted a grouping of the MSS. in three classes, each of which is based on a lost archetype. The three archetypes are ultimately derived from an original archetype of the first or second century. The claim is made that a reading found in the MSS. of two classes should take precedence over that found in only one. The three classes are distinguished from one another by the degree of systematic alteration and interpolation to which they have been subjected.

This elaborate classification of Keller and Holder's has proved too complicated and has failed to win general acceptance. A simpler and more satisfactory grouping has been attempted by Professor Vollmer of Munich in his recension of 1906 (2nd edition 1912) in which the editor, returning to the principles of Bentley, endeavours to reconstruct the sixth century Mavortian [a] edition, beyond which, however far this may have departed from the original Horatian text, one can hardly hope to go. Vollmer enumerates only fifteen MSS., which he divides into two groups, I. and II. In Class I. he includes *K*, a codex not known

---

[a] The name of Mavortius, who was consul in A.D. 527, appears in association with that of Felix, *orator urbis Romae*, as an *emendator* or διορθωτής, in eight MSS., including *A*, λ, *l*, and *Goth*.

INTRODUCTION

to Keller and Holder. The *vetustissimus* (*V*) he places in Class II. along with a Vatican MS., *R*, of the ninth century and the *Gothanus* of the fifteenth century, which reveals its kinship with *V*. The readings of Class II. are often to be preferred to those of Class I.

In 1912, in revising for the Clarendon Press Wickham's text edition of Horace, Mr. H. W. Garrod of Oxford carried this simplification still further. He adopts Vollmer's classification, but drops some MSS. which he finds to have little significance, viz. from Class I., *A*, which is a mere duplicate of *a*, and *K*; while from Class II. he omits *R*, *Goth.*, λ (Parisinus 7972), and *l* (= Leidensis Lat. 28). On the other hand, he recalls *M*, which Keller had overestimated but Vollmer had rejected as of little value. *V*, placed outside the two classes, is held in high esteem.

The MSS. cited in this edition are as follows:

a = codex Ambrosianus 136, from Avignon, now in Milan. Tenth century. Available for *Satires* and *Epistles*, except from *Sat.* ii. 7. 27 to ii. 8. 95.

A = Parisinus 7900 a. Tenth century. Used for *Epistles* i. (here by a second hand), and to supplement *a*.

B = codex Bernensis 363; in Bern, Switzerland. Written by an Irish scribe at the end of the ninth century. Available for *Satires* up to i. 3. 135, and for *Ars Poet.* up to l. 441.

C and *E* = codex Monacensis 14685 (two parts). Eleventh century. *C* is available from *Sat.* i. 4. 122 up to i. 6. 40; for *Sat.* ii. 8; and for *Ars Poet.* up to l. 441. *E* is available for *Satires* and *Epistles*, except for *Sat.* ii. 5. 87 up to ii. 6. 33; and for *Ars Poet.*, except ll. 441 to 476.

D = codex Argentoratensis. Destroyed at Strasburg 1870. Tenth century. Available for *Satires* and *Epistles*,

except from *Sat*. ii. 2. 132 to ii. 3. 75 ; from *Sat*. ii. 5. 95
to *Epist*. ii. 2. 112.   Not available for *Ars Poet*.

K = codex S. Eugendi, now St. Claude.   Eleventh century.
Available for *Satires* up to ii. 2. 25, and for *Ars Poet*.

M = codex Mellicensis.   Eleventh century.   Available for
Satires, except from ii. 5. 95 and a portion of ii. 3 ;
and for *Epistles*, except from i. 6. 57 to i. 16. 35.

The above MSS. constitute Class I.

R = Vaticanus Reginae 1703.   Ninth century.   Available
for *Satires* and *Epistles*, except from *Sat*. i. 3. 28 to
i. 8. 4, and from *Sat*. ii. 1. 16 to ii. 8. 95.

δ = codex Harleianus 2725.   Ninth century.   Available
for *Satires* up to i. 2. 114 ; and for *Epistles* up to
i. 8. 8, and from ii. 2. 19 to the end of *Ars Poetica*.

λ = Parisinus 7972.   Tenth century.   Complete.

l = Leidensis Lat. 28.   Ninth century.   Complete.

π = codex Parisinus 10310.   Ninth or tenth century.
Available for *Epistles* and *Ars Poetica*, but for *Satires*
only up to i. 2. 70.

ϕ = codex Parisinus 7974.   Tenth century.   Complete.

ψ = codex Parisinus 7971.   Tenth century.   Complete.

Goth. = Gothanus.   Fifteenth century.   This lacks the
Ars Poetica.

These constitute Class II.

Besides these, account must be taken (through the
edition of Cruquius) of the four lost Blandinian MSS.
(designated as *Bland.*), the chief of which was V
(= *vetustissimus*).   In a number of cases V alone (or
in conjunction with *Goth.*) preserved the correct
reading.   The most striking instance of this is given
in *Sat*. i. 6. 126, but other examples are afforded by
Sat. i. 1. 108 ; ii. 2. 56 ; ii. 3. 303 ; ii. 4. 44 ; ii. 8. 88 ;
Epist. i. 10. 9 ; i. 16. 43.   On the whole, however,
V was probably just as faulty as are most of the

extant MSS., no one of which stands out as conspicuous for accuracy. Yet, as a group, the MSS. of Class I. are distinctly superior to those of Class II., though not infrequently the latter preserve correct readings which the former had lost.

Collections of Horatian *scholia*, or explanatory notes, have come down to us from antiquity under the names of Porphyrio and Acron. These scholars lived probably in the third century of our era, Acron being the earlier of the two, but the *scholia* now surviving under Acron's name are as late as the fifth century. Both collections are largely interpolated. Both, however, precede our MSS. in point of time, and are therefore valuable in determining the priority of conflicting readings.

The term Commentator Cruquianus is given to a collection of notes gathered by Cruquius from the marginalia in his Blandinian MSS.

E. Editions and Bibliography

The *editio princeps* of Horace appeared in Italy, without date or name of place, about 1470, and was followed by the annotated edition by Landinus, Florence, 1482. Lambin's, which first appeared in 1561, was frequently republished in Paris and elsewhere. The complete edition by Cruquius was issued at Antwerp, 1578. Modern editions may be said to begin with Heinsius, Leyden, 1612. Bentley's (Cambridge, 1711, Amsterdam 1713, and frequently republished) marks an epoch in Horatian study. Among nineteenth-century editors may be mentioned Döring (Leipzig, 1803), Lemaire (Paris, 1829), Peerlkamp

INTRODUCTION

(Harlem, 1834), Dillenburger (Bonn, 1844), Duentzer (Brunswick, 1849) and Orelli, whose text and commentary (revised by Baiter 1852, then by Hirschfelder and Mewes—fourth large edition, Berlin, 1892) became the standard. Ritter's edition is dated 1856–1857, Leipzig. Keller and Holder's (*editio maior*, Leipzig, 1864–70 ; *editio minor*, 1878) is based on an exhaustive study of the MSS. Vollmer's important edition (2nd, 1912, Leipzig) has a serviceable *apparatus criticus*. One of the best annotated editions is A. Kiessling's, Berlin, 1884 and later ; revised by Heinze, 1910. Another good one is that of Schütz, Berlin, 1880–83, and one by L. Müller, Leipzig, 1891–1893. English editions are Macleane's, London, 1869 (4th, 1881) ; Wickham's, 2 vols., annotated, Oxford, 1878 and 1891, and the Page, Palmer and Wilkins edition, London and New York, 1896. Wickham's text edition, Oxford, 1900, was revised by Garrod, 1912 (see p. xxv). In America the best complete editions are those by C. L. Smith and J. B. Greenough, Boston, 1894, and by C. H. Moore and E. P. Morris, New York, 1909. In France, there is the Waltz edition, Paris, 1887. Of the Plessis and Lejay edition only the volume of *Satires* by Lejay has thus far appeared (Paris, 1911). The best complete edition in Italy is Fumagalli's, Rome, 5th, 1912.

Special editions of the *Satires* and *Epistles* are numerous. A few that we may mention are those by A. Palmer, *Satires*, London and New York, 1883 ; A. S. Wilkins, *Epistles*, London and New York, 1885 ; J. Gow, *Satires*, i. Cambridge, 1901 ; J. C. Rolfe, Boston, 1901 ; P. Rasi, Milan, 1906–07 ; Sabbadini, Turin, 1906 ; E. P. Morris, New York, 1909–11.

INTRODUCTION

Among other works of importance for the study of Horace may be mentioned the following :

F. Hauthal, *Acronis et Porphyrionis commentarii in Horatium*, Berlin, 1864–66.

W. Meyer, *Porphyrionis commentarii in Horatium*, Leipzig, 1874.

R. M. Hovenden, *Horace's Life and Character*, London, 1877.

O. Keller, *Epilegomena zu Horaz*, Leipzig, 1879–80.

W. Y. Sellar, *Horace, Roman Poets of the Augustan Age*, Oxford, 1892.

R. Y. Tyrrell, *Latin Poetry* ; Johns Hopkins Lectures, 1893.

J. W. Mackail, *Latin Literature*, New York, 1895.

Gaston Boissier, *The Country of Horace and Virgil*, translated by Fisher, New York, 1896.

A. Cartault, *Étude sur les Satires d'Horace*, Paris, 1899.

O. Keller, *Pseudacronis scholia in Horatium vetustiora*, Leipzig, 1902–4.

F. Marx, *C. Lucilii carminum reliquiae*, 2 vol., Leipzig, 1904–5.

C. Cichorius, *Untersuchungen zu Lucilius*, Berlin, 1908.

J. W. Duff, *Literary History of Rome*, London, 1909.

F. Leo, *Geschichte der römischen Literatur*, Berlin, 1913.

Courtand, *Horace, sa vie et sa pensée à l'époque des Épîtres*, Paris, 1914.

Lane Cooper, *A Concordance to the Works of Horace*, Washington (The Carnegie Institution), 1916.

Mary Rebecca Thayer, *The Influence of Horace on the Chief English Poets of the Nineteenth Century*, New Haven, 1916.

J. F. D'Alton, *Horace and his Age*, London and New York, 1917.

G. C. Fiske, *Lucilius and Horace : a Study in the Classical Theory of Imitation*, Madison, Wisconsin, 1920.

Grant Showerman, *Horace and his Influence*, Boston, 1922.

H. N. Fowler, *A History of Roman Literature*, New York, 1923 (2nd edition).

E. E. Sikes, *Roman Poetry*, London, 1923.

INTRODUCTION

A. Y. Campbell, *Horace, a new Interpretation*, London, 1924.

Elizabeth H. Haight, *Horace and his Art of Enjoyment*, New York, 1925.

There are also many pamphlets and periodical articles, too numerous to record, which must be consulted by an editor of Horace.

F. Abbreviations

A.J.P. = *American Journal of Philology*.

A.P.A. = Transactions and Proceedings of the American Philological Association.

C.P. = *Classical Philology*.

C.R. = *Classical Review*.

C.W. = *Classical Weekly*.

Fiske = *Lucilius and Horace*, by G. C. Fiske.

Harv. St. = *Harvard Studies in Classical Philology*.

J.P. = *Journal of Philology*.

Rh. M. = *Rheinisches Museum für klassische Philologie*.

Editions of Horace are often referred to by the name of the editor alone, e.g. Lejay = the Lejay edition of the *Satires*.

SATIRES

I

THE RACE FOR WEALTH AND POSITION

THE opening Satire serves as a dedication of the whole book to Maecenas, and deals with a conspicuous feature of social life in the Augustan age.

Everybody, says Horace, is discontented with his lot and envies his neighbour. Yet, if some god were to give men a chance to change places, they would all refuse. The cause of this restlessness is the longing for wealth. Men will assure you that the only reason why they toil unceasingly is that they may secure a competence and then retire. They claim to be like the ant, which provides so wisely for the future; but the ant enjoys its store when winter comes, whereas the money-seeking man never ceases from his labours, so long as there is one richer than himself (1-40).

And yet what is the use of large possessions? If a man has enough, more wealth will prove a burden and a peril. The miser claims that the wealthier he is the more highly will men think of him. I will not argue the point, says Horace, but will leave him to his self-esteem. He is like Tantalus, tortured with thirst though the waters are so near. Your avaricious man suffers all the pain, and enjoys none of the pleasure that money can buy. There is indeed

2

no more certain cause of misery than avarice. Yet one must not run to the other extreme, but should observe the golden mean (41-107).

To return to the starting-point: everybody is trying to outstrip his neighbour in the race for wealth. People are never satisfied, and therefore we seldom see a man who is ready to quit the banquet of life like a guest who has had enough (108-119).

But enough of this preaching, or you will think that I have rifled the papers of Crispinus (120, 121).

Palmer thinks that this Satire "was probably the last composed of those in the first book," and Morris speaks of its "maturity of style and treatment." Campbell, however, points out "distinct signs of immaturity," such as the Lucretian echo in ll. 23-26, a passage which "smacks of the novice in satire-writing" (cf. Lucr. i. 936 ff.), the weakness of l. 108, and the "lame conclusion" in ll. 120, 121 (*Horace*, p. 165). Lejay thinks that our author composed the discussion of *avaritia* (28-117) first, and later, when dedicating his book to Maecenas, added the beginning and the end. This is a very plausible view.

A minute analysis of this Satire is given by Charles Knapp in the *Transactions of the American Philological Association*, xlv. pp. 91 ff.

SERMONUM

LIBER PRIMUS

I.

Qui fit, Maecenas, ut nemo, quam sibi sortem
seu ratio dederit seu fors[1] obiecerit, illa
contentus vivat, laudet diversa sequentis ?
" o fortunati mercatores ! " gravis annis[2]
miles ait, multo iam fractus membra labore.   5
contra mercator, navem iactantibus Austris,
" militia est potior. quid enim ? concurritur : horae
momento cita mors venit aut victoria laeta."
agricolam laudat iuris legumque peritus,
sub galli cantum consultor ubi ostia pulsat.   10
ille, datis vadibus qui rure extractus in urbem est,
solos felices viventis clamat[3] in urbe.
cetera de genere hoc, adeo sunt multa, loquacem
delassare valent Fabium. ne te morer, audi
quo rem deducam. si quis deus " en ego " dicat, 15

---

[1] fors *V MSS.* : sors *B.*
[2] annis *MSS.* : armis *conjectured by Bouhier and accepted
by Vollmer.*   [3] cantat *B.*

---

[a] The reference is not so much to the professional lawyer
as to the influential citizen, whose humble clients come
at daybreak to ask for advice. Such a citizen would
commonly have had a good legal training. With him is

SATIRES

BOOK I

Satire I

How comes it, Maecenas, that no man living is
content with the lot which either his choice has
given him, or chance has thrown in his way, but
each has praise for those who follow other paths?
"O happy traders!" cries the soldier, as he feels
the weight of years, his frame now shattered with
hard service. On the other hand, when southern
gales toss the ship, the trader cries: "A soldier's
life is better. Do you ask why? There is the battle
clash, and in a moment of time comes speedy death
or joyous victory." One learned in law and statutes
has praise for the farmer, when towards cockcrow a
client comes knocking at his door.[a] The man
yonder, who has given surety and is dragged into
town from the country cries that they only are happy
who live in town. The other instances of this kind
—so many are they—could tire out the chatterbox
Fabius. To be brief with you, hear the conclusion
to which I am coming. If some god were to say:[b]

contrasted a countryman, who is a defendant in some case
and must, therefore, come to the city against his will.

[b] Horace imagines a dramatic scene where a god appears
ex machina. *Cf. Sat.* ii. 7. 24 ; *Ars Poetica*, 191.

" iam faciam, quod voltis : eris tu, qui modo miles,
mercator ; tu, consultus modo, rusticus ; hinc vos,
vos hinc mutatis discedite partibus : eia !
quid statis ? "—nolint.[1] atqui licet esse beatis.
quid causae est, merito quin illis Iuppiter ambas   20
iratus buccas inflet neque se fore posthac
tam facilem dicat, votis ut praebeat aurem ?

    Praeterea, ne sic, ut qui iocularia, ridens[2]
percurram : quamquam ridentem dicere verum
quid vetat ? ut pueris olim dant crustula blandi   25
doctores, elementa velint ut discere prima :
sed tamen amoto quaeramus seria ludo :
ille gravem duro terram qui vertit aratro,
perfidus hic caupo, miles nautaeque per omne
audaces mare qui currunt, hac mente laborem   30
sese ferre, senes ut in otia tuta recedant,
aiunt, cum sibi sint congesta cibaria : sicut
parvola, nam exemplo est, magni formica laboris
ore trahit quodcumque potest atque addit acervo
quem struit, haud ignara ac non incauta futuri.   35
quae, simul inversum contristat Aquarius annum,
non usquam prorepit et illis utitur ante
quaesitis sapiens,[3] cum te neque fervidus aestus
demoveat lucro neque hiems, ignis, mare, ferrum,
nil obstet tibi, dum ne sit te ditior alter.   40

    Quid iuvat immensum te argenti pondus et auri
furtim defossa timidum deponere terra ?
" quod si comminuas, vilem redigatur ad assem."

[1] nolent *B.*
[2] *ll.* 22, 23 *with order inverted BK.*
[3] sapiens *V, II* : patiens *I.*

---

[a] The sun enters the sign of Aquarius in January, the
chilliest month of a Roman winter, when the year's cycle
begins anew.

" Here I am ! I will grant your prayers forthwith.
You, who were but now a soldier, shall be a trader ;
you, but now a lawyer, shall be a farmer. Change
parts ; away with you—and with you ! Well ! Why
standing still ? " They would refuse. And yet
'tis in their power to be happy. What reason is
there why Jove should not, quite properly, puff out
both cheeks at them in anger, and say that never
again will he be so easy-going as to lend ear to their
prayers ?

²³ Furthermore, not to skim over the subject
with a laugh like a writer of witticisms—and yet
what is to prevent one from telling truth as he laughs,
even as teachers sometimes give cookies to children
to coax them into learning their A B C ?—still, putting
jesting aside, let us turn to serious thoughts : yon
farmer, who with tough plough turns up the heavy
soil, our rascally host here, the soldier, the sailors
who boldly scour every sea, all say that they bear
toil with this in view, that when old they may retire
into secure ease, once they have piled up their pro-
visions ; even as the tiny, hard-working ant (for she
is their model) drags all she can with her mouth,
and adds it to the heap she is building, because she
is not unaware and not heedless of the morrow. Yet
she, soon as Aquarius saddens the upturned year,ᵃ
stirs out no more but uses the store she gathered
beforehand, wise creature that she is ; while as for
you, neither burning heat, nor winter, fire, sea,
sword, can turn you aside from gain—nothing stops
you, until no second man be richer than yourself.

⁴¹ What good to you is a vast weight of silver
and gold, if in terror you stealthily bury it in a hole
in the ground ? " But if one splits it up, it would

7

at ni id fit, quid habet pulchri constructus acervus ?
milia frumenti tua triverit area centum,   45
non tuus hoc capiet venter plus ac[1] meus ; ut si
reticulum panis venalis inter onusto
forte vehas umero, nihilo plus accipias quam
qui nil portarit.

        Vel dic, quid referat intra
naturae finis viventi, iugera centum an   50
mille aret ? " at suave est ex magno tollere acervo."
dum ex parvo nobis tantundem haurire relinquas,
cur tua plus laudes cumeris granaria nostris ?
ut tibi si sit opus liquidi non amplius urna
vel cyatho, et dicas " magno de flumine mallem[2]   55
quam ex hoc fonticulo tantundem sumere." eo fit,
plenior ut si quos delectet copia iusto,
cum ripa simul avolsos ferat Aufidus acer.
at qui tantuli eget, quanto est opus, is neque limo
turbatam haurit aquam, neque vitam amittit in undis.

   At[3] bona pars hominum decepta cupidine falso 61
" nil satis est " inquit, " quia tanti quantum habeas
    sis."
quid facias illi ? iubeas miserum esse, libenter
quatenus id facit : ut quidam memoratur Athenis
sordidus ac dives, populi contemnere voces   65
sic solitus : " populus me sibilat, at mihi plaudo
ipse domi, simul ac nummos contemplor in arca."

   Tantalus a labris sitiens fugientia captat
flumina—quid rides ? mutato nomine de te

        [1] ac *B* : quam *aDEM.*
      [2] malle *B* : malim, *II, Bentley, Vollmer.*
        [3] at *K*[2] : ut *MSS.* : *Vollmer.*

---

   [a] Here and below, the miser speaks for himself.
   [b] The picture is that of a gang of slaves driven to the
market for sale. One of them carries the provisions for all.
   [c] The Aufidus, a stream in Horace's native Apulia, at
times became a raging torrent, undermining its banks.

dwindle to a paltry penny." [a] Yet if that is not done, what beauty has the piled-up heap? Suppose your threshing-floor has threshed out a hundred thousand bushels of grain; your stomach will not on that account hold more than mine: 'tis as if in the slave-gang you by chance should carry the heavy bread-bag on your shoulder, yet you would receive no more than the slave who carries nothing. [b]

[49] Or, tell me, what odds does it make to the man who lives within Nature's bounds, whether he ploughs a hundred acres or a thousand? "But what a pleasure to take from a large heap!" So long as you let us take just as much from our little one, why praise your granaries above our bins? It is as if you needed no more than a jug or a cup of water, and were to say, "I'd rather have taken the quantity from a broad river than from this tiny brook." So it comes about that when any find pleasure in undue abundance, raging Aufidus sweeps them away, bank and all; while the man who craves only so much as he needs, neither draws water thick with mud, nor loses his life in the flood. [c]

[61] But a good many people, misled by blind desire, say, "You cannot have enough: for you get your rating from what you have." What can you do to a man who talks thus? Bid him be miserable, since that is his whim. He is like a rich miser in Athens who, they say, used thus to scorn the people's talk: "The people hiss me, but at home I clap my hands for myself, once I gaze on the moneys in my chest."

[68] Tantalus, thirsty soul, catches at the streams that fly from his lips—why laugh? Change but

fabula narratur : congestis undique saccis   70
indormis inhians, et tamquam parcere sacris
cogeris aut pictis tamquam gaudere tabellis.
nescis quo valeat nummus, quem praebeat usum ?
panis ematur, holus, vini sextarius ; adde
quis humana sibi doleat natura negatis.   75
an vigilare metu exanimem, noctesque diesque
formidare malos fures, incendia, servos,
ne te compilent fugientes, hoc iuvat ?   horum
semper ego optarim[1] pauperrimus esse bonorum.
  " At si condoluit temptatum frigore corpus   80
aut alius casus lecto te adfixit,[2] habes qui
adsideat, fomenta paret, medicum roget, ut te
suscitet ac reddat gnatis[3] carisque propinquis."
non uxor salvum te vult,[4] non filius ; omnes
vicini oderunt, noti, pueri atque puellae.   85
miraris, cum tu argento post omnia ponas,
si nemo praestet quem non merearis amorem ?
an si[5] cognatos, nullo Natura labore
quos tibi dat, retinere velis servareque amicos,
infelix operam perdas, ut si quis asellum   90
in Campo doceat parentem currere frenis ?
  Denique sit finis quaerendi, cumque habeas plus,
pauperiem metuas minus et finire laborem
incipias, parto quod avebas,[6] ne facias quod
Ummidius quidam.[7] non longa est fabula : dives   95

---

[1] optarem, *I.*
[2] adfixit *K, so Bentley and most editors* : adflixit *most MSS.*
[3] gnatis reddat *Goth.*   [4] te vult salvum *D.*
[5] an si] at si *K*: an sic *Goth.*
[6] habebas *B.*   [7] quidam] qui tam *Bentley.*

the name, and the tale is told of you. You sleep with open mouth on money-bags piled up from all sides, and must perforce keep hands off as if they were hallowed, or take delight in them as if painted pictures. Don't you know what money is for, what end it serves? You may buy bread, greens, a measure of wine, and such other things as would mean pain to our human nature, if withheld. What, to lie awake half-dead with fear, to be in terror night and day of wicked thieves, of fire, of slaves, who may rob you and run away—is this so pleasant? In such blessings I could wish ever to be poorest of the poor.

80 "But if your body is seized with a chill and racked with pain, or some other mishap has pinned you to your bed, have you some one to sit by you, to get lotions ready, to call in the doctor so as to raise you up and restore you to your children and dear kinsmen?" No, your wife does not want you well, nor does your son: every one hates you, neighbours and acquaintances, boys and girls. Can you wonder, when you put money above all else, that nobody pays you the love you do not earn? Or, when Nature gives you kinsfolk without trouble, if you sought to hold and keep their love, would it be as fruitless a waste of effort, as if one were to train an ass to race upon the Campus *a* obedient to the rein?

92 In short, set bounds to the quest of wealth, and as you increase your means let your fear of poverty lessen, and when you have won your heart's desire, begin to bring your toil to an end, lest you fare like a certain Ummidius—'tis a short story—so

a The Campus Martius.

ut metiretur nummos ; ita sordidus, ut se
non umquam servo melius vestiret ; ad usque
supremum tempus, ne se penuria victus
opprimeret, metuebat. at hunc liberta securi
divisit medium, fortissima Tyndaridarum.　　　100

　" Quid mi igitur suades ? ut vivam Naevius aut sic
ut Nomentanus ? "　pergis pugnantia secum
frontibus adversis componere. non ego, avarum
cum veto te fieri, vappam iubeo ac nebulonem.
est inter Tanain quiddam socerumque Viselli :　105
est modus in rebus, sunt certi denique fines,
quos ultra citraque nequit consistere rectum.

　Illuc, unde abii, redeo, qui nemo, ut[1] avarus,
se probet ac potius laudet diversa sequentis,
quodque aliena capella gerat distentius uber,　110
tabescat, neque se maiori pauperiorum
turbae comparet, hunc atque hunc superare laboret.
sic festinanti semper locupletior obstat,
ut, cum carceribus missos rapit ungula currus,
instat equis auriga suos[2] vincentibus, illum　115
praeteritum temnens extremos inter euntem.
inde fit ut raro, qui se vixisse beatum

---

[1] qui nemo ut *V* : nemon ut *mss.*, *Porph.* : cum nemo ut
Keck, *Vollmer*.　*For other attempts to improve the text see
Knapp*, loc. cit. *pp.* 102 *ff.*
　[2] suis *aDEM*.

---

　[a] *i.e.* instead of counting it. The idea was proverbial,
cf. Xen. *Hellen.* iii. 2. 27 ; Petronius, *Sat.* 37.
　[b] Clytemnestra, daughter of Tyndareus, slew her husband
Agamemnon with an axe. Possibly the freedwoman's name
was Tyndaris.
　[c] Both of these names were used by Lucilius. The men
represent the spendthrift type.

rich that he measured his money,[a] so miserly that he dressed no better than a slave ; up to his last hour he feared he would die of starvation. Yet a freed-woman cleft him in twain with an axe, bravest of the Tyndarid breed.[b]

[101] " What, then, would you have me do ? Live as a Naevius or a Nomentanus ? "[c] You go on to set opposites in head to head conflict with each other.[d] When I call on you not to be a miser, I am not bidding you become a worthless prodigal. There is some mean between a Tanais and the father-in-law of Visellius.[e] There is measure in all things. There are, in short, fixed bounds, beyond and short of which right can find no place.

[108] I return to my starting-point, how it comes that no man because of his greed is self-contented, but rather does each praise those who follow other paths, pines away because his neighbour's goat shows a more distended udder, and, instead of matching himself with the greater crowd of poorer men, strives to surpass first one and then another. In such a race there is ever a richer in your way. 'Tis[f] as when chariots are let loose from the barriers and swept onwards behind the hoofed steeds : hard on the horses that outstrip his own presses the charioteer, caring naught for that other whom he has passed and left in the rear. Thus it comes that seldom can we find one who says he has had a happy

---

[a] The figure is taken, not so much from gladiators, as from rams or bulls. Knapp takes *componere* as " reconcile " (*loc. cit.* p. 101).
[e] Tanais is said to have been a freedman of Maecenas. The other person is unknown.
[f] This passage closely resembles Virgil, *Georg.* i. 512 ff.

dicat et exacto contentus tempore vita[1]
cedat uti conviva satur, reperire queamus.

    Iam satis est.   ne me Crispini scrinia lippi   120
compilasse putes, verbum non amplius addam.

---

[1] vitae *D.*

---

   [a] *Cf.* Lucretius, iii. 938,
     Cur non ut plenus vitae conviva recedis,
     Aequo animoque capis securam, stulte, quietem?

life, and who, when his time is sped, will quit life in contentment, like a guest who has had his fill.*

120 Well, 'tis enough. Not a word more will I add, or you will think I have rifled the rolls of blear-eyed Crispinus.*

b The *scrinia* were the cylindrical boxes in which rolls of manuscript were kept. Crispinus, according to the scholiasts, was an *aretalogus*, one who babbled about virtue. He wrote, we are told, in verse.

II

THE FOLLY OF RUNNING TO EXTREMES

MEN seldom keep the golden mean, but run from one extreme to another. Especially may this be illustrated by victims of sensual indulgence and by people guilty of adultery, a vice which has become a shocking feature of the age.

This immature and forbidding sketch, coarse and sensational in tone, and doubtless one of Horace's earliest efforts, is closely associated with the Lucilian type of satire. It abounds in personalities, freely handled, and Horace himself (in *Sat.* i. 4. 92) cites it later as an illustration of the kind of writing which had aroused enmity against the author. Even Maecenas, if we are to believe the scholiasts, is thinly disguised in the Maltinus of l. 25.

In his introduction to this Satire, Lejay has shown how dependent it ultimately is " upon the erotic literature of the Hellenistic period as expressed in the popular Cynic philosophy, in the New Comedy, and in the *Anthology* " (Fiske, p. 251). There is a striking parallel between it and a poem on love in the *Oxyrhynchus Papyri* by the Cynic Cercidas of Megalopolis, who lived in the latter part of the third century B.C. See Chapter I. of Powell and Barber's *New Chapters in the History of Greek Literature* (Oxford, 1921).

II.

Ambubaiarum collegia, pharmacopolae,
mendici, mimae, balatrones, hoc genus omne
maestum ac sollicitum est cantoris morte Tigelli :
quippe benignus erat.   contra hic, ne prodigus esse
dicatur metuens, inopi dare nolit amico,   5
frigus quo duramque famem propellere[1] possit.
hunc si perconteris, avi cur atque parentis
praeclaram ingrata stringat malus ingluvie rem,
omnia conductis coemens obsonia nummis :
sordidus atque animi quod parvi nolit haberi,   10
respondet.   laudatur ab his, culpatur ab illis.
Fufidius vappae famam timet ac nebulonis,
dives agris, dives positis in faenore nummis : [2]
quinas hic capiti mercedes exsecat,[3] atque
quanto perditior quisque est, tanto acrius urget ;   15
nomina sectatur modo sumpta veste virili
sub patribus duris tironum.   "maxime" quis non
" Iuppiter ! " exclamat, simul atque audivit ?   " at
     in se
pro quaestu sumptum facit hic.[4]   vix credere possis

[1] depellere, *II.*
[2] *l.* 13 (= *Ars Poet.* 421) *rejected by Sanadon, Holder.*
[3] exigit E^2.
[4] facit. Hic ? *some editors.*   hic] hoc δφψ.

---

[a] The usual rate was one per cent a month, twelve per

18

Satire II

The flute-girls' guilds, the drug-quacks, beggars,
actresses, buffoons, and all that breed, are in grief and
mourning at the death of the singer Tigellius. He
was, they say, so generous. On the other hand,
here's one who, fearing to be called a prodigal,
would grudge a poor friend the wherewithal to banish
cold and hunger's pangs. Should you ask another
why, in his thankless gluttony, he recklessly strips
the noble estate of his sire and grandsire, buying
up every dainty with borrowed money, he answers
that it is because he would not like to be thought
mean and of poor spirit. He is praised by some,
blamed by others. Fufidius, rich in lands, rich in
moneys laid out at usury, fears the repute of a
worthless prodigal ; five times the interest he slices
away from the principal,[a] and the nearer a man is
to ruin, the harder he presses him ; he aims to get
notes-of-hand from youths who have just donned
the toga of manhood, and have stern fathers.
" Great Jove ! " who does not cry as soon as he
hears it ? " but surely he spends on himself in pro-
portion to his gains ? " You would hardly believe

cent a year, but Fufidius charged five times that rate,
and took it in advance as in discounting, so that the sum
actually received by the borrower was only forty per cent
of the amount borrowed.

19

quam sibi non sit amicus, ita ut pater ille, Terenti   20
fabula quem miserum gnato vixisse fugato
inducit, non se peius cruciaverit atque hic.

Si quis nunc quaerat "quo res haec pertinet?" illuc:
dum vitant stulti vitia, in contraria currunt.
Maltinus tunicis demissis ambulat ; est qui   25
inguen ad obscenum subductis usque[1] facetus.
pastillos Rufillus olet, Gargonius hircum.
nil medium est. sunt qui nolint[2] tetigisse nisi illas
quarum subsuta talos tegat instita veste :
contra alius nullam nisi olenti in fornice stantem. 30
quidam notus homo cum exiret fornice, " macte
virtute esto " inquit sententia dia Catonis :
" nam simul ac venas inflavit taetra libido,
huc[3] iuvenes aequum est descendere, non alienas
permolere uxores." " nolim laudarier," inquit   35
" sic me," mirator cunni Cupiennius albi.

Audire est operae pretium, procedere recte
qui moechis non voltis, ut omni parte laborent,
utque illis multo corrupta dolore voluptas
atque haec rara[4] cadat dura inter saepe pericla.   40
hic se praecipitem tecto dedit ; ille flagellis
ad mortem caesus ; fugiens hic decidit acrem
praedonum in turbam, dedit hic pro corpore nummos,
hunc perminxerunt calones ; quin etiam illud

---

[1] *Punctuation after* usque, *Vollmer.*
[2] nolunt *aD.*   [3] hac, *II.*   [4] rata *E.*

---

[a] In the *Heauton Timorumenos*, or *Self-Tormentor*, the father, Menedemus, seized with remorse for his harshness to his son Clinias, punishes himself with hard labour.

[b] *i.e.*, married women who dress as such.

how poor a friend he is to himself, so that the father whom Terence's play pictures as having lived in misery after banishing his son, never tortured himself worse than he.[a]

23 Should one now ask, "What is the point of all this?" 'tis this: in avoiding a vice, fools run into its opposite. Maltinus walks with his garments trailing low; another, a man of fashion, wears them tucked up indecently as far as his waist. Rufillus smells like a scent-box, Gargonius like a goat. There is no middle course. Some men would deal only with women whose ankles are hidden by a robe with low-hanging flounce;[b] another is found only with such as live in a foul brothel. When from such a place a man he knew was coming forth, "A blessing on thy well-doing!" runs Cato's revered utterance; "for when shameful passion has swelled the veins, 'tis well that young men come down hither, rather than tamper with other men's wives." "I should not care to be praised on that count," says Cupiennius, an admirer of white-robed lechery.[c]

37 It is worth your while,[d] ye who would have disaster wait on adulterers, to hear how on every side they fare ill, and how for them pleasure is marred by much pain, and, rare as it is, comes oft amid cruel perils. One man has thrown himself headlong from the roof; another has been flogged to death; a third, in his flight, has fallen into a savage gang of robbers; another has paid a price to save his life; another been abused by stable-boys; nay, once it

c Roman matrons dressed usually in white.
d Cf. Ennius:
    audire est operae pretium procedere recte
    qui rem Romanam Latiumque augescere voltis.

accidit, ut quidam testis caudamque salacem   45
demeteret ferro. " iure " omnes : Galba negabat.

  Tutior at quanto merx est in classe secunda,
libertinarum dico, Sallustius in quas
non minus insanit quam qui moechatur. at hic[1] si,
qua res, qua ratio suaderet, quaque modeste   50
munifico[2] esse licet, vellet bonus atque benignus
esse, daret quantum satis esset, nec sibi damno
dedecorique foret. verum hoc se amplectitur uno,
hoc amat et laudat : " matronam nullam ego tango."
ut quondam Marsaeus, amator Originis ille,   55
qui patrium mimae donat fundumque laremque,
" nil fuerit mi " inquit " cum uxoribus umquam
    alienis."
verum est cum mimis, est cum meretricibus, unde
fama malum gravius quam res trahit. an tibi abunde
personam satis est, non illud quicquid ubique   60
officit evitare ? bonam deperdere famam,
rem patris oblimare, malum est ubicumque. quid inter-
est in matrona, ancilla peccesne[3] togata ?

  Villius in Fausta Syllae gener, hoc miser uno
nomine deceptus, poenas dedit usque superque   65
quam satis est, pugnis caesus ferroque petitus,
exclusus fore, cum Longarenus foret intus.
huic si mutonis verbis mala tanta videnti

    [1] at K : ut most MSS.   [2] munificum K[2].
        [3] -ve MSS., Porph.

---

  [a] Galba was at once an adulterer and (according to the scholiasts) a *iuris consultus*.

  [b] *i.e.* of adulterer. The reputation of adulterer would come from association with *matronae*, but not with *meretrices*.

  [c] *Meretrices* wore the *toga* (*cf.* v. 82), in contrast with the *stola*, worn by matrons, *cf.* v. 71. The *ancilla* is a slave-girl who had become a *meretrix*.

22

so befell that a man mowed down with the sword the testicles and lustful member. "That's the law," cry all, Galba dissenting.[a]

[47] But how much safer is trafficking in the second class—with freedwomen, I mean; after whom Sallustius runs just as wild as an adulterer. Yet he, if he wished to be good and generous, so far as his means and reason would direct, and so far as one might be liberal in moderation, would give a sum sufficient, not such as would mean for him shame and ruin. But no; because of this one thing he hugs himself, admires and plumes himself, because, says he, "I meddle with no matron." Just as was once said by Marsaeus, Origo's well-known lover, who gave his paternal home and farm to an actress: "Never may I have dealings with other men's wives!" But you have with actresses and with courtesans, through whom your name loses more than does your estate. Or is it enough for you to avoid the rôle,[b] but not the thing, which in any case works harm? To throw away a good name, to squander a father's estate, is at all times ruinous. What matters it, whether with matron you offend, or with long-gowned maid[c]?

[64] Villius, son-in-law of Sulla, was punished richly and more than enough because of Fausta[d]—by this name alone was the wretch misled—being smitten with the fist, assailed with the sword, and shut out of doors while Longarenus was within. If while facing such evils a man's mind were thus to plead on

---

[d] The reference is to a scandal of earlier days. Fausta, daughter of Sulla, was the wife of Milo, but had other lovers, among them Longarenus and Villius, who is called *Sullae gener* in derision. Fausta's name indicates her noble birth.

diceret haec animus : " quid vis tibi ? numquid ego
   a te
magno prognatum deposco consule cunnum   70
velatumque stola, mea cum conferbuit ira ? "
quid responderet ? " magno patre nata puella est."
at quanto meliora monet pugnantiaque istis
dives opis natura suae, tu si modo recte
dispensare velis ac non fugienda petendis   75
immiscere. tuo vitio rerumne labores,
nil referre putas ? quare, ne paeniteat te,
desine matronas sectarier,[1] unde laboris
plus haurire mali est quam ex re decerpere fructus.
nec magis huic inter niveos viridisque lapillos   80
(sit licet hoc, Cerinthe, tuum[2]) tenerum est femur aut
   crus
rectius, atque etiam melius persaepe togatae est.[3]
adde huc quod mercem sine fucis gestat, aperte
quod venale habet ostendit, nec, si quid honesti est,
iactat habetque palam, quaerit quo turpia celet. 85
regibus hic mos est, ubi equos mercantur : opertos[4]
inspiciunt, ne, si facies, ut saepe, decora
molli fulta pede est, emptorem inducat hiantem,
quod pulchrae clunes, breve quod caput, ardua cervix.
hoc illi recte : ne corporis optima Lyncei[5]   90
contemplere oculis, Hypsaea caecior illa
quae mala sunt spectes. " o crus, o bracchia ! "
   verum

---

   [1] sectari matronas *aBD.*
   [2] *Housman (J. P.* vol. xxxv.) *conjectures* aesque, Corinthe,
tuum.   [3] est *omitted, most* MSS.
   [4] *This verse begins a new sermo in some* MSS. *For* regibus
Kiessling conjectured Threcibus.
   [5] lynceis *EK.*

his passion's behalf; "What wouldst thou? Do I ever, when my rage is at its worst, ask you for a dame clad in a stola,[a] the offspring of a great consul?" What would he answer? "The girl is a noble father's child." But how much better—how utterly at variance with this—is the course that nature, rich in her own resources, prompts, if you would only manage wisely, and not confound what is to be avoided with what is to be desired! Do you think it makes no difference, whether your trouble is due to your own fault or to circumstances? Wherefore, that you may have no reason to repent, cease to court matrons, for thence one may derive pain and misery, rather than reap enjoyment in the reality. Though this may not be your opinion, Cerinthus, yet not softer or finer are a woman's limbs amidst snowy pearls and green emeralds—nay, often the advantage is with the strumpet. She, moreover, presents her wares without disguise; what she has for sale she openly displays; and if she has some charm, she does not boastfully show it off, while carefully concealing all unsightliness. This is the way with the rich when they buy horses; they inspect them covered, so that if a beautiful shape, as often, is supported by a tender hoof, it may not take in the buyer, as he gapes at the comely haunches, the small head, the stately neck. In this they act wisely. So do not survey bodily perfections with the eyes of a Lynceus[b] and be blinder than Hypsaea, when you gaze upon deformities. "What a leg! what arms!" you cry,

---

[a] The *stola* was a long over-garment, caught in at the waist by a girdle.

[b] The keen-sighted Argonaut. Nothing is known of the blind Hypsaea.

depugis, nasuta, brevi latere ac pede longo est.
matronae praeter faciem nil cernere possis,
cetera, ni Catia est, demissa veste tegentis.   95
si interdicta petes, vallo circumdata (nam te
hoc facit insanum), multae tibi tum[1] officient[2] res,
custodes, lectica, ciniflones, parasitae,
ad talos stola demissa et circumdata palla,
plurima quae invideant pure apparere tibi rem.   100
altera, nil obstat ; Cois tibi paene videre est
ut nudam, ne crure malo, ne sit pede turpi ;
metiri possis oculo latus.   an tibi mavis
insidias fieri pretiumque avellier ante
quam mercem ostendi ? " leporem venator ut alta 105
in nive sectetur, positum sic tangere nolit,"
cantat et apponit " meus est amor huic similis ; nam
transvolat in medio posita et fugientia captat."
hiscine versiculis speras tibi posse dolores
atque aestus curasque gravis e pectore pelli[3] ?   110

   Nonne, cupidinibus statuat natura modum quem,
quid latura sibi, quid sit dolitura negatum,
quaerere plus prodest et inane abscindere[4] soldo ?

       [1] dum, *II.*   [2] officiunt φψλ*l.*
      [3] tolli *VBK.*   [4] abscedere *B.*

---

  a A kind of transparent silk was made in the island of
Cos.

  b Horace makes use of an epigram of the poet Callimachus
(*Anthologia Palatina*, xii. 102), in which the lover is compared
to a hunter who will go to great trouble to catch game, but
scorns it when it is caught and lies outstretched upon the
ground (so Orelli).   The Greek runs thus :

    ὡγρευτής, Ἐπίκυδες, ἐν οὔρεσι πάντα λαγωὸν
      διφᾷ καὶ πάσης ἴχνια δορκαλίδος,

but there are thin hips, a long nose, a short waist and
a long foot. In a matron one can see only her face,
for unless she be a Catia, her long robe conceals all
else. But if you seek forbidden charms that are
invested with a rampart—for this it is that drives you
crazy—many obstacles will then be in your way—
attendants, the sedan, hairdressers, parasites, the
robe dropping to the ankles, and, covered with a wrap,
a thousand things which hinder you from a clear
view. In the other—no obstacle. In her Coan silk [a]
you may see her, almost as if naked, so that she
may not have a poor leg, an unsightly foot ; you may
measure her whole form with your eye. Or would
you rather have a trick played upon you and your
money extorted before the wares are shown ? The
gallant sings how [b] " the huntsman pursues the hare
mid the deep snow, but declines to touch it when
thus outstretched," and adds : " My love is like unto
this, for it passes over what is served to all, and chases
flying game." Do you suppose that with verses
such as these, sorrow and passion and the burden of
care can be lifted from your breast ?

111 Would it not be more profitable to ask what
limit nature assigns to desires, what satisfaction she
will give herself, what privation will cause her pain,
and so to part the "void" from what is "solid" ?[c] Or,
when thirst parches your jaws, do you ask for cups of

στίβῃ καὶ νιφετῷ κεχρημένος· ἢν δέ τις εἴπῃ,
  "τῇ, τόδε βέβληται θηρίον," οὐκ ἔλαβεν.
χοὖμὸς ἔρως τοιόσδε· τὰ μὲν φεύγοντα διώκειν
  οἶδε, τὰ δ' ἐν μέσσῳ κείμενα παρπέτεται.

The *positum sic* represents τόδε βέβληται θηρίον, while *in medio
posita* translates ἐν μέσσῳ κείμενα.

[c] A reference to Epicurean physics, according to which the
universe is composed of "void" (*inane*) and "solid" atoms.

27

num, tibi cum fauces urit sitis, aurea quaeris
pocula ?   num esuriens fastidis omnia praeter   115
pavonem rhombumque ?   tument tibi cum inguina,
　　num, si
ancilla aut verna est praesto puer, impetus in quem
continuo fiat, malis tentigine rumpi ?
non ego : namque parabilem amo Venerem facilem-
　　que.   119
illam " post paulo," " sed pluris," " si exierit vir,"
Gallis, hanc Philodemus ait sibi, quae neque magno
stet pretio neque cunctetur cum est iussa venire.
candida rectaque sit ; munda hactenus, ut neque longa
nec magis alba velit quam dat[1] natura videri.
haec ubi supposuit dextro corpus mihi laevum,   125
Ilia et Egeria est ; do nomen quodlibet illi,
nec vereor[2] ne, dum futuo, vir rure recurrat,
ianua frangatur, latret canis, undique magno
pulsa domus strepitu resonet, vepallida[3] lecto
desiliat[4] mulier, miseram se conscia clamet,   130
cruribus haec metuat, doti deprensa, egomet mi.
discincta tunica fugiendum est et pede nudo,
ne nummi pereant aut puga aut denique fama.
deprendi miserum est : Fabio vel iudice vincam.

---

[1] det *D.*   [2] metuo, *II.*
[3] vae pallida *MSS.* : vepallida *known to Acron* : ne pallida
Bentley.   [4] dissiliat, *II.*

---

[a] These were priests of Cybele, who mutilated themselves,
cf. the *Attis* of Catullus.   Horace is here quoting and sum-
marizing an epigram by Philodemus, a Greek philosopher,
and a client of the L. Calpurnius Piso who was assailed by

gold ? When hungry, do you disdain everything save peacock and turbot ? When your passions prove unruly, would you rather be torn with desire ? I should not, for the pleasures I love are those easy to attain. " By and by," " Nay more," " If my husband goes out "—a woman who speaks thus is for the Galli,[a] says Philodemus ; for himself he asks for one who is neither high-priced nor slow to come when bidden. She must be fair and straight, and only so far arranged that she will not wish to seem taller or fairer than nature allows. When she and I embrace, she is to me an Ilia or an Egeria[b] : I give her any name. No fears have I in her company, that a husband may rush back from the country, the door burst open, the dog bark, the house ring through and through with the din and clatter of his knocking ; that the woman, white as a sheet, will leap away, the maid in league with her cry out in terror, she fearing for her limbs, her guilty mistress for her dowry, and I for myself. With clothes dishevelled and bare of foot, I must run off, dreading disaster in purse or person or at least repute. To be caught is an unhappy fate : this I could prove, even with Fabius [c] as umpire.

Cicero in his *In Pisonem*, where Philodemus is characterized in 68 ff. The epigram is discussed by G. L. Hendrickson in *A.J.P.* xxxlx. (1918) pp. 27 ff., and by F. A. Wright, xlii. (1921) pp. 168, 169.

[b] Ilia, mother of Romulus, and Egeria, the nymph who inspired Numa, here represent women of highest rank.

[c] *Cf. Sat.* i. 1. 14. This writer on Stoicism is said to have been detected in adultery.

III

ON MUTUAL FORBEARANCE

THE connexion between this satire and the preceding one is indicated at the outset, for the musician Tigellius is again introduced as a person who well illustrates the foibles and inconsistencies of a large class of people. But, says Horace, some one may ask me, "Have you yourself no faults?" Yes, I have, though they may not be as bad as his. I trust I am not like Maenius, who laid bare the faults of others, but overlooked his own. Self-satisfaction of this sort well deserves to be satirized. A man should examine himself and search out his own faults before criticizing others (1-37).

Think how blind is the lover to the defects of his beloved, or how tenderly a fond father treats his child's deformities. Even so we should be indulgent to the weaknesses of our friends. On the contrary, we often look upon real virtues as faults, calling for example modest behaviour stupidity, and simplicity boorishness. We must exercise mutual forbearance and also discriminate between failings, for a mere impropriety is not as serious as a heinous crime (38-95).

In fact the Stoic paradox that all offences are equal, "omnia peccata paria esse" (Cicero, *De finibus*,

30

iv. 19. 55), besides being repugnant to common sense, is historically unsound, our social ethics being the result of a process of evolution. Yet your Stoic would punish all offences alike, if he were a king (96-124).

" If he were a king," did I say ? Why, according to another of his paradoxes, the Stoic is already a king, even as he is rich and handsome and everything else that is good. " Yes," he would explain, " I am a king potentially, even as Hermogenes is a singer, though he does not open his lips." " Well," replies Horace, " I cannot see that your crown wins you esteem or saves you from ill-treatment. For myself, not being a philosopher, I will remain a private citizen, and live on terms of mutual forbearance with others " (124-142).

In striking contrast with Satire II., this one is kindly and genial in tone, and it would seem that the author was disarming criticism by his assurance that he was not disposed to be over-censorious, as we learn from ll. 63 ff. Horace has now become acquainted with Maecenas, and this improvement in his worldly prospects may to some extent account for the change of tone, and the doffing of the severity of Lucilian invective.

III.

Omnibus hoc vitium est cantoribus, inter amicos
ut numquam inducant animum cantare rogati,
iniussi numquam desistant.   Sardus habebat
ille Tigellius hoc.   Caesar, qui cogere posset,
si peteret per amicitiam patris atque suam, non   5
quicquam proficeret ; si collibuisset, ab ovo
usque ad mala citaret " io Bacche[1] ! " modo summa
voce, modo hac, resonat[2] quae chordis quattuor ima.
nil aequale homini fuit illi : saepe velut qui
currebat fugiens hostem, persaepe velut qui[3]   10
Iunonis sacra ferret ; habebat saepe ducentos,
saepe decem servos ; modo reges atque tetrarchas,
omnia magna loquens, modo " sit mihi mensa tripes et
concha salis puri et toga, quae defendere frigus
quamvis crassa queat."   deciens centena dedisses   15
huic parco, paucis contento, quinque diebus
nil erat in loculis.   noctes vigilabat ad ipsum
mane, diem totum stertebat.   nil fuit umquam
sic impar sibi.

[1] Bacchae *BE*.   [2] resonet $\psi\lambda l$.
[3] *B omits l.* 10; *see* C.R. *xxx. p.* 15.

---

[a] A dinner opened with the *gustatio* or *promulsis*, supposed
to whet the appetite.   In this eggs played a part.   Fruit
was served as a dessert just as with us.

[b] The refrain of a drinking-song.

[c] Editors commonly take *summa* and *ima* as defining the
position of strings on the lyre, *summa* = ὑπάτη and *ima* =
νήτη ; the former therefore being " lowest," and the latter
" highest," and *voce* being " the note."   But see Clement L.
Smith in *C.R.* xx. (1906) pp. 397 ff.

Satire III

All singers have this fault : if asked to sing among
their friends they are never so inclined ; if unasked,
they never leave off. That son of Sardinia, Tigellius,
was of this sort. If Caesar, who might have forced
him to comply, should beg him by his father's friend-
ship and his own, he could make no headway. If the
man took the fancy, then from the egg-course to the
fruit *a* he would keep chanting " Io Bacche ! " *b* now
with highest voice and now with one responding in
lowest pitch to the tetrachord.*c* There was nothing
consistent in the fellow. Often he would run as if
fleeing from a foe ; very often he would stalk as
slowly as some bearer of Juno's holy offerings.*d*
Often he would keep two hundred slaves, often only
ten. Now he would talk of kings and tetrarchs,
everything grand, and now he'd say, " Give me a
three-legged table, a shell of clean salt, and a coat
that, however coarse, can keep out the cold." Sup-
pose you had given a million *e* to this thrifty gentle-
man, contented with so little ; in a week there was
nothing in his pockets. All night, till dawn, he
would stay awake ; all day would snore. Never
was a creature so inconsistent.

d A reference to the κανηφόροι, or basket-bearers, who
in religious processions walked with slow and stately stride.
e i.e. sesterces. The sum in question would amount,
roughly speaking, to £10,000 or $50,000.

Nunc aliquis dicat mihi : " quid tu ?   19
nullane habes vitia ? " immo alia et fortasse minora.[1]
Maenius absentem Novium cum carperet, " heus tu "
quidam ait, " ignoras te, an ut ignotum dare nobis
verba putas ? " " egomet mi ignosco " Maenius
   inquit.
stultus et improbus hic amor est dignusque notari.

   Cum tua pervideas[2] oculis mala[3] lippus inunctis, 25
cur in amicorum vitiis tam cernis acutum
quam aut aquila aut serpens Epidaurius ?   at[4] tibi
   contra
evenit, inquirant vitia ut tua rursus et illi.

   Iracundior est paulo, minus aptus acutis[5]
naribus horum hominum ; rideri possit eo, quod   30
rusticius tonso toga defluit et male laxus
in pede calceus haeret : at est bonus, ut melior vir
non alius quisquam, at tibi amicus, at ingenium ingens
inculto latet hoc sub corpore.[6]   denique te ipsum
concute, num qua tibi vitiorum inseverit[7] olim   35
natura aut etiam consuetudo mala ; namque
neglectis urenda filix innascitur agris.

   Illuc praevertamur, amatorem quod amicae[8]
turpia decipiunt caecum vitia, aut etiam ipsa haec
delectant, veluti Balbinum polypus Hagnae.   40
vellem in amicitia sic erraremus, et isti
errori nomen virtus[9] posuisset honestum.

---

[1] *B omits l.* 20.
[2] praevideas *Bentley.*   [3] male *Bentley.*
[4] ac *MSS.*   [5] aduncis *Bentley.*
[6] pectore, *II.*   [7] insederit, *II.*   [8] amici, *II.*
[9] victus *Housman, in* J.P. xviii. p. 3.

---

[a] Epidaurus was famous for the worship of Aesculapius,
whose symbol was a serpent or δράκων, a word supposed to
come from δέρκομαι, "to see."

¹⁹ Now someone may say to me : " What about yourself ? Have you no faults ? " Why yes, but not the same, and perhaps lesser ones. When Maenius once was carping at Novius behind his back, " Look out, sir," said someone, " do you not know yourself ? Or do you think you impose on us, as one we do not know ? " " I take no note of myself," said Maenius. Such self-love is foolish and shameless, and deserves to be censured.

²⁵ When you look over your own sins, your eyes are rheumy and daubed with ointment ; why, when you view the failings of your friends, are you as keen of sight as an eagle or as a serpent of Epidaurus ᵃ ? But, on the other hand, the result for you is that they, too, in turn peer into *your* faults.

²⁹ " He is a little too hasty in temper, ill-suited to the keen noses of folk nowadays. He might awake a smile because his hair is cut in country style, his toga sits ill, and his loose shoe will hardly stay on his foot." ᵇ But he's a good man, none better ; but he's your friend ; but under that uncouth frame are hidden great gifts. In a word, give yourself a shaking and see whether nature, or haply some bad habit, has not at some time sown in you the seeds of folly ; for in neglected fields there springs up bracken, which you must burn.

³⁸ Let us turn first to this fact, that the lover, in his blindness, fails to see his lady's unsightly blemishes, nay is even charmed with them, as was Balbinus with Hagna's wen. I could wish that we made the like mistake in friendship and that to such an error our ethics had given an honourable name. At any

ᵇ The scholiasts suggest that this may be a description either of Virgil or of Horace himself.

at[1] pater ut gnati, sic nos debemus amici[2]
si quod sit vitium non fastidire. strabonem
appellat paetum pater, et pullum, male parvus   45
si cui filius est, ut abortivus fuit olim
Sisyphus ; hunc varum distortis cruribus, illum
balbutit scaurum pravis fultum male talis.
parcius hic vivit : frugi dicatur. ineptus
et iactantior hic paulo est : concinnus amicis   50
postulat ut videatur. at est truculentior atque
plus aequo liber : simplex fortisque habeatur.
caldior est : acris inter numeretur. opinor,
haec res et iungit, iunctos et servat amicos.
at nos virtutes ipsas invertimus atque   55
sincerum cupimus[3] vas incrustare.[4] probus quis
nobiscum vivit, multum demissus homo : illi[5]
tardo cognomen, pingui, damus. hic fugit omnis
insidias nullique malo latus obdit apertum,
cum genus hoc inter vitae versemur,[6] ubi acris   60
invidia atque vigent ubi crimina : pro bene sano
ac non incauto fictum astutumque vocamus.
simplicior quis et est qualem me saepe libenter
obtulerim tibi, Maecenas, ut[7] forte legentem
aut tacitum impellat[8] quovis sermone molestus[9] :   65
" communi sensu plane caret " inquimus. eheu,

---

[1] at] ac *BDEM Vollmer.*   [2] amicis *B.*
[3] fugimus *B* : furimus *Goth.*, *Vollmer.*   [4] incurtare *BDE.*
  [5] ille *V.*   [6] versemur *V Bentley* : versetur *MSS.*
            [7] ut] aut *or* haut, *II.*
  [8] impediat *Bentley. Some editors punctuate after* sermone.
            [9] modestus, *II.*

---

[a] The pet names used, viz. *paetus, pullus, varus, scaurus,*
are all adjectives denoting a less objectionable form of the
defect referred to, but they were also *cognomina* in well-
known family names. " Paetus " is associated with the
Aelii and Papirii, " Pullus " with the Fabii and the Iunii,
" Varus " with the Quintilii, and " Scaurus " with the

rate, we should deal with a friend as a father with
his child, and not be disgusted at some blemish. If a
boy squints, his father calls him " Blinky " ; if his
son is sadly puny, like misbegotten Sisyphus of
former days, he styles him " Chickabiddy." One
with crooked legs he fondly calls " Cruikshank," and
one that can hardly stand on twisted ankles, " Curly-
legs." [a] Is a friend somewhat close ? Let us call
him thrifty. Does another fail in tact and show off
a bit too much ? He wants his friends to think him
agreeable. Or is he somewhat bluff and too out-
spoken ? Let him pass for frank and fearless. Hot-
headed is he ? Let him be counted a man of spirit.
This, I take it, is how to make friends, and to keep
them when made. But we turn virtues themselves
upside down, and want to soil a clean vessel. Does
there live among us an honest soul, a truly modest
fellow ? We nickname him slow and stupid. Does
another shun every snare and offer no exposed side
to malice, seeing that we live in that kind of a world
where keen envy and slanders are so rife ? Instead
of his good sense and prudence we speak of his
craftiness and insincerity. Is one somewhat simple
and such as often I have freely shown myself to you,
Maecenas, interrupting you perhaps while reading
or thinking with some annoying chatter ? " He is
quite devoid of social tact," [b] we say. Ah, how

Aemilii and Aurelii. For the passage as a whole we may
compare Plato, *Rep.* v. 474 D, Lucretius, iv. 1100 ff., Ovid,
Ars Am. ii. 657 ; and among modern writers, Molière,
Misanthrope, Act ii. Sc. 5, *e.g.* " Ils comptent les défauts
pour des perfections."

   [b] The expression *communis sensus* does not mean precisely
the same as the phrase we have derived from it, viz. "common
sense." It is rather social sense, a sense of propriety in
dealing with our fellows, or what the French call *savoir faire.*

quam temere in nosmet legem sancimus iniquam !
nam vitiis nemo sine nascitur : optimus ille est,
qui minimis urgetur. amicus dulcis, ut aequum est,
cum mea compenset vitiis bona, pluribus hisce, 70
si modo plura mihi bona sunt, inclinet, amari
si volet : hac lege in trutina ponetur eadem.
qui ne tuberibus propriis offendat amicum
postulat, ignoscet[1] verrucis illius : aequum est
peccatis veniam poscentem reddere rursus. 75

Denique, quatenus excidi penitus vitium irae,[2]
cetera item nequeunt stultis haerentia, cur non
ponderibus modulisque suis ratio utitur, ac res
ut quaeque est, ita suppliciis delicta coercet ?
si quis eum servum, patinam qui tollere iussus 80
semesos piscis tepidumque ligurrierit ius,
in cruce suffigat, Labeone insanior inter
sanos dicatur. quanto hoc[3] furiosius atque
maius peccatum est : paulum deliquit amicus,
quod nisi concedas, habeare insuavis : acerbus[4] 85
odisti et fugis ut Rusonem debitor aeris,
qui nisi, cum tristes misero venere Kalendae,
mercedem aut nummos unde unde extricat, amaras
porrecto iugulo historias captivus ut audit.
comminxit lectum potus, mensave catillum 90

---

[1] ignoscat *B*.   [2] *B omits* 76-80.
[3] hoc *omitted EM* : *deleted in V.*
[4] *Some punctuate after* acerbus ; *so Orelli and Ritter.*

---

[a] According to the Stoics only the ideal sage, the *sapiens*,
is excepted from the class of *stulti*. Horace places himself
in the majority.   [b] Labeo was a crazy jurisconsult.

[c] Ruso, the usurer, has literary aspirations and writes
histories. The fate of the debtor, who is in Ruso's power,
and must therefore listen while Ruso reads to him from his
works, is humorously regarded as most horrible. *Cf.*
Macaulay's story of the criminal, who went to the galleys
rather than read the history of Guicciardini. ("Burleigh

lightly do we set up an unjust law to our own harm !
For no living wight is without faults : the best is he
who is burdened with the least. My kindly friend
must, as is fair, weigh my virtues against my faults,
if he wishes to gain my love, and must turn the scales
in their favour as being the more numerous—if only
my virtues are the more numerous. On that con-
dition he shall be weighed in the same scale. One
who expects his friend not to be offended by his
own warts will pardon the other's pimples. It is
but fair that one who craves indulgence for failings
should grant it in return.

[76] In fine, since the fault of anger, and all the
other faults that cleave to fools[a] cannot be wholly
cut away, why does not Reason use her own weights
and measures, and visit offences with punishment
suited to each ? If one were to crucify a slave who,
when bidden to take away a dish, has greedily licked
up the half-eaten fish and its sauce, now cold, sane
men would call him more insane than Labeo.[b] How
much madder and grosser a sin is this : a friend has
committed a slight offence, which you would be
thought ungracious not to pardon ; you hate him
bitterly and shun him, as Ruso is shunned by his
debtor, who, poor wretch, if at the coming of the sad
Kalends he cannot scrape up from some quarter
either interest or principal, must offer his throat like
a prisoner of war and listen to his captor's dreary
histories ![c] What if in his cups my friend has wet
the couch or knocked off the table a bowl once

and his Times " in *Critical and Historical Essays*.) *Cf.*
Juvenal's

> mille pericula saevae
> urbis et Augusto recitantes mense poetas
>
> (*Sat.* iii. 8).

Euandri manibus tritum deiecit[1] : ob hanc rem,
aut positum ante mea[2] quia pullum in parte catini
sustulit esuriens, minus hoc iucundus amicus
sit mihi ? quid faciam si furtum fecerit, aut si
prodiderit commissa fide sponsumve negarit ?   95
quis paria esse fere placuit peccata, laborant
cum ventum ad verum est : sensus moresque repug-
    nant
atque ipsa Utilitas, iusti prope mater et aequi.

Cum prorepserunt primis animalia terris,
mutum et turpe pecus, glandem atque cubilia propter
unguibus et pugnis, dein fustibus, atque ita porro   101
pugnabant armis, quae post fabricaverat usus,
donec verba, quibus voces sensusque notarent,[3]
nominaque invenere ; dehinc absistere bello,
oppida coeperunt munire et ponere leges,   105
ne quis fur esset, neu latro, neu quis adulter.
nam fuit ante Helenam cunnus taeterrima belli
causa, sed ignotis perierunt mortibus illi,
quos venerem incertam rapientis more ferarum
viribus editior caedebat ut in grege taurus.   110
iura inventa metu iniusti fateare necesse est,
tempora si fastosque velis evolvere mundi.
nec Natura potest iusto secernere iniquum,
dividit ut bona diversis, fugienda petendis ;
nec vincet Ratio hoc, tantundem ut peccet idemque

[1] proiecit *B*.

[2] me, *II* : *B* omits 92, *as well as* 95-100, *and* 111-124.

[3] quibus sensus, vocesque, notarent *Housman* (*cf. Lucr.*
v. 1041 *ff.*)

---

[a] *i.e.* of great antiquity and consequently very valuable.

[b] This was a doctrine of the Stoics ; *cf.* Cicero, *De fin.* iv.
19. 55, " recte facta omnia aequalia, omnia peccata paria esse."

[c] Appeal is here made to the Epicureans, whose moral
philosophy rested on a distinctly utilitarian basis.

fingered by Evander,[a] is he for such offence, or because when hungry he snatched up first a pullet served on my side of the dish, to be less pleasing in my eyes? What shall I do if he commits a theft, or betrays a trust, or disowns his bond? Those whose creed is that all sins are much on a par [b] are at a loss when they come to face facts. Feelings and customs rebel, and so does Expedience herself, the mother, we may say, of justice and right.[c]

[99] When living creatures [d] crawled forth upon primeval earth, dumb, shapeless beasts, they fought for their acorns and lairs with nails and fists, then with clubs, and so on step by step with the weapons which need had later forged, until they found words and names [e] wherewith to give meaning to their cries and feelings. Thenceforth they began to cease from war, to build towns, and to frame laws that none should thieve or rob or commit adultery. For before Helen's day a wench was the most dreadful cause of war, but deaths unknown to fame were theirs whom, snatching fickle love in wild-beast fashion, a man stronger in might struck down, like the bull in a herd. If you will but turn over the annals and records of the world, you must needs confess that justice was born of the fear of injustice.[f] Between right and wrong Nature can draw no such distinction as between things gainful and harmful, what is to be sought and what is to be shunned; nor will Reason ever prove this, that the sin is one and the

[d] The doctrine of the evolution of society, as here set forth, is based on Lucretius, *De rerum natura*, v. 780 ff.

[e] Or "verbs and nouns," the two main divisions of human speech. *Cf. A.P.* 234-5.

[f] According to the utilitarian theory of ethics, the sense of right and wrong is not innate in us.

qui teneros caules alieni fregerit horti 116
et qui nocturnus sacra divum[1] legerit.   adsit
regula, peccatis quae poenas inroget aequas,
ne scutica dignum horribili sectere flagello.
nam ut ferula caedas meritum maiora subire 120
verbera non vereor, cum dicas esse pares res
furta latrociniis et magnis parva mineris
falce recisurum simili te, si tibi regnum
permittant homines.
       Si dives, qui sapiens est,
et sutor bonus et solus formosus et est rex, 125
cur optas quod habes ?   "non nosti quid pater " inquit
" Chrysippus dicat : sapiens crepidas sibi numquam
nec soleas fecit ; sutor tamen est sapiens."   qui[2] ?
" ut quamvis tacet Hermogenes cantor tamen atque
optimus est modulator ; ut Alfenus vafer omni 130
abiecto instrumento artis clausaque taberna[3]
tonsor[4] erat, sapiens operis sic optimus omnis
est opifex solus, sic rex."   vellunt tibi barbam
lascivi pueri ; quos tu nisi fuste coerces,
urgeris turba circum te stante miserque[5] 135
rumperis et latras, magnorum maxime regum.

---

[1] divum sacra *aK*.   [2] qui *B* : quo *other MSS.*
[3] ustrina *V*.   [4] tonsor *V* : sutor *MSS., Porph.*
[5] *Beginning with* 135, *B is lacking up to the end of Book II. of the* Epistles.

---

[a] For another interpretation see T. G. Tucker in *C.R.*
1920, p. 156.
[b] The sixth Stoic Paradox according to Cicero, is " solum
sapientem esse divitem."   The Stoics held that the truly
wise man or philosopher was perfect : he was therefore
rich, as well as beautiful, accomplished, and a king among
men.   Horace ridicules these claims here and elsewhere,

same to cut young cabbages in a neighbour's garden and to steal by night the sacred emblems of the gods. Let us have a rule to assign just penalties to offences, lest you flay with the terrible scourge what calls for the strap. For [a] as to your striking with the rod one who deserves sterner measures, I am not afraid of that, when you say that theft is on a par with highway robbery, and when you threaten to prune away all crimes, great and small, with the same hook, if men would but give you royal power.

[124] If the wise man is rich,[b] and a good cobbler, and alone handsome and a king, why crave what you already have? [c] "You do not know," he answers, "what our father Chrysippus [d] means. The wise man has never made himself shoes or sandals ; yet the wise man is a cobbler." How so ? "As Hermogenes, however silent, is still the best of singers and musicians ; as shrewd Alfenus, after tossing aside every tool of his art and closing his shop, was a barber [e] ; so the wise man—he alone— is the best workman of every craft, so is he king." Mischievous boys pluck at your beard, and unless you keep them off with your staff, you are jostled by the crowd that surrounds you, while you, poor wretch, snarl and burst with rage, O mightiest of mighty

as in *Epist.* i. 1. 106. *Cf.* the account of the wise man of the Stoics given in Plutarch, *Mor.* p. 1057, and for St. Paul's application of the principle see 2 Cor. 6. 4-10.

[c] The Stoic has just admitted that he is not a king.

[d] Chrysippus was regarded as the second founder of Stoicism, the first being Zeno.

[e] The reading *tonsor* is preferred to *sutor*. As the Stoic tries to prove that the wise man is a cobbler, he naturally turns elsewhere for illustrations, *e.g.* to Hermogenes the musician, and to Alfenus the barber.

ne longum faciam : dum tu quadrante lavatum
rex ibis neque te quisquam stipator ineptum
praeter Crispinum sectabitur, et mihi dulces
ignoscent, si quid peccaro stultus, amici,   140
inque vicem illorum patiar delicta libenter,
privatusque magis vivam te rege beatus.

---

^a Like a Persian king, βασιλεὺς βασιλέων.
^b *Cf. Sat.* i. 1. 120.

kings!ᵃ In short, while you, a king, go to your penny
bath, and no escort attends you except crazy Cris-
pinus,ᵇ my kindly friends will pardon me if I, your
foolish man,ᶜ commit some offence, and in turn I
shall gladly put up with their shortcomings, and in
my private station shall live more happily than Your
Majesty.

ᶜ *i.e. stultus*, as the Stoics used it, the opposite of *sapiens*.

IV

A DEFENCE OF SATIRE

THE writers of Old Attic Comedy assailed the vicious with the utmost freedom. In Roman literature, Lucilius shows the same spirit and boldness, but his metrical forms are different, and his verse is uncouth. He was careless and verbose, more interested in the quantity than in the quality of his work (1-13).

Similar in this last respect is Crispinus, who challenges the poet to a scribbling contest, but Horace declines to compete with such poetasters, even as he refuses to emulate the self-satisfied Fannius by reading his verses in public, because this kind of writing is not popular. Men do not like to have their weaknesses exposed. " Give such a poet a wide berth," they cry (14-38).

" Listen to my defence," says Horace. " In the first place, a man who composes verses as I do, verses that are really more like conversation, should not be called a poet. The true poet has imaginative power and lofty utterance. This is why the question has been raised whether comedy is poetry, for even in its most spirited passages, as rendered on the stage, we are really dealing with pure conversation, such as would be suitable to similar scenes in daily life " (38-56).

" So it is with the verses of Lucilius and my own. Take away the metrical element, change the word-order, and you have plain prose. But the question whether satire is poetry must be postponed. At present let us consider the question of its unpopularity " (56-65).

46

SATIRES, I. iv.

" You look upon me as an informer, but even if
you are a rogue I am no informer. My friends will
acquit me of such a charge. I am not writing for
the general public, and my object is not to give
pain. Yet it is my habit to observe the conduct of
others, and to profit thereby, for I was trained to
do so by my father, and have always continued the
practice. To be sure, I jot down my thoughts, but
what of that ? Nowadays everybody writes, and
you, my critic, willy-nilly, will take to writing
yourself " (65-143).

On the appearance of his first *Satires* (and it is
to be noticed that the carefully chosen subjunctive
habeat in l. 71 does not preclude their publication),
the poet's critics had accused Horace of being a
malevolent scandal-monger. They also contrasted
him unfavourably with Lucilius, who in his open war-
fare used the weapons of Old Comedy, was familiar
with the Greek moralists and philosophers, and had
the pen of a ready writer. In his reply, Horace
maintains that his own satire is not personal, but
rather social and general in its application. He does
not indulge in the invective of Old Comedy, but
rather follows the New in spirit as well as in style.
His teacher in morals, if not a great philosopher (*cf.
sapiens*, l. 115), was a representative of the fine, old-
fashioned Roman virtues, even his own father. As for
the copiousness of Lucilius, that was his predecessor's
chief fault, which he himself would carefully avoid.

This is one of the early Satires, and in view of the
citation in l. 92 is to be associated closely with the
Second. As there is no reference to Maecenas, it
was probably composed before the poet's introduction
to the statesman in 38 B.C.

IV.

Eupolis atque Cratinus Aristophanesque poetae
atque alii, quorum comoedia prisca virorum est,
si quis erat dignus describi, quod malus ac fur,
quod moechus foret aut sicarius aut alioqui
famosus, multa cum libertate notabant.   5
hinc omnis pendet Lucilius, hosce secutus
mutatis tantum pedibus numerisque ; facetus,
emunctae naris, durus componere versus.
nam fuit hoc vitiosus : in hora saepe ducentos,
ut magnum, versus dictabat stans pede in uno ;   10
cum flueret lutulentus, erat quod tollere velles ;
garrulus atque piger scribendi ferre laborem,
scribendi recte : nam ut multum, nil moror.   ecce,
Crispinus minimo me provocat : " accipe, si vis,
accipiam[1] tabulas : detur[2] nobis locus, hora,   15
custodes ; videamus uter plus scribere possit."
di bene fecerunt, inopis me quodque pusilli
finxerunt animi, raro et perpauca loquentis.
at tu conclusas hircinis follibus auras
usque laborantis, dum ferrum molliat ignis,   20
ut mavis, imitare.

[1] accipe iam, *I, but not in harmony with* hora.   [2] dentur, *II.*

---

a For the emphasis on *poetae* (denied by Ullman, *A.P.A.*
xlviii. p. 115) see *Epist.* ii. 1. 247.

b Proverbial for " doing without effort."

c For Crispinus see *Sat.* i. 1. 120. He offers to bet a

Satire IV

Eupolis and Cratinus and Aristophanes, true poets,[a] and the other good men to whom Old Comedy belongs, if there was anyone deserving to be drawn as a rogue and thief, as a rake or cut-throat, or as scandalous in any other way, set their mark upon him with great freedom. It is on these that Lucilius wholly hangs ; these he has followed, changing only metre and rhythm. Witty he was, and of keen-scented nostrils, but harsh in framing his verse. Herein lay his fault : often in an hour, as though a great exploit, he would dictate two hundred lines while standing, as they say, on one foot.[b] In his muddy stream there was much that you would like to remove. He was wordy, and too lazy to put up with the trouble of writing—of writing correctly, I mean ; for as to quantity, I let that pass. See, Crispinus challenges me at long odds[c] : " Take your tablets, please ; I'll take mine. Let a place be fixed for us, and time and judges ; let us see which can write the most." The gods be praised for fashioning me of meagre wit and lowly spirit, of rare and scanty speech ! But do you, for such is your taste, be like the air shut up in goat-skin bellows, and ever puffing away until the fire softens the iron.

large sum against a small one on my part. Bentley conjectured *nummo* for *minimo*, *i.e.* " bets me a sesterce," that being all his poverty would allow.

Beatus Fannius ultro
delatis capsis et imagine, cum mea nemo
scripta legat volgo recitare timentis ob hanc rem,
quod sunt quos genus hoc minime iuvat, utpote pluris
culpari dignos. quemvis media elige[1] turba :   25
aut ob avaritiam[2] aut misera[3] ambitione laborat.
hic nuptarum insanit amoribus, hic puerorum ;
hunc capit argenti splendor ; stupet Albius aere ;
hic mutat merces surgente a sole ad eum quo
vespertina tepet[4] regio ; quin per mala praeceps   30
fertur uti pulvis collectus turbine, ne quid
summa deperdat metuens aut ampliet ut rem :
omnes hi metuunt versus, odere poetas.
" faenum habet in cornu : longe fuge ! dummodo risum
excutiat sibi, non hic[5] cuiquam parcet amico ;   35
et quodcumque semel chartis illeverit, omnis
gestiet a furno redeuntis scire lacuque
et pueros et anus."

Agedum, pauca accipe contra.
primum ego me illorum, dederim quibus esse poetas,[6]
excerpam numero : neque enim concludere versum 40
dixeris esse satis ; neque, si qui scribat uti nos
sermoni propiora, putes hunc esse poetam.

[1] erue *K, Vollmer* : eripe 3 *Bland.* : arripe *Bentley.*
[2] ab avaritia, *see Rolfe*, C.P. vii. p. 246.
[3] miser *K, II.*   [4] patet, *II.*
[5] non non, *II, adopted by Vollmer and Garrod.*
[6] poetis *R and scholia on Sat.* i. 6. 25 ; *so Vollmer.*

[a] Fannius, a petty poet, brought his writings (kept in
capsae or cylindrical boxes), together with his portrait, into
prominence, but in what way he did so is now unknown.

²¹ Happy fellow, Fannius, who has delivered his books and bust unasked ! *a* My writings no one reads, and I fear to recite them in public, the fact being that this style *b* is abhorrent to some, inasmuch as most people merit censure. Choose anyone from amid a crowd : he is suffering either from avarice or some wretched ambition. One is mad with love for somebody's wife, another for boys. Here is one whose fancy the sheen of silver catches ; Albius *c* dotes on bronzes ; another trades his wares from the rising sun to regions warmed by his evening rays ; nay, through perils he rushes headlong, like dust gathered up by a whirlwind, fearful lest he lose aught of his total, or fail to add to his wealth. All of these dread verses and detest the poet : " He carries hay on his horns,*d* give him a wide berth. Provided he can raise a laugh for himself, he will spare not a single friend, and whatever he has once scribbled on his sheets he will rejoice to have all know, all the slaves and old dames as they come home from bakehouse and pond." *e*

³⁸ Come now, listen to a few words in answer. First I will take my own name from the list of such as I would allow to be poets. For you would not call it enough to round off a verse, nor would you count anyone poet who writes, as I do, lines more

Probably he presented them to private libraries. At this time the only public library in Rome was the one founded by Asinius Pollio in 38 B.C., and the only living writer whose works were admitted to it was Varro. Another view is that Fannius's admirers presented the poet with book-cases and bust. *b i.e.*, Satire.

c The extravagance of Albius impoverishes his son (l.109).

d Dangerous cattle were thus distinguished.

e i.e. the common people, as they went to get bread from the public bakery and water from the public tanks. Agrippa set up seven hundred *lacus* or reservoirs in Rome.

ingenium cui sit, cui mens divinior atque os
magna sonaturum, des nominis huius honorem.
idcirco quidam Comoedia necne poema   45
esset quaesivere, quod acer spiritus ac vis
nec verbis nec rebus inest, nisi quod pede certo
differt sermoni, sermo merus. " at pater ardens
saevit, quod meretrice nepos insanus[1] amica
filius uxorem grandi[2] cum dote recuset,   50
ebrius et, magnum quod dedecus, ambulet ante
noctem cum facibus." numquid Pomponius istis
audiret leviora, pater si viveret ? ergo
non satis est puris[3] versum perscribere verbis,
quem si dissolvas, quivis stomachetur eodem   55
quo personatus pacto pater. his, ego quae nunc,
olim quae scripsit Lucilius, eripias si
tempora certa modosque, et quod prius ordine
    verbum[4] est,
posterius facias, praeponens ultima primis,
non, ut si solvas " postquam Discordia taetra   60
Belli ferratos postis portasque refregit,"
invenias etiam disiecti membra poetae.

Hactenus haec : alias iustum sit necne poema,
nunc illud tantum quaeram, meritone tibi sit
suspectum genus hoc scribendi. Sulcius acer   65
ambulat et Caprius, rauci male cumque libellis,
magnus uterque timor latronibus : at bene si quis
et vivat puris manibus, contemnat utrumque.

[1] insanit, *II.*   [2] grandem, *II.*   [3] pueris, *II.*   [4] versum, *II.*

---

[a] Who Pomponius was is unknown, but in real life he
corresponds to the prodigal in the play, and the language
used by his father under the circumstances would be similar
to that in the scene from Comedy.

[b] The passage cited is from Ennius and refers to the
temple of Janus, which was opened in time of war. It
is imitated in Virgil, *Aen.* vii. 622.

akin to prose. If one has gifts inborn, if one has a
soul divine and tongue of noble utterance, to such
give the honour of that name. Hence some have
questioned whether Comedy is or is not poetry;
for neither in diction nor in matter has it the fire
and force of inspiration, and, save that it differs
from prose-talk in its regular beat, it is mere prose.
"But," you say, "there is the father storming in
passion because his spendthrift son, madly in love
with a wanton mistress, rejects a wife with large
dower, and in drunken fit reels abroad—sad scandal
—with torches in broad daylight." Would Pom-
ponius hear a lecture less stern than this, were his
father alive? [a] And so 'tis not enough to write out
a line of simple words such that, should you break
it up, any father whatever would rage in the same
fashion as the father in the play. Take from the
verses which I am writing now, or which Lucilius
wrote in former days, their regular beat and rhythm
—change the order of the words, transposing the
first and the last—and it would not be like breaking
up:

> When foul Discord's din
> War's posts and gates of bronze had broken in,

where, even when he is dismembered, you would find
the limbs of a poet.[b]

63 Of this enough. Some other time we'll see
whether this kind of writing is true poetry or not.
To-day the only question I'll ask is this, whether
you are right in viewing it with distrust. Keen-
scented Sulcius and Caprius stalk about, horribly
hoarse and armed with writs, both a great terror to
robbers, but if a man is honest of life and his hands

ut sis tu similis Caeli Birrique latronum,
non ego sim[1] Capri neque Sulci : cur metuas me ? 70
nulla taberna meos habeat neque pila libellos,
quis manus insudet volgi Hermogenisque Tigelli ;
nec[2] recito cuiquam nisi amicis, idque coactus,
non ubivis coramve quibuslibet. in medio qui
scripta foro recitent, sunt multi, quique lavantes : 75
suave locus voci resonat conclusus. inanis
hoc iuvat, haud illud quaerentis, num sine sensu,
tempore num faciant alieno.

                            " Laedere gaudes "
inquit,[3] "et hoc studio pravus facis."   Unde petitum
hoc in me iacis ?   est auctor quis denique eorum   80
vixi cum quibus ?   absentem qui rodit amicum,
qui non defendit alio culpante, solutos
qui captat risus hominum famamque dicacis,
fingere qui non visa potest, commissa tacere
qui nequit : hic niger est, hunc tu, Romane, caveto. 85
saepe tribus lectis videas cenare quaternos,
e quibus unus[4] amet[5] quavis aspergere cunctos
praeter eum qui praebet aquam ; post hunc quoque
      potus,
condita cum verax aperit praecordia Liber.

----

[1] sum *Porph*.   [2] non, *II*.   [3] inquis *M, II*.   [4] imus, *II*.
[5] amet 1 *Bland.*, *Bentley* : avet *mss.* ; *a subjunctive is
necessary here.*

----

  a Sulcius and Caprius are commonly supposed to have
been professional informers, hoarse from bawling in the
courts, but Ullman (*A.P.A.* xlviii. p. 117) takes them to be
contemporary satirists, who recite their long-winded poems
and carry about copies for free distribution.
  b For Tigellius see *Sat*. i. 3. 129. The scholiasts iden-
tify him with the Tigellius of *Sat*. i. 2. 3, and i. 3. 4,
and Ullman convincingly upholds this view (*C.P.* x. pp.
270 ff.). He was now dead, but Horace treats him as the
poet of the *volgus*. See note on *Sat*. i. 10. 90. Book-stalls

clean, he may scorn them both.[a] Though you be like Caelius and Birrius, the robbers, I need not be like Caprius or Sulcius : why should you fear me ? I want no stall or pillar to have my little works, so that the hands of the crowd—and Hermogenes Tigellius [b]—may sweat over them. Nor do I recite them to any save my friends, and then only when pressed—not anywhere or before any hearers. Many there are who recite their writings in the middle of the Forum, or in the baths. How pleasantly the vaulted space echoes the voice ! That delights the frivolous, who never ask themselves this, whether what they do is in bad taste or out of season.

[78] " You like to give pain," says one, " and you do so with spiteful intent." Where have you found this missile to hurl at me ? Does anyone whatever with whom I have lived vouch for it ? The man who backbites an absent friend ; who fails to defend him when another finds fault ; the man who courts the loud laughter of others, and the reputation of a wit ; who can invent what he never saw ; who cannot keep a secret—that man is black of heart ; of him beware, good Roman. Often on each of the three couches you may see four at dinner,[c] among whom one loves to bespatter in any way everyone present except the host who provides the water, and later him as well, when he has well drunk and the truthful god of free speech [d] unlocks the heart's secrets.

were usually in arcades, the pillars of which were doubtless used for advertising the books within. One may compare the Parisian kiosques.

[c] Three was the usual number, so that this was a large party. Cicero speaks of five as a great crush: *Graeci stipati, quini in lectulis* (*In Pis.* 27. 67).

[d] The god Liber was identified with Bacchus. *Cf.* the proverbs οἶνος καὶ ἀλάθεα (Alcaeus), and *in vino veritas*.

hic tibi comis et urbanus liberque videtur,   90
infesto nigris. ego si risi, quod ineptus
pastillos Rufillus olet, Gargonius hircum,
lividus et mordax videor tibi ? mentio si quae[1]
de Capitolini[2] furtis iniecta Petilli
te coram fuerit, defendas ut tuus est mos :   95
" me Capitolinus convictore usus amicoque
a puero est, causaque mea permulta rogatus
fecit, et incolumis laetor quod vivit in urbe ;
sed tamen admiror quo pacto iudicium illud
fugerit." hic nigrae sucus lolliginis, haec est   100
aerugo mera. quod vitium procul afore chartis
atque animo prius, ut[3] si quid promittere de me
possum aliud vere, promitto.
                                        Liberius si
dixero quid, si forte iocosius, hoc mihi iuris
cum venia dabis. insuevit pater optimus hoc me, 105
ut fugerem exemplis vitiorum quaeque notando.
cum me hortaretur, parce frugaliter atque
viverem uti contentus eo, quod mi ipse parasset :
" nonne vides, Albi ut male vivat filius, utque
Baius inops ? magnum documentum, ne patriam rem
perdere quis velit." a[4] turpi meretricis amore   111
cum deterreret : " Scetani dissimilis sis."
ne sequerer moechas, concessa cum venere uti
possem : " deprensi non bella est fama Treboni,"

---

¹ qua *KM, II.*   ² capitolinis *DE, II.*
³ animo, prius ut, (= ut prius) *Housman.* ⁴ aut *E, II* : at *M.*

ᵃ Cited from *Sat.* i. 2. 27.   *Hic* in l. 90 is Lucilius, who
must have described such a banqueting-scene (ll. 86-89) in
the first person. See *Sat.* i. 10. 65, and note.
   ᵇ The crime of which Petillius is said to have been
accused, that of stealing the gold crown of Jupiter on the
Capitol, was a proverbial one, as is seen from the allusions

Such a man you think genial and witty and frank —you who hate the black of heart. As for me, if I have had my laugh because silly " Rufillus smells like a scent-box, Gargonius like a goat," [a] do you think I am a spiteful, snappish cur ? If in your presence somebody hinted at the thefts of Petillius Capitolinus, you would defend him after *your* fashion : " Capitolinus has been a comrade and friend of mine from boyhood ; much has he done to serve me when asked, and I rejoice that he is alive and out of danger here in Rome—but still I *do* wonder how he got out of that trial." [b] Here is the very ink of the cuttlefish ; here is venom unadulterate. That such malice shall be far from my pages, and first of all from my heart, I pledge myself, if there is aught that I can pledge with truth.

[103] If in my words I am too free, perchance too light, this bit of liberty you will indulgently grant me. 'Tis a habit the best of fathers taught me, for, to enable me to steer clear of follies, he would brand them, one by one, by his examples.[c] Whenever he would encourage me to live thriftily, frugally, and content with what he had saved for me, " Do you not see," he would say, " how badly fares young Albius,[d] and how poor is Baius ? A striking lesson not to waste one's patrimony ! " When he would deter me from a vulgar amour, " Don't be like Scetanus." And to prevent me from courting another's wife, when I might enjoy a love not forbidden, " Not pretty," he would say,

to it in Plautus, *e.g. Trinummus* 83, *Menaechmi* 941. The cognomen *Capitolinus* gave a handle to his assailants.

[c] The *hoc* of l. 105 refers to Horace's freedom of speech (*liberius si dixero*), while the clause *ut fugerem* expresses the father's purpose with *notando*.

[d] *Cf.* l. 28 above.

aiebat. " sapiens, vitatu quidque petitu   115
sit melius, causas reddet tibi : mi satis est, si
traditum ab antiquis morem servare tuamque,
dum custodis eges, vitam famamque tueri
incolumem possum ; simul ac duraverit aetas
membra animumque tuum, nabis sine cortice." sic me
formabat puerum dictis, et sive iubebat,   121
ut facerem quid, " habes auctorem quo facias hoc,"
unum ex iudicibus selectis[1] obiciebat ;
sive vetabat, " an hoc inhonestum et inutile factu[2]
necne sit addubites, flagret rumore malo cum   125
hic atque ille ? " avidos[3] vicinum funus ut aegros
exanimat mortisque metu sibi parcere cogit,
sic teneros animos aliena opprobria saepe
absterrent vitiis.
     Ex hoc ego sanus ab illis,
perniciem quaecumque ferunt, mediocribus et quis 130
ignoscas[4] vitiis teneor. fortassis et istinc
largiter abstulerit[5] longa aetas, liber amicus,
consilium proprium ; neque enim, cum lectulus aut me
porticus excepit, desum mihi : " rectius hoc est :
hoc faciens vivam melius : sic dulcis amicis   135
occurram : hoc quidam non belle : numquid ego illi
imprudens olim faciam simile ? " haec ego mecum
compressis agito labris ; ubi quid datur oti,

---

    [1] electis *M, II* : electi *E.*   [2] factum *aDEM.*
  [3] vides, *II.*   [4] ignoscat, *II.*   [5] abstulerint *aDEM.*

---

   [a] A reference to the list of jurors, men of high character,
annually empanelled by the praetor to serve in the trial
of criminal cases.

is the repute of Trebonius, caught in the act. Your philosopher will give you theories for shunning or seeking this or that : enough for me, if I can uphold the rule our fathers have handed down, and if, so long as you need a guardian, I can keep your health and name from harm. When years have brought strength to body and mind, you will swim without the cork." With words like these would he mould my boyhood ; and whether he were advising me to do something, " You have an example for so doing," he would say, and point to one of the special judges ; [a] or were forbidding me, " Can you doubt whether this is dishonourable and disadvantageous or not, when so and so stands in the blaze of ill repute ? " As a neighbour's funeral scares gluttons when sick, and makes them, through fear of death, careful of themselves, so the tender mind is oft deterred from vice by another's shame.

129 Thanks to this training I am free from vices which bring disaster, though subject to lesser frailties such as you would excuse. Perhaps even from these much will be withdrawn by time's advance, candid friends, self-counsel ; for when my couch welcomes me or I stroll in the colonnade,[b] I do not fail myself : " This is the better course : if I do that, I shall fare more happily : thus I shall delight the friends I meet : that was ugly conduct of so and so : is it possible that some day I may thoughtlessly do anything like that?" Thus, with lips shut tight, I debate with myself ; and when I find a bit of leisure, I trifle with my

[b] The colonnades, or porticoes, were a striking architectural feature of ancient Rome, and much used for promenading in. The *lectulus* was an easy couch for reclining upon while reading, corresponding to our comfortable arm-chairs.

illudo[1] chartis.   hoc est mediocribus illis
ex vitiis unum : cui si concedere nolis,   140
multa poetarum veniat[2] manus, auxilio quae
sit mihi (nam multo plures sumus), ac veluti te
Iudaei cogemus in hanc concedere turbam.

[1] incumbo, *II*: *Röhl conjectures* includo.
[2] veniet *Acron, Bentley.*

---

[a] Horace toys with his papers by jotting down his random thoughts.

[b] For the eagerness of the Jews to proselytize *cf.* St. Matthew xxiii. 15.

[c] Among the numerous articles that contain a discussion of this Satire, reference may be made to the following :—

papers.[a] This is one of those lesser frailties I spoke of, and if you should make no allowance for it, then would a big band of poets come to my aid—for we are the big majority—and we, like the Jews,[b] will compel you to make one of our throng.[c]

G. L. Hendrickson, "Horace, *Sermones* i. 4. A Protest and a Programme," *A.J.P.* xxi. pp. 121 ff.; "Satura—the Genesis of a Literary Form," *C.P.* vi. pp. 129 ff.;

Charles Knapp, "The Sceptical Assault on the Roman Tradition concerning the Dramatic *Satura*," *A.J.P.* xxxiii. pp. 125 ff.;

H. R. Fairclough, "Horace's View of the Relations between Satire and Comedy," *A.J.P.* xxxiv. pp. 183 ff.;

B. L. Ullman, "Horace on the Nature of Satire," *A.P.A.* xlviii. pp. 111 ff.; "Dramatic Satura," *C.P.* ix. pp. 1 ff.

V

A JOURNEY TO BRUNDISIUM

This Satire is modelled upon one by Lucilius, who in his third book had described a journey from Rome to Capua and thence to the Sicilian straits.

Horace's journey was associated with an embassy on which Maecenas and others were sent in 38 B.C. by Octavian, to make terms with Marcus Antonius, who, notwithstanding the so-called treaty of Brundisium, made between the rivals of two years earlier, was again somewhat estranged.

The travellers left Rome by the Appian Way, and made a night-journey from Appii Forum to Anxur by canal-boat through the Pomptine marshes. From Capua their road took them over the Apennines into the Apulian hill-country of Horace's birth, whence they passed on to Italy's eastern coast, reaching Brundisium in fifteen days. The journey had been pursued in a leisurely fashion, for if necessary it might have been covered in less than half that time.

Although the mission of Maecenas was a political one, Horace steers clear of political gossip. The account reads like a compilation of scanty notes from a diary, and yet leaves a delightful impression about the personal relations of men distinguished in literature and statesmanship. Some of the character-

62

istics of the sketch are doubtless due to Horace's
adherence to the satiric type. Thus the encounter
of the two buffoons (51-69) is a dramatic scene, treated
in a mock-heroic fashion, where the comparison made
between Sarmentus and a unicorn recalls the Lucilian
description of a rhinoceros with a projecting tooth,

> dente adverso eminulo hic est
> rinoceros
>
> (117 f. ed. Marx.)

while the four disfiguring lines (82-85) are parallel to
a similar incident recorded by Lucilius. This close
dependence of Horace upon Lucilius throughout is
clearly shown both by Lejay, in his introduction to
this Satire, and by Fiske in his *Lucilius and Horace*,
pp. 306 ff.

Professor Tenney Frank, in *Classical Philology*,
xv. (1920) p. 393, has made the plausible suggestion
that Heliodorus, the *rhetor, Graecorum longe doctis-
simus*, of ll. 2 and 3, is really Apollodorus, who was
chosen by Julius Caesar to be the teacher of Octavian,
and who is called by Wilamowitz " the founder of
the classical school of Augustan poetry." The name
Apollodorus cannot be used in hexameters, and
Helios would be an easy substitution for Apollo.
This scholar would have been a not unworthy mem-
ber of the distinguished literary group who accom-
panied Maecenas to Brundisium.

V.

Egressum magna me accepit[1] Aricia Roma
hospitio modico ; rhetor comes Heliodorus,
Graecorum longe[2] doctissimus : inde Forum Appi,
differtum nautis, cauponibus atque malignis.
hoc iter ignavi divisimus, altius ac nos   5
praecinctis unum : minus est gravis Appia tardis.
hic ego propter aquam, quod erat deterrima, ventri
indico bellum, cenantis haud animo aequo
expectans comites.
                        Iam nox inducere terris
umbras et caelo diffundere signa parabat.   10
tum pueri nautis, pueris convicia nautae
ingerere : " huc appelle ! " " trecentos inseris."
        " ohe,
iam satis est." dum aes exigitur, dum mula ligatur,
tota abit hora. mali culices ranaeque palustres
avertunt somnos, absentem ut[3] cantat amicam   15
multa prolutus vappa nauta atque viator
certatim. tandem fessus dormire viator
incipit ac missae pastum retinacula mulae

---

[1] excepit *D, II.*   [2] linguae *K, II.*   [3] ut *omitted by CDK.*

ᵃ The " Market of Appius," for which see Acts xxviii. 15,
was at the head of the canal which ran through the Pomptine
marshes to Feronia.

ᵇ *i.e.* from Rome to Appii Forum, nearly forty miles. The
phrase *altius praecinctis* means literally "higher girt," *cf.*
the Biblical " gird up your loins."

Satire V

Leaving mighty Rome, I found shelter in a modest
inn at Aricia, having for companion Heliodorus the
rhetorician, far most learned of all Greeks. Next
came Appii Forum,[a] crammed with boatmen and
stingy tavern-keepers. This stretch[b] we lazily cut
in two, though smarter travellers make it in a single
day: the Appian Way is less tiring, if taken slowly.
Here owing to the water, for it was villainous, I
declare war against my stomach, and wait impatiently
while my companions dine.

[9] Already night was beginning to draw her curtain
over the earth and to sprinkle the sky with stars.
Then slaves loudly rail at boatmen, boatmen at
slaves: " Bring to here ! " " You're packing in
hundreds ! " " Stay, that's enough ! " What with
collecting fares and harnessing the mule[c] a whole
hour slips away. Cursed gnats and frogs of the fens
drive off sleep, the boatman, soaked in sour wine,
singing the while of the girl he left behind, and a
passenger[d] taking up the refrain. The passenger
at last tires and falls asleep, and the lazy boatman

---

[c] The mule was to pull the boat through the canal.

[d] Some take *viator* to mean a driver of the mule along
the tow-path, but, according to ll. 18, 19, it would seem to
be the boatman who drives the mule and who drops his
work to take a nap on the bank.

nauta piger saxo religat stertitque supinus.
iamque dies aderat, nil cum procedere lintrem   20
sentimus, donec cerebrosus prosilit unus
ac mulae nautaeque caput lumbosque saligno
fuste dolat.

       Quarta vix demum exponimur hora.
ora manusque tua lavimus, Feronia, lympha.
milia tum pransi tria repimus atque subimus   25
impositum saxis late candentibus Anxur.
huc venturus erat Maecenas optimus atque
Cocceius, missi magnis de rebus uterque
legati, aversos soliti componere amicos.
hic oculis ego nigra meis collyria lippus   30
illinere. interea Maecenas advenit atque
Cocceius Capitoque simul Fonteius, ad unguem
factus homo, Antoni non ut magis alter amicus.

Fundos Aufidio Lusco praetore libenter
linquimus, insani ridentes praemia scribae,   35
praetextam et latum clavum prunaeque vatillum.
in Mamurrarum lassi deinde urbe manemus,
Murena praebente domum, Capitone culinam.
postera[1] lux oritur multo gratissima : namque
Plotius et Varius[2] Sinuessae Vergiliusque   40
occurrunt, animae qualis neque candidiores
terra tulit, neque quis me sit devinctior alter.

    [1] proxima *a*.   [2] varus *K, II*.

---

   [a] The word *soliti* implies at least one previous experience of this sort and probably refers to the treaty of Brundisium, 40 B.C.

   [b] The Latin expression involves a metaphor from sculpture, for the artist would pass his finger-nail over the marble, to test the smoothness of its joints.

   [c] The chief official at Fundi was doubtless an aedile

turns his mule out to graze, ties the reins to a stone, and drops a-snoring on his back. Day was now dawning when we find that our craft was not under way, until one hot-headed fellow jumps out, and with willow cudgel bangs mule and boatman on back and head.

23 At last, by ten o'clock we are barely landed, and wash face and hands in thy stream, Feronia. Then we breakfast, and crawling on three miles climb up to Anxur, perched on her far-gleaming rocks. Here Maecenas was to meet us, and noble Cocceius, envoys both on business of import, and old hands at settling feuds between friends.[a] Here I put black ointment on my sore eyes. Meanwhile Maecenas arrives and Cocceius, and with them Fonteius Capito, a man without flaw,[b] so that Antony has no closer friend.

34 Fundi, with its "praetor"[c] Aufidius Luscus, we quit with delight, laughing at the crazy clerk's gewgaws, his bordered robe, broad stripe, and pan of charcoal. Next, wearied out we stop in the city of the Mamurrae,[d] Murena providing shelter and Capito the larder. Most joyful was the morrow's rising, for at Sinuessa there meet us Plotius, Varius, and Virgil, whitest souls earth ever bore, to whom none can be more deeply attached than I. O the

but as he gave himself airs, Horace dubs him "praetor." Aufidius, like Horace himself, had once been a humble *scriba* at Rome. In his present exalted position he wears a toga with a purple border, and a tunic with a broad purple stripe. Burning charcoal is carried before him, probably in case some ceremonial sacrifice is seen to be appropriate on the occasion of this visit of Maecenas.

[d] Mamurra, a notorious favourite of Julius Caesar, came from Formiae.

o qui complexus et gaudia quanta fuerunt !
nil ego contulerim[1] iucundo sanus amico.

    Proxima Campano ponti quae villula, tectum   45
praebuit, et parochi quae debent ligna salemque.
hinc muli Capuae clitellas tempore ponunt.
lusum it Maecenas, dormitum ego Vergiliusque :
namque pila lippis inimicum et ludere crudis.
hinc nos Coccei recipit plenissima villa,   50
quae super est Caudi[2] cauponas.

                         Nunc mihi paucis
Sarmenti scurrae pugnam Messique Cicirri,
Musa, velim memores, et quo patre natus uterque
contulerit litis.   Messi clarum genus Osci ;
Sarmenti domina exstat : ab his maioribus orti   55
ad pugnam venere. prior Sarmentus : " equi te
esse feri similem dico." ridemus, et ipse
Messius " accipio," caput et movet. " o tua cornu
ni foret exsecto frons," inquit, " quid faceres, cum
sic mutilus minitaris[3] ? " at illi foeda cicatrix   60
saetosam laevi frontem turpaverat oris.
Campanum in morbum, in faciem permulta iocatus,
pastorem saltaret uti Cyclopa rogabat :
nil illi larva[4] aut tragicis opus esse cothurnis.

                  [1] praetulerim *C*.
         [2] caudi *DK Porph.* : claudi *most* MSS.
   [3] miniteris *DEM*.   [4] barba *DR*.

---

   [a] The *villula* was probably a small house built for the convenience of persons travelling on public business, where officers were stationed whose duty it was to provide ordinary necessaries. For these officers Horace uses a Greek word (*parochi* from παρέχειν), the regular Latin word, according to Porphyrio, being *copiarii*.

   [b] In mock-heroic style Horace describes a battle of wit between two buffoons, one of whom, Sarmentus, is a freedman of Maecenas, while the other, Cicirrus, or " game-cock," is of the native Oscan stock of Samnium.

embracing! O the rejoicing! Nothing, so long as I am in my senses, would I match with the joy a friend may bring.

45 The little house close to the Campanian bridge put a roof above our heads, and the state-purveyors,[a] as in duty bound, furnished fuel and salt. Next, at Capua, our mules lay aside their saddle-bags at an early hour. Maecenas goes off to ball-playing, Virgil and I to sleep, for such play is hard on the sore-eyed and the dyspeptic. Another stage, and we are taken in at the well-stocked villa of Cocceius, lying above the inns of Caudium.

51 Now, O Muse, recount in brief the contest of Sarmentus the jester and Messius Cicirrus, and the lineage of the two who engaged in the fray.[b] Messius was of famous stock, an Oscan; the mistress of Sarmentus is still living: from such ancestry sprung,[c] they entered the lists. And first Sarmentus: " You, I say, are like a wild horse." We laugh, and Messius himself, " I grant you," and tosses his head. " Oh ! " says Sarmentus, " if only the horn had not been cut out of your forehead, what would you do, when you can threaten, thus dehorned ? " Now an unsightly scar had disfigured the left side of his bristly brow. With many a joke on his Campanian disease[d] and on his face, he begged him to dance the Cyclops shepherd-dance : he would need neither mask nor

---

[e] The scholiast on Juvenal, *Sat.* v. 3, tells us that a certain Sarmentus had been a slave, who on the proscription and death of his master Favonius had been bought by Maecenas and set free. If the Sarmentus of this scene is the same man, the *domina* is the widow of Favonius.

[d] The scholiast in Cruquius explains this of warts, which left scars when removed.

multa Cicirrus ad haec : donasset iamne catenam 65
ex voto Laribus, quaerebat ; scriba quod esset,
nilo deterius dominae[1] ius esse ; rogabat
denique, cur umquam fugisset, cui satis una
farris libra foret, gracili sic tamque pusillo.
prorsus iucunde cenam producimus illam. 70

    Tendimus hinc recta[2] Beneventum ; ubi sedulus hospes
paene macros arsit dum turdos versat in igni ;
nam vaga per veterem dilapso[3] flamma culinam
Volcano summum properabat lambere tectum.
convivas avidos cenam servosque timentis 75
tum rapere atque omnis restinguere velle videres.

    Incipit ex illo montis Apulia notos
ostentare mihi, quos torret[4] Atabulus et quos
numquam erepsemus, nisi nos vicina Trivici
villa recepisset, lacrimoso non sine fumo, 80
udos cum foliis ramos urente camino.
hic ego mendacem stultissimus usque puellam
ad mediam noctem exspecto : somnus tamen aufert
intentum veneri ; tum immundo somnia visu
nocturnam vestem maculant ventremque supinum. 85

    Quattuor hinc rapimur viginti et milia raedis,
mansuri oppidulo, quod versu dicere non est,
signis perfacile est : venit vilissima rerum
hic aqua ; sed panis longe pulcherrimus, ultra
callidus ut soleat umeris portare viator. 90

      [1] domini *C*.   [2] recte *D, II.*
        [3] delapso *CK, II.*   [4] terret *CE.*

---

   [a] *Altino* is to-day the local Apulian term for the hot
scirocco, which Horace calls the "Atabulus."

   [b] The name is not recorded, at least correctly, but Horace
has in mind a passage in Lucilius, viz. :

70

tragic buskin. Much had Cicirrus to say to this. Had he yet, he inquired, made a votive offering of his chain to the Lares? Clerk though he was, yet his mistress's claim was not less strong. At the last he asked why he had ever run away, since a pound of meal was enough for one so lean and so puny. Right merrily did we prolong that supper.

[71] Thence we travel straight to Beneventum, where our bustling host was nearly burned out while turning lean thrushes over the fire. For as Vulcan slipped out through the old kitchen the vagrant flame hastened to lick the roof. Then you might have seen the hungry guests and frightened slaves snatching up the dinner, and all trying to quench the blaze.

[77] From this point Apulia begins to show to my eyes her familiar hills, which the Altino[a] scorches, and over which we had never crawled had not a villa near Trivicum taken us in, but not without smoke that brought tears, as green wood, leaves and all, was burning in the stove. Here I, utter fool that I am, await a faithless girl right up to midnight. Then, after all, sleep carries me off still thinking upon love, and evil dreams assail me.

[86] From here we are whirled in carriages four and twenty miles, to spend the night in a little town I cannot name in verse, though 'tis quite easy to define it by tokens.[b] Here water, nature's cheapest product, is sold, but the bread is far the best to be had, so that the knowing traveller is wont to shoulder

servorum est festus dies hic
quem plane hexametro versu non dicere possis
(vi. 228, ed. Marx),
"This is the slaves' festal day, which one cannot freely name in hexameter verse."

nam Canusi lapidosus (aquae non ditior urna),
qui locus a forti Diomede est conditus olim.[1]
flentibus hinc Varius discedit maestus amicis.

Inde Rubos fessi pervenimus, utpote longum
carpentes iter et factum corruptius imbri.   95
postera tempestas melior, via peior ad usque
Bari moenia piscosi.   dein[2] Gnatia lymphis
iratis exstructa dedit risusque iocosque,
dum flamma sine tura liquescere limine sacro
persuadere cupit.   credat[3] Iudaeus Apella,   100
non ego : namque deos didici securum agere aevum,
nec, si quid miri faciat natura, deos id
tristis ex alto caeli demittere[4] tecto.
Brundisium longae finis chartaeque viaeque est.

---

[1] *Line 92 was deleted by Bentley.*   [2] dehinc, *II.*
[3] credet *CK Goth.*   [4] dimittere *DE.*

---

[a] This implies that Gnatia had no springs.   Pliny (*N.H.* ii.
111) mentions the miracle of wood, placed on a sacred stone,
taking fire spontaneously.   The stone would seem to have
been at the entrance of a temple.

[b] The Jews, who were very numerous in Rome under

a load for stages beyond; for at Canusium, a place founded long ago by brave Diomede, it is gritty, and as to water, the town is no better off by a jugful. Here Varius leaves us, to the grief of his weeping friends.

94 Thence we come to Rubi, very weary after covering a long stage much marred by the rain. Next day's weather was better, but the road worse, right up to the walls of Barium, a fishing town. Then Gnatia, built under the wrath of the water-nymphs,[a] brought us laughter and mirth in its effort to convince us that frankincense melts without fire at the temple's threshold. Apella, the Jew,[b] may believe it, not I; for I " have learned that the gods lead a care-free life," [c] and if Nature works any marvel, the gods do not send it down from their heavenly home aloft when in surly mood [d] ! Brundisium is the end of a long story and of a long journey.

Augustus, were regarded by the Romans as peculiarly superstitious.

[c] Horace is quoting from Lucretius, *De rerum nat.* v. 82.

[d] Horace uses *tristis* of the gods as Virgil speaks of Charon as *tristis, Aen.* vi. 315.

VI

ON SOCIAL AND POLITICAL AMBITION

This Satire, addressed to the poet's patron, is mainly autobiographical. Horace, now an intimate friend of Maecenas, has become an object of suspicion and envy to many people whose social and political aspirations were unsatisfied. He therefore disclaims such ambition for himself, sets forth the principles upon which Maecenas chooses his friends, and pays a noble tribute to his own father, to whom he is indebted for all that he is, both in character and education. Himself the son of a freedman, he has no wish to change places with a man of patrician birth. As it is, he lives a simple and care-free life, and is far more happy than if he had the burden of noble ancestry on his shoulders.

As this interesting Satire contains no allusion to the Sabine farm, it was probably composed before 33 b.c., the year when Maecenas presented him with the estate. In its subject and treatment it is to be grouped with the third, fourth, and tenth Satires. It is at once a defence of Maecenas, who did not look down upon men of lowly birth, and of the poet himself, who is not ashamed of his humble origin, but is proud of his freedman father, who had given him the intellectual and moral training which won for him a place in the circle of his patron.

For the influence of Lucilius upon this Satire see Introduction C.

VI.

Non quia, Maecenas, Lydorum quidquid Etruscos
incoluit finis, nemo generosior est te,
nec quod avus tibi maternus fuit atque paternus,
olim qui magnis legionibus imperitarent,[1]
ut plerique solent, naso suspendis adunco   5
ignotos,[2] ut[3] me libertino patre natum.[4]
Cum referre negas quali sit quisque parente
natus, dum ingenuus, persuades hoc tibi vere,
ante potestatem Tulli atque ignobile regnum
multos saepe viros nullis maioribus ortos   10
et vixisse probos, amplis et honoribus auctos ;
contra Laevinum, Valeri genus, unde Superbus
Tarquinius regno pulsus[5] fugit, unius assis
non umquam pretio pluris licuisse, notante
iudice quo nosti populo, qui stultus honores   15
saepe dat indignis et famae servit ineptus,
qui stupet in titulis et imaginibus.   quid oportet
nos facere a volgo longe longeque[6] remotos ?
Namque esto, populus Laevino mallet honorem

---

[1] imperitarint, *I, accepted by Vollmer.*
[2] ignoto *Palmer.*   [3] ut *D:* aut *aM, II;* aut ut *C:* at ut *E.*
[4] natus *or* natos *aCDE.*
[5] pulsus regno *CK.*   [6] lateque *Goth.*

---

[a] Cf. *Odes*, i. 1. 1.   The Etruscans, according to the
tradition commonly accepted in antiquity, came from Lydia.

[b] The reference is to Servius Tullius, the sixth king of
Rome, said to have been the son of a female slave.   See,
however, Livy, i. 39. 5.

Satire VI

Though of all the Lydians that are settled in Tuscan lands none is of nobler birth than you,[a] and though grandsires of yours, on your mother's and father's side alike, commanded mighty legions in days of old, yet you, Maecenas, do not, like most of the world, curl up your nose at men of unknown birth, men like myself, a freedman's son.

[7] When you say it matters not who a man's parent is, if he be himself free-born, you rightly satisfy yourself of this, that before the reign of Tullius and his lowly kingship,[b] numbers of men, sprung from ancestors of no account, often lived upright lives and were honoured with high office ; that Laevinus, on the other hand, descendant of that Valerius through whom Tarquin the Proud was driven from his throne to exile, was never valued higher by the price of a single penny, even when rated by the people—the judge you know so well, who in folly often gives office to the unworthy, is stupidly enslaved to fame, and dazzled by titles of honour and waxen masks.[c] What, then, should we [d] do, we who are set far, far above the vulgar ?

[19] For let us grant that the people would rather

[c] Waxen masks of ancestors with accompanying inscriptions would imply the antiquity and nobility of one's family.

[d] The plural is generic, meaning intelligent and educated people.

quam Decio mandare novo, censorque moveret   20
Appius, ingenuo si non essem patre natus :
vel merito, quoniam in propria non pelle quiessem.
sed fulgente trahit constrictos Gloria curru
non minus ignotos generosis.   quo tibi, Tilli,
sumere depositum clavum fierique tribuno ?   25
invidia accrevit, privato quae minor esset.
nam ut quisque insanus nigris medium impediit[1] crus
pellibus et latum demisit[2] pectore clavum,
audit continuo : " quis homo hic est[3] ? " " quo patre
     natus ? "

ut[4] si qui aegrotet quo morbo Barrus, haberi   30
et cupiat formosus, eat quacumque, puellis
iniciat[5] curam quaerendi singula, quali
sit facie, sura, quali pede, dente, capillo :
sic qui promittit civis, urbem sibi curae,
imperium fore et Italiam, delubra deorum,   35
quo patre sit natus, num ignota matre inhonestus,
omnis mortalis curare et quaerere cogit.[6]
" tune, Syri, Damae, aut Dionysi filius, audes
deicere de saxo civis aut tradere Cadmo ? "
" at Novius collega gradu post me sedet uno :   40

---

¹ impediit *Porph.* : impediet *MSS.*   ² dimisit *DEK.*
     ³ est *aDE* : et *CK* : aut *Bentley.*   ⁴ et *φ.*
     ⁵ iniciat *CK Goth.*   ⁶ cogit *K* : cogat *MSS.*

ᵃ A reference to the well-known fable of the Ass in the Lion's
Skin. P. Decius Mus, first of a plebeian family to become a
consul, sacrificed himself in the Latin war (Livy, viii. 9).

ᵇ The laticlave or broad stripe (*cf. Sat.* i. 5. 36) of purple
on the tunic was a mark of the senatorian order. Tillius,
according to the scholiasts, was removed from the senate

give office to a Laevinus than to an unknown Decius, and that an Appius as censor would strike out my name if I were not the son of a free-born father— and quite rightly, for not having stayed quiet in my own skin.[a] The truth is, Vanity drags all, bound to her glittering car, the unknown no less than the well known. What good was it to you, Tillius, to assume the stripe once doffed and become a tribune ?[b] Envy fastened on you afresh, but would be less, were you in a private station. For as soon as any man is so crazy as to bind the black thongs half way up his leg,[c] and to drop the broad stripe down his breast, at once he hears : "What fellow is this ? What was his father ?" Just as, if one should suffer from the same malady as Barrus, and long to be thought handsome, then wherever he went he would make the girls eager to ask about details— what his face was like, his ankle, his foot, his teeth, his hair : so he who takes it upon himself to look after his fellow-citizens and the city, the empire and Italy and the temples of the gods, compels all the world to take an interest, and to ask who was his father, and whether he is dishonoured through an unknown mother. "Do you, the son of a Syrus, a Dama, a Dionysius,[d] dare to fling from the rock[e] or to hand over to Cadmus citizens of Rome ?" "But," you say, "Novius, my colleague, sits one row

by Julius Caesar, but after the Dictator's death resumed this dignity and also became a military tribune.

[c] Senators wore a peculiar shoe, fastened by four black thongs bound about the leg.

[d] These are common slave-names.

[e] *i.e.* the Tarpeian rock from which criminals were sometimes thrown by order of a tribune. Cadmus was a public executioner.

namque est ille, pater quod erat meus." " hoc tibi
　　Paulus
et Messalla videris ?　at hic, si plostra ducenta
concurrantque foro tria funera magna, sonabit[1]
cornua quod vincatque tubas : saltem tenet hoc nos."

　　Nunc ad me redeo libertino patre natum,　　　　45
quem rodunt omnes libertino patre natum,[2]
nunc, quia sim[3] tibi, Maecenas, convictor, at olim,
quod mihi pareret legio Romana tribuno.
dissimile hoc illi est, quia non, ut forsit honorem
iure mihi invideat quivis, ita te quoque amicum,　　50
praesertim cautum dignos adsumere, prava
ambitione procul.　felicem dicere non hoc
me possim,[4] casu quod te sortitus amicum :
nulla etenim mihi te fors obtulit ; optimus olim
Vergilius, post hunc Varius, dixere quid essem.　　55
ut veni coram, singultim pauca locutus,
infans namque pudor prohibebat plura profari,
non ego me claro natum patre, non ego circum
me Satureiano vectari rura caballo,
sed quod eram narro.　respondes, ut tuus est mos,　60
pauca : abeo, et revocas nono post mense iubesque
esse in amicorum numero.　magnum hoc ego duco,
quod placui tibi, qui turpi secernis honestum
non patre praeclaro, sed vita et pectore puro.

　　Atqui si vitiis mediocribus ac mea[5] paucis　　　65

---

[1] funera, magna sonabit; *so Palmer, Wickham, Vollmer.*
　　[2] natus *aD.*　　　　　　　　　[3] sum *D.*
　　[4] possunt *com. Cruq., Bentley.*　　[5] aut mea, *II.*

---

[a] Seats in the theatre were assigned according to rank,
knights occupying the first fourteen rows, and the senators
the orchestral space.

[b] Horace was a tribune in the army of Brutus, but each
legion had six tribunes.

behind me,[a] for he is only what my father was."
"Do you therefore fancy yourself a Paulus or a
Messala? Why, this Novius, if two hundred carts
and three big funerals come clashing in the Forum,
will shout loud enough to drown horns and trumpets:
that at least takes with us."

⁴⁵ Now to return to myself, "son of a freedman
father," whom all carp at as "son of a freedman
father"—now, because I consort with you, Maecenas;
but in other days, because as tribune I had a Roman
legion under my command.[b] This case and that are
different, for though perchance anyone may rightly
grudge me the office, yet he should not grudge me
your friendship as well—the less so, as you are
cautious to choose as friends only the worthy, who
stand aloof from base self-seeking. Fortunate I could
not call myself as having won your friendship by some
chance; for 'twas no case of luck throwing you in my
way; that best of men, Virgil, some time ago, and after
him Varius, told you what manner of man I was.
On coming into your presence I said a few faltering
words, for speechless shame stopped me from saying
more. My tale was not that I was a famous father's
son, not that I rode about my estate on a Saturian[c]
steed: I told you what I was. As is your way, you
answered little and I withdrew; then, nine months
later, you sent for me again and bade me join your
friends. I count it a great honour that I pleased you,
who discern between fair and foul, not by a father's
fame, but by blamelessness of life and heart.

⁶⁵ And yet, if the flaws that mar my otherwise
sound nature are but trifling and few in number,

[c] *i.e.* Tarentine, Saturium being the district in which
Tarentum was founded. The adjective belongs quite as
much to *rura* as to *caballo*.

mendosa est natura, alioqui[1] recta, velut si
egregio inspersos reprehendas corpore naevos,
si neque avaritiam neque sordes nec[2] mala lustra
obiciet vere quisquam mihi, purus et insons,
ut me collaudem, si et vivo carus amicis ;   70
causa fuit pater his, qui macro pauper agello
noluit in Flavi ludum me mittere, magni
quo pueri magnis e[3] centurionibus orti,
laevo suspensi loculos tabulamque lacerto,
ibant octonos referentes Idibus aeris,[4]   75
sed puerum est ausus Romam portare, docendum
artis, quas doceat quivis eques atque senator
semet prognatos.   vestem servosque sequentis,
in magno ut populo, si qui[5] vidisset, avita
ex re praeberi sumptus mihi crederet illos.   80
ipse mihi custos incorruptissimus omnis
circum doctores aderat.   quid multa ?   pudicum,
qui primus virtutis honos, servavit[6] ab omni
non solum facto, verum opprobrio quoque turpi ;
nec timuit, sibi ne vitio quis verteret, olim   85
si praeco parvas aut, ut fuit ipse, coactor
mercedes sequerer : neque ego essem questus : at
     hoc[7] nunc
laus illi debetur et a me gratia maior.

    Nil me paeniteat sanum patris huius, eoque
non, ut magna dolo factum negat esse suo pars,   90
quod non ingenuos habeat clarosque parentis,
sic me defendam.   longe mea discrepat istis

    [1] alioquin, *I, but cf.* Sat. i. 4. 4.
[2] nec (mala) *V*: ac *MSS.*: aut *Porph., Bentley.*   [3] et *a.*
    [4] octonis . . . aera *M, II, retained by Wickham.*
[5] si quis *K, Goth.*   [6] servabat, *II.*   [7] ad hoc *MSS.*

    [a] The pupils paid their small school fee on the Ides of
each month. The reading *octonis* would imply that the
school-year lasted eight months.

even as you might find fault with moles spotted over a comely person—if no one will justly lay to my charge avarice or meanness or lewdness; if, to venture on self-praise, my life is free from stain and guilt and I am loved by my friends—I owe this to my father, who, though poor with a starveling farm, would not send me to the school of Flavius, to which grand boys used to go, sons of grand centurions, with slate and satchel slung over the left arm, each carrying his eightpence on the Ides[a]—nay, he boldly took his boy off to Rome, to be taught those studies that any knight or senator would have his own offspring taught. Anyone who saw my clothes and attendant slaves—as is the way in a great city[b]—would have thought that such expense was met from ancestral wealth. He himself, a guardian true and tried, went with me among all my teachers. Need I say more? He kept me chaste—and that is virtue's first grace—free not only from every deed of shame, but from all scandal. He had no fear that some day, if I should follow a small trade as crier or like himself as tax-collector, somebody would count this to his discredit. Nor should I have made complaint, but, as it is, for this I owe him praise and thanks the more.

[89] Never while in my senses could I be ashamed of such a father, and so I will not defend myself, as would a goodly number, who say it is no fault of theirs that they have not free-born and famous parents. Far different from this is what I say and what I think:

[b] I take this to mean that on going to Rome Horace's father did as the Romans did. At Venusia Horace would have gone unattended, carrying his own books. Some, however, take the words *in magno ut populo* with *vidisset, i.e.* " had anyone noticed—so far as one could notice such things in a great throng."

et vox et ratio : nam si natura iuberet
a certis annis aevum remeare peractum
atque alios legere ad fastum quoscumque parentis 95
optaret sibi quisque,[1] meis contentus honestos[2]
fascibus et sellis nollem mihi sumere, demens
iudicio volgi, sanus fortasse tuo, quod
nollem onus haud umquam solitus portare molestum.
nam mihi continuo maior quaerenda foret res 100
atque salutandi plures, ducendus et unus
et comes alter, uti ne solus rusve peregreve[3]
exirem, plures calones atque caballi
pascendi, ducenda petorrita. nunc mihi curto
ire licet mulo vel si libet usque Tarentum, 105
mantica cui lumbos onere ulceret atque eques armos :
obiciet nemo sordes mihi, quas tibi, Tilli,
cum Tiburte via praetorem quinque sequuntur
te pueri, lasanum portantes oenophorumque.
hoc ego commodius quam tu, praeclare senator, 110
milibus atque aliis vivo.

                 Quacumque libido est,
incedo solus ; percontor quanti holus ac far ;
fallacem Circum vespertinumque[4] pererro
saepe Forum ; adsisto divinis ; inde domum me
ad porri et ciceris refero laganique catinum. 115
cena ministratur pueris tribus, et lapis albus
pocula cum cyatho duo sustinet ; adstat echinus
vilis, cum patera gutus, Campana supellex.
deinde eo dormitum, non sollicitus mihi quod cras

---

[1] si quisque, *II.*   [2] (h)onustos.
[3] peregre aut *MSS.*: *Housman conjectures* ne rus solusve
peregre.   [4] vespertinusque.

---

[a] The *fasces* were insignia of the consuls and praetors ;
the curule *sellae* were a privilege of the aediles and censors
as well.

for if after a given age Nature should call upon us to traverse our past lives again, and to choose in keeping with our pride any other parents each might crave—content with my own, I should decline to take those adorned with the rods and chairs of state.[a]   And though the world would deem me mad, you, I hope, would think me sane for declining to shoulder a burden of trouble to which I have never been accustomed.   For at once I should have to enlarge my means, to welcome more callers, to take one or two in my company so as not to go abroad or into the country alone; I should have to keep more pages and ponies, and take a train of wagons.   To-day, if I will, I may go on a bob-tailed mule even to Tarentum, the saddle-bag's weight galling his loins, and the rider his withers.   No one will taunt me with meanness as he does you, praetor Tillius,[b] when on the Tibur road five slaves follow you, carrying a commode and case of wine.   In this and a thousand other ways I live in more comfort than you, illustrious senator.

[111] Wherever the fancy leads, I saunter forth alone. I ask the price of greens and flour; often toward evening I stroll round the cheating Circus [c] and the Forum.   I listen to the fortune-tellers; then homeward betake me to my dish of leeks and peas and fritters.   My supper is served by three boys, and a white stone-slab supports two cups with a ladle.   By them stand a cheap salt-cellar, a jug and saucer of Campanian ware.   Then I go off to sleep, untroubled with the thought that I must rise early on the morrow

[b] Apparently the man mentioned in l. 24 above.
[c] The stalls in the outer wall of the Circus Maximus were used by fortune-tellers, confidence-men, and the like.

surgendum sit mane, obeundus Marsya, qui se   120
voltum ferre negat Noviorum posse minoris.
ad quartam iaceo ; post hanc vagor ; aut ego, lecto
aut scripto quod me tacitum iuvet, unguor olivo,
non quo fraudatis immundus Natta lucernis.
ast ubi me fessum sol acrior ire lavatum   125
admonuit, fugio Campum lusumque trigonem.[1]
pransus non avide, quantum interpellet inani
ventre diem durare, domesticus otior.

                           Haec est
vita solutorum misera ambitione gravique ;
his me consolor victurum[2] suavius ac si   130
quaestor avus pater atque meus patruusque[3] fuissent.

  [1] fugio campum lusumque trigonem V^1, *Goth.* (lusitque):
fugio rabiosi tempora signi MSS. *Porph.*   *Bannier* (*in* Rh. M.
lxxiii. *neue Folge, pp.* 65 *ff.*) *makes the interesting claim that*
both readings are correct, the original passage having been
such as the following :

    admonuit fugio campum lusumque trigonem
      providus et fugio rabiosi tempora signi.

  [2] victurus *Goth.*
  [3] *For* patruus *Bücheler conjectured* praetor.

---

  [a] A statue of the Satyr Marsyas stood in the Forum near
the praetor's tribunal.   The usurer Novius had his table

and pass before Marsyas, who says he cannot stand the face of Novius Junior.[a]   I lie a-bed till ten ; then I take a stroll, or after reading or writing something that will please me in quiet moments I anoint myself with oil—not such as filthy Natta steals from the lamps.   But when I am weary and the fiercer sun has warned me to go to the baths, I shun the Campus and the game of ball.[b]   After a slight luncheon, just enough to save me from an all-day fast, I idle away time at home.

[128] Such is the life of men set free from the burden of unhappy ambition.   Thus I comfort myself with the thought that I shall live more happily than if my grandfather had been a quaestor, and my father and uncle likewise.

near by and so gives the poet an opportunity to put his own interpretation on the attitude or facial expression of Marsyas, who, after defeat in a musical contest with Apollo, was flayed alive.   Extant copies of Myron's Marsyas show him with right hand uplifted and a face expressive of pain.

[b] The *trigo* was a game of ball in which *three* players took part.   The phrase *lusum trigonem* means properly "the playing of ball," and implies a transitive use of *ludere* (*cf.* "post decisa negotia," *Ep.* i. 7. 59 ; also *Sat.* ii. 3. 248). See Jefferson Elmore, *A.P.A.* xxxv. p. xcii.

VII

HO FOR A REGICIDE!

THE incident recorded here occurred, probably in 43 B.C., at Clazomenae in Asia Minor, when Brutus, as propraetor of the Province, was holding court, and Horace was serving as tribune in his army. The poem gives us a single scene, a battle of wit between two litigants, Rupilius Rex, of Praeneste, a man proscribed by Antony and Octavius, and Persius, a half-Greek, half-Roman merchant of Clazomenae. The main point of the story is found in Persius' pun on the name Rex (king), which he cleverly links up with the propraetor and the propraetor's most famous ancestor. The latter had driven out of Rome the ancient Tarquin kings, and Brutus himself had slain Caesar.

This little poem, similar, perhaps, to the farcical and dramatic scenes of early *Satura*, is probably the first of Horace's *Sermones*, and must have been composed before the battle of Philippi (42 B.C), and the tragic death of Brutus.

VII.

Proscripti Regis Rupili pus atque venenum
hybrida quo pacto sit Persius ultus, opinor
omnibus et lippis notum et tonsoribus esse.
Persius hic permagna negotia dives habebat
Clazomenis, etiam litis cum Rege molestas,   5
durus homo atque odio qui posset vincere Regem,
confidens, tumidus,[1] adeo sermonis amari,
Sisennas, Barros ut equis praecurreret albis.
    Ad Regem redeo.   postquam nihil inter utrumque
convenit (hoc etenim sunt omnes iure molesti,   10
quo fortes, quibus adversum bellum incidit : inter
Hectora Priamiden, animosum atque inter Achillem
ira fuit capitalis, ut ultima divideret mors,
non aliam ob causam, nisi quod virtus in utroque
summa fuit : duo si discordia vexet inertis,   15
aut si disparibus bellum incidat, ut Diomedi
cum Lycio Glauco, discedat pigrior,[2] ultro
muneribus missis), Bruto praetore tenente
ditem Asiam, Rupili et Persi par pugnat, uti non

---

[1] tumidusque, *II.*
[2] pigrior *VK* : pulchrior *MSS.*

---

[a] He was half-Greek and half-Roman.

Satire VII

How the mongrel [a] Persius took vengeance on the foul and venomous Rupilius Rex (" king "), an outlawed man, is a tale well known, methinks, to every blear-eyed man and barber.[b] This Persius, a rich man, had a very large business at Clazomenae, also a troublesome lawsuit with Rex. A rough man he was, the sort that in offensiveness could outdo Rex, bold and blustering and so bitter of speech as to outstrip a Sisenna or a Barrus with the speed of white coursers.[c]

To return to Rex. When he and Persius could come to no terms—(for quarrelsome folk all claim the same right as heroes who meet front to front in battle : between Hector, son of Priam, and the wrathful Achilles, the anger was so deadly, that death alone could part them, and for this sole reason that the valour of each was supreme : if two cowards chance to quarrel, or an ill-matched pair meet in war, as Diomede and Lycian Glaucus,[d] the less valiant man gives way and sends gifts to boot)—well, when Brutus was praetor in charge of rich Asia, Persius

[b] The shops of apothecaries and barbers were favourite places of gossip.

[c] A proverbial expression, white horses being regarded as the swiftest of their kind. *Cf.* Virgil, *Aen.* xii. 83 ff.

[d] See Index under Glaucus. The reference is to a famous scene in the sixth *Iliad*.

compositum[1] melius cum Bitho Bacchius. in ius[2]   20
acres procurrunt,[3] magnum spectaculum uterque.

   Persius exponit causam ; ridetur ab omni
conventu ; laudat Brutum laudatque cohortem ;
solem Asiae Brutum appellat, stellasque salubris
appellat comites, excepto Rege ; Canem illum,   25
invisum agricolis sidus, venisse.   ruebat
flumen ut hibernum, fertur quo rara securis.
tum Praenestinus salso multoque[4] fluenti
expressa arbusto regerit convicia, durus
vindemiator et invictus, cui saepe viator   30
cessisset magna compellans voce cuculum.

   At Graecus, postquam est Italo perfusus aceto,
Persius exclamat : " per magnos, Brute, deos te
oro, qui reges consueris tollere, cur non
hunc Regem iugulas ? operum hoc, mihi crede,
   tuorum est."   35

   [1] compositus *DK*.   [2] in ius] intus *V*.
   [3] procurrunt *VK, II* : concurrunt *aDEM*.
                [4] multumque, *II*.

   a In *par* and *compositum* Horace uses terms appropriate
to gladiators, to which class Bacchius and Bithus belonged.
   b *i.e.* in some mountain gorge, which wood-choppers
cannot enter.

and Rupilius clashed, a pair [a] not less well matched than Bacchius and Bithus. Keenly they rush into court, each wondrous to behold.

22 Persius sets forth his case : all the assembly laugh. He praises Brutus, he praises his staff. The "sun of Asia" he calls Brutus, and "healthful stars" his suite—all except Rex, who had come like the Dog-star, hated of husbandmen. On he rushed like some winter torrent, whither the axe is seldom borne.[b] Then, in answer to his full flood of wit, the man of Praeneste flings back abuse, the very essence of the vineyard, like some vine-dresser, tough and invincible, to whom the wayfarer has often had to yield, when loudly hooting at him " Cuckoo ! "[c]

32 But the Greek Persius, now soused with Italian vinegar, cries out : " By the great gods, I implore you, O Brutus, since it is in your line to take off " kings," why not behead this Rex ?[d] This, believe me, is a task meet for you."

[c] In calling out "Cuckoo!" the passer-by implies that the vine-dresser is late in his pruning, which should be finished before the cuckoo arrives in the spring.
[d] It was a Brutus who had driven out the Tarquins, and it was a Brutus who had slain Caesar.

VIII

HOW PRIAPUS PUT WITCHES TO ROUT

Horace lays the scene of this incident in that part of the Esquiline which lay outside the famous *Agger*, or Mound of Servius, on the north-east side of Rome. In this district there had long been a burial-place, used especially for criminals and paupers, where, among the tombs, witches practised their weird and infernal rites. Here, however, Maecenas, co-operating with Augustus in the work of city improvement, had laid out beautiful gardens, in which he later built himself a palace with a conspicuous tower.[a]

The incident must be supposed to have occurred before the transformation from a squalid and repulsive site had been completed. A wooden statue, however, of Priapus, the god of gardens, had already been set up.

The gruesome story of the witches' incantations comes to a ridiculous end when the wood of the statue cracked, and the noise of the explosion drove the hags away in terror.

The Satire is closely connected in subject with Epodes 5 and 17. Virgil's eighth Eclogue may also be compared, as well as the three *Priapea* to be found among the minor poems attributed to Virgil.

[a] *Cf.* "molem propinquam nubibus arduis," *Odes* iii. 29. 10.

VIII.

Olim truncus eram ficulnus, inutile lignum,
cum faber, incertus scamnum faceretne Priapum,
maluit esse deum. deus inde ego, furum aviumque
maxima formido ; nam fures dextra coercet
obscenoque ruber porrectus ab inguine palus ;   5
ast importunas volucres in vertice harundo
terret fixa vetatque novis considere in hortis.
huc prius angustis eiecta cadavera cellis
conservus vili[1] portanda locabat in arca ;
hoc miserae plebi stabat commune sepulcrum,   10
Pantolabo scurrae Nomentanoque nepoti.
mille pedes in fronte, trecentos cippus in agrum
hic dabat, heredes monumentum ne sequeretur.[2]
nunc licet Esquiliis habitare salubribus atque
Aggere in aprico spatiari, quo[3] modo tristes   15
albis informem spectabant ossibus agrum ;

¹ vilis *K, II.*   ² sequerentur *K, II.*   ³ qua *Bentley.*

ᵃ *Cf.* Isaiah xliv. 10 ff., especially 17 " and the residue
thereof he maketh a god."

ᵇ A wooden statue of Priapus, the garden-god, was used
as a scarecrow.

ᶜ On the Esquiline Hill, just outside the Servian Wall, was a
cemetery largely used for the pauper and criminal classes.
Here, however, Maecenas laid out his *Horti*, or gardens,
which became one of the beauty-spots of Imperial Rome.

ᵈ This verse may come from Lucilius. It is repeated in
Sat. ii. 1. 22 and Nomentanus is mentioned in *Sat.* i. 1. 102.

Once I was a fig-wood stem, a worthless log, when the carpenter, doubtful whether to make a stool or a Priapus, chose that I be a god.[a] A god, then, I became, of thieves and birds the special terror[b]; for thieves my right hand keeps in check, and this red stake, protruding from unsightly groin; while for the mischievous birds, a reed set on my head affrights them and keeps them from lighting in the new park.[c] Hither in other days a slave would pay to have carried on a cheap bier the carcasses of his fellows, cast out from their narrow cells. Here was the common burial-place fixed for pauper folk, for Pantolabus the parasite, and spendthrift Nomentanus.[d] Here a pillar assigned a thousand feet frontage and three hundred of depth, and provided that the graveyard should pass to no heirs.[e] To-day one may live on a wholesome Esquiline, and stroll on the sunny Rampart,[f] where of late one sadly looked out on ground ghastly with bleaching bones. For myself,

  [e] Horace puts into verse form the common inscription, which defined the dimensions of a plot of ground assigned for burial purposes and often closed with the abbreviated formula H. M. H. N. S. (*Hoc monumentum heredes non sequetur*).
  [f] This is the famous *Agger*, an embankment and fosse of nearly a mile in length, which on the Esquiline level was a part of the Servian Wall system.

H

cum mihi non tantum furesque feraeque suetae
hunc vexare locum curae sunt[1] atque labori,
quantum carminibus quae versant atque venenis
humanos animos : has nullo perdere[2] possum   20
nec prohibere modo, simul ac vaga Luna decorum
protulit os, quin ossa legant herbasque nocentis.

Vidi egomet nigra succinctam vadere palla
Canidiam, pedibus nudis passoque capillo,
cum Sagana maiore ululantem : pallor utrasque   25
fecerat horrendas aspectu. scalpere terram
unguibus et pullam divellere mordicus agnam
coeperunt ; cruor in fossam confusus, ut inde
manis elicerent, animas responsa daturas.
lanea et effigies erat, altera cerea : maior   30
lanea, quae poenis compesceret inferiorem ;
cerea suppliciter stabat, servilibus ut quae
iam peritura modis. Hecaten vocat altera, saevam
altera Tisiphonen : serpentes atque videres
infernas errare canes, Lunamque rubentem,   35
ne foret his testis, post magna latere sepulcra.
mentior at si quid, merdis caput inquiner albis
corvorum, atque in me veniat mictum atque cacatum
Iulius et fragilis Pediatia furque Voranus.
singula quid memorem, quo pacto alterna loquentes 40
umbrae cum Sagana resonarint[3] triste et acutum,
utque lupi barbam variae cum dente colubrae
abdiderint furtim terris, et imagine cerea
largior arserit ignis, et ut non testis inultus

---

[1] sint *D*.   [2] pellere *Heinsius*.
      [3] resonarint *Bentley* : resonarent MSS.

---

[a] The passage is mock-heroic and based upon the famous
scene in the eleventh book of the *Odyssey* (36 ff.), where the
blood poured into a trench brought the spirits up from
Erebus.

'tis not so much the thieves and beasts wont to infest the place that cause me care and trouble, as the witches who with spells and drugs vex human souls : these in no wise can I bring to naught or stop from gathering bones and harmful herbs, as soon as the roving Moon has uplifted her beauteous face.

[23] My own eyes have seen Canidia walk with black robe tucked up, her feet bare, her hair dishevelled, shrieking with the elder Sagana. Their sallow hue had made the two hideous to behold. Then they began to dig up the earth with their nails, and to tear a black lamb to pieces with their teeth ; the blood was all poured into a trench, that therefrom they might draw the sprites, souls that would give them answers.[a] One image there was of wool, and one of wax, the woollen one the larger, to curb and punish the smaller ; the waxen stood in suppliant guise, as if awaiting death in slavish fashion. One witch calls on Hecate, the other on fell Tisiphone. You might see serpents and hell-hounds roaming about, and the blushing Moon, that she might not witness such deeds, hiding behind the tall tombs. Nay, if I lie in aught, may my head be defiled by ravens' white ordure, and may Julius and the weakling Pediatia and the thief Voranus come to water and befoul me ! Why tell each detail—how in converse with Sagana the shades made echoes sad and shrill, how the two stealthily buried in the ground a wolf's beard and the tooth of a spotted snake,[b] how the fire blazed higher from the image of wax, and how as witness I shuddered at the words and deeds

[b] With this passage cf. the famous witch scene in Macbeth IV. i.

horruerim voces Furiarum et facta duarum ?   45
nam displosa sonat quantum vesica pepedi
diffissa nate ficus : at illae currere in urbem.
Canidiae dentes, altum Saganae caliendrum
excidere atque herbas atque incantata lacertis
vincula cum magno risuque iocoque videres.   50

of the two Furies—though not unavenged ? For as loud as the noise of a bursting bladder was the crack when my fig-wood buttock split. Away they ran into town. Then amid great laughter and mirth you might see Canidia's teeth and Sagana's high wig come tumbling down, and from their arms the herbs and enchanted love-knots.

IX

AN UNWELCOME COMPANION

WHILE taking a morning stroll, Horace is joined by a mere acquaintance, who insists on accompanying him, hoping through closer intimacy to secure an introduction to Maecenas. The poet vainly endeavours to shake him off, and it is only when the man's adversary in a lawsuit appears on the scene—a genuine *deus ex machina*—that Horace is rescued from his unhappy position.

The delightful humour, the skilful dramatic treatment of the theme, and the poet's well-established position in Maecenas's circle which is assumed, indicate that this is one of the latest Satires, in point of composition, in the first book. It may be compared with the sixth Satire, in which Horace gives an account of his introduction to Maecenas.

For the connexion of this Satire with Lucilius see Introduction C.

IX.

Ibam forte Via Sacra, sicut meus est mos
nescio quid meditans nugarum, totus in illis.
accurrit[1] quidam notus mihi nomine tantum,
arreptaque manu, " quid agis, dulcissime rerum ? "
" suaviter, ut nunc est," inquam, " et cupio omnia
    quae vis."   5
   Cum adsectaretur, " num quid vis ? " occupo. at ille,
" noris nos," inquit ; " docti sumus." hic ego, " pluris
hoc," inquam, " mihi eris." misere discedere quaerens,
ire modo ocius, interdum consistere, in aurem
dicere nescio quid puero, cum sudor ad imos[2]   10
manaret talos. " o te, Bolane, cerebri
felicem ! " aiebam tacitus, cum quidlibet ille
garriret, vicos,[3] urbem laudaret.
                     Ut illi
nil respondebam, " misere cupis," inquit, " abire ;
iamdudum video ; sed nil agis ; usque tenebo ; 15
persequar[4] hinc quo nunc iter est tibi." " nil opus
    est te

---

  [1] occurrit.
  [2] *Bentley punctuated so as to take* cum . . . manaret *with*
aiebam.
  [3] ficos, *II, Charisius.*
  [4] prosequar *D, II, Bentley.*

---

  [a] The Sacra Via was the oldest and most famous street in
Rome, running into the Forum ; see Via Sacra in Index.

SATIRE IX

I was strolling by chance along the Sacred Way,[a] musing after my fashion [b] on some trifle or other, and wholly intent thereon, when up there runs a man I knew only by name and seizes my hand: "How d'ye do, my dearest fellow?" "Pretty well, as times are now," I answer, "I hope you get all you want."

[6] As he kept dogging me, I break in with, "Nothing you want, is there?" [c] But he: "You must know me; I'm a scholar." To this I say, "Then I'll esteem you the more." Dreadfully eager to get away I now walk fast, at times stop short, then whisper a word in my slave's ear, while the sweat trickled down to my very ankles. "O Bolanus," I kept saying to myself, "how lucky to have your temper!" while the fellow rattled on about everything, praising the streets and the city.

[13] As I was making him no answer, "You're dreadfully anxious to be off," said he, "I have long seen that; but it's no use, I'll stick to you; I'll stay with you to your journey's end."

"There's no need of your being dragged about;

[b] In view of *forte*, Wickham rightly associates *sicut* ... *mos* with *meditans*, not with *ibam*. So too Lejay.
[c] The question *num quid vis?* is a polite formula of dismissal.

circumagi : quendam volo visere non tibi notum ;
trans Tiberim longe cubat is, prope Caesaris hortos."
" Nil habeo quod agam et non sum piger : usque
    sequar te."
    Demitto auriculas, ut iniquae mentis asellus,   20
cum gravius dorso subiit onus.

                            Incipit ille :
" si bene me novi, non Viscum pluris amicum,
non Varium facies : nam quis me scribere pluris
aut citius possit versus ?   quis membra movere
mollius ? invideat quod et Hermogenes, ego canto."
    Interpellandi locus hic erat : " est tibi mater,   26
cognati, quis te salvo est opus ? "

                          " Haud mihi quisquam :
omnis composui."

                   " Felices ! nunc ego resto.
confice ; namque instat fatum mihi triste, Sabella
quod puero cecinit divina mota[1] anus urna :   30
' hunc neque dira venena nec hosticus auferet ensis
nec laterum dolor aut tussis nec tarda podagra ;
garrulus hunc quando consumet cumque ; loquaces,
si sapiat, vitet, simul atque adoleverit aetas.' "
    Ventum erat ad Vestae, quarta iam parte diei   35
praeterita, et casu tunc respondere vadato
debebat ; quod ni fecisset, perdere litem.
" si me amas," inquit, " paulum hic ades."

                  [1] mota divina *Bentley.*

---

   [a] These gardens, on the right bank of the Tiber, were
left by Julius Caesar to the people of Rome.
   [b] Qualifications despised by Horace ; *cf. Sat.* i. 4. 12 ff.
   [c] See *Sat.* i. 4. 72.

I want to visit a man you do not know. He's ill abed, a long way off across the Tiber, near Caesar's gardens." *a*

"I've nothing to do, and I'm not a poor walker; I'll keep on with you to the end."

Down drop my poor ears like a sulky donkey's, when he has come under a load too heavy for his back.

21 Then he begins: "If I do not deceive myself, you will not think more of Viscus or of Varius as a friend than of me: for who can write more verses or write more quickly than I ? *b* Who can dance more daintily ? Even Hermogenes *c* might envy my singing."

26 Here was my chance to break in: "Have you a mother or kindred who are dependent upon your welfare ?"

"Not one; I have laid them all to rest."

"O happy they! now I am left. Finish me; for now draws near to me that sad fate, which a Sabine dame, shaking her divining urn, sang for me in my boyhood:

> No wicked drug shall prove his end,
> No foeman's sword shall death him send,
> No cough or pleurisy or gout—
> A chatterbox shall talk him out:
> And if he's wise, as he grows old,
> He'll steer quite clear of talkers bold.

35 We had come to Vesta's temple, a fourth of the day being now past, and by chance at that hour he was due to give answer to a plaintiff, on pain of losing his suit, should he fail to appear. "As you love me," he says, "do help me here a while!"

"Interim, si

aut valeo stare[1] aut novi civilia iura ;
et propero quo scis."

"Dubius sum quid faciam," inquit, 40
"tene relinquam an rem." "me, sodes." "non
     faciam," ille,
et praecedere coepit. ego, ut contendere durum[2]
cum victore, sequor.

"Maecenas quomodo tecum ?"
hinc repetit : "paucorum hominum et mentis bene
     sanae.
nemo dexterius fortuna est usus. haberes   45
magnum adiutorem, posset qui ferre secundas,
hunc hominem velles si tradere ; dispeream, ni
summosses omnis."

"Non isto vivimus[3] illic
quo tu rere modo ; domus hac nec purior ulla est
nec magis his aliena malis ; nil mi[4] officit, inquam, 50
ditior hic aut est quia doctior ; est locus uni
cuique suus."

"Magnum narras, vix credibile !" "atqui[5]
sic habet."

"Accendis, quare cupiam magis illi
proximus esse."

"Velis tantummodo : quae tua virtus,
expugnabis ; et est qui vinci possit, eoque   55
difficilis aditus primos habet."

"Haud mihi deero :
muneribus servos corrumpam ; non, hodie si
exclusus fuero, desistam ; tempora quaeram,

---

[1] ista re *Verrall*.   [2] durum est.   [3] vivitur.
   [4] mi *omitted by VK Goth.*   [5] atque, *II*.

" Confound me if I either have strength to stand up,[a] or know the laws of the land ! and besides I must hurry, you know where."

" I wonder," said he, " what I ought to do, whether to leave my suit or you." " Me, I pray ! " " No, I won't," said he, and started to go ahead. As for me, since 'tis hard to fight with one's master, I follow.

43 " How stands Maecenas with you," he thus begins afresh, " a man of few friends and right good sense ? No one ever made wiser use of his luck. You might have a strong backer, who could be your understudy, if you would introduce your humble servant. Hang me, if you wouldn't find that you had cleared the field ! "

" We don't live there on such terms as *you* think. No house is cleaner or more free from such intrigues than that. It never hurts me, I say, that one is richer or more learned than I. Each has his own place."

" That's a strange tale, I can scarce believe it."

" And yet 'tis so."

" You add flame to my desire to get closer to him."

" You have only to wish it ; such is your valour, you will carry the fort. He's a man who can be won, and that is why he makes the first approaches so difficult."

" I'll not fail myself. I'll bribe his slaves. If shut out to-day, I'll not give up. I'll look for the

---

[a] As he would have to do in court. That this is the sense of *stare* seems to follow from *valeo*. Some, however, take *stare* as a synonym of *adesse*, " to appear in court," or as meaning " to be successful," *i.e.* in law.

occurram in triviis, deducam.   nil sine magno
vita labore dedit mortalibus."
                                        Haec dum agit, ecce 60
Fuscus Aristius occurrit, mihi carus et illum
qui pulchre nosset.   consistimus.   " unde venis ? " et
" quo tendis ? " rogat et respondet.   vellere coepi
et pressare[1] manu lentissima bracchia, nutans,
distorquens oculos, ut me eriperet.   male salsus   65
ridens dissimulare ;   meum iecur urere bilis.[2]
" certe nescio quid secreto velle loqui te
aiebas mecum."
                  " Memini bene, sed meliore
tempore dicam ;   hodie tricesima sabbata : vin tu
curtis Iudaeis oppedere ? "
                                " Nulla mihi," inquam, 70
" religio est."
                  " At mi ;   sum paulo infirmior, unus
multorum.   ignosces ;   alias loquar."
                                          Huncine solem
tam nigrum surrexe mihi !   fugit improbus ac me
sub cultro linquit.
                      Casu venit obvius illi
adversarius, et, " quo tu turpissime ? " magna   75
inclamat voce, et " licet antestari ? "   ego vero
oppono auriculam.   rapit in ius ;   clamor utrimque,
undique concursus.   sic me servavit Apollo.

---

[1] pressare *DK, Porph.*: prensare *V, Bentley.*   [2] bellis, *II.*

---

[a] Probably a quotation from some poet.   The sentiment
is found as early as Hesiod, *Works and Days,* 287.
[b] This is probably pure nonsense, no particular Sabbath
being intended.   Perhaps, however, the Sabbath fell on the
thirtieth of the month.
[c] A bystander, consenting to act as witness, allowed the

fitting time ; I'll meet him in the streets ; I'll escort him home.

Life grants no boon to man without much toil." [a]

⁶⁰ While he is thus running on, lo ! there comes up Aristius Fuscus, a dear friend of mine, who knew the fellow right well. We halt. " Whence come you ? Whither go you ? " he asks and answers. I begin to twitch his cloak and squeeze his arms—they were quite unfeeling—nodding and winking hard for him to save me. The cruel joker laughed, pretending not to understand. I grew hot with anger. " Surely you said there was something you wanted to tell me in private."

" I mind it well, but I'll tell you at a better time. To-day is the thirtieth Sabbath.[b] Would you affront the circumcised Jews ? "

" I have no scruples," say I.

" But I have. I'm a somewhat weaker brother, one of the many. You will pardon me ; I'll talk another day."

To think so black a sun as this has shone for me ! The rascal runs away and leaves me under the knife.

⁷⁴ It now chanced that the plaintiff came face to face with his opponent. " Where go you, you scoundrel ? " he loudly shouts, and to me : " May I call you as witness ? " I offer my ear to touch.[c] He hurries the man to court. There is shouting here and there, and on all sides a running to and fro. Thus was I saved by Apollo.[d]

litigant to touch the tip of his ear. The custom was an old one and is referred to in Plautus.

[d] Apollo was the god who befriended poets. The expression comes, however, from Homer (*Iliad*, xx. 443), τὸν δ' ἐξήρπαξεν Ἀπόλλων, words which Lucilius had also used.

X

ON SATIRE

Horace resumes a discussion of the main subject of his fourth Satire, which had brought down considerable censure upon him from the critics, who upheld the excellence of early Latin poetry, and to these he now makes reply.

He reminds them that, while he had found fault with Lucilius's verse, he had also credited it with great satiric power. In this he was quite consistent, for one may admire good mimes without holding them to be good poems. You may make people laugh, but you must also have a terse style and a proper mixture of the grave and the gay, such as is seen in the robust writers of Old Attic Comedy, whom Hermogenes and his school never read. But Lucilius is admired for his skill in blending Greek and Latin. "Nonsense!" cries Horace, "such a mixture is a serious blemish, and no more acceptable in poetry than in oratory" (1-30).

The poet here confesses that at one time he had thought of writing in Greek instead of Latin, but realized in time that this would be like carrying faggots to the forest (31-35).

So while Bibaculus essays something grand and lofty, Horace is less ambitious and turns to a more modest field. If we survey contemporary literature, comedy is pre-empted by Fundanius; Pollio has won fame in tragedy and Varius in the epic ; Virgil is simple and charming in his pastorals. Satire alone was open to Horace, for Varro Atacinus and others had tried it and failed, while Horace has met with success, however short he may come of the first in the field (36-49).

It is true that Horace had criticized Lucilius, just as Lucilius had pointed out defects in Accius and Ennius. His verse *is* faulty—his stream is muddy, he lacks finish, he wrote too freely. If we were to compare him with a writer who is carving out a new species of verse quite untouched by the Greeks, we might attribute to him some polish, but the fact remains that had he lived in the Augustan age, he would have filed away his roughnesses, and learned " the last and greatest art, the art to blot " (50-71).

A writer should aim at pleasing, not the multitude, but a small circle of good critics. If he wins their approval, he may bid the cheap teachers of the lecture-room go hang ! (72-91).

With this statement of his conviction, Horace puts the finishing touch to his First Book (92).

In this satire Horace is a spokesman for the chief writers of the Augustan era, setting forth some of their ideals in contrast with the ignorance and vulgarity of popular scribblers, as represented by men like Tigellius. Among the requisites of good satire Horace speaks of the appropriate use of humour, together with the qualities of brevity, clearness, purity of diction and smoothness of composition, all of which are characteristic of the so-called plain style, or *genus tenue*, of poetry as of oratory. For a full discussion see papers by Hendrickson and Ullman ; also Fiske, *Lucilius and Horace*, pp. 336 ff.)

I

X.

[Lucili, quam sis mendosus, teste Catone
defensore tuo pervincam, qui male factos
emendare parat versus ; hoc lenius ille,
quo melior vir est, longe subtilior illo,
qui multum puer et loris et funibus udis   5
exoratus, ut esset opem qui ferre poetis
antiquis posset contra fastidia nostra,
grammaticorum equitum doctissimus. ut redeam
  illuc :][1]

Nempe incomposito dixi pede currere versus
Lucili. quis tam Lucili fautor inepte est,
ut non hoc fateatur ? at idem, quod sale multo
urbem defricuit, charta laudatur eadem.
  Nec tamen hoc tribuens dederim quoque cetera ;
    nam[2] sic   5
et Laberi mimos ut pulchra poemata mirer.
ergo non satis est risu diducere[3] rictum

---

[1] *Ll.* 1-8. *These awkward verses are found in* MSS. *of class
II only, but are not commented on by the scholiasts. Persius,
an imitator of Horace, begins his third satire with* nempe.
In l. 4, vir, *used by the writer as a long syllable, appears as*
vir et *in a few later* MSS.

[2] num *a M, II.*   [3] deducere *K, II.*

---

a The first eight lines are regarded as spurious, and the
only reason for reproducing them is that they are given in
many MSS., though not in the best. The Cato referred to is
Valerius Cato, a poet and critic of the late Republic, but who
the *grammaticorum equitum doctissimus* was is not known.

SATIRE X

[Lucilius, how faulty you are I will prove clearly by the witness of Cato, your own advocate, who is setting to work to remove faults from your ill-wrought verses. This task is done so much more gently by him, as he is a better man, of much finer taste than the other, who as a boy was ofttimes gently entreated by the lash and moist ropes, so that later he might give aid to the poets of old against our present daintiness, when he had become the most learned of pedagogic knights. But to return [a] :]

[1] To be sure I did say [b] that the verses of Lucilius run on with halting foot. Who is a partisan of Lucilius so in-and-out of season as not to confess this ? And yet on the self-same page the self-same poet is praised because he rubbed the city down with much salt.

[5] Yet, while granting this virtue, I would not also allow him every other ; for on those terms I should also have to admire the mimes of Laberius as pretty poems.[c] Hence it is not enough to make your

[a] It is surely impossible " by reaching back over the relative clause intervening " to refer these words to Cato, as does Hendrickson, who upholds the genuineness of these verses.

[b] In *Sat.* i. 4, which may be compared with this Satire throughout.

[c] Mimes were dramatic scenes from low life, largely farcical and grotesque in character. Laberius, a Roman knight, who was compelled by Julius Caesar to act in his own mimes, was no longer living when Horace wrote.

115

auditoris ; et est quaedam tamen hic quoque virtus :
est brevitate opus, ut currat sententia neu se
impediat verbis lassas onerantibus auris ;   10
et sermone opus est modo tristi, saepe iocoso,
defendente vicem modo rhetoris atque poetae,
interdum urbani,[1] parcentis viribus atque
extenuantis eas consulto.   ridiculum acri
fortius et melius magnas plerumque secat res.   15
illi scripta quibus comoedia prisca viris est
hoc stabant, hoc sunt imitandi ; quos neque pulcher
Hermogenes umquam legit neque simius iste
nil praeter Calvum et doctus cantare Catullum.

    " At magnum fecit, quod verbis Graeca Latinis   20
miscuit."

         O seri studiorum, quine putetis
difficile et mirum, Rhodio quod Pitholeonti
contigit !

         " At sermo lingua concinnus utraque
suavior, ut[2] Chio nota si commixta Falerni est."

    Cum versus facias, te ipsum percontor, an et cum   25
dura tibi peragenda rei sit causa Petilli ?
scilicet oblitus[3] patriaeque patrisque, Latine[4]
cum Pedius causas exsudet Publicola atque

           [1] urbane, *II.*   [2] et, *II.*
      [3] oblitos *Bentley ; so Holder, Vollmer.*
      [4] Latine *comm. Cruq.*: Latini *V, I, Bentley.*

---

    [a] This, according to Porphyrio, is the Demetrius mentioned
in l. 90 below.   Hendrickson thinks it is Bibaculus (*C.P.*
xii. p. 87).
    [b] For *cantare* " to satirize " *cf. Sat.* ii. 1. 46.   These words
are not, as commonly believed, said in depreciation of Calvus
and Catullus, for there was no opposition toward them
on the part of the Augustan poets.   See Rand, " Catullus
and the Augustans," *Harv. St.* xvii. p. 28, and Ullman,
" Horace, Catullus, and Tigellius," *C.P.* x. pp. 270 ff.

hearer grin with laughter—though even in that there is some merit. You need terseness, that the thought may run on, and not become entangled in verbiage that weighs upon wearied ears. You also need a style now grave, often gay, in keeping with the rôle, now of orator or poet, at times of the wit, who holds his strength in check and husbands it with wisdom. Jesting oft cuts hard knots more forcefully and effectively than gravity. Thereby those great men who wrote Old Comedy won success ; therein we should imitate them—writers whom the fop Hermogenes has never read, nor that ape,[a] whose skill lies solely in droning Calvus and Catullus.[b]

20 But that was a great feat," you say, " his mixing of Greek and Latin words."

O ye late learners ![c] ye who really think that a hard and wondrous knack, which Pitholeon of Rhodes achieved !

" But a style, where both tongues make a happy blend, has more charm, as when the Falernian wine is mixed with Chian."

25 In your verse-making only (I put it to yourself), or does the rule also hold good when you have to plead the long, hard case of the defendant Petillius ? Would you forsooth forget fatherland and father, and, while Pedius Publicola and Corvinus sweat over their causes in Latin, would

---

[c] *Seri studiorum* is a translation of ὀψιμαθεῖς, used of those who make a show of their newly acquired knowledge. In the words following, -*ne* should not be regarded as interrogative. It is an affirmative particle, as Priscian held it to be. Nothing is known about Pitholeon, but Bentley plausibly supposed he was the same as Pitholaus, who assailed Julius Caesar in verse (Suet. *Jul.* 75).

Corvinus, patriis intermiscere petita
verba foris malis, Canusini more bilinguis? 30
    Atque[1] ego cum Graecos facerem, natus mare citra,
versiculos, vetuit me tali voce Quirinus,
post mediam noctem visus, cum somnia vera:
" In silvam non ligna feras insanius ac si
magnas Graecorum malis implere catervas." 35
    Turgidus Alpinus iugulat dum Memnona dumque
defingit[2] Rheni luteum caput, haec ego ludo,
quae neque in aede sonent certantia iudice Tarpa,
nec redeant iterum atque iterum spectanda[3] theatris.
    Arguta meretrice potes Davoque Chremeta 40
eludente senem comis garrire libellos
unus vivorum, Fundani ; Pollio regum
facta canit pede ter percusso ; forte epos acer,
ut nemo, Varius ducit ; molle atque facetum
Vergilio adnuerunt[4] gaudentes rure Camenae. 45
hoc erat, experto frustra Varrone Atacino
atque quibusdam aliis, melius quod scribere possem,[5]
inventore minor ; neque ego illi detrahere ausim
haerentem capiti cum multa laude coronam.

[1] atqui *Bentley.*
[2] defingit, *I* : diffingit *K, II, Porph.*
[3] spectata *K, II.*
[4] adnuerant *a* : adnuerint *D.*   [5] possim, *II.*

---

  [a] At Canusium, in Apulia, both Greek and Oscan were spoken.
  [b] A sarcastic reference to M. Furius Bibaculus, who wrote an epic on Caesar's Gallic Wars, and also an *Aethiopis,* in which Memnon is slain by Achilles. The references would be more intelligible if the poems of Bibaculus were extant, but his bombastic style is clearly parodied. See further, *Sat.* ii. 5. 41.
  [c] *i.e.* the Temple of the Muses, where new poetry could be read. For Tarpa see Index, under Maecius.
  [d] A reference to New Comedy, as handled by Terence.

118

you prefer to jumble with your native speech words imported from abroad, like the Canusian's jargon [a] ?

[31] I, too, though born this side of the sea, once took to writing verses in Greek; but after midnight, when dreams are true, Quirinus appeared and forbade me with words like these : " 'Tis just as foolish to carry timber to a wood as to wish to swell the crowded ranks of the Greeks."

[36] So while the pompous poet of the Alps murders Memnon and botches with mud the head of the Rhine,[b] I am toying with these trifles, which are neither to be heard in the Temple[c] as competing for Tarpa's verdict, nor are to come back again and again to be witnessed on the stage.

[40] You alone of living poets, Fundanius, can charm us with the chit-chat of comedies, where the artful mistress and Davus fool old Chremes.[d] In measure of triple beat Pollio sings of kings' exploits.[e] Surpassing all in spirit, Varius moulds the valorous epic.[f] To Virgil the Muses rejoicing in rural life have granted simplicity and charm.[g] This satire, which Varro of the Atax and some others had vainly tried, was what I could write with more success, though falling short of the inventor [h] ; nor would I dare to wrest from him the crown that clings to his brow with so much glory.

---

[e] Pollio used the iambic trimeter in his tragedies.

[f] This was written before Virgil had composed his *Aeneid*.

[g] A reference to the *Eclogues*. Professor C. N. Jackson has won wide acceptance for his view that in *molle atque facetum*, commonly rendered as "tenderness and grace," Horace refers to distinctive features of the *genus tenue*, or plain style of writing (*Harv. St.* xxv. pp. 117 ff.).

[h] Lucilius.

At[1] dixi fluere hunc lutulentum, saepe ferentem 50
plura quidem tollenda relinquendis. age, quaeso,[2]
tu nihil in magno doctus reprehendis Homero ?
nil comis tragici mutat Lucilius Acci ?
non ridet versus Enni gravitate minores,[3]
cum de se loquitur non ut maiore reprensis ? 55
quid vetat et nosmet Lucili scripta legentis
quaerere, num illius, num rerum dura negarit
versiculos natura magis factos[4] et euntis
mollius, ac[5] si quis, pedibus quid claudere senis,
hoc tantum contentus, amet scripsisse ducentos 60
ante cibum versus, totidem cenatus ? Etrusci
quale fuit Cassi rapido ferventius amni
ingenium, capsis quem fama est esse librisque
ambustum propriis.
              Fuerit Lucilius, inquam,
comis et urbanus,[6] fuerit limatior idem 65
quam rudis et Graecis intacti carminis auctor
quamque poetarum seniorum turba : sed ille,
si foret hoc nostrum fato delapsus[7] in aevum,
detereret sibi multa, recideret omne quod ultra
perfectum traheretur, et in versu faciendo 70
saepe caput scaberet, vivos et roderet unguis.
Saepe stilum vertas, iterum quae digna legi sint
scripturus, neque te ut miretur turba labores,

---

[1] at *or* ad] et λlψ. [2] quaero, *I*. [3] minoris *Goth.*
  [4] altos *Goth.* [5] et *a*. [6] urbanis, *II*.
  [7] delapsus *V, adopted by Vollmer and Lejay* : dilatus *one*
Bland., Bentley and generally accepted : dilapsus *MSS.*

---

[a] *i.e.* hexameters. [b] On Cassius see p. 277, note [b].
  [c] *Cf. Sat.* i. 4. 90. The coincidence implies that there the
hic is Lucilius. So Tenney Frank in *A.J.P.* xlvi. (1925)
p. 72. [d] *Cf.* Quintilian, x. 1. 93 "satura tota nostra est."
  [e] The phrase *stilum vertere* means to erase what has been
written on the wax tablet, because the blunt end of the
120

⁵⁰ But I did say his stream runs muddy, and often carries more that you would rather remove than leave behind. Come, pray, do you, a scholar, criticize nothing in the great Homer? Does your genial Lucilius find nothing to change in the tragedies of Accius? Does he not laugh at the verses of Ennius as lacking in dignity, though he speaks of himself as no greater than those he has blamed? And as we read the writings of Lucilius, what forbids us, too, to raise the question whether it was his own genius, or whether it was the harsh nature of his themes that denied him verses more finished and easier in their flow than if one were to put his thoughts into six feet *a* and, content with this alone, were proud of having written two hundred lines before and two hundred after supping? Such was the gift of Tuscan Cassius,*b* more headstrong than a rushing river, whose own books and cases, so 'tis told us, made his funeral pile.

⁶¹ Grant, say I, that Lucilius was genial and witty *c* : grant that he was also more polished than you would expect one to be who was creating a new style quite untouched by the Greeks,*d* and more polished than the crowd of older poets : yet, had he fallen by fate upon this our day, he would smooth away much of his work, would prune off all that trailed beyond the proper limit, and as he wrought his verse he would oft scratch his head and gnaw his nails to the quick.

⁷² Often must you turn your pencil to erase,*e* if you hope to write something worth a second reading, and you must not strive to catch the wonder of the crowd,

stilus was used to smooth out the surface traced by the sharp end.

contentus paucis lectoribus. an tua demens
vilibus[1] in ludis dictari carmina malis ?   75
non ego ; nam satis est equitem mihi plaudere, ut
    audax,
contemptis aliis, explosa Arbuscula dixit.

  Men moveat cimex Pantilius, aut cruciet quod
vellicet absentem Demetrius, aut quod ineptus
Fannius Hermogenis laedat conviva Tigelli ?   80
Plotius et Varius, Maecenas Vergiliusque,
Valgius et probet haec Octavius optimus atque
Fuscus et haec utinam Viscorum laudet uterque !
ambitione relegata te dicere possum,
Pollio, te, Messalla, tuo cum fratre, simulque   85
vos, Bibule et Servi, simul his te, candide Furni,
compluris alios, doctos ego quos et amicos
prudens praetereo ; quibus haec, sint qualiacumque,
adridere velim, doliturus. si placeant spe
deterius nostra. Demetri, teque, Tigelli,   90
discipularum[2] inter iubeo plorare cathedras.

  I, puer, atque meo citus haec subscribe libello.

[1] milibus ψλl.   [2] discipularum MSS. Porph.: discipulorum.

  [a] *i.e.* Aristius Fuscus. Octavius is Octavius Musa, poet
and historian.
  [b] The phrase *iubeo plorare* is a satiric substitute for *iubeo
valere* ("I bid farewell to"). *Cf.* οἴμωζε in Aristophanes, as
in *Plut.* 257.
  [c] In this paragraph Horace contrasts writers of low
literary standards, represented by Tigellius, with members
of the three circles of Maecenas, Pollio and Messalla. He
himself, like Virgil, belongs to the circle of Maecenas.
Tibullus, a member of Messalla's circle, is perhaps at this
time too young to be named. (See Ullman, *C.P.* x. (1910)
pp. 270 ff.)
  [d] The last verse, addressed to the slave who acts as
secretary, serves as an epilogue to the whole book. "The
farewell (or rather 'fare-ill') to Tigellius is the last shot in
the war, and Tigellius is never mentioned again. The last

but be content with the few as your readers. What, would you be so foolish as to want your poems dictated in common schools? Not so I. " 'Tis enough if the knights applaud me "—to quote dauntless Arbuscula's scornful remark, when the rest of the house hissed her.

[78] Am I to be troubled by that louse Pantilius? Or tortured because Demetrius carps at me behind my back, or because silly Fannius, who sponges on Hermogenes Tigellius, girds at me? Let but Plotius and Varius approve of these verses; let Maecenas, Virgil, and Valgius; let Octavius and Fuscus,[a] best of men; and let but the Viscus brothers give their praise! With no desire to flatter, I may name you, Pollio; you, Messalla, and your brother; also you, Bibulus and Servius; also you, honest Furnius, and many another scholar and friend, whom I purposely pass over. In their eyes I should like these verses, such as they are, to find favour, and I should be grieved if their pleasure were to fall short of my hopes. But you, Demetrius, and you, Tigellius, I bid you go whine[b] amidst the easy chairs of your pupils in petticoats![c]

[92] Go,[d] lad, and quickly add these lines to my little book.[e]

line of the first book represents the triumph of an artistic ideal " (Ullman, loc. cit. p. 279).

[e] In connexion with this Satire reference may be made to articles mentioned on p. 61, as well as to the following: Hendrickson, G. L., " Horace and Lucilius. A Study of Horace, Serm. i. 10," in Gildersleeve Studies, pp. 151 ff.; " Horace and Valerius Flaccus " (three articles), C.P. xi. and xii.; B. L. Ullman, " Horace, Catullus and Tigellius," C.P. x. pp. 270 ff.; E. K. Rand, " Catullus and the Augustans," Harv. St. xvii. pp. 15 ff.; C. F. Jackson, " Molle atque Facetum," Harv. St. xxiv. pp. 117 ff.

BOOK II

I

HORACE'S PARTING SHOT AT HIS CRITICS

THIS Satire continues the subject of the fourth and tenth Satires of the First Book. That book had aroused much criticism, which the poet meets in this prologue to his Second Book.

The Satire assumes the form of an imaginary dialogue between Horace and C. Trebatius Testa, a famous lawyer of Cicero's time, whose legal advice on the subject of satiric writing Horace is professedly anxious to secure. Trebatius advises him to give up writing altogether, or if that is impossible, to take up epic poetry (1-12).

" I have no gift for the epic," says Horace, " and yet I must write, and must write satire, even as Lucilius used to do. I belong to a frontier stock, but am armed for defence, not offence, using the pen when attacked as naturally as the bull its horns " (13-60).

TREBATIUS. Then you will come to grief. Some of your great friends will freeze you to death.

HORACE. Did those of Lucilius desert him, when he attacked great and small ? Nay, he lived on intimate terms with Scipio and Laelius, and though

I fall short of him in social rank and ability, yet I, too, have illustrious friends (60-79).

TRE. But let me remind you of the law. You are forbidden to write bad—that is, libellous— verses against anyone.

HOR. Of course not. But what if they are good, like mine, and win Caesar's approval ?

TRE. Then such a charge will be laughed out of court (79-86).

In view of *Caesaris invicti* of l. 11, it would seem that this Satire was written after the Battle of Actium, and therefore shortly before the publication of this Second Book in 30 B.C. Horace is now thirty-five years of age and has won recognition and an assured position in Roman literature. He no longer finds it necessary to defend his satire very seriously, but, as Lejay, in his introduction to this Satire, has clearly shown, " the legal conditions under which satire could be produced in the Augustan age formed a very real restriction upon the freedom of speech traditional in satire. . . . There is a touch of serious anxiety beneath the jest upon the *mala* and *bona carmina* with which the Satire closes " (Fiske, *Lucilius and Horace*, p. 370).

LIBER SECUNDUS

I.

Sunt quibus in satura videar[1] nimis acer et ultra
legem tendere opus ; sine nervis altera, quidquid
composui, pars esse putat similisque meorum
mille die versus deduci[2] posse. Trebati,
quid faciam, praescribe.

     " Quiescas."

         Ne faciam, inquis, 5

omnino versus ?

     " Aio."

        Peream male, si non
optimum erat ; verum nequeo dormire.

            " Ter uncti

transnanto Tiberim, somno quibus est opus alto,
irriguumque mero sub noctem corpus habento.
aut si tantus amor scribendi te rapit, aude 10
Caesaris invicti res dicere, multa laborum
praemia laturus."

       Cupidum, pater optime, vires
deficiunt : neque enim quivis horrentia pilis
agmina nec fracta peruntis cuspide Gallos
aut labentis equo describat[3] volnera Parthi. 1§

---

   [1] videor φψ.   [2] diduci, *II.*
    [3] describat *aEM* : -it *D, II* : -et *K.*

---

  [a] We may infer from one letter of Cicero's (*Ad fam.* vii. 22

BOOK II

Satire I

HORACE. There are some critics who think that I am too savage in my satire and strain the work beyond lawful bounds. The other half of them hold that all I have composed is "nerveless," and that verses as good as mine could be turned out a thousand a day. Give me advice, Trebatius. What am I to do?

TREBATIUS. Take a rest.

HOR. Not write verses at all, you mean?

TRE. Yes.

HOR. Confound me, if that would not be best! But I cannot sleep.

TRE. Let those who need sound sleep oil themselves and swim across the Tiber thrice; then, as night comes on, let them steep themselves in wine.ᵃ Or if such a passion for writing carries you away, bravely tell of the feats of Caesar, the unvanquished. Many a reward for your pains will you gain.

HOR. Would that I could, good father, but my strength fails me. Not everyone can paint ranks bristling with lances, or Gauls falling with spear-heads shattered, or wounded Parthian slipping from his horse.

that Trebatius was a hard drinker, and we learn from another (ib. vii. 10) that he was fond of swimming, *studiosissinus homo natandi*.

" Attamen et iustum poteras et scribere fortem,
Scipiadam ut sapiens Lucilius."

                         Haud mihi dero,
cum res ipsa feret : nisi dextro tempore, Flacci
verba per attentam non ibunt Caesaris aurem,
cui male si palpere, recalcitrat[1] undique tutus.   20
   " Quanto rectius hoc, quam tristi laedere versu
Pantolabum scurram Nomentanumque[2] nepotem,
cum sibi quisque timet, quamquam est intactus, et
    odit."
   Quid faciam ? saltat Milonius, ut semel icto
accessit fervor capiti numerusque lucernis ;   25
Castor gaudet equis, ovo prognatus eodem
pugnis ; quot capitum vivunt, totidem studiorum
milia : me pedibus delectat claudere verba
Lucili ritu, nostrum melioris utroque.
ille velut fidis arcana sodalibus olim   30
credebat libris, neque si male cesserat,[3] usquam
decurrens alio, neque si bene ; quo fit, ut omnis
votiva pateat veluti descripta tabella
vita senis.
        Sequor hunc, Lucanus an Apulus, anceps :
nam Venusinus arat finem sub utrumque colonus, 35
missus ad hoc, pulsis, vetus est ut fama, Sabellis,
quo ne per vacuum Romano incurreret hostis,
sive quod Apula gens seu quod Lucania bellum
incuteret violenta. sed hic stilus haud petet ultro

---

      [1] recalcitret.   [2] -que] -ve, *II, Porph.*
           [3] cesserat *K* : gesserat *MSS.*

---

   [a] A line quoted, with change of case, from *Sat.* i. 8. 11.
   [b] Coming as he does of frontier stock, Horace humorously

TRE. But you might write of himself, at once just and valiant, as wise Lucilius did of Scipio.

HOR. I will not fail myself, when the occasion itself prompts. Only at an auspicious moment will the words of a Flaccus find with Caesar entrance to an attentive ear. Stroke the steed clumsily and back he kicks, at every point on his guard.

21 TRE. How much wiser this than with bitter verse to wound "Pantolabus, the parasite, and spendthrift Nomentanus," [a] whereupon everybody is afraid for himself, though untouched, and hates you.

24 HOR. What am I to do? Milonius starts a-dancing once the heat has mounted to his wine-smitten brain and the lamps twinkle double. Castor finds joy in horses; his brother, born from the same egg, in boxing. For every thousand living souls, there are as many thousand tastes. My own delight is to shut up words in feet, as did Lucilius, a better man than either of us. He in olden days would trust his secrets to his books, as if to faithful friends, never turning elsewhere for recourse, whether things went well with him or ill. So it comes that the old poet's whole life is open to view, as if painted on a votive tablet.

34 He it is I follow—I, a Lucanian or Apulian,[b] I know not which, for the settlers in Venusia plough close to the borders of both lands. Thither they were sent, as the old story goes, when the Samnites were driven out, and to this end, that no foe might ever assail the Romans through an open frontier, whether the Apulian race or whether Lucania lawlessly threatened any war. But this, both my dagger

claims that this is why he is so pugnacious and takes to satire.

quemquam animantem et me veluti custodiet ensis 40
vagina tectus ; quem cur destringere[1] coner
tutus ab infestis latronibus ? o pater et rex
Iuppiter, ut pereat positum robigine telum,[2]
nec quisquam noceat cupido mihi pacis ! at ille,
qui me commorit (melius non tangere, clamo),   45
flebit et insignis tota cantabitur urbe.

  Cervius iratus leges minitatur et urnam,
Canidia Albuci quibus est inimica venenum,
grande malum Turius, si quid se iudice certes.[3]
ut quo quisque valet suspectos terreat, utque   50
imperet hoc natura potens, sic collige mecum :
dente lupus, cornu taurus petit ; unde, nisi intus
monstratum ?   Scaevae vivacem crede nepoti
matrem ; nil faciet sceleris pia dextera : mirum,
ut neque calce lupus quemquam neque dente petit[4]
    bos :   55
sed mala[5] tollet anum vitiato melle cicuta.
ne longum faciam : seu me tranquilla senectus
exspectat seu mors atris circumvolat alis,
dives, inops, Romae, seu fors ita iusserit, exsul,
quisquis erit vitae scribam color.
                              " O puer, ut sis   60
vitalis metuo, et maiorum ne quis amicus
frigore te feriat." quid ? cum est Lucilius ausus
primus in hunc operis componere carmina morem,
detrahere et pellem, nitidus qua quisque per ora

---

[1] distringere, *II.*
[2] telum MSS.: ferrum *Priscian.*
[3] quis . . . certet *DK, II.*   [4] petat *Dφψl.*
[5] mala MSS.: male *EM.*

---

  [a] The *stilus*, a pointed instrument, could be used either
as a pen or as a weapon.   For the latter sense *cf. stiletto.*

and pen,[a] shall never of my free will assail any man alive but shall protect me, like a sword laid up in its sheath. Why should I try to draw it, while I am safe from robbers' assaults? O Jupiter, Sire and King, let perish with rust the discarded weapon, and let no man injure me, a lover of peace! But if one stir me up ("Better not touch me!" I shout), he shall smart for it and have his name sung up and down the town.

[47] Cervius, when angry, threatens his foes with laws and the judge's urn; Canidia with the poison of Albucius; Turius with a big fine, if you go to court when he is judge. How everyone, using the weapon in which he is strong, tries to frighten those whom he fears, and how this is at Dame Nature's own command, you must infer—as I do—thus: the wolf attacks with fangs, the bull with horns—how was each taught, if not by instinct? Suppose you entrust to the spendthrift Scaeva a long-lived mother: his filial hand will commit no crime. How marvellous! no more so than that a wolf assails none with his heels, nor an ox with his teeth; but deadly hemlock in drugged honey will carry the old crone off. To be brief—whether peaceful age awaits me, or Death hovers round with sable wings, rich or poor, in Rome, or, if chance so bid, in exile, whatever the colour [b] of my life, write I must.

[60] TRE. My lad, I fear your life will be brief. One of your great friends will strike you with a killing frost.

HOR. What! when Lucilius first dared to compose poems after this kind, and to strip off the skin with which each strutted all bedecked before the eyes of

[b] *i.e.* bright or dark, with good or bad fortune.

cederet, introrsum turpis, num Laelius et[1] qui   65
duxit ab oppressa meritum Karthagine nomen
ingenio offensi aut laeso doluere Metello
famosisque Lupo cooperto versibus ? atqui
primores populi arripuit populumque tributim,[2]
scilicet uni aequus Virtuti atque eius amicis.   70
quin ubi se a volgo et scaena in secreta remorant
virtus Scipiadae et mitis sapientia Laeli,
nugari cum illo et discincti ludere, donec
decoqueretur holus, soliti.   quicquid sum ego, quam-
     vis
infra Lucili censum ingeniumque, tamen me   75
cum magnis vixisse invita fatebitur usque
invidia, et fragili quaerens inlidere dentem
offendet solido, nisi quid tu, docte Trebati,
dissentis.
      " Equidem nihil hinc diffindere[3] possum.
sed tamen ut monitus caveas, ne forte negoti   80
incutiat tibi quid sanctarum inscitia legum :
si mala condiderit in quem quis carmina, ius est
iudiciumque."
         Esto, si quis mala ; sed bona si quis
iudice condiderit laudatus Caesare ? si quis
opprobriis dignum latraverit, integer ipse ?   85
" Solventur risu tabulae, tu missus abibis."

    [1] et *DK* : aut *aE*.
    [2] tributim *aK* : tributum *DE*.
    [3] diffindere *VDM, II, Porph.* : diffingere *a* : diffundere *E* :
diffidere.

---

   [a] The younger Scipio Africanus.
   [b] In l. 82 Horace uses the very phraseology of the XII.
Tables as cited by Pliny, " qui malum carmen incantassit"
(*Hist. Nat.* xxviii. 4. 18), and Cicero, " sive carmen condi-

men, though foul within, was Laelius offended at
his wit, or he who took his well-earned name from
conquered Carthage ?[a] Or were they hurt because
Metellus was smitten, and Lupus buried under a
shower of lampooning verses ? Yet he laid hold
upon the leaders of the people, and upon the people
in their tribes, kindly in fact only to Virtue and her
friends. Nay, when virtuous Scipio and the wise
and gentle Laelius withdrew into privacy from the
throng and theatre of life, they would turn to folly,
and flinging off restraint would indulge with him in
sport while their dish of herbs was on the boil. Such as
I am, however far beneath Lucilius in rank and native
gifts, yet Envy, in spite of herself, will ever admit
that I have lived with the great, and, while trying
to strike her tooth on something soft, will dash upon
what is solid. But maybe you, learned Trebatius,
disagree.

[79] TRE. Indeed, I can take no exception to this. But
for all that, let me warn you to beware, lest haply
ignorance of our sacred laws bring you into trouble.
If a man write ill verses against another,[b] there is a
right of action and redress by law.

HOR. To be sure, in case of ill verses. But what
if a man compose good verses, and Caesar's judge-
ment approve ? If he has barked at someone who
deserves abuse, himself all blameless ?

TRE. The case will be dismissed with a laugh.[c]
You will get off scot-free.

disset" (*De republica*, iv. 10. 12). Horace is, of course,
punning on the use of *malum*, which can mean both
"libellous" and "of bad quality."

[c] Literally, "the official records will be cancelled." See
Jefferson Elmore, *C.R.* xxxiii. p. 102.

II

A DISCOURSE ON PLAIN LIVING

Horace puts the discourse in the mouth of Ofellus, an old neighbour of the poet's, and a representative of the simplicity and other sturdy qualities of the Apulian farmers. As a whole, however, the Satire is mainly a collection of commonplaces taken from the teachings of the various philosophic schools, though the theme and even the mode of handling it were probably suggested by Lucilius. It stands midway between dialogue and monologue, and perhaps indicates that the author is still experimenting in regard to the form. It is probably the first one of this book in the order of composition.

The argument is as follows : Learn from me, or rather from my authority, Ofellus—a plain but shrewd countryman—the value of simple living. Let us learn the lesson before we break our fast.

A man never despises frugal fare after heavy exercise, because the pleasure of eating lies, not in costly food, but in oneself. The most tempting dainties lose their flavour for the man who has no appetite. People foolishly prefer a peacock to a pullet, simply because it has a fine tail and costs more money. So, too, a three-pound mullet is admired, while a big pike is scorned. The former is an unnatural rarity, the latter is common, and the well-fed stomach scorns things common. Some day we shall find roast gulls in fashion (1-52).

Plain living is not the same as mean living, and you must not avoid one fault merely to fall into another. There is a happy mean between stinginess and extravagance (53-69).

A simple fare means health of body, a good digestion, sound and refreshing sleep, mental vigour. It allows one to indulge himself occasionally, as when the holidays come, or in times of ill-health, or when old age arrives. In the good old days dainties were reserved for hospitality (70-93).

A luxurious life leads to disgrace and ruin. "That may be true of others," says one, "but I can well afford to be extravagant." Then why not use your money for better ends? And what about the changes and chances of life? Which of the two will meet them best, the man accustomed to every comfort, or the one who is content with little (94-111)?

I knew Ofellus in my boyhood, when he was the well-to-do owner of the land on which he now pays rent. In those days he lived the same simple life that he does now, and when misfortunes came, he faced them bravely and in true philosophic fashion (113-136).

Kiessling has pointed out how closely this Satire reproduces some ideas found in the well known letter of Epicurus to Menoecus (Diog. Laert. x. 131), but Lejay has also called attention to striking parallels in Cicero's philosophical writings. Even the phrase *tenuis victus* (l. 53) is Ciceronian (*cf. Tusc. Disp.* iii. 49. 5; v. 26. 89, etc.). "Cicéron," says Lejay (p. 380), "est peut-être encore plus complètement l'inspiration des grandes lignes de la satire."

II.

Quae virtus et quanta, boni, sit vivere parvo
(nec meus hic sermo est, sed quae praecepit Ofellus
rusticus, abnormis[1] sapiens crassaque Minerva),
discite, non inter lances mensasque nitentis,
cum stupet insanis acies fulgoribus et cum   5
acclinis falsis animus meliora recusat,
verum hic impransi mecum disquirite.   " cur hoc ? "
dicam, si potero.   Male verum examinat omnis
corruptus iudex.   leporem sectatus equove
lassus ab indomito vel, si Romana fatigat   10
militia adsuetum graecari, seu pila velox
molliter austerum studio fallente laborem,
seu te discus agit (pete cedentem aëra disco)—
cum labor extuderit fastidia, siccus, inanis
sperne cibum vilem ; nisi Hymettia mella Falerno   15
ne biberis diluta.   foris est promus et atrum
defendens piscis hiemat mare : cum sale panis
latrantem stomachum bene leniet.   unde putas aut
qui partum ?   non in caro nidore voluptas

---

¹ abnormi *aEK Acr.*: ab normis *Vollmer and Lejay.*

---

   a For *Romana militia*, or training for the Roman army,
cf. Cicero, *De nat. deor.* ii. 64, "ut exerceamur in venando
ad similitudinem bellicae disciplinae," and for the contrast
with Greek games see *Odes*, iii. 24. 54 ff.
   b According to Macrobius, *Saturn.* vii. 12, the best

SATIRE II

WHAT and how great, my friends, is the virtue of frugal living—now this is no talk of mine, but is the teaching of Ofellus, a peasant, a philosopher unschooled and of rough mother-wit—learn, I say, not amid the tables' shining dishes, when the eye is dazed by senseless splendour, and the mind, turning to vanities, rejects the better part ; but here, before we dine, let us discuss the point together. " Why so ? " I will tell you, if I can.

[8] Every judge who has been bribed weighs truth badly. After hunting the hare or wearily dismounting from an unbroken horse, or else, if Roman army-exercises [a] are fatiguing to one used to Greek ways, it may be the swift ball takes your fancy, where the excitement pleasantly beguiles the hard toil, or it may be the discus (by all means hurl the discus through the yielding air)—well, when toil has knocked the daintiness out of you ; when you are thirsty and hungry, despise, if you can, plain food ; refuse to drink any mead, unless the honey is from Hymettus, and the wine from Falernum.[b] The butler is out ; the sea, dark and stormy, protects its fish ; bread and salt will suffice to appease your growling belly. Whence or how do you think this comes about ? The chiefest pleasure lies, not in the costly savour, but in

mead was made of new Hymettian honey and old Falernian wine.

summa, sed in te ipso est.   tu pulmentaria quaere 20
sudando : pinguem vitiis albumque neque ostrea
nec scarus aut poterit peregrina iuvare lagois.

Vix tamen eripiam, posito pavone velis quin
hoc potius quam gallina tergere palatum,
corruptus vanis rerum, quia veneat auro   25
rara avis et picta pandat spectacula cauda ;
tamquam ad rem attineat quicquam.   num vesceris
    ista
quam laudas pluma ?   cocto num adest honor[1] idem ?
carne tamen quamvis distat nil, hac[2] magis illam[3]
imparibus formis deceptum te petere[4] !   esto :   30
unde datum sentis, lupus hic Tiberinus an alto
captus hiet, pontisne inter iactatus an amnis
ostia sub Tusci ?   laudas, insane, trilibrem
mullum, in singula quem minuas pulmenta necesse
    est.
ducit te species, video.   quo pertinet ergo   35
proceros odisse lupos ?   quia scilicet illis
maiorem natura modum dedit, his breve pondus.
ieiunus raro stomachus volgaria temnit.

 " Porrectum magno magnum spectare catino
vellem," ait Harpyiis gula digna rapacibus.   at vos, 40
praesentes Austri, coquite horum obsonia.   quam-
    quam[5]
putet aper rhombusque recens, mala copia quando

---

[1] color *Goth.*   [2] haec.
[3] illam *E Goth., Porph.* : illa *aD, II.*
[4] petere *aDEK Porph.* : patet *D²M, Orelli.*
[5] quamvis, *II.*

---

a Cicero (*Ad fam.* ix. 20. 2) implies that a peacock was
regarded as an essential feature of a banquet.

yourself. So earn your sauce with hard exercise. The man who is bloated and pale from excess will find no comfort in oysters or trout or foreign grouse.

²³ Yet, if a peacock be served,^a I shall hardly root out your longing to tickle your palate with it rather than with a pullet. You are led astray by the vain appearance, because the rare bird costs gold and makes a brave show with the picture of its outspread tail—as though that had aught to do with the case ! Do you eat the feathers you so admire ? Does the bird look as fine when cooked ? Yet, though in their meat they are on a par, to think that you crave the one rather than the other, duped by the difference in appearance ! Very well. But what sense tells you whether this pike gasping here was caught in the Tiber or in the sea, whether in the eddies between the bridges ^b or just at the mouth of the Tuscan ^c river ? You foolish fellow, you praise a three-pound mullet, which you must needs cut up into single portions. 'Tis the look, I see, that takes you. Why then detest a very long pike ? It is, of course, because nature has made the pike large, and the mullet light of weight. Only a stomach that seldom feels hunger scorns things common.

³⁹ "But a big fish on a big dish outstretched ! That's what I'd like to see ! " cries a gullet worthy of the greedy Harpies. Nay, come in your might, ye southern gales, and taint these gluttons' dainties ! And yet they are already rank, yon boar and fresh

---

^b *i.e.* off the *Insula Tiberina*. The two bridges, *Pons Cestius* and *Pons Fabricius*, connected the island with the right and left banks of the Tiber.
^c The Tiber rises in Etruria.

aegrum sollicitat stomachum, cum rapula plenus
atque acidas mavolt inulas. necdum omnis abacta
pauperies epulis regum : nam vilibus ovis   45
nigrisque est oleis hodie locus. haud ita pridem
Galloni praeconis erat acipensere mensa
infamis. quid? tunc[1] rhombos minus aequor alebat[2]?
tutus erat rhombus tutoque ciconia nido,
donec vos auctor docuit praetorius. ergo   50
si quis nunc mergos suavis edixerit assos,
parebit pravi docilis Romana iuventus.

Sordidus a tenui victu distabit,[3] Ofello
iudice ; nam frustra vitium vitaveris illud,
si te alio pravum detorseris. Avidienus,   55
cui Canis ex vero ductum[4] cognomen adhaeret,
quinquennis oleas est et silvestria corna,
ac nisi mutatum parcit defundere[5] vinum, et
cuius odorem olei[6] nequeas perferre, licebit
ille repotia, natalis aliosve dierum   60
festos albatus celebret, cornu ipse bilibri
caulibus instillat, veteris non parcus aceti.
quali igitur victu sapiens utetur, et horum
utrum imitabitur? hac urget lupus, hac canis, aiunt.[7]
mundus erit, qua[8] non offendat sordibus, atque   65
in neutram partem cultus miser. hic neque servis,
Albuci senis exemplo, dum munia didit,[9]

---

[1] tum, *II*.   [2] aequora alebant *EM*.
      [3] distabit *early editors* : distabat *MSS*.
            [4] ductum *V* : dictum *MSS*.
[5] fundere, *II*.   [6] olet, *II*.   [7] angit *D²*.
            [8] qui, *II*.   [9] dedit *DEM*.

---

a Lucilius had satirized Gallonius for serving a huge
sturgeon at dinner.

b According to Porphyrion, the reference is to one Rufus
who set the fashion of eating storks, and who was defeated

turbot, since cloying plenty worries the jaded stomach, which, sated as it is, prefers radishes and tart pickles the while. Nor is the poor man's fare yet wholly banished from the feasts of kings, for cheap eggs and black olives still have a place. 'Tis not so long ago that by reason of a sturgeon the table of Gallonius the auctioneer won ill repute.[a] What? Was the sea less a home for turbots in those days? The turbot was safe, and safe was the nest of the stork, till a praetor's sanction taught you the lesson.[b] So now, should someone decree that roasted gulls are delicacies, our Roman youth, quick to learn ill ways, will obey.

[53] A mean style of living will differ, so Ofellus thinks, from a simple one; for it will be idle for you to shun one fault, if you turn aside into another crooked path. Avidienus, to whom the nickname " Dog " quite rightly clings, eats his olives five years old with cornels from the wood, and is chary of drawing his wine till it has soured; as to his oil, you couldn't bear its smell, yet even if in his whitened garb [c] he keeps a wedding or birthday feast or some other holiday, he drops it on the salad from a two-pound horn with his own hands, though his old vinegar he does not stint. What style then will the wise man adopt, and which of these two will he copy? On the one side, as the saying is, a wolf attacks, on the other a dog. He will be neat, so far as not to shock us by meanness, and in his mode of living will be unhappy in neither direction. He will neither, like old Albucius, be cruel to his slaves, as he assigns

for the praetorship. The word *praetorius* is therefore used in irony.

[c] *i.e.* in holiday attire, and wearing a freshly cleaned toga.

saevus erit ; nec sic ut simplex Naevius unctam
convivis praebebit aquam : vitium hoc quoque mag-
    num.   69

   Accipe nunc, victus tenuis quae quantaque secum
adferat. imprimis valeas bene. nam variae res
ut noceant homini credas, memor illius escae,
quae simplex olim tibi sederit : at simul assis
miscueris elixa, simul conchylia turdis,
dulcia se in bilem vertent stomachoque tumultum 75
lenta feret pituita. vides ut pallidus omnis
cena desurgat dubia ? quin corpus onustum
hesternis vitiis animum quoque praegravat una
atque adfigit humo divinae particulam aurae.
alter, ubi dicto citius curata sopori   80
membra dedit, vegetus praescripta ad munia surgit.
hic tamen ad melius poterit transcurrere quondam,
sive diem festum rediens advexerit annus,
seu recreare volet tenuatum corpus, ubique
accedent anni,[1] tractari mollius aetas   85
imbecilla volet : tibi quidnam accedet ad istam
quam puer et validus praesumis mollitiem, seu
dura valetudo inciderit seu tarda senectus ?

   Rancidum aprum antiqui laudabant, non quia nasus
illis nullus erat, sed, credo, hac mente, quod hospes
tardius adveniens vitiatum[2] commodius quam   91

---

    [1] anni et *Bentley*.   [2] vitiaret *VaEM*.

---

   [a] The phrase *cena dubia* (used by Terence, *Phormio*, 342)
had become proverbial. It means a dinner so varied that
you don't know what to take.
   [b] Horace is using the language of high philosophy. The
animus is a part of the universal divine spirit imprisoned in
the body ; *cf.* Cicero, *De senectute*, 21. 78, " ex universa
mente delibatos animos." In *adfigit humo* Horace echoes
Plato, who, in *Phaedo* 83 D, says that every pleasure and
142

their tasks, nor, like careless Naevius, will he offer greasy water to his guests: this too is a great blunder.

70 Now learn what and how great are the blessings that simple living brings in its train. First of all, good health. For how harmful to a man a variety of dishes is, you may realize, if you recall that plain fare which agreed with you in other days. But as soon as you mix boiled and roast, shell-fish and thrushes, the sweet will turn to bile, and the thick phlegm will cause intestine feud. Do you see how pale rises each guest from his "puzzle feast" *a* ? Nay more, clogged with yesterday's excess, the body drags down with itself the mind as well, and fastens to earth a fragment of the divine spirit.*b* The other, when after refreshment he has surrendered his limbs to sleep sooner than you can speak,*c* rises up in vigour for his appointed tasks. Yet at times he will be able to pass over to better cheer, whether the revolving year brings some holiday, or he wants to renew a shrunken frame, and when, as time advances, the frailty of age looks for more indulgent treatment. But as for you, if ill-health come, or enfeebling age, what will you bring to add to that indulgence which, while young and hale, you thus forestall ?

89 Our fathers used to praise a boar when high ; not that they had no noses, but with this thought, I suppose, that a guest arriving behind time could more conveniently eat it when tainted than the

very pain is a sort of nail, which nails (προσηλοῖ) the soul to the body.

c The proverbial expression *dicto citius*, "quicker than a word," is like the English "before you can say Jack Robinson." The phrase *curare membra* or *curare corpus* is often used of taking refreshment.

143

integrum edax dominus consumeret. hos utinam inter
heroas natum tellus me prima tulisset !

Das aliquid famae, quae carmine gratior aurem
occupet[1] humanam : grandes rhombi patinaeque   95
grande ferunt una cum damno dedecus ; adde
iratum patruum, vicinos, te tibi iniquum
et frustra mortis cupidum, cum derit egenti
as, laquei pretium.   " iure," inquit, " Trausius istis
iurgatur verbis : ego vectigalia magna   100
divitiasque habeo tribus amplas regibus."   ergo
quod superat non est melius quo insumere possis ?
cur eget indignus quisquam, te divite ?   quare
templa ruunt antiqua deum ?   cur, improbe, carae
non aliquid patriae tanto emetiris acervo ?   105
uni nimirum recte[2] tibi semper erunt res,
o magnus posthac inimicis risus !   uterne
ad casus dubios fidet sibi certius ?   hic qui
pluribus adsuerit mentem corpusque superbum,
an qui contentus parvo metuensque futuri   110
in pace, ut sapiens, aptarit idonea bello ?

Quo magis his credas, puer[3] hunc ego parvus Ofellum
integris opibus novi non latius usum
quam nunc accisis.   videas metato[4] in agello
cum pecore et gnatis fortem mercede colonum,   115

---

[1] occupat, *II*.   [2] rectae *V*.
[3] puer λ *Goth.* : puerum, *I*.   [4] metatum, *II*.

---

[a] Horace says that their ancestors kept the boar till it
was " high," a practice which he attributes to their hospitality
or desire to have something in store should a guest arrive.

[b] In Latin literature the uncle is the regular type of the
stern and severe relative.

[c] This jest, found in Plautus, *e.g. Pseud.* 88, doubtless
comes from Attic comedy.

[d] The word means " measured off," *i.e.* for confiscation.

greedy master, while still fresh. Oh, that the early world had given me birth among heroes such as those ! [a]

[94] You set some store by good repute, which, sweeter than song, charms the human ear. Big turbots and dishes bring a big scandal and loss. Add the angry uncle,[b] the angry neighbours, your hatred of self, your vain longing for death, when in your need you lack a penny to buy a halter with.[c] " 'Tis all right," he answers, " for Trausius to be scolded in such language, but I have large revenues, and riches ample for three kings." Well, is there no better object on which you can spend your surplus ? Why is any worthy man in want, while you are rich ? Why are the ancient temples of the gods in ruin ? Why, shameless man, do you not measure out something from that great heap for your dear country ? You alone, of course, will always find things go well. Oh, what a laughing-stock you will be some day for your enemies ! Which of the two, in face of changes and chances, will have more self-confidence—he who has accustomed a pampered mind and body to superfluities, or he who, content with little and fearful of the future, has in peace, like a wise man, provided for the needs of war ?

[112] That you may give more credit to such words, I will tell you how, when I was a little boy, this Ofellus, as I well know, used his full means on no larger scale than he does now, when they are cut down. You may see him on his little farm, now assigned to others,[d] with his cattle and his sons, a

It was assigned to the veteran Umbrenus (ii. 133). Probably Ofellus was dispossessed of his farm when Horace, like Virgil, lost his own property, in 41 B.C.

" non ego," narrantem, " temere edi luce profesta
quicquam praeter holus fumosae cum pede pernae.
ac mihi seu longum post tempus venerat hospes,
sive operum vacuo gratus conviva per imbrem
vicinus, bene erat non piscibus urbe petitis,   120
sed pullo atque haedo ; tum[1] pensilis uva secundas
et nux ornabat mensas cum duplice ficu.
post hoc ludus erat culpa[2] potare magistra,
ac venerata Ceres, ita culmo surgeret alto,
explicuit vino contractae seria frontis.   125
saeviat atque novos moveat Fortuna tumultus :
quantum[3] hinc imminuet? quanto aut ego parcius
     aut vos,
o pueri, nituistis,[4] ut huc novus incola venit ?
nam propriae telluris erum natura neque illum
nec me nec quemquam statuit : nos expulit ille ; 130
illum aut nequities aut vafri inscitia iuris,
postremum expellet certe vivacior heres.[5]
nunc ager Umbreni sub nomine, nuper Ofelli
dictus, erit nulli proprius, sed cedet in usum
nunc mihi, nunc alii.[6] quocirca vivite fortes, 135
fortiaque adversis opponite pectora rebus."

[1] tunc, *I* : tum, *II, Priscian.*
[2] culpa *MSS., Porph.* : cupa *Bentley, who also suggested*
nulla : captu . . . magistro *Housman.*
[3] quantum *DM, II* : *Peerlkamp conjectured* quando.
[4] instituistis *D²φλ.*
[5] *From here D is wanting up to* ii. 3. 75.   [6] aliis *λ.*

---

  [a] Instead of the formalities of a banquet, where a *magister
bibendi* prescribed the rules, any shirking would be punished
by a forfeit.

  [b] *Usus* is probably put for *ususfructus,* which was the right

sturdy tenant-farmer, and this is his story: " I was not the man to eat on a working day, without good reason, anything more than greens and the shank of a smoked ham, and if after long absence a friend came to see me, or if in rainy weather, when I could not work, a neighbour paid me a visit—a welcome guest—we fared well, not with fish sent for from town, but with a pullet or a kid; by and by raisins and nuts and split figs set off our dessert. Then we had a game of drinking, with a forfeit to rule the feast,[a] and Ceres, to whom we made our prayer—" so might she rise on lofty stalk!"—smoothed out with wine the worries of a wrinkled brow. Let Fortune storm and stir fresh turmoils; how much will she take off from this? How much less sleek have I been, or you, my lads, since this new landlord came? Nature, in truth, makes neither him nor me nor anyone else lord of the soil as his own. He drove us out, and he will be driven out by villainy, or by ignorance of the quirks of the law, or in the last resort by an heir of longer life. To-day the land bears the name of Umbrenus; of late it had that of Ofellus; to no one will it belong for good, but for use it will pass, now to me and now to another.[b] Live, then, as brave men, and with brave hearts confront the strokes of fate."

of using and enjoying property, but not of owning it. The latter was called *dominium*. For the thought *cf.* the famous verse in Lucretius (iii. 971), " Life is granted to none in fee-simple, to all on lease,"

vitaque mancipio nulli datur, omnibus usu.

III

THE FOLLIES OF MANKIND

ACCORDING to the Stoics, everyone save the wise man is mad; πᾶς ἄφρων μαίνεται. Horace makes this paradox his text and assails the follies of the world.

The Satire takes the form of a dialogue between the poet and Damasippus. Horace is at his newly acquired Sabine farm, to which he has retired to avoid the excitement of the Saturnalia in Rome. Damasippus, of whom we hear in Cicero's Epistles, is a bankrupt speculator and dealer in works of art, who, having fallen into the depths of despair, had been rescued by the Stoic sage Stertinius, was converted by him to philosophy, and so made into the wise man he has now become. He reports a long discourse of Stertinius upon the text, " all men, save only the wise, are mad " (1-81).

The sermon of Stertinius may be divided into four parts, dealing with avarice (82-157), ambition (158-223), self-indulgence (225-280), and superstition (281-295), all of which are phases of madness.

The avaricious are the largest class of madmen. They believe poverty to be the greatest possible disgrace, and suppose that wealth can confer every blessing (91-97). Avarice, as well as its opposite,

149

prodigality, are illustrated by the story of the two sons of Servius Oppidius (168-178).

The ambitious are mad. Agamemnon, slaying his daughter for the sake of power and position, was just as mad as Ajax, who slew sheep under the delusion that they were his enemies (193-213).

The madness of self-indulgence is illustrated by the spendthrift Nomentanus, who wastes the fortune he has inherited (224-238); by the son of Aesopus, who swallows the precious pearl of his mistress which he has dissolved in vinegar (239-241); by the sons of Arrius, who breakfast on costly nightingales (243-246); and especially by the follies of lovers, who are often as crazy as would be a grown-up man if he indulged in the sports of children (247-254). Better for them to follow the example of Polemon, who listened to the voice of reason and cast away the tokens of his malady (254-257). The love passion may even lead to bloodshed, as we saw the other day when Marius murdered his mistress and took his own life (275-280).

The madness of superstition is illustrated by the old freedman who prayed for immortality, and by the mother whose sick son recovers only to be killed through her foolish vow (281-295).

" And what," asks Horace, as Damasippus brings this long sermon of Stertinius to a close, " is my madness? I think I am sane."

DAMASIPPUS. So Agave thought, when she was carrying in her hands the head of her unfortunate son.

HORACE. Well, what is my madness?

DAM. You are aping the great, like the frog in the fable. You write verses, you have a bad temper, you live beyond your means, you are always falling in love.

HOR. You greater madman, spare the lesser! (296-326).

This is not only the longest, but also the best constructed of Horace's Satires. Notwithstanding the long discourse which makes up the main body of the poem, the dialogue-form serves as a framework for the whole, and allows the poet to employ a light, humorous vein in both beginning and end, where he turns the laugh against himself. Note that while the writer's main aim throughout is to portray striking forms of human folly, a second one is to ridicule the airs and manners of the Stoic preachers of the day. The Satire was probably written in 33 B.C., because in l. 185 there is a reference to the curule aedileship of Agrippa, held in that year and distinguished by magnificence of display.

III.

" Sic[1] raro scribis,[2] ut toto non quater anno
membranam poscas, scriptorum quaeque retexens,
iratus tibi, quod vini somnique benignus
nil dignum sermone canas ; quid fiet ?   at[3] ipsis
Saturnalibus huc fugisti.   sobrius ergo[4]   5
dic aliquid dignum promissis : incipe. nil est :
culpantur frustra calami, immeritusque laborat
iratis natus paries dis atque poetis.
atqui voltus erat multa et praeclara minantis,
si vacuum tepido cepisset villula tecto.   10
quorsum pertinuit stipare Platona Menandro,
Eupolin, Archilochum, comites educere tantos ?
invidiam placare paras virtute relicta ?
contemnere, miser.   vitanda est improba Siren
desidia, aut quidquid vita meliore parasti   15
ponendum aequo animo." di te, Damasippe, deaeque

¹ sic : si *E.*
² scribis *M* : scribes *aE.   Bentley read* si scribes.
³ at *V, II* : ab, *I.*   ⁴ *Bentley punctuated after* sobrius.

---

a Parchment would be needed for the final form of his
words, after the poet had written and corrected his notes
on the tablets.

b Horace is probably thinking of Penelope's web.

c The wall suffers because the poet pounds it in his vain
efforts at composition.

d Though Orelli supposed that Plato the philosopher is
here meant, it seems certain that Horace is speaking of
Plato the poet, leader of the so-called Middle Attic Comedy.

Satire III

DAMASIPPUS. So seldom do you write, that not four times in all the year do you call for the parchment,[a] while you unweave the web of all you have written,[b] and are angry with yourself because, while so generous of wine and of sleep, you turn out no poetry worth talking about. What will be the end ? Why, you say, even in the Saturnalia you fled here for refuge. Well then, in your sober mood, tell something worthy of your promises. Begin. Nothing comes. In vain you blame the pen ; and the innocent wall, begotten when gods and poets were angry, must suffer.[c] Yet you had the look of one who threatened great and glorious things, if once you were care-free and your country cottage welcomed you under its warm roof. What was the use of packing Plato[d] with Menander, and of taking out of town Eupolis and Archilochus, such weighty comrades ? Think you to lay Envy low by deserting Virtue ? You will earn contempt, poor wretch. You must shun the wicked Siren, Sloth, or be content to drop whatever honour you have gained in nobler hours.

HORACE. May the gods and goddesses give you,

Thus he would take with him to the country representatives of Old (Eupolis), Middle, and New (Menander) Comedy, as well as the great iambic poet, Archilochus.

verum ob consilium donent tonsore. sed unde
tam bene me nosti ?

        " Postquam omnis res mea Ianum
ad medium fracta est, aliena negotia curo,
excussus propriis. olim nam quaerere amabam,   20
quo vafer[1] ille pedes lavisset Sisyphus aere,
quid sculptum infabre, quid fusum durius esset ;
callidus huic signo ponebam milia centum ;
hortos egregiasque domos mercarier unus
cum lucro noram ; unde frequentia Mercuriale   25
imposuere mihi cognomen compita." novi,
et miror morbi purgatum te illius. " atqui
emovit veterem mire novus, ut solet, in cor
traiecto lateris miseri capitisve[2] dolore,
ut lethargicus hic cum fit pugil et medicum urget." 30
dum ne quid simile huic, esto ut libet. " o bone, ne te
frustrere, insanis et tu stultique prope omnes,
si quid Stertinius veri[3] crepat, unde ego mira
descripsi docilis praecepta haec, tempore quo me
solatus iussit sapientem pascere barbam   35
atque a Fabricio non tristem ponte reverti.

[1] vafer, *I, Porph.*: faber, *II.*
[2] -ve] -que *a, II.*   [3] verum, *II.*

---

[a] Being a philosopher, Damasippus grows a long beard.
See l. 35 below.
[b] The temple of Janus stood on the north side of the
Forum, at the entrance to the street called Argiletum.
This street, centre of the banking business of Rome, is here
called " Janus " after the temple, and was probably lined
with a colonnade or arcade. Horace elsewhere uses the
expression *Ianus summus ab imo* (*Epist.* i. 1. 54).
[c] He was a connoisseur in antiques and *objets d'art.*

Damasippus, for your sound advice — a barber[a]! But how come you to know me so well ?

DAM. Ever since the wreck of all my fortunes at the Central Arcade,[b] I have looked after other people's business, after being flung overboard from my own. There was a time when my hobby[c] was to look out for the bronze in which shrewd old Sisyphus had washed his feet, and to see what work of art was crude in the carving, what was too rough in the casting. As an expert, I valued this or that statue at a hundred thousand. As to gardens and fine houses, I was the one man that knew how to buy them at a bargain ; hence the crowded streets gave me the nickname of " Mercury's pet."[d]

HOR. I know it, and am surprised to find you cured of that disorder.

DAM. Nay, what is surprising is that a new disorder drove out the old, as is the way when the pain of aching side or head passes into the stomach, or when the lethargic patient here turns boxer and pummels the doctor.

HOR. As long as you do nothing of that sort, be it as you please.

DAM. My good sir, don't deceive yourself; you, too, are mad, and so, I may say, are all fools, if there is any truth in the preaching of Stertinius, from whom I took down these wondrous lessons that I learned, the very day that he consoled me, and bade me grow a wise man's beard, and go home from the Fabrician bridge,[e] no longer sad. For after my

[d] Mercury was the god of gain ; cf. l. 68.
[e] This bridge, between the island in the Tiber, and the old Campus Martius, still stands. The inscription on it says that it was built by L. Fabricius, *curator viarum*.

nam male re gesta cum vellem mittere operto
me capite in flumen, dexter stetit et :

> 'Cave faxis

te quicquam indignum : pudor,' inquit, ' te malus
    angit,[1]

insanos qui inter vereare insanus haberi.   40

primum nam inquiram, quid sit furere : hoc si erit·
    in te

solo, nil verbi, pereas quin fortiter, addam.

   ' Quem mala stultitia et quemcumque inscitia veri

caecum agit, insanum Chrysippi porticus et grex   44

autumat.   haec populos, haec magnos formula reges,

excepto sapiente, tenet.

> 'Nunc accipe, quare

desipiant omnes aeque ac tu, qui tibi nomen

insano posuere.   velut silvis, ubi passim

palantis error certo de tramite pellit,

ille sinistrorsum, hic dextrorsum abit, unus utrique[3] 50

error, sed variis illudit partibus ; hoc te

crede modo insanum, nihilo ut sapientior ille,

qui te deridet, caudam trahat.[4]

> 'Est genus unum

stultitiae nihilum metuenda timentis, ut ignis,

ut rupes fluviosque in campo obstare queratur :   55

alterum et huic varum et nihilo sapientius ignis

per medios fluviosque ruentis.   clamet amica

mater,[5] honesta soror cum cognatis, pater, uxor :

" hic fossa est ingens, hic rupes maxima : serva ! "

---

  [1] angit 4 *Bland.* : urget, *II.*   [2] si erit] siet, *II.*
  [3] utrisque *EM, a not legible.*   [4] trahit.
  [5] amica mater *joined by Porph. Some editors separate*
them.

---

  [a] The discourse of Stertinius extends from here, l. 38, to
l. 295.

business failed, and I wanted to cover up my head and fling myself into the river, he stood at my right hand and said [a] :

" Beware of doing anything unworthy of yourself. 'Tis a false shame that tortures you, for among madmen you fear to be thought mad. For first of all I will ask, What is madness ? If this is found in you alone, I will not add another word to save you from dying bravely.

" Every man whom perverse folly, whom ignorance of the truth drives on in blindness, the Porch [b] of Chrysippus and his flock pronounce insane. This definition takes in whole nations, this takes in mighty kings, all save only the sage.

46 " Now learn why all, who have given you the name of madman, are quite as crazy as yourself. Just as in a forest, where some error drives men to wander to and fro from the proper path, and this one goes off to the left and that one to the right : both are under the same error, but are led astray in different ways : so believe yourself to be insane only so far that he who laughs at you drags a tail behind him, no whit the wiser man.[c]

53 " One class of fools fear where there is nothing at all to fear, crying out that fires, that rocks and rivers stop their course over an open plain. Another class, diverging from this, but no whit more wisely, would rush through the midst of fire and flood. Though a fond mother, a noble sister, father, wife and kindred, cry out : ' Here's a broad ditch, here's a huge rock,

[b] The term Stoic is derived from the σrοá (= porticus) in Athens, where Zeno and his successors taught.
[c] A reference to the trick played by children of tying a tail to people without their knowing it.

non magis audierit quam Fufius ebrius olim,   60
cum Ilionam edormit, Catienis mille ducentis
"mater, te appello!" clamantibus. huic ego volgus[1]
errori similem cunctum insanire docebo.

'Insanit veteres statuas Damasippus emendo:
integer est mentis Damasippi creditor? esto.   6
"accipe quod numquam reddas mihi," si tibi dicam,
tune insanus eris si acceperis? an magis excors
reiecta praeda, quam praesens Mercurius fert?
scribe decem a Nerio[2]: non est satis; adde Cicutae
nodosi tabulas centum, mille adde catenas: 70
effugiet tamen haec[3] sceleratus vincula Proteus.
cum rapies in ius[4] malis ridentem alienis,
fiet aper, modo avis, modo saxum et, cum volet, arbor.
si male rem gerere insani est, contra bene sani,
putidius multo cerebrum est, mihi crede, Perelli   75
dictantis, quod tu numquam rescribere possis.

'Audire atque togam iubeo componere, quisquis
ambitione mala aut argenti pallet amore,
quisquis luxuria tristive superstitione

---

[1] vulgum *a*: vultum φψ.   [2] Anerio *known to scholiasts.*
    [3] hic *E*.   [4] in iura *a, II.*

---

[a] Fufius played the part of the sleeping heroine in the *Ilione* of Pacuvius, but when the ghost of her murdered son (a part taken by Catienus) called upon her, he was so sound asleep that he did not hear, though the audience, taking up the actor's words, joined in the appeal.

[b] These words are addressed to the creditor, who is shown to be more foolish than the borrower, for whatever notes or bonds are involved in the transaction, they prove to be worthless in the end. With *decem* understand *tabulas*, Nerius being, like Cicuta and Perellius, a money-lender. They are all supposed to be uncommonly shrewd. Many

look out!' they would no more give ear than once did
drunken Fufius,[a] as he over-slept the part of Ilione,
while twelve hundred Catieni shouted, 'Mother, on
thee I call!' Like such folly is the madness of all
the world, as I shall prove.

[64] "Damasippus is mad in buying old statues; the
creditor of Damasippus, is he sound of mind? Be it
so! But if I say to you, 'Take this sum which you
need never return to me,' will you be a madman if
you take it? Or will you be more senseless if you
spurn the booty which propitious Mercury offers?
'Write out ten bonds drawn up by Nerius.'[b] That's
not enough; add a hundred of the cunning Cicuta—
add a thousand fetters! yet your scoundrelly Proteus
will slip out from all these ties. When you drag him
to court, he will laugh at your expense;[c] he will
turn into a boar, then into a bird, then into a stone,
or, if he likes, a tree. If it be the mark of a madman
to manage an estate badly, but of a sane man to
manage well, then much more addled, believe me, is
the brain of a Perellius, who dictates the bond, which
you can never pay.

[77] "Now give heed, I bid you, arrange your robes,[d]
and whoever of you is pale with sordid ambition or
avarice, whoever is feverish with extravagance or

prefer to supply *sestertia* with *decem*, taking Nerius to
be a banker who pays out money on an order from the
creditor.

[c] Horace's phrase *malis ridentem alienis*, "laugh with alien
jaws," is an echo of Homer's γναθμοῖσι γελοίων ἀλλοτρίοισιν
(*Od.* xx. 347), which, however, referred to forced, unnatural
laughter.

[d] Stertinius now assumes that he is addressing a class,
and therefore bids his hearers prepare for a formal discourse,
such as Stoic teachers frequently delivered.

aut alio mentis morbo calet : huc propius me,　　80
dum doceo insanire omnis vos ordine, adite.
　' Danda est ellebori multo pars maxima avaris ;
nescio an Anticyram ratio illis destinet omnem.
heredes Staberi summam incidere sepulcro,
ni sic fecissent, gladiatorum dare centum　　　　85
damnati populo paria atque epulum arbitrio Arri,
frumenti quantum metit Africa.　" sive ego prave
seu recte hoc volui, ne sis patruus mihi : " credo,
hoc Staberi prudentem animum vidisse.　" quid ergo
sensit, cum summam patrimoni insculpere saxo　90
heredes voluit ? "　quoad vixit, credidit ingens
pauperiem vitium et cavit nihil acrius, ut, si
forte minus locuples uno quadrante perisset,[1]
ipse videretur sibi nequior.　omnis enim res,
virtus, fama, decus, divina humanaque pulchris　95
divitiis parent ; quas qui construxerit,[2] ille
clarus erit, fortis, iustus.　" sapiensne[3] ? " etiam, et rex
et quidquid volet.[4]　hoc, veluti virtute paratum,
speravit magnae laudi fore.
　　　　　　　　　　　' Quid simile isti
Graecus Aristippus, qui servos proicere aurum　100
in media iussit Libya, quia tardius irent
propter onus segnes ?　uter est insanior horum ?

---

　　　[1] periret, I, adopted by Palmer.
　　　　[2] contraxerit, II, 3 Bland.
　　[3] -ne] -que DEM.　　　　　　[4] velut in, II.

---

　　a The ancient specific for insanity ; cf. Ars Poetica,
300.　For Anticyra see Index.
　　b This unusual number would be exhibited at the funeral
feast.　Q. Arrius entertained many thousands of people
at the extravagant funeral feast which he gave in honour
of his father.
　　c Cf. Sat. ii. 2. 97.　Staberius means that his heirs are
not to criticize him for what may seem to them an idiotic will.

gloomy superstition, or some other mental disorder. Hither, come nearer to me, while I prove that you are mad, all of you from first to last.

[82] " To the covetous must we give far the largest dose of hellebore : [a] wisdom, I rather think, would assign to them all Anticyra. The heirs of Staberius had to engrave upon his tomb the sum of his estate : should they fail to do so, they were bound to provide for the people a hundred pairs of gladiators,[b] with such a feast as Arrius would direct, and as much corn as Africa reaps. ' Whether I am right or wrong in willing this,' he wrote, ' don't play the uncle [c] with me.' That, I take it, is what Staberius in his wisdom foresaw. ' Well,' you ask, ' what was his intent when he willed that his heirs should carve on stone the sum of his estate ? ' All his life long he thought poverty a monstrous evil, and shunned nothing more earnestly, so that, if haply he had died less rich by a single penny, so far would he have thought himself the worse man. For all things—worth, repute, honour, things divine and human—are slaves to the beauty of wealth, and he who has made his ' pile ' will be famous, brave and just. ' And wise too ? ' Yes, wise, and a king and anything else he pleases.[d] His riches, as though won by worth, would bring him, he hoped, great renown.

[99] " What is the likeness between such a man and the Greek Aristippus, who in mid Libya bade his slaves throw away his gold, because, said he, freighted with the burden, they journeyed too slowly ? Which of the two is the madder ? Useless is an instance which

---

Hoc in l. 89 refers to this censorious attitude, not to the substance of ll. 94 f., as Keightley, Wickham and Lejay hold.
  [d] *Cf. Sat.* i. 3. 124 and note.

nil agit exemplum, litem quod lite resolvit.
si quis emat citharas, emptas comportet in unum,
nec studio citharae nec Musae deditus ulli,　　　　　105
scalpra et formas non sutor, nautica vela
aversus mercaturis, delirus et amens
undique dicatur merito.　qui[1] discrepat istis,[2]
qui nummos aurumque recondit, nescius uti
compositis metuensque velut contingere sacrum ?　110
　' Si quis ad ingentem frumenti semper acervum
porrectus[3] vigilet cum longo fuste, neque illinc
audeat esuriens dominus contingere granum,
ac potius foliis parcus vescatur[4] amaris ;
si positis intus Chii veterisque Falerni　　　　　115
mille cadis—nihil est, tercentum milibus—acre
potet acetum ;　age, si et stramentis incubet, unde-
octoginta annos natus, cui stragula vestis,
blattarum ac tinearum epulae, putrescat in arca ;
nimirum insanus paucis videatur, eo quod　　　　120
maxima pars hominum morbo iactatur eodem.
filius aut etiam haec libertus ut ebibat heres,
dis inimice senex, custodis ?　ne tibi desit ?
quantulum enim summae curtabit quisque dierum,
unguere si caulis oleo meliore caputque　　　　　125
coeperis impexa foedum porrigine ?　quare,
si quidvis satis est, periuras, surripis, aufers
undique ?　tun[5] sanus !
　　　　　　　　　' Populum si caedere saxis
incipias servosve tuos,[6] quos aere pararis,

----

　　　　[1] quid *DE*.　　　　[2] iste, *II*.　　　　[3] proiectus.
　　　　　　[4] vexatur *aE* : pascatur *M*.
　　　[5] tunc *D* : tu insanus *M, II*.　　　　[6] tuo *Goth*.

----

　　　　[a] For l. 122 *cf. Od.* ii. 14. 25 :
　　　　　　absumet heres Caecuba dignior
　　　　　　servata centum clavibus, etc.

solves puzzle by puzzle. If a man were to buy harps, and soon as bought were to pile them together, though feeling no interest in the harp or any Muse; if, though no cobbler, he did the same with shoe-knives and lasts; with ships' sails, though set against a trader's life—everyone would call him crazy and mad, and rightly too. How differs from these the man who hoards up silver and gold, though he knows not how to use his store, and fears to touch it as though hallowed?

¹¹¹ " If beside a huge corn-heap a man were to lie outstretched, keeping ceaseless watch with a big cudgel, yet never dare, hungry though he be and the owner of it all, to touch one grain thereof, but rather feed like a miser on bitter herbs; if, with a thousand jars—that's nothing, say three hundred thousand—of Chian and old Falernian stored in his cellars, he were to drink sharp vinegar; nay if, when but a year short of eighty, he should lie on bed of straw, though rich coverlets, prey of moths and worms, lay mouldering in his chest; few, doubtless, would think him mad, because the mass of men toss about in the same kind of fever. Is it that a son or even a freedman heir may drink it up that you, you god-forsaken dotard, are guarding it? ª Is it that you fear want? Why, how tiny a sum will each day dock off, if you begin with better oil to dress your salad, as well as your head, foul with uncombed scurf? Why, if anything is enough for you, do you perjure, steal, plunder on every side? You sane!

¹²⁸ " If you were to take to pelting stones at the crowd, or at your own slaves, for whom you've paid

insanum te omnes pueri clamentque puellae :   130
cum laqueo uxorem interemis matremque veneno,
incolumi capite es ?   quid enim ?   neque tu hoc facis
    Argis,
nec ferro ut demens genetricem occidis Orestes.
an tu reris eum occisa insanisse parente,
ac non ante malis dementem actum Furiis quam   135
in matris iugulo ferrum tepefecit acutum ?
quin ex quo est habitus male tutae mentis Orestes
nil sane fecit, quod tu reprehendere possis :
non Pyladen ferro violare aususve sororem
Electran, tantum maledicit utrique vocando   140
hanc Furiam, hunc aliud, iussit quod splendida bilis.
  ' Pauper Opimius[1] argenti positi intus et auri,
qui Veientanum festis potare diebus
Campana solitus trulla vappamque profestis,
quondam lethargo grandi est oppressus, ut heres   145
iam circum loculos et clavis laetus ovansque
curreret.   hunc medicus multum celer atque fidelis
excitat hoc pacto : mensam poni iubet atque
effundi saccos nummorum, accedere pluris
ad numerandum. hominem sic erigit, addit et
    illud :   150
" ni tua custodis, avidus iam haec auferet heres."
" men vivo ? "   " ut vivas igitur, vigila. hoc age."
    " quid[2] vis ? "
" deficient[3] inopem venae te, ni cibus atque
ingens accedit[4] stomacho fultura ruenti.

      [1] Opimius *Porph.* : opimus, *II.*
    [2] quod *D, II.*   [3] deficiant *E.*   [4] accedat *Dλ.*

---

  [a] The argument is ironical. Such an incident as this matricide might savour of high tragedy, but, of course, in the tragedy of Orestes both the place and the manner of killing were different. As a matter of fact, these differences are quite unessential.

164

in cash, all would hoot at you as mad, lads and lasses alike. When you strangle your wife and poison your mother, are you sound in head ? Why not ? You're not doing this at Argos, nor killing a mother with a sword, as mad Orestes did.[a] Or do you suppose he went mad after killing his parent, and was not spurned to frenzy by the wicked Furies before he warmed his sharp steel in his mother's throat ? Nay, from the moment that Orestes was held to be of unsafe mind, he did nothing whatever that you can condemn. He did not dare to attack with the sword Pylades or his sister Electra. He merely threw ill words at both, calling her a Fury, and him by some other name which his gleaming choler prompted.[b]

142 " Opimius, a poor man for all his gold and silver hoarded up within, would on holidays, from ladle of Campanian ware,[c] drink wine of Veii, and on working days soured wine. Now once he fell into a lethargy so deep that already his heir was running in joy and triumph round about his keys and coffers. But his physician, a man of very quick wit and a loyal friend, revives him by this device. He has a table brought in and bags of coin poured out, and bids many draw near to count it. Thus he brings the man to, and adds, ' Unless you guard your wealth, your greedy heir will be off with it forthwith.' ' What, while I'm alive ? ' ' Well, if you mean to live, wake up. Come now ! ' ' What would you have me do ? ' ' You are weak, and your veins will fail you, unless food and strong support be given your sinking stomach. Do

---

[b] The expression here used belongs to medical language. Black bile, which the ancients supposed to be a cause of madness (cf. μελαγχολία), has a glittering appearance.

[c] Cf. Campana supellex (Sat. i. 6. 118).

tu cessas ? agedum, sume hoc tisanarium oryzae." 155
" quanti emptae[1] ? " " parvo." " quanti ergo ? "
   " octussibus." " eheu !
quid refert, morbo an furtis pereamque rapinis ? "
   ' " Quisnam igitur sanus ? " qui non stultus.
   " quid avarus ? "
stultus et insanus. " quid, si quis non sit avarus,
continuo sanus ? " minime. " cur, Stoice ? " dicam. 160
non est cardiacus (Craterum dixisse putato)
hic aeger : recte est igitur surgetque ? negabit,
quod latus aut renes morbo temptentur[2] acuto.
non est periurus neque sordidus : immolet aequis
hic porcum Laribus : verum ambitiosus et audax : 165
naviget Anticyram. quid enim differt, barathrone
dones quidquid habes an numquam utare paratis ?
   ' Servius Oppidius Canusi duo praedia, dives
antiquo censu, gnatis divisse duobus
fertur et hoc[3] moriens pueris dixisse vocatis 170
ad lectum : " postquam te talos, Aule, nucesque
ferre sinu laxo, donare et ludere vidi,
te, Tiberi, numerare, cavis abscondere tristem,
extimui ne vos ageret vesania[4] discors,
tu Nomentanum, tu ne sequerere Cicutam. 175
quare per divos oratus uterque Penatis,
tu cave ne minuas, tu ne maius facias id
quod satis esse putat pater et natura coercet.
praeterea, ne vos titillet gloria, iure
iurando obstringam ambo : uter aedilis fueritve 180

---

[1] empti, *II*.   [2] temptantur *Priscian*.   [3] haec.
   [4] insania, *I, adopted by Orelli and Palmer*.

---

[a] *Cf.* ll. 82, 83, above.

you hold back ?   Come now, take this drop of rice-gruel.' 'What's the cost ? ' 'Oh, a trifle.' 'How much, I say ? ' 'Eight pence.' 'Alack ! what matters it, whether I die by sickness, or by theft and robbery ? '

158 "' Who, then, is sane ? ' He who is no fool. 'What of the covetous ? ' He is fool and madman. 'Well, if a man is not covetous, is he then and there sane ? ' By no means. 'Why, good Stoic ? ' I will tell you. 'This patient,' suppose Craterus to have said, ' is no dyspeptic.' He is well then and may get up ? 'No,' he will say, ' for his lungs or his kidneys are afflicted with acute disease.' Here's one who is no perjurer or miser. Let him slay a hog to the kind Lares. But he is ambitious and headstrong. Let him take ship for Anticyra.ᵃ For what is the difference, whether you throw all you have into a pit, or never make use of your savings ?

168 "There's a story that Servius Oppidius, a rich man, as incomes once were, divided his two farms at Canusium between his two sons, and on his death-bed called them to him and said : ' Ever since I saw you, Aulus, carrying your taws and nuts in a loose toga, giving and gambling them away—and you, Tiberius, anxiously counting them and hiding them in holes, I have greatly feared that madness of different kinds might plague you—that you, my son, might follow after Nomentanus, and you after Cicuta. I therefore adjure you both, by our house-hold gods, the one not to reduce, the other not to increase, what your father thinks enough, and what nature sets as a limit. Further, that ambition may not tickle your fancy, I shall bind you both by an oath : whichever of you becomes aedile or praetor,

vestrum praetor, is intestabilis et sacer esto.
in cicere atque faba bona tu perdasque lupinis,
latus ut in circo spatiere aut[1] aeneus ut stes,
nudus agris, nudus nummis, insane, paternis ?
scilicet ut plausus, quos fert Agrippa, feras tu,   185
astuta ingenuum volpes imitata leonem."—

   " ' Ne quis humasse velit Aiacem, Atrida, vetas
      cur ? "

   "Rex sum."

           "Nil ultra quaero[2] plebeius."

                      "Et aequam
rem imperito ; at[3] si cui videor non iustus, inulto
dicere quod[4] sentit permitto."

                  " Maxime regum,   190
di tibi dent capta classem[5] reducere[6] Troia.
ergo consulere et mox respondere licebit ? "

   " Consule."

           " Cur Aiax, heros ab Achille secundus,
putescit, totiens servatis clarus Achivis ?
gaudeat ut populus Priami Priamusque inhumato,   195
per quem tot iuvenes patrio caruere sepulcro ? "

   " Mille ovium insanus morti dedit, inclitum Ulixen
et Menelaum una mecum se occidere clamans."

   " Tu cum pro vitula statuis dulcem Aulide gnatam
ante aras spargisque mola caput, improbe, salsa,   200
rectum animi servas cursum[7] ? insanus quid enim Aiax

---

[1] et, *II.*   [2] quaere *V, Bentley.*   [3] at *V* : ac *MSS.*
[4] quae *D.*   [5] classem capta *E.*   [6] deducere.
[7] cursum *Bothe* : quorsum *MSS. and retained by Orelli,
Kiessling, Wickham, Morris, etc.* : quorum *Goth., Porph.*

---

   [a] These would be given to the people by way of largess
by aediles and praetors. Such an expense might be serious
enough for people of small fortunes.
   [b] The dialogue which begins here and continues to l. 207

let him be outlawed and accursed. Would you waste your wealth on vetches, beans, and lupines,[a] that you may play the swell and strut in the Circus, or be set up in bronze, though stripped of the lands, stripped, madman, of the money your father left : to the end, oh yes, that *you* may win the applause which Agrippa wins—a cunning fox mimicking the noble lion ? '

[187] " Son of Atreus,[b] you forbid us to think of burying Ajax. Why is this ?

" ' I am king.'

" I, a common man, ask no more.

" ' And my command is fair, but if anyone deems me unjust, I permit him to say freely what he thinks.'

" Mightiest of kings, may the gods grant you to take Troy and bring your fleet safe home ! May I then ask questions and answer in turn ?

" ' Pray, do.'

" Why does Ajax, a hero second only to Achilles, lie rotting, though so often he won glory by saving the Greeks ? Is it that Priam and Priam's people may exult in that man's lacking burial, through whom so many of their sons were bereft of burial in their native land ?

" ' The madman slew a thousand sheep, crying that he was slaying famed Ulysses, Menelaus, and myself.'

" And you, when at Aulis you brought your sweet child to the altar in a heifer's stead, and sprinkled her head with salt meal, O shameless one, did you keep your mind in its sound course ? Why, what did the madman Ajax do, when he slew the flock

is between the Stoic Stertinius and Agamemnon, and is suggested by the scene at the end of the *Ajax* of Sophocles, where Menelaus forbids Teucer to bury his brother Ajax.

fecit cum stravit ferro pecus ? abstinuit vim
uxore et gnato : mala multa precatus Atridis
non ille aut Teucrum aut ipsum violavit Ulixen."

" Verum ego, ut haerentis adverso litore navis 205
eriperem, prudens placavi sanguine divos."

" Nempe tuo, furiose."

" Meo, sed non furiosus."—

' Qui species alias veris scelerisque[1] tumultu
permixtas capiet, commotus habebitur, atque
stultitiae erret, nihilum distabit, an ira.   210
Aiax immeritos cum[2] occidit desipit agnos :
cum prudens scelus ob titulos admittis inanis,
stas animo et purum est vitio tibi, cum tumidum est,
    cor ?
si quis lectica nitidam gestare amet agnam,   214
huic vestem, ut gnatae, paret ancillas, paret aurum,
Rufam aut[3] Posillam[4] appellet fortique marito
destinet uxorem, interdicto huic omne adimat ius
praetor et ad sanos abeat tutela propinquos.
quid ? si quis gnatam pro muta devovet agna,
integer est animi ? ne dixeris. ergo ubi prava 220
stultitia, hic summa est insania ; qui sceleratus,
et furiosus erit ; quem cepit vitrea fama,
hunc circumtonuit gaudens Bellona cruentis.

' Nunc age, luxuriam et Nomentanum arripe mecum :

---

[1] MSS. have veri sceleris or veris celeris (V) : (veris sceleris
Goth.).   [2] cum immeritos D, II.
[3] et V.   [4] posillam V : pusillam MSS.

---

[a] *Adverso litore* : the shore refused to let the ships depart.
[b] The *species* (= φαντασίας) are ideas or mental concepts,
which may be true or false, and become confused when
some guilty impulse causes disturbance. At l. 208 Stertinius
still addresses Agamemnon, but gradually slides into a
continuation of his lecture.
[c] Like Agamemnon.   [d] Like Ajax.

with the sword? He withheld violence from wife and child. His curses on the Atridae were copious, but no harm did he do either to Teucer or even to Ulysses.

"'But I, in order to free the ships that clung to a hostile [a] shore, purposely appeased the gods with blood.'

"Yes, with your own, maniac.

"'My own blood; but no maniac I.'

208 "He who conceives ideas that are other than true, and confused by the turmoil due to sin,[b] will be held distraught and, whether he go astray from folly [c] or from rage,[d] it will not matter. Ajax, when he slays harmless lambs, is insane. When *you* purposely commit a crime for empty glory, are you sound of mind, and is your heart, when swollen with pride, free from fault? Suppose one chose to carry about in a litter a pretty lamb, and, treating it as a daughter, provided it with clothes, maids, gold, called it 'Goldie' or 'Teenie,' and planned to have it wed a gallant husband: the praetor by injunction would take from him all control, and the care of him would pass to his sane relations. Well, if a man offers up his daughter, as if she were a dumb lamb, is he sound of mind? Say not so. Thus, where there is perverse folly, there is the height of madness. The man who is criminal, will also be a maniac; he who is caught by the glitter of fame has about his head the thunder of Bellona, who delights in bloodshed.[e]

224 "Now, come, arraign with me extravagance and Nomentanus; for Reason will prove that spend-

[e] Bellona's votaries were fanatics, who gashed their bodies with knives.

vincet[1] enim stultos ratio insanire nepotes.   225
hic simul accepit patrimoni mille talenta,
edicit, piscator uti, pomarius, auceps,
unguentarius ac Tusci turba impia vici,
cum scurris fartor, cum Velabro omne macellum
mane domum veniant.   quid tum ?   venere fre-
        quentes.   230
verba facit leno : " quidquid mihi, quidquid et horum
cuique domi est, id crede tuum et vel nunc pete vel
        cras."
accipe quid contra haec iuvenis responderit aequus :
" tu[2] nive Lucana dormis ocreatus, ut aprum
cenem ego ; tu piscis hiberno ex aequore verris.[3] 235
segnis ego, indignus qui tantum possideam : aufer !
sume tibi deciens ; tibi tantundem ; tibi triplex,
unde uxor media currit de nocte vocata.[4] "

   ' Filius Aesopi detractam ex aure Metellae,
scilicet ut deciens solidum absorberet,[5] aceto   240
diluit insignem bacam : qui sanior ac si
illud idem in rapidum flumen iaceretve cloacam ?
Quinti progenies Arri, par nobile fratrum,
nequitia et nugis, pravorum et amore gemellum,
luscinias soliti impenso prandere coemptas,   245
quorsum abeant ? sani ut[6] creta, an carbone notati ?

   ' Aedificare casas, plostello adiungere mures,
ludere par impar, equitare in harundine longa,
si quem delectet[7] barbatum, amentia verset.
si[8] puerilius his ratio esse evincet amare,   250

---

[1] vincit, *II*.   [2] tu *Bentley for* in *of* MSS.
            [3] vellis, *I, Acron.*
      [4] citata *Porph., who knows also* vocata.
            [5] obsorberet *a:* exsorberet, *II.*
   [6] sani ut] sani *or* sanii, *II.*   [7] delectat, *II.*   [8] sic *E.*

---

         a Cf. *Sat.* ii. 2. 51.

thrifts are fools and madmen. This man, soon as
he received his patrimony of a thousand talents,
decreed, in praetor-fashion,[a] that fishmonger, fruit-
seller, fowler, perfumer, the Tuscan Street's vile
throng, cooks and parasites, the whole market and
Velabrum, should come to him next morning. What
next ? They came in crowds. A pimp was spokes-
man. 'Whatever I have, whatever any of these
have at home, believe me, is at your service. Send
for it to-day or to-morrow.' Hear the honest youth's
reply : 'Amid Lucanian snows you sleep well-
booted, that I may have a boar for dinner. You
sweep the stormy seas for fish. I am lazy and un-
worthy to possess so much. Away with it. You
take a million—you, the same—and you, from whose
house your wife comes running when called at
midnight, thrice that sum.'

239 " The son of Aesopus took from Metella's ear
a wondrous pearl, and meaning, forsooth, to swallow
a million at a gulp, steeped it in vinegar.[b] How
was he more sane than if he had flung that same
thing into a running river or a sewer ? The sons of
Quintus Arrius, a famous pair of brothers, twins in
wickedness, folly, and perverted fancies, used to
breakfast on nightingales, bought up at vast cost.
Into which list are they to go ? Marked with chalk
as sane, or with charcoal ? [c]

247 " Building toy-houses, harnessing mice to a wee
cart, playing odd and even, riding a long stick—if
these things delighted a bearded man, lunacy would
plague him. If reason prove that being in love is

[b] The same absurd story is told of Cleopatra. See Pliny,
N.H. ix. 58. 117.
[c] White was associated with good fortune, black with ill-
luck.

nec quicquam differre, utrumne in pulvere, trimus[1]
quale prius, ludas opus, an meretricis amore
sollicitus plores : quaero, faciasne quod olim
mutatus Polemon ?   ponas insignia morbi,
fasciolas, cubital,[2] focalia, potus ut ille   255
dicitur ex collo furtim carpsisse coronas,
postquam est impransi correptus voce magistri ?
porrigis irato puero cum poma, recusat :
" sume, catelle ! " negat ; si non des, optet. amator
exclusus qui distat, agit ubi secum, eat an non,   260
quo rediturus erat non arcessitus, et haeret
invisis foribus ?   " nec nunc, cum me[3] vocet[4] ultro,
accedam ?   an potius mediter finire dolores ?
exclusit ; revocat : redeam ?   non, si obsecret." ecce
servus non paulo sapientior : " o ere, quae res   265
nec modum habet neque consilium, ratione modoque
tractari non volt. in amore haec sunt mala, bellum,
pax rursum : haec si quis tempestatis prope ritu
mobilia et caeca fluitantia sorte laboret
reddere certa sibi, nihilo plus explicet ac si   270
insanire paret certa ratione modoque."
quid ?   cum Picenis excerpens semina pomis
gaudes, si cameram percusti forte, penes te es ?
quid ?   cum balba feris annoso verba palato,

---

[1] primus *V*.   [2] cubital *Porph*. *V* : cubitale *MSS*.
        [3] ne *Goth*.   [4] vocat.

---

[a] Only effeminate men would wear these things.

[b] This was Xenocrates, whose lecture on temperance converted the young profligate to a sober, philosophic life, so that he afterwards succeeded his master as head of the Academy.

[c] Horace here reproduces, almost literally, a scene from the *Eunuchus* (46-63) of Terence, where Phaedria debates with Parmeno, his slave, whether he is to go back to Thais.

more childish than such ways, that it makes no
difference whether you play at building in the sand,
as you did when three years old, or whine in anxiety
for love of a mistress, I ask you, will you do as once
Polemon did, when converted ? Will you lay aside
the tokens of your malady, garters, elbow-cushion,
neck-wrap,[a] even as he, 'tis said, stealthily plucked
the chaplets from his neck after a carouse, the moment
he was arrested by the voice of his fasting master ?[b]
When you offer apples to a sulky child, he refuses
them. ' Take them, pet.' He says, ' No.' Were
you not to offer them, he would crave them. How
differs the lover who, when shut out, debates with
himself whether to go or not to where, though not
invited, he meant to return, and hangs about the
hated doors ?[c] ' Shall I not go even now, when she
invites me of her own accord ? Or rather, shall I think
of putting an end to my affliction ? She shut me out.
She calls me back. Shall I return ? No—not if she
implores me.' Now listen to the slave, wiser by
far of the two : ' My master, a thing that admits of
neither method nor sense cannot be handled by rule
and method. In love inhere these evils—first war,
then peace : things almost as fickle as the weather,
shifting about by blind chance, and if one were to
try to reduce them to fixed rule for himself, he would
no more set them right than if he aimed at going
mad by fixed rule and method.' Why, when you
pick the pips from Picenian apples,[d] and are glad if
by chance you have hit the vaulted roof, are you
master of yourself ? Why, when on your old palate

[a] If a lover could hit the ceiling with an apple-seed, shot
from between his thumb and finger, he supposed his love
was returned.

aedificante casas qui sanior ? adde cruorem   275
stultitiae, atque ignem gladio scrutare.   modo, in-
    quam,
Hellade percussa Marius cum praecipitat se
cerritus fuit ; an commotae crimine mentis
absolves hominem et sceleris damnabis eundem,
ex more imponens cognata vocabula rebus ?   280
    ' Libertinus erat, qui circum compita siccus
lautis mane senex manibus currebat et, " unum,"
(" quid tam magnum ? " addens) " unum me surpite
    morti,
dis etenim facile est ! " orabat ; sanus utrisque
auribus atque oculis : mentem, nisi litigiosus,   285
exciperet dominus, cum venderet. hoc quoque volgus[1]
Chrysippus ponit fecunda in gente Meneni.
" Iuppiter, ingentis qui das adimisque dolores,"
mater ait pueri mensis iam quinque cubantis,
" frigida si puerum quartana reliquerit, illo   290
mane[2] die, quo tu indicis ieiunia, nudus
in Tiberi stabit."   casus medicusve[3] levarit
aegrum ex praecipiti, mater delira necabit
in gelida fixum ripa febremque reducet.
quone malo mentem concussa ? timore deorum.'   295
    Haec mihi Stertinius, sapientum octavus, amico

---

  [a] Horace gives his own turn to the Pythagorean rule πῦρ μαχαίρᾳ μὴ σκαλεύειν, which probably means, " excit not an angry man to violence."
  [b] See Index under Hellas.
  [c] According to the Stoics, crime and madness wer identical (see l. 221). The different names given to ther (e.g. insania and scelus) were thus synonyms.
  [d] He would follow the ritual of fasting and ceremonia washing, and pray at the shrines of the Lares of the crossway. the Lares Compitales.

you strike out baby-talk, how are you wiser than
the child that builds toy-houses ? Add blood to folly,
and stir the fire with a sword.[a] The other day, for
instance, when Marius killed Hellas and then flung
himself headlong, was he crazy ?[b] Or will you
acquit the man of a disordered mind and condemn
him for crime, giving to things, as we often do,
names of kindred meaning ?[c]

[281] " A freedman there was who in old age, fasting
and with washed hands, would in early hours run to all
street-shrines and pray :[d] ' Save me, me alone
" Is it not a little boon ? " he would add), save me
alone from death. 'Tis an easy matter for the gods.'
The man was sound in both ears and eyes ; but as to
his mind, his master, if selling him, would not have
vouched for that, unless bent on a lawsuit. All this
crowd[e] also Chrysippus will place in the prolific
family of Menenius. ' O Jupiter, who givest and
takest away sore afflictions,' cries the mother of a
child that for five long months has been ill abed, ' if
he quartan chills leave my child, then on the morning
of the day on which thou appointest a fast,[f] he shall
stand naked in the Tiber.' Should chance or the
doctor raise the sick lad up from his peril, his crazy
mother will kill him by planting him on the cold bank
and bringing back his fever. What is the malady
that has stricken her mind ? Fear of the gods.' "

[296] Such were the weapons which my friend Ster
nius, eighth of the wise men, put in my hands, that

---

[e] *i.e.* the superstitious who are also insane, like Menenius,
f whom, however, nothing is known.
    [f] This would be *dies Iovis*, corresponding to our Thursday
Thor's day). The Jews, whose practices are here referred
), fasted on this day.

arma dedit, posthac ne compellarer inultus.
dixerit insanum qui me, totidem audiet atque
respicere ignoto discet pendentia tergo."

Stoice, post damnum sic vendas omnia pluris,   300
qua me stultitia, quoniam non est genus unum,
insanire putas ?   ego nam videor mihi sanus.

  " Quid ? caput abscisum manibus cum portat[1]
    Agave
gnati infelicis, sibi tunc[2] furiosa videtur ? "

Stultum me fateor (liceat concedere veris)   305
atque etiam insanum : tantum hoc edissere, quo me
aegrotare putes animi vitio.
                  " Accipe. primum
aedificas, hoc est, longos imitaris, ab imo
ad summum totus moduli bipedalis, et idem
corpore maiorem rides Turbonis in armis   310
spiritum et incessum : qui ridiculus minus illo ?
an quodcumque facit Maecenas, te quoque verum est
tantum[3] dissimilem et tanto certare minorem ?

  Absentis ranae pullis vituli pede pressis,
unus ubi effugit, matri denarrat, ut ingens   315
belua cognatos eliserit : illa rogare,
quantane ? num tantum,[4] sufflans se, magna fuisset ?

---

[1] abscissum manibus cum portat *Goth.* : manibus portavit
V : demens cum portat *MSS.* *Bentley restored* manibus t*
text.
  [2] tum, *II.*   [3] tantum *V* : tanto *MSS.*
  [4] tantum *VE Porph.* : tandem *aD²M, omitted in* D¹.

---

  [a] A reference to the fable of the two wallets. We se*
only the one in front which holds our neighbours' faults
But *cf.* l. 53 above.
  [b] In the *Bacchae* of Euripides, Agave appears with th*
head of her son Pentheus, whom she and the other frenzie*
Maenads have torn to pieces.

no one thereafter might call me names with impunity. Whoso dubs me madman shall hear as much in reply, and shall learn to look behind on what is hanging from his back, that is never noticed.[a]

300 HORACE. Good Stoic—as I pray that after your losses you may sell all you have at a profit !—in what folly, since there are so many kinds, do you think my madness appears ? For to myself I seem sane.

DAMASIPPUS. What ? When Agave is carrying in her hands the head of her luckless son,[b] which she has cut off, does she even then think herself mad ?

HOR. I confess my folly—let me yield to the truth —and my madness too. This only unfold : from what mental failing do you think I suffer ?

DAM. Listen. First, you are building,[c] which means, you try to ape big men, though from top to toe your full height is but two feet ;[d] and yet you laugh at the strut and spirit of Turbo in his armour, as though they were too much for his body. How are you less foolish than he ? Is it right that whatever Maecenas does, you also should do, so unlike him as you are and such a poor match for him ?

314 A mother frog[e] was away from home when her young brood were crushed under the foot of a calf. One only escaped to tell the tale to his mother, how a huge beast had dashed his brothers to death. " How big was it ? " she asks ; " as big as this ? " puffing herself out. " Half as big again." " Was it big like this ? " as she swelled herself out more and more.

---

[c] Probably on his Sabine farm.
[d] For Horace's short stature see *Epist.* i. 20. 24, *corporis exigui.*
[e] Horace reproduces, with variations, the well-known Aesopian fable of the Ox and the Frogs.

' maior dimidio.' ' num tanto[1] ? ' cum magis atque
se magis inflaret, ' non, si te ruperis,' inquit,
' par eris.' haec a te non multum abludit imago.   320
adde poemata nunc, hoc est, oleum adde camino
quae si quis sanus fecit, sanus facis et[2] tu.
non dico[3] horrendam rabiem,"

Iam desine !

" Cultum

maiorem censu,"

Teneas, Damasippe, tuis te !

" Mille puellarum, puerorum mille furores."   325
O maior tandem parcas, insane, minori !

[1] tanto *MSS.* : tantum.

[2] facis et] facies *D,* 3 *Bland.*   [3] dicam *D.*

" Though you burst yourself," said he, " you'll never be as large." Not badly does this picture hit you off. Now throw in your verses—that is, throw oil on the fire. If any man ever wrote verses when sane, then you are sane in writing yours. I say nothing of your awful temper—

HOR. Stop now !

DAM. Your style beyond your means—

HOR. Mind your own business, Damasippus.

DAM. Your thousand passions for lads and lasses.

HOR. O greater one, spare, I pray, the lesser madman !

IV

THE ART OF GOOD LIVING

" Where is the man that can live without dining?"
In the Rome of the Augustan Age cookery seems
to have held the place it had occupied in Greece in
the degenerate days of the Middle and New Attic
Comedy, when, as Mahaffy says,[a] " it was no mere
trade, but a natural gift, a special art, a school of
higher philosophy." This false importance given to
the subject is gently satirized by Horace, who repre-
sents himself as meeting one Catius, just as the latter
is hurrying home to arrange his notes upon a wonder-
ful lecture on gastronomy, which he has just heard,
and of which Horace induces him to repeat the main
points. Horace professes profound admiration for so
much learning, and begs his friend to take him to
hear the lecturer himself, who must be what Epicurus
was to Lucretius, the fountain-head of wisdom in
regard to right living.

There has been much speculation, both as to who
Catius was or represents and as to the main purport
of this Satire. Among the *Saturae* of Ennius there
was one with the formidable title *Heduphagetica*,
which dealt with gastronomical matters and was based
on the ῾Ηδυπάθεια of Archestratus of Gela. It is clear

[a] *Social Life in Greece*, p. 299.

183

from his fragments that Lucilius handled the same topic, and we find among the titles of Varro's *Menippean Satires* that of Περὶ ἐδεσμάτων. It is probable therefore that Horace is simply trying his hand upon a traditional satiric theme.

But it is possible that the Satire has a greater significance than this. In the preceding Satire Horace deals in his own humorous fashion with the Stoics ; in this he seems to be playing with the Epicureans. In the concluding verses the reference to Lucretius is unmistakable, while scattered through the Satire are philosophical terms, such as *natura* (7, 21, 45, 64), *praecepta* (11), *ratio* (36), and *ingenium* (47), which are conspicuous in Lucretius's great poem. Palmer can see no reference to Epicureanism here, because Horace was himself an Epicurean, but Horace was never firmly wedded to any school. He was a free lance,

> nullius addictus iurare in verba magistri
> (*Epist.* i. 1. 14),

and even if he was an orthodox Epicurean, what was there to prevent his satirizing those of the school whose idea of the *vita beata* was to have good things to eat and drink ? Even Metrodorus, intimate friend of Epicurus, is reported to have said that " it is our business, not to seek crowns by saving the Greeks, but to enjoy ourselves in good eating and drinking " (Plutarch, *Adv. Col.* 1125 D).

As to Catius, the scholiasts tell us that he was an Epicurean and (like Lucretius) the author of a *De rerum natura*, but in commenting on l. 47 they also refer to another Catius who had written a book on the baker's art. There is a Catius, an Insubrian and an

Epicurean, spoken of by Cicero as lately dead (*Ad fam.* xv. 16 ; *cf.* Quintilian, **x.** 1. 124), and it is highly probable that for this dramatic purpose Horace here introduces a person of an earlier generation in much the same way in which he uses Trebatius in the first, and Damasippus in the third, Satires of this book.

IV.

Unde et quo Catius ?

           " Non est mihi tempus aventi
ponere signa novis praeceptis, qualia vincent[1]
Pythagoran Anytique reum doctumque Platona."

Peccatum fateor, cum te sic tempore laevo
interpellarim[2] ; sed des veniam bonus, oro.   5
quod si interciderit tibi nunc aliquid, repetes mox,
sive est naturae hoc sive artis, mirus utroque.

    " Quin id erat curae, quo pacto cuncta tenerem,
utpote res tenuis, tenui sermone peractas."

Ede hominis nomen, simul et, Romanus an hospes. 10

" Ipsa[3] memor praecepta canam, celabitur[4] auctor.

Longa quibus facies ovis erit, illa memento,
ut suci melioris et ut magis alba rotundis,
ponere ; namque marem cohibent callosa vitellum.
caule suburbano qui siccis crevit in agris   15
dulcior ; irriguo nihil est elutius horto.

Si vespertinus subito te oppresserit hospes,

---

    [1] vincent *V, II* : vincunt, *I* : vincant.
    [2] interpellarem.   [3] ipse *D.*   [4] celebrabitur, *II.*

---

    [a] Socrates.
    [b] The word *canam* suggests that the rules that follow are
to be treated like an oracle. They may be grouped roughly
under four heads : (*a*) the antepast, or *gustatio* (12-34) ;
(*b*) the main dinner, or *mensa prima* (35-69) ; (*c*) the dessert,
or *mensa secunda* (70-75) ; (*d*) details of service (76-87).

Satire IV

HORACE. Whence and whither, Catius?

CATIUS. I have no time to stop, so keen am I to make a record of some new rules, such as will surpass Pythagoras, and the sage *a* whom Anytus accused, and the learned Plato.

HOR. I confess my fault in thus breaking in on you at an awkward moment, but kindly pardon me, I pray. If aught has slipped from you now, you will soon recover it ; whether your memory is due to nature or to art, in either case you are a marvel.

CAT. Nay, I was just thinking how to keep all in mind, for it was a subtle theme handled in subtle style.

HOR. Tell me the man's name, whether he is a Roman or a stranger.

11 CAT. The rules themselves I will recite *b* from memory ; the professor's name must be withheld.

Give good heed to serve eggs of an oblong shape, for they have a better flavour and are whiter than the round ; they are firm and enclose a male yoke. Cabbage grown on dry lands is sweeter than from farms *c* near the city ; nothing is more tasteless than a watered garden's produce.

If a friend suddenly drops in upon you of an

---

c These would be irrigated artificially.

ne gallina malum responset[1] dura palato,
doctus eris vivam mixto[2] mersare Falerno ;
hoc teneram faciet.

Pratensibus optima fungis   20
natura est ; aliis male creditur.

Ille salubris   •
aestates peraget,[3] qui nigris prandia moris
finiet, ante gravem quae legerit arbore solem.

Aufidius forti miscebat mella Falerno,
mendose ; quoniam vacuis committere venis   25
nil nisi lene decet ; leni praecordia mulso
prolueris melius. si dura morabitur alvus,
mitulus et viles pellent obstantia conchae
et lapathi brevis herba, sed albo non sine Coo.

Lubrica nascentes implent conchylia lunae ;   30
sed non omne mare est generosae fertile testae :
murice Baiano melior Lucrina peloris,
ostrea Circeiis, Miseno oriuntur echini,
pectinibus patulis iactat se molle Tarentum.

Nec sibi cenarum quivis temere arroget artem,   35
non prius exacta tenui ratione saporum.
nec satis est cara piscis averrere[4] mensa
ignarum quibus est ius aptius et quibus assis
languidus in cubitum iam se conviva reponet.[5]

Umber et iligna nutritus glande rotundas   40
curvat aper lances carnem vitantis[6] inertem ;
nam Laurens malus est, ulvis et harundine pinguis.

[1] respondet *DEM* : responsat *a*.
[2] mixto *MSS.* : musto *Bentley, widely adopted.*
[3] peragit, *I*.   [4] avertere *DM*.
[5] reponit, *II*.   [6] vitiantis.

---

   a i.e., to continue eating. This is more probable than, as taken by Palmer, " which ones being broiled, the guest, after eating his fill of them, shall at length replace himself on his elbow."

188

evening, and you fear that a tough fowl may answer ill to his taste, you will be wise to plunge it alive into diluted Falernian : this will make it tender.

Mushrooms from the meadows are best ; others are not to be trusted.

A man will pass his summers in health, who will finish his luncheon with black mulberries which he has picked from the tree before the sun is trying.

Aufidius used to mix his honey with strong Falernian—unwisely ; for when the veins are empty one should admit nothing to them that is not mild. With mild mead you will do better to flood the stomach. If the bowels be costive, limpet and common shell-fish will dispel the trouble, or low-growing sorrel—but not without white Coan wine.

New moons swell the slippery shell-fish, but it is not every sea that yields the choicest kind. The Lucrine mussel is better than the Baian cockle. Oysters come from Circeii, sea-urchins from Misenum, luxurious Tarentum plumes herself on her broad scallops.

35 It is not everyone that may lightly claim skill in the dining art, without first mastering the subtle theory of flavours. Nor is it enough to sweep up fish from the expensive stall, not knowing which are better with sauce, and which, if broiled, will tempt the tired guest to raise himself once more upon his elbow.[a]

From Umbria, fed on holm-oak acorns, comes the boar that makes the round dish bend, when the host would shun tasteless meat ; for the Laurentian is a poor beast, being fattened on sedge and reeds.[b]

[b] Cf. Macaulay, " Battle of Lake Regillus " :

> From the Laurentian jungle,
> The wild hog's reedy home.

Vinea submittit capreas non semper edulis.
fecundae[1] leporis sapiens sectabitur armos.
piscibus atque avibus[2] quae natura et foret aetas,   45
ante meum nulli patuit quaesita palatum.

Sunt quorum ingenium nova tantum[3] crustula
   promit.
nequaquam satis in re una consumere curam ;
ut si quis solum hoc, mala ne sint vina, laboret,
quali perfundat[4] piscis securus olivo.   50

Massica si caelo suppones vina sereno,
nocturna, si quid crassi est, tenuabitur aura,
et decedet odor nervis inimicus ; at illa
integrum perdunt lino vitiata saporem.
Surrentina vafer qui miscet faece Falerna   55
vina,[5] columbino limum bene colligit ovo,
quatenus ima petit volvens aliena vitellus.

Tostis marcentem squillis recreabis et Afra
potorem coclea ; nam lactuca innatat acri
post vinum stomacho ; perna magis et[6] magis hillis 60
flagitat immorsus refici, quin omnia malit
quaecumque immundis fervent allata popinis.

Est operae pretium duplicis pernoscere iuris
naturam.   simplex e dulci constat olivo,
quod pingui miscere mero muriaque decebit   65
non alia quam qua[7] Byzantia putuit orca.

---

¹ fecundae *V* : fecundi MSS.
² atque pavis.   ³ tamen, *II.*
   ⁴ profundat.   ⁵ vinum.
      ⁶ ac *EM.*   ⁷ quae *aD, II.*

ᵃ The *ius duplex*, or compound sauce, consists of (1) the
simplex, viz. sweet olive oil, and (2) the other ingredients
named in ll. 65 ff.   The passage, however, is not clear.
Some prefer to take *ius duplex* as meaning two kinds of
sauce, one of which, the *simplex*, described in ll. 64-66,

Roes bred in a vineyard are not always eatable.
The connoisseur will crave the wings of a hare
when in young. As to fish and fowl, what their
qualities and age should be is a question never made
clear to any palate before mine.

Some there are whose talent lies only in finding
new sweets ; 'tis by no means enough to spend all
one's care on a single point—just as if someone were
anxious only that his wines be good, but cared not
what oil he poured upon his fish.

If you set Massic wine beneath a cloudless sky,
all its coarseness will be toned down by the night
air, and the scent, unfriendly to the nerves, will pass
off ; but the same wine, when strained through
linen, is spoiled, losing its full flavour. Surrentine
wine a knowing man mixes with lees of Falernian,
and carefully collects the sediment with pigeons'
eggs, for the yolk sinks to the bottom, carrying with
it all foreign matter.

A jaded drinker you will rouse afresh by fried
prawns and African snails ; for after wine lettuce
rises on the acid stomach. By ham and by sausages
rather does it crave to be pricked and freshened.
Nay, it would prefer any viands brought smoking
hot from untidy cookshops.

It is worth while to study well the nature of the
compound sauce.[a] The simple consists of sweet
olive oil, which should be mixed with thick wine and
with brine, such as that of which your Byzantine jar

consists of oil, wine, and brine, while the compound adds
to these the chopped herbs, saffron, and Venafran oil of
ll. 67-69.

hoc ubi confusum sectis inferbuit herbis
Corycioque croco sparsum stetit, insuper addes[1]
pressa Venafranae quod baca remisit olivae.

Picenis cedunt pomis Tiburtia suco ;　　　　　　　　70
nam facie praestant.　Venucula convenit ollis ;
rectius Albanam fumo duraveris uvam.
hanc ego cum malis, ego faecem primus et allec,
primus et invenior[2] piper album cum sale nigro
incretum puris circumposuisse catillis.　　　　　　75
immane est vitium dare milia terna macello
angustoque vagos piscis urgere catino.
magna movet[3] stomacho fastidia, seu puer unctis
tractavit calicem manibus, dum furta ligurrit,
sive gravis veteri craterae[4] limus adhaesit.　　　80
vilibus in scopis, in mappis, in scobe quantus
consistit sumptus ?　neglectis, flagitium ingens.
ten lapides varios lutulenta[5] radere palma
et Tyrias dare circum illuta toralia vestis,
oblitum, quanto curam sumptumque minorem　　85
haec habeant, tanto reprehendi iustius illis,
quae nisi divitibus nequeunt[6] contingere mensis ! ''

Docte Cati, per amicitiam divosque rogatus,
ducere me auditum, perges quocumque, memento.
nam quamvis memori referas mihi pectore cuncta,　90
non tamen interpres tantundem iuveris.　adde
voltum habitumque hominis, quem tu vidisse beatus

[1] addens, *II*.	[2] inveni *aM* : inventor *E*.
[3] movent, *I*.	[4] creterrae *Vφψ*.
[5] luculenta, *φψl*.	[6] nequeant *Bentley*.

---

[a] Byzantium was an important centre for the fishing
industry of the Black Sea, and the brine in which the fish
were sent was held in high esteem.

smells so strong.[a] When this, mixed with chopped herbs, has been boiled, and, after being sprinkled with Corycian saffron, has been left to stand, you are to add besides some of the juice yielded by the pressed berry of the Venafran olive.

Apples from Tibur yield to the Picenian in flavour, but in look are finer. The Venuculan grape suits the preserving jar; the Alban you had better dry in the smoke. This last you will find that I was the first to serve round the board with apples, as I was the first to serve up wine-lees and caviare, white pepper and black salt sifted on to dainty little dishes. It is a monstrous sin to spend three thousand on the fish market, and then to cramp those roving fishes in a narrow dish. It strongly turns the stomach, if a slave has handled the drinking cup with hands greasy from licking stolen snacks; or if vile mould clings to your ancient bowl.[b] Common brooms, napkins, and sawdust, how little do they cost! But if neglected, how shocking is the scandal! To think of your sweeping mosaic pavements with a dirty palm-broom, or putting unwashed coverlets over Tyrian tapestries, forgetting that the less care and cost these things involve, the more just is blame for their neglect than for things which only the tables of the rich can afford!

HOR. O learned Catius, by our friendship and by the gods I beg you, remember to take me to a lecture, wherever you go to one. For however faithful the memory with which you tell me all, yet as merely reporting you cannot give me the same pleasure. And there is the man's look and bearing!

[b] If the bowl was an antique and therefore valuable, there was all the more reason for its being kept clean.

non magni pendis, quia contigit : at mihi cura
non mediocris inest, fontis ut adire remotos
atque haurire queam vitae praecepta beatae.   95

---

^a Horace here parodies a famous passage in Lucretius :

   iuvat integros accedere fontes atque haurire.

                                   (*De rerum nat.* i. 927-8.)

You think little of having seen him, lucky fellow, because you have had that good fortune, but I have no slight longing to be able to draw near to the sequestered fountains, and to drink in the rules for living happily.[a]

THE ART OF LEGACY-HUNTING

THE practice of seeking legacies, especially from those who had no family connexions, seems to have been common in Rome at the beginning of the Imperial period. Horace, therefore, in true satiric fashion, undertakes to lay down rules for the guidance of those who may need advice in playing the game.

The Satire takes the form of a dialogue, and is a burlesque continuation of a famous scene in the Eleventh Odyssey (90–149), where Odysseus (Ulysses), in the lower world, learns from the Theban seer Tiresias that he will return to his home in Ithaca, but only when reduced to poverty. The hero, therefore, desires to ascertain how he may again enrich himself, and the seer instructs him in the lucrative ways of fortune-hunting.

From the obvious reference to Actium in *tellure marique magnus* (l. 63) we infer that the Satire was not composed before 30 B.C. The skilful parody of epic style shows Horace's satiric power at its best, and it is well to recall the fact that the travestying of heroic themes is traditional in both satire and comedy. The *Amphitryo* of Plautus, based on some play of the New Attic Comedy, is a good example. Both Lucilius and Varro made use of parody, and it is a prominent feature of the prose satire of Lucian, upon which many modern satires have been modelled, such as Disraeli's *Ixion in Heaven* and *The Infernal Marriage*, and Bangs's *Houseboat on the Styx*. Lucian's resemblances to Horace, which, according to Lejay, are due to a direct knowledge of the Roman poet on the part of Lucian, may really be the result of their common indebtedness to Menippus of Gadara (*cf.* Fiske, *Lucilius and Horace*, p. 401). Sellar describes the poem before us as " the most trenchant of all the Satires " of Horace, who doubtless conceived the utmost contempt for the fortune-hunters of his day. No analysis is necessary.

V.

Hoc quoque, Teresia,[1] praeter narrata petenti
responde, quibus amissas reparare queam res
artibus atque modis.   quid rides ?
        " Iamne doloso
non satis est Ithacam revehi patriosque Penates
adspicere ? "
     O nulli quicquam mentite, vides ut   5
nudus inopsque domum redeam[2] te vate, neque illic
aut apotheca procis intacta est aut pecus ; atqui[3]
et genus et virtus, nisi cum re, vilior alga est.
 " Quando pauperiem missis ambagibus horres,
accipe qua ratione queas ditescere.
        " Turdus   10
sive aliud privum dabitur tibi, devolet illuc,
res ubi magna nitet domino sene ; dulcia poma
et quoscumque feret cultus tibi fundus honores,
ante Larem gustet venerabilior Lare dives ;
qui quamvis periurus erit, sine gente, cruentus   15
sanguine fraterno, fugitivus, ne tamen illi
tu comes exterior, si postulet, ire recuses."
 Utne[4] tegam spurco Damae latus ?   haud ita Troiae

---

[1] Tiresia *M.*   [2] redeat.   [3] aut qui, *II.*   [4] visne.

---

 [a] By *doloso* Horace translates πολύτροπος, or one of the
several Homeric epithets such as πολύμητις, πολυμήχανος,
ποικιλόμητις, applied to Odysseus.

198

Satire V

ULYSSES. One more question pray answer me, Tiresias, besides what you have told me. By what ways and means can I recover my lost fortune? Why laugh?

TIRESIAS. What! not enough for the man of wiles *a* to sail back to Ithaca and gaze upon his household gods?

ULY. O you who have never spoken falsely to any man, you see how I am returning home, naked and in need, as you foretold; and there neither cellar nor herd is unrifled by the suitors. And yet birth and worth, without substance, are more paltry than seaweed.

TIR. Since, in plain terms, 'tis poverty you dread, hear by what means you can grow rich.

Suppose a thrush or other dainty be given you for your own, let it wing its way to where grandeur reigns and the owner is old. Your choice apples or whatever glories your trim farm bears you, let the rich man taste before your Lar; more to be reverenced than the Lar is he.*b* However perjured he may be, though low of birth, stained with a brother's blood, a runaway slave, yet, if he ask you to walk with him, do not decline to take the outer side.

ULY. What! give the wall to some dirty Dama?

---

b First-fruits were offered to the Lares.

199

me gessi, certans semper melioribus.

" Ergo
pauper eris."

Fortem hoc animum tolerare iubebo ; 20
et quondam maiora tuli.   tu protinus, unde
divitias aerisque ruam[1] dic, augur, acervos.

" Dixi equidem et dico : captes astutus ubique
testamenta senum, neu,[2] si vafer unus et alter
insidiatorem praeroso fugerit hamo, 25
aut spem deponas aut artem illusus omittas.
magna minorve foro si res certabitur olim,
vivet uter locuples sine gnatis, improbus, ultro
qui meliorem audax vocet in ius, illius esto
defensor ; fama civem causaque priorem 30
sperne, domi si gnatus erit fecundave coniunx.
'Quinte,' puta, aut 'Publi' (gaudent praenomine
        molles
auriculae), " tibi me virtus tua fecit amicum ;
ius anceps novi, causas defendere possum ;
eripiet quivis oculos citius mihi quam te 35
contemptum cassa[3] nuce pauperet ; haec mea cura est,
ne quid tu perdas neu sis iocus." ire domum atque
pelliculam curare iube ; fi cognitor ipse ;
persta atque obdura, seu rubra Canicula findet
infantis statuas, seu pingui tentus omaso 40
Furius hibernas cana nive conspuet Alpis.
" nonne vides," aliquis cubito stantem prope tangens

---

[1] eruam E.   [2] seu.   [3] cassa Acr.: quassa MSS.

---

  [a] Cf. κρείσσοσιν ἶφι μάχεσθαι (Iliad, xxi. 486), one of the
Homeric echoes in the Satire. Dama is a common slave name.
  [b] So Odysseus speaks in Od. xx. 18 :
        τέτλαθι δὴ κραδίη· καὶ κύντερον ἄλλο ποτ' ἔτλης.

  [c] Horace makes satiric use of some verses from Furius
Bibaculus (cf. Sat. i. 10. 36, with note). In Bibaculus, as

Not so at Troy did I bear myself, but ever was matched with my betters.[a]

TIR. Then you will be a poor man.

ULY. I'll bid my valiant soul endure this. Ere now worse things have I borne.[b] Go on, O prophet, and tell me how I am to rake up wealth and heaps of money.

TIR. Well, I have told you, and I tell you now. Fish craftily in all waters for old men's wills, and though one or two shrewd ones escape your wiles after nibbling off the bait, do not give up hope, or drop the art, though baffled. If some day a case, great or small, be contested in the Forum, whichever of the parties is rich and childless, villain though he be, who with wanton impudence calls the better man into court, do you become his advocate ; spurn the citizen of the better name and cause, if he have a son at home or a fruitful wife. Say : " Quintus " it may be, or " Publius " (sensitive ears delight in the personal name), " your worth has made me your friend. I know the mazes of the law ; I can defend a case. I will let anyone pluck out my eyes sooner than have him scorn you or rob you of a nutshell. This is my concern, that you lose nothing, and become not a jest." Bid him go home and nurse his precious self ; become yourself his counsel. Carry on, and stick at it, whether

> " the Dog-star red
> Dumb statues split," [c]

or Furius, stuffed with rich tripe,

> " With hoary snow bespew the wintry Alps."

" Do you not see," says someone, nudging a neighbour

we know from Quintilian, viii. 6. 17, the second citation opened with *Iuppiter* as subject.

inquiet, ' ut patiens, ut amicis aptus, ut acer?'
plures adnabunt thynni et cetaria crescent.

" Si cui praeterea validus male filius in re   45
praeclara sublatus aletur, ne manifestum
caelibis obsequium nudet te, leniter in spem
adrepe[1] officiosus, ut et[2] scribare secundus
heres et, si quis casus puerum egerit Orco,
in vacuum venias : perraro haec alea fallit.   50

" Qui testamentum tradet tibi cumque legendum,
abnuere et tabulas a te removere memento,
sic tamen, ut limis rapias, quid prima secundo
cera velit versu ; solus multisne coheres,
veloci percurre oculo. plerumque recoctus   55
scriba ex quinqueviro corvum deludet hiantem,
captatorque dabit risus Nasica Corano."

Num furis? an prudens ludis me obscura canendo?

" O Laërtiade, quidquid dicam, aut erit aut non :
divinare etenim magnus mihi donat Apollo."   60

Quid tamen ista velit sibi fabula, si licet,[3] ede.

" Tempore, quo iuvenis Parthis horrendus, ab alto
demissum genus Aenea, tellure marique

---

[1] arripe *a, II.*   [2] ut et] ut *Goth.* : uti *Heindorf.*
[3] si licet] scilicet *aD.*

---

a Cf. *Epist.* i. 1. 79, " excipiantque senes quos in vivaria
mittant." The *cetaria* were artificial preserves. The tunnies
represent the rich fools who may be caught when needed,
cf. captes l. 23, and *captator* in l. 57.

b It was an old Roman custom for fathers to take up in
their arms such new-born children as they wished to rear.
Sublatus, therefore, might be rendered as " recognized."

c *i.e.* as substitute heir, to be called to the inheritance
in case the heir first named dies.

d The will, it is supposed, would be written on wax tablets
and sealed. On the inside of the first tablet would appear
the name of the testator, followed in the second line by the
name of the heir.

with his elbow, " how steady he is, how helpful to his friends, how keen ? " More tunnies will swim up, and your fish-ponds swell.[a]

[45] Again, if one with a fine fortune rears a sickly son whom he has taken up,[b] then for fear lest open devotion to a childless man betray you, by your attentions worm your way to the hope that you may be named as second heir,[c] and if some chance send the child to his grave, you may pass into his place. Seldom does this game fail.

[57] Suppose someone gives you his will to read, be sure to decline and push the tablets from you ; yet in such a way that with a side glance you may catch the substance of the second line on the first page.[d] Swiftly run your eye across to see whether you are sole heir or share with others. Quite often a constable, new-boiled into a clerk, will dupe the gaping raven, and Nasica the fortune-hunter will make sport for Coranus.[e]

ULY. Are you mad ? or do you purposely make fun of me with your dim oracle ?

TIR. O son of Laertes, whatever I say will or will not be [f] ; for prophecy is great Apollo's gift to me.

ULY. But what means that story ? Tell me, if you may.

TIR. In the days when a youthful hero,[g] the Parthian's dread, scion of high Aeneas's lineage, shall

[a] In *recoctus* there is a reference to the legend of Medea, who restored his youth to Aeson by boiling him in a caldron. The *quinqueviri* were very humble police officials. Coranus had been one of these, but later had become a public clerk, like Horace himself (*Sat.* ii. 6. 36). In *corvum hiantem*, there is a reference to the fable of the raven which the fox flattered for its singing, and so caused it to drop the cheese.

[f] A burlesque on oracular utterances.

[g] *i.e.* the young Octavius, born 63 B.C.

magnus erit, forti nubet procera Corano
filia Nasicae, metuentis reddere soldum.   65
tum gener hoc faciet : tabulas socero dabit atque
ut legat orabit ; multum Nasica negatas
accipiet tandem et tacitus leget, invenietque
nil sibi legatum praeter plorare suisque.

   " Illud ad haec iubeo : mulier si forte dolosa   70
libertusve senem delirum temperet, illis
accedas socius ; laudes, lauderis ut absens ;
adiuvat hoc quoque, sed vincit[1] longe prius ipsum
expugnare caput.   scribet[2] mala carmina vecors :
laudato.   scortator erit : cave te roget ; ultro   75
Penelopam facilis potiori trade."
                              Putasne,
perduci poterit tam frugi tamque pudica,
quam nequiere[3] proci recto depellere cursu ?

   " Venit enim magnum donandi parca iuventus,
nec tantum Veneris quantum studiosa culinae.   80
sic tibi Penelope frugi est ; quae si semel uno
de sene gustarit tecum partita lucellum,
ut canis a corio numquam absterrebitur uncto.

   " Me sene quod dicam factum est.   anus improba
      Thebis
ex testamento sic est elata : cadaver   85
unctum oleo largo nudis umeris tulit heres,

------

   [1] vincet *a Goth*.   [2] scribit.
                [3] nequivere MSS.

------

   [a] The story, which was doubtless familiar to the readers
of Horace's own day, is now obscure.   Nasica probably
owed money to Coranus, and gave him his daughter in
marriage, hoping that the son-in-law would by will free him
from his debt.   This would seem to imply that the son-in-law
was older than the father-in-law.

be mighty by land and sea, the tall daughter of Nasica, who dreads paying up in full, shall wed gallant Coranus. Then shall the son-in-law thus proceed: to his father-in-law he shall give the tablets of his will, and pray him to read them. After many a refusal at length Nasica shall take them, and read them to himself, and shall find that nothing is left to him and his but—to whine.[a]

⁷⁰ Here's another hint I give you. If it so chance that some crafty dame or freedman sways an old dotard, make common cause with them. Praise them, that they may praise you behind your back. This too helps; but far better is it to storm the citadel itself. Will the idiot write poor verses? Praise them. Is he a libertine? See that he has not to ask you; yourself obligingly hand over Penelope to your better.

ULY. You think so! Can she be tempted,—she so good, so pure, whom the suitors could not turn from the straight course?

TIR. Yes, for the young suitors who came were sparing of their gifts; their thoughts were not so much on loving as on eating. So it is your Penelope is virtuous; but if just once she gets from one old man a taste of gain in partnership with you, then she will be like the hound, which can never be frightened away from the greasy hide.[b]

⁸⁴ I will tell you something that happened when I was old.[c] A wicked old crone at Thebes, by the terms of her will, was buried thus: her corpse, well oiled, her heir carried on his bare shoulders. She

---

[b] *i.e.* a hide to which pieces of fat still cling.
The speaker, now long dead, is a shade in the lower world.

scilicet elabi si[1] posset mortua ; credo,
quod nimium institerat[2] viventi.

                 " Cautus adito :
neu desis operae neve immoderatus abundes.
difficilem et morosum offendet[3] garrulus ; ultra[4]   90
non etiam sileas. Davus sis comicus atque
stes capite obstipo, multum similis metuenti.
obsequio grassare ; mone, si increbruit aura,
cautus uti velet carum caput ; extrahe turba
oppositis umeris ; aurem substringe loquaci.   95
importunus amat laudari : donec ' ohe iam ! '
ad caelum manibus sublatis dixerit, urge,
crescentem tumidis infla sermonibus utrem.

     " Cum te servitio longo curaque levarit,
et certum vigilans, ' quartae sit partis Ulixes,'   100
audieris, ' heres ' : ergo nunc Dama sodalis
nusquam est ? unde mihi tam fortem tamque
     fidelem ? '
sparge subinde et, si paulum potes, illacrimare ; est[5]
gaudia prodentem[6] voltum[7] celare. sepulcrum
permissum arbitrio sine sordibus exstrue : funus   105
egregie factum laudet vicinia. si quis
forte coheredum senior male tussiet, huic tu
dic, ex parte tua seu fundi sive domus sit
emptor, gaudentem nummo te addicere.

                     " Sed me
imperiosa trahit Proserpina : vive valeque."   110

---

[1] si] ut sic *V*.   [2] extiterat.   [3] offendit $\phi\psi l$.
    [4] ultro.   [5] est *deleted in a.*
      [6] prudentem.   [7] multum $\phi\psi l$.

---

[a] *Cf.* " Davoque Chremeta eludente," *Sat.* i. 10. 40.

206

wanted, of course, to see whether she could give him the slip when dead. I suppose, when she was living, he had borne too hard upon her.

88 Be cautious in your approach; neither fail in zeal, nor show zeal beyond measure. A chatterbox will offend the peevish and morose; yet you must not also be silent beyond bounds. Act the Davus of the comedy,[a] and stand with head bowed, much like one overawed. With flattery make your advances; warn him, if the breeze stiffens, carefully to cover up his precious pate; shoulder a way and draw him out of a crowd; make a trumpet of your ear when he is chattering. Does he bore you with his love of praise? Then ply him with it till with hands uplifted to heaven he cry "enough!" and blow up the swelling bladder with turgid phrases.

99 And when from your long care and servitude he sets you free, and wide awake you hear the words, "To one-fourth let Ulysses be heir," then, now and again, scatter about such words as these, "Ah! is my old friend Dama now no more? Where shall I find one so firm, so faithful?" and if you can do a bit of it, drop in some tears. If your face betray joy, you can hide it. If the tomb is left to your discretion, build it in style: let the neighbours praise the handsome funeral. If one of your co-heirs happens to be older than you, and has a bad cough, say to him that if he would like to buy land or a house that is in your share, you would gladly knock it down to him for a trifle.

But Proserpine, our queen, calls me back. Live and fare well!

VI

TOWN AND COUNTRY LIFE

This famous Satire, which has been so happily imitated by Pope, contrasts the annoyances and discomforts of life in Rome with the peace and happiness enjoyed by the poet on his beloved Sabine farm.

It is probably owing to its peculiarly personal tone that for this Satire Horace does not set up a dialogue framework, but reverts to the monologue form of the First Book, although a large portion of the poem, viz. the fable of the Town and the Country Mouse, is put into the mouth of another speaker.

Kiessling has pointed out how the hours of morning (1-23) and of evening (60-76), as spent in the country, suggest the two side-pictures of a triptych, which enclose the central and larger picture, that of a day passed in Rome (23-59). The contrast thus presented between the peacefulness of rural life and the restlessness of city life is then summed up in the delightful allegory with which the Satire concludes (79-117). Nothing could be more artistic than such an arrangement.

Besides being one of the most charming of Horace's compositions, this Satire is important for settling some of the chronology of Horace's life. Thus l. 38

seems to refer to the time which included the Battle of Actium and succeeding events, when Maecenas, in the absence of Octavian, had full control in Rome and Italy. The mention of the Dacians in l. 53 reminds us that these people wavered between Octavian and Antony and that Crassus was sent against them in 30 B.C. Again, the assignment of lands to the veterans, referred to in l. 55, is doubtless the reward promised for services at Actium. In this connexion some of the soldiers mutinied in the winter of 31 B.C. The Satire therefore was composed late in 31 B.C. or early in 30 B.C., and it follows from l. 40 ff. that Horace entered the circle of Maecenas in 39 or 38 B.C. The Sabine farm was given to the poet some six years later.

VI.

Hoc erat in votis : modus agri non ita magnus,
hortus ubi et tecto vicinus iugis aquae fons
et paulum silvae super his foret.   auctius atque
di melius fecere.   bene est.   nil amplius oro,
Maia nate, nisi ut propria haec mihi munera faxis.
si neque maiorem feci ratione mala rem
nec sum facturus vitio culpave[1] minorem,
si veneror stultus nihil horum : " o si angulus ille
proximus accedat, qui nunc denormat agellum !
o[2] si urnam argenti fors quae mihi monstret, ut illi,   10
thesauro invento qui mercennarius agrum
illum ipsum mercatus aravit, dives amico
Hercule ! " si quod adest gratum iuvat, hac prece t᷄
      oro :
pingue pecus domino facias et cetera praeter
ingenium, utque soles, custos mihi maximus adsis ! 15
   Ergo ubi me in montes et in arcem ex urbe removi
quid prius illustrem saturis Musaque pedestri ?
nec mala me ambitio perdit nec plumbeus Auster
autumnusque gravis, Libitinae quaestus acerbae.

---

   a In the opening words Horace gives utterance to a feeling
of deep satisfaction as he contemplates the scene before him
in the morning sunshine.   His former prayer has been
realized.   Hence the past tense of *erat*.
   b Mercury was god of luck and gain ; Hercules the god
of treasure-trove (see ll. 12, 13 below).

Satire VI

This is what I prayed for! [a]—a piece of land not so very large, where there would be a garden, and near the house a spring of ever-flowing water, and up above these a bit of woodland. More and better than this have the gods done for me. I am content. Nothing more do I ask, O son of Maia,[b] save that thou make these blessings last my life long. If I have neither made my substance larger by evil ways, nor mean to make it smaller by excesses or neglect; if I offer up no such foolish prayers as these: " O if there could be added that near corner, which now spoils the shape of my little farm! O that some lucky strike would disclose to me a pot of money, like the man who, having found a treasure-trove, bought and ploughed the self-same ground he used to work on hire, enriched by favour of Hercules "!—if what I have gives me comfort and content, then thus I pray to thee: make fat the flocks I own, and all else save my wit, and, as thou art wont, still be my chief guardian!

[16] So, now that from the city I have taken myself off to my castle in the hills, to what should I sooner give renown in the Satires of my prosaic Muse? Here no wretched place-hunting worries me to death, nor the leaden scirocco, nor sickly autumn, that brings gain to hateful Libitina.[c]

[c] The old Italian goddess Libitina, sometimes identified with Persephone, presided over funerals.

Matutine pater, seu " Iane " libentius audis,   20
unde homines operum primos vitaeque labores
instituunt (sic dis placitum), tu carminis esto
principium. Romae sponsorem mc rapis : " heia,
ne prior officio quisquam respondeat, urge."
sive Aquilo radit terras seu bruma nivalem   25
interiore diem gyro trahit, ire necesse est.
postmodo, quod mi obsit, clare certumque locuto
luctandum in turba et facienda iniuria tardis.
" quid tibi vis, insane, et quam rem¹ agis ? " improbus
   urget
iratis precibus : " tu pulses omne quod obstat,   30
ad Maecenatem memori si mente recurras."

Hoc iuvat et melli² est, non mentiar. at simul atras
ventum est Esquilias, aliena negotia centum
per caput et circa saliunt latus. " ante secundam
Roscius orabat sibi adesses ad Puteal cras."   35
" de re communi scribae magna atque nova te
orabant hodie meminisses, Quinte, reverti."
" imprimat his, cura, Maecenas signa tabellis."
dixeris, " experiar " : " si vis, potes," addit et instat
Septimus octavo propior³ iam fugerit annus,   40

¹ quam rem *Bentley*: MSS. *show* quas res, *which can be
kept if* tibi *or* agis *is deleted. Thus Orelli, Wickham, Lejay.*
² mel, *II.*   ³ propior *E* : proprior *a.*

ᵃ *Cf.* Milton's " Or hear'st thou rather pure ethereal
stream " (*Par. Lost*, iii. 6). The language is mock heroic,
and the apostrophe of the god of the morn, or of beginnings,
indicates the time of day when Horace was writing.

ᵇ Horace gives an illustration of early morning duties in
Rome.

ᶜ The circles apparently traced by the sun get smaller
up to the winter solstice.

ᵈ Probably the *sponsor* was directed by the court to speak
thus.

ᵉ *i.e.* this recognition of his intimacy with Maecenas.

[20] O Father of the dawn, or Janus, if so thou hearest rather,[a] from whom men take the beginnings of the work and toil of life—such is Heaven's will— be thou the prelude of my song! At Rome thou hurriest me off to be surety[b] : "Come! bestir yourself, lest someone answer duty's call before you." Whether the North-wind sweeps the earth, or winter drags on the snowy day in narrower circle,[c] go I must. Later, when I have said in clear and certain tones[d] what may work me harm, I must battle in the crowd and do damage to the slow of pace. "What do you mean, madman? What are you driving at?" So some ruffian assails me with angry curses : "You would jostle everything in your way, should you be posting back to Maecenas, thinking only of him."

[32] That[e] gives pleasure and is like honey, I'll not deny. But as soon as I come to the gloomy[f] Esquiline, a hundred concerns of others dance through my head and all about me : "Roscius begs you to meet him to-morrow at Libo's Wall[g] before seven o'clock." "The clerks beg you, Quintus, to be sure to return to-day on some fresh and important business of common interest.[h]" "Have Maecenas put his seal to these papers." If you say, "I'll try," "You can, if you will," he adds insistently.

[40] The seventh year—nay, nearer the eighth—will

[f] "Gloomy," because of the old associations of the place. See *Satire* i. 8. 14, note c.

[g] The praetor's tribunal was near the *Puteal Libonis*, a place in the Forum, which, having been struck by lightning, was enclosed by a wall, and regarded as sacred.

[h] Horace, being himself a member of the guild of *scribae*, is addressed on familiar terms. He had been a member of the quaestor's staff.

ex quo Maecenas me coepit habere suorum
in numero, dumtaxat ad hoc, quem tollere raeda
vellet iter faciens, et cui concredere nugas
hoc genus :   "hora quota est?"   "Thraex est
    Gallina Syro par?"
"matutina parum cautos iam frigora mordent;"   45
et quae rimosa bene deponuntur[1] in aure.
per totum hoc tempus subiectior in diem et horam
invidiae noster. ludos spectaverat[2] una,
luserat[3] in Campo: "Fortunae filius!" omnes.
frigidus a rostris manat per compita rumor: 50
quicumque obvius est me consulit: "o bone, nam te
scire, deos quoniam propius[4] contingis, oportet,
numquid de Dacis audisti?" "nil equidem." "ut tu
semper eris derisor!" "at[5] omnes di exagitent me,
si quicquam."   "quid? militibus promissa Triquetra
praedia Caesar an est Itala tellure daturus?"   56
iurantem me scire nihil mirantur[6] ut unum
scilicet egregii mortalem altique silenti.

    Perditur haec inter misero lux non sine votis:
o rus, quando ego te aspiciam! quandoque licebit   60
nunc veterum libris, nunc somno et inertibus horis,[7]
ducere sollicitae iucunda oblivia vitae!
o quando faba Pythagorae cognata simulque

[1] disponuntur *E.*   [2] spectaverit.   [3] luserit.   [4] proprius $\phi\psi\lambda$.
[5] at *Goth.*: ad *MSS.*   [6] miratur $\phi\psi$.   [7] hortis $\phi\psi$.

---

    [a] The reference is to some sporting event of the day.
The men mentioned were gladiators, one being armed like
a Thracian.

    [b] This colloquial use of *noster* = "I", for which we have
examples in Plautus, enables the writer to avoid a tone of
egoism. *Cf.* ἀνὴρ ὅδε.

    [c] Sicily. After the battle of Actium the soldiers who had
served with Octavius had lands allotted to them. The
expression used for Sicily is probably an echo of Lucretius
(i. 717) "insula . . . triquetris terrarum . . . in oris."

soon have sped, since Maecenas began to count me
among his friends—merely thus far, as one he would
like to take in his carriage when on a journey, and
confide to his ears trifles like this: "What's the
time?" "Is the Thracian Chicken a match for
Syrus?"[a] "The morning frosts are nipping now,
if people are careless," and such chat as is safely
dropped into a leaky ear. For all these years, every
day and hour, our friend[b] has been more and more
the butt of envy. Has he viewed the games, or
played ball in the Campus with Maecenas? "For-
tune's favourite!" all cry. Does a chilly rumour
run from the Rostra through the streets? Whoever
comes my way asks my opinion: "My good sir,
you must know—you come so much closer to the
gods: you haven't heard any news about the
Dacians, have you?" "None whatever." "How
you will always mock at us!" But heaven confound
me, if I have heard a word! "Well, is it in the
three-cornered isle,[c] or on Italian soil, that Caesar
means to give the soldiers their promised lands?"
When I swear I know nothing, they marvel at me
as, forsooth, the man of all men remarkably and
profoundly reticent.

[59] Amid such trifling, alas! I waste my day, pray-
ing the while: O rural home: when shall I behold
you! When shall I be able, now with books of the
ancients, now with sleep and idle hours, to quaff
sweet forgetfulness of life's cares! O when shall
beans, brethren of Pythagoras,[d] be served me, and

---

[d] Pythagoras forbade the eating of beans as well as of
the flesh of animals, in the latter case because of his doctrine
of transmigration of souls. Horace humorously applies
this doctrine to beans as well. *Cf.* Gellius, iv. 11.

uncta satis pingui ponentur holuscula lardo !
o noctes cenaeque deum ! quibus ipse meique   65
ante Larem proprium vescor vernasque procaces
pasco libatis dapibus.   prout cuique libido est,
siccat inaequalis calices conviva, solutus
legibus insanis, seu quis capit acria fortis
pocula, seu modicis uvescit[1] laetius. ergo   70
sermo oritur, non de villis domibusve alienis,
nec male necne Lepos saltet ; sed quod magis ad nos
pertinet et nescire malum est, agitamus : utrumne
divitiis homines an sint virtute beati ;
quidve ad amicitias, usus rectumne, trahat nos ;   75
et quae sit natura boni summumque quid eius.
  Cervius haec inter vicinus[2] garrit anilis
ex re fabellas. si quis nam laudat Arelli
sollicitas ignarus opes, sic incipit : " olim
rusticus urbanum murem mus paupere fertur   80
accepisse cavo, veterem vetus hospes amicum,
asper et attentus quaesitis, ut tamen artum
solveret hospitiis animum. quid multa ? neque ille
sepositi ciceris nec longae invidit avenae,
aridum et ore ferens acinum semesaque lardi   85
frusta[3] dedit, cupiens varia fastidia cena
vincere tangentis male singula dente superbo ;
cum pater ipse domus palea porrectus in horna
esset ador loliumque, dapis meliora relinquens.
tandem urbanus ad hunc, " quid te iuvat," inquit,
  " amice,   90

---

[1] humescit *E*.   [2] vicino *E* : vicinos *V*.
    [3] frustra *Eφλ Goth.* : furta *Peerlkamp*.

---

  a Another plausible interpretation of *libatis dapibus* is
" after due offering," *i.e.* to the Lares, before the *mensa
secunda* with its wine-drinking began.

with them greens well larded with fat bacon! O
nights and feasts divine! When before my own
Lar we dine, my friends and I, and feed the
saucy slaves from the barely tasted dishes.[a] Each
guest, as is his fancy, drains cups big or small, not
bound by crazy laws, [b] whether one can stand strong
bumpers in gallant style, or with mild cups mellows
more to his liking. And so begins a chat, not about
other men's homes and estates, nor whether Lepos
dances well or ill; but we discuss matters which
concern us more, and of which it is harmful to be in
ignorance—whether wealth or virtue makes men
happy, whether self-interest or uprightness [c] leads
us to friendship, what is the nature of the good and
what is its highest form.

[77] Now and then our neighbour Cervius rattles off
old wives' tales that fit the case. Thus, if anyone,
blind to its anxieties, praises the wealth of Arellius,
he thus begins: " Once on a time—such is the tale
—a country mouse welcomed a city mouse in his
poor hole, host and guest old friends both. Roughly
he fared, frugal of his store, yet could open his thrifty
soul in acts of hospitality. In short, he grudged not
his hoard of vetch or long oats, but bringing in his
mouth a dried raisin and nibbled bits of bacon he
served them, being eager by varying the fare to
overcome the daintiness of a guest, who, with squeam-
ish tooth, would barely touch each morsel. Mean-
while, outstretched on fresh straw, the master of
the house himself ate spelt and darnel, leaving the
titbits to his friend. At last the city mouse cries
to him: " What pleasure can you have, my friend,

[b] Cf. Sat. ii. 2. 123 and note.
[c] Fundamental questions of ethical philosophy.

praerupti nemoris patientem vivere dorso ?
vis tu homines urbemque feris praeponere silvis ?
carpe viam, mihi crede, comes.   terrestria quando
mortalis animas vivunt sortita, neque ulla est
aut magno aut parvo leti fuga, quo, bone,[1] circa,   95
dum licet, in rebus iucundis vive beatus ;
vive memor, quam sis aevi brevis."   haec ubi dicta
agrestem pepulere, domo levis exsilit ; inde
ambo propositum peragunt iter, urbis aventes
moenia nocturni subrepere.
                Iamque tenebat
nox medium caeli spatium, cum ponit uterque
in locuplete domo vestigia, rubro ubi cocco
tincta super lectos canderet vestis eburnos,
multaque de magna superessent fercula cena,
quae procul exstructis inerant hesterna canistris. 105
ergo ubi purpurea porrectum in veste locavit
agrestem, veluti succinctus cursitat hospes
continuatque dapes, nec non verniliter[2] ipsis[3]
fungitur officiis, praelambens omne quod adfert.[4]
ille cubans gaudet mutata sorte bonisque   110
rebus agit laetum convivam, cum subito ingens
valvarum strepitus lectis excussit utrumque.
currere per totum pavidi conclave, magisque
exanimes trepidare, simul domus alta Molossis
personuit canibus.   tum rusticus, " haud mihi vita 115
est opus hac," ait " et valeas : me silva cavusque
tutus ab insidiis tenui solabitur ervo."

       [1] bene *E.*   [2] vernaliter.
       [3] ipse *Lambinus.*   [4] afflat φψλ.

in living so hard a life on the ridge of a steep wood?
Wouldn't you put people and the city above these
wild woods? Take my advice: set out with me.
Inasmuch as all creatures that live on earth have
mortal souls, and for neither great nor small is there
escape from death, therefore, good sir, while you
may, live happy amid joys; live mindful ever of how
brief your time is!" These words struck home with
the rustic, who lightly leaped forth from his house.
Then both pursue the journey as planned, eager to
creep under the city walls by night.

100 And now night was holding the mid space of
heaven, when the two set foot in a wealthy palace,
where covers dyed in scarlet glittered on ivory
couches, and many courses remained over from a
great dinner of the evening before, in baskets piled
up hard by. So when the town mouse has the
rustic stretched out on purple covers, he himself
bustles about in waiter-style, serving course after
course, and doing all the duties of the home-bred
slave, first tasting everything he serves. The other,
lying at ease, enjoys his changed lot, and amid the
good cheer is playing the happy guest, when of a
sudden a terrible banging of the doors tumbled them
both from their couches. In panic they run the
length of the hall, and still more terror-stricken were
they, as the lofty palace rang with the barking of
Molossian hounds. Then says the rustic: "No use
have I for such a life, and so farewell: my wood
and hole, secure from alarms, will solace me with
homely vetch."

VII

ONLY THE WISE ARE FREE

The scene is laid in Rome during the Saturnalia, when slaves were treated with great indulgence (l. 4 and *Sat.* ii. 3. 5). Davus, the slave of Horace, is therefore permitted to speak his mind freely to his master (1-5).

He remarks that some men are consistent in their vices, others waver between vice and virtue. Horace is an inconsistent man. He praises the good old times, but would not go back to them if he could. In town he pines for the country, in the country he longs for the town. If not invited out, he pretends to be glad, but if an invitation from Maecenas comes at a late hour, off he runs in great excitement, leaving his expectant parasites in the lurch, and proving that he is no better than they (6-42).

"What," asks Davus, "if you, the master, be found to be a greater fool than I, your slave?" Such an audacious remark provokes Horace's wrath, but Davus is allowed to report the lessons of wisdom, which a servant of Crispinus had overheard at the door of his master's lecture-room, and had passed on to him (42-45).

The so-called master, victim of his passions, pursues intrigues, stoops to mean devices to gain his

221

ends, runs all sorts of risks, and sacrifices character
and everything else that he has. He is a real slave
whom no manumission can free, and his Davus is but
his fellow-slave. He is a mere puppet, worked by
wires that others pull (46-82).

Who, then, is free? Only the wise man, who is
complete master of himself. He who is subject to
passion is never that (83-94).

Again, the so-called master is not above his slave
in other faults. The latter wastes time gazing on
crude posters, the former is crazy over some great
artist's paintings. The slave likes pasties and gets
a thrashing, the master loves grand suppers and
suffers from indigestion. The slave swaps the brush
he has stolen for a bunch of grapes, the master sells
off his estates to fill his belly. Why, this master
cannot bear his own company. He is a runaway, a
vagabond, ever seeking, though in vain, to baffle care
(95-115).

This is too much for the angered master, who
threatens to send his slave out to his Sabine farm
(116-118).

This Satire is a close companion of the third, and
deals with another Stoic paradox, viz. that only the
philosopher is free, ὅτι μόνος ὁ σοφὸς ἐλεύθερος. The
Satires have the Saturnalia—a time of free speech—
as their setting, and are much alike in substance,
both dealing with the follies of mankind, and handling
the theme in a very similar dramatic fashion.
the Stoic teacher Crispinus corresponds to Stertinius.
The slave Davus, who finds that, being wise, is
free, takes the place of the social outcast Damasippus,
who discovered that he was no more mad than other
men. In both Satires Horace is the auditor.

sermon, the lessons of which he must apply to himself.
In both he feigns an outburst of anger.

Though Horace thus allows his own name to be
used, the dialogue is really between *any* slave and
any master. It is true that, to heighten the humour
of the scene, he introduces, at the beginning and
perhaps at the end of the criticism of the master
(so ll. 22-35 ; 111-115), some of the atmosphere of
reality, but so far as the main features of the master's
portrait are concerned, it would be more correct to
regard the slave Davus, the preacher of wisdom, as
the Horace of real life. That the poet is not describ-
ing himself with any consistency is clear from ll. 102,
ff., where he is accused of gluttony, whereas we
know that he was very abstemious (*cf. Sat.* i. 5. 7-9).
The seeming self-accusation as to serious offences,
therefore, we may put down to dramatic necessity or
to comic exaggeration.

The dialogue form is maintained throughout,
though during the delivery of Crispinus's lecture it
is held in suspense.

VII.[1]

" Iamdudum ausculto et cupiens tibi dicere servus
pauca reformido." Davusne ? " ita, Davus, amicum
mancipium domino et frugi quod sit satis, hoc est,
ut vitale putes." age, libertate Decembri,
quando ita maiores voluerunt, utere ; narra.   5

" Pars hominum vitiis gaudet constanter et urget
propositum ; pars multa natat, modo recta capessens,
interdum pravis obnoxia. saepe notatus
cum tribus anellis, modo laeva Priscus inani,
vixit inaequalis, clavum ut mutaret in horas,   10
aedibus ex magnis subito se conderet, unde
mundior exiret vix libertinus honeste ;
iam moechus Romae, iam mallet doctus[2] Athenis
vivere, Vertumnis, quotquot sunt, natus iniquis.
scurra Volanerius, postquam illi iusta cheragra   15
contudit articulos, qui pro se tolleret atque
mitteret in phimum[3] talos, mercede diurna

---

[1] The Bland. MSS. make no division between this and the
previous Satire ; so too Bentley : not so aEλ or Porph.

[2] doctor V, II ; so Lejay.

[3] pyrgum Goth. ; no doubt a gloss.

---

[a] The Satire begins like a scene in comedy. The slave
has had to listen to his master's preaching, and now would
like to have his turn at fault-finding.

[b] Alluding to the familiar saying that the good die young.

[c] During the Saturnalia, which came in December, slaves
were allowed great freedom, because, in the age of Saturn,
all men were equal.

[d] As senator, Priscus would wear a broad stripe ; as eques,

224

DAVUS. I've been listening some time, and wishing to say a word to you, but as a slave I dare not.[a]

HORACE. Is that Davus?

DAV. Yes, Davus, a slave loyal to his master, and fairly honest—that is, so that you need not think him too good to live.[b]

HOR. Come, use the licence December allows,[c] since our fathers willed it so. Have your say.

DAV. Some men persist in their love of vice and stick to their purpose; the greater number waver, now aiming at the right, at times giving way to evil. Thus Priscus, who often attracted notice by wearing three rings, but once in a while by wearing none, was so fickle in his life, that he would change his stripe every hour.[d] Passing from a stately mansion, he would bury himself in a den, from which a decent freedman could scarcely emerge without shame. Now he would choose to live in Rome as a rake, now as a sage in Athens—a man born when every single Vertumnus was out of sorts.[e] Volanerius, the jester, when the gout he had earned crippled his finger-joints, kept a man, hired at a daily wage, to pick

a narrow one. Rings were worn on the left hand (*laeva*); only a fop would wear more than one.

[e] Vertumnus, god of the changing year, could assume any shape he pleased. For the form of expression *cf.* "lymphis iratis," *Sat.* i. 5. 97.

conductum pavit; quanto constantior isdem[1]
in vitiis, tanto levius[2] miser ac prior[3] illo,[4]
qui iam contento, iam[5] laxo fune laborat."   20
 Non dices hodie, quorsum haec tam putida tendant,
furcifer? " ad te, inquam." quo pacto, pessime?
           " Laudas
fortunam et mores antiquae plebis, et idem,
si quis ad illa deus subito te agat, usque recuses,
aut quia non sentis quod clamas rectius esse,   25
aut quia non firmus rectum defendis, et haeres
nequiquam caeno cupiens evellere plantam.
Romae rus optas; absentem rusticus urbem
tollis ad astra levis. si nusquam es forte vocatus
ad cenam, laudas securum holus ac, velut usquam   30
vinctus eas, ita te felicem dicis amasque,
quod nusquam tibi sit potandum. iusserit ad se
Maecenas serum sub lumina prima venire
convivam: 'nemon oleum feret[6] ocius? ecquis[7]
audit?' cum magno blateras clamore fugisque.[8]   35
Mulvius et scurrae, tibi non referenda precati,
discedunt. ' etenim fateor me,' dixerit ille,
' duci ventre levem, nasum nidore supinor,'[9]

---

[1] idem *E*λ.   [2] levius] est melius, *II*.
[3] ac prior] acrior *aE Goth*.
[4] illo φ² *one Bland*.: ille *best MSS., yet an error*.
[5] iam . . . iam] tam . . . quam φψ: *second* iam *omitted*
E; *becomes* quam *a*.
[6] fert *El Vollmer*.   [7] et quis *E*.
[8] furisque *V*.   [9] supino, *II*.

---

 [a] The source of the figure is probably an animal tied by
a rope, and pulled up with a jerk, as it tries to get free.
 [b] We are to suppose that Horace, who is already dining
at home, gets a late invitation from Maecenas to fill a vacant
place. The oil he calls for is needed for the lantern to light
him through the streets.

226

up the dice for him and put them in the box. As he was the more persistent in his vices, so he was the less unhappy and the better man, than the one who, with rope now taut, now loose, is in distress.[a]

HOR. Are you to take all day, you scape-gallows, in telling me the point of such rot?

DAV. 'Tis you, I say.

HOR. How so, villain?

DAV. You praise the fortune and manners of the men of old; and yet, if on a sudden some god were for taking you back to those days, you would refuse every time; either because you don't really think that what you are ranting is sounder, or because you are wobbly in defending the right, and, though vainly longing to pull your foot from the filth, yet stick fast in it. At Rome you long for the country; in the country, you extol to the stars the distant town, you fickle one! If so it be that you are asked out nowhere to supper, you praise your quiet dish of herbs, and, as though you were in chains when you do go anywhere, you call yourself lucky, and hug yourself, because you have not to go out for some carousal. Let but Maecenas bid you at a late hour come to him as a guest, just at lamp-lighting time: "Won't someone bring me oil this instant?[b] Does nobody hear me?" So you scream and bawl, then tear off. Mulvius and his fellow-jesters sneak off with curses for you that I cannot repeat.[c] "Yes," he would say, "'tis true that I'm a fickle creature, led by my stomach. I curl up my nose for a savoury

---

[c] Mulvius was a parasite, who had come to share Horace's dinner and is now disappointed. His quoted remarks show that Davus looked upon Horace himself as a parasite at the table of Maecenas.

imbecillus, iners, si quid vis, adde, popino.
tu cum sis quod ego et fortassis nequior, ultro   40
insectere velut melior verbisque decoris
obvolvas vitium ? '   quid, si me stultior ipso[1]
quingentis empto drachmis deprenderis ?   aufer
me voltu terrere ; manum stomachumque teneto,
dum quae Crispini docuit me ianitor edo.   45

    " Te coniunx aliena capit, meretricula Davum.
peccat uter nostrum cruce dignius ?   acris ubi me
natura intendit,[2] sub clara nuda lucerna
quaecumque excepit turgentis verbera caudae,
clunibus aut agitavit equum lasciva supinum,   50
dimittit neque famosum neque sollicitum ne
ditior aut formae melioris meiat eodem.
tu[3] cum proiectis insignibus, anulo equestri
Romanoque habitu, prodis ex iudice Dama
turpis, odoratum caput obscurante lacerna,[4]   55
non es quod simulas ?   metuens induceris atque
altercante[5] libidinibus tremis ossa pavore.
quid refert, uri virgis ferroque necari
auctoratus eas, an turpi clausus in arca,
quo te demisit[6] peccati conscia erilis,   60
contractum genibus tangas caput ?   estne marito
matronae peccantis in ambo[7] iusta potestas ?
in corruptorem vel iustior.   illa tamen se

---

[1] ipse *E.*   [2] incendit *Goth.*   [3] te, *II.*   [4] lucerna *E.*
[5] alternante *Goth.*   [6] dimisit, *II.*   [7] ambos.

---

  [a] Roughly equivalent to £20, or $100, a low price for a slave.

  [b] Davus is a σπερμολόγος, " a picker up of learning's crumbs," and he has picked them up, not from the Stoic Crispinus himself, but at second-hand from his door-keeper, who would be in a position to catch some scraps of the lectures delivered in the school-room.

  [c] The term *iudex* implies a citizen of good standing.

smell. I am weak, lazy, and, if you like to add, a toper. But you, since you are just the same and maybe worse, would you presume to assail me, as though you were a better man, and would you throw over your own vices a cloak of seemly words?" What if you are found to be a greater fool than even I, who cost you five hundred drachmas?[a] Don't try to scare me by your looks. Hold back your hand and temper, while I set forth the lessons taught me by the porter of Crispinus.[b]

46 You are the slave of another man's wife; Davus of a poor harlot. Which of us commits a sin more deserving of the cross? When vehement nature drives me, she who satisfies my passion sends me away neither disgraced nor anxious lest some richer or more handsome man possess her. You, when you have cast aside your badges, the ring of knighthood and your Roman dress, and step forth, no longer a judge,[c] but a low Dama, with a cape hiding your perfumed head, are you not what you pretend to be? Full of fear, you are let into the house, and you tremble with a terror that clashes with your passions. What matters it, whether you go off in bondage,[d] to be scourged and slain with the sword, or whether, shut up in a shameful chest, where the maid, conscious of her mistress's sin, has stowed you away, you touch your crouching head with your knees? Has not the husband of the erring matron a just power over both? Over the seducer a still juster? Yet she

See note on *Sat.* i. 4. 123. That Horace could claim equestrian rank, and was even a "potential senator," is maintained by Lily Ross Taylor in an article on "Horace's Equestrian Career" in *A.J.P.* xlvi. (1925) pp. 161 ff. So, too, Haight, *Horace*, etc. p. 38.

[d] The word *auctoratus* is technical, being applicable to one who sold himself as a gladiator.

non habitu mutatve loco peccatve[1] superne,
cum te formidet mulier neque credat amanti.   65
ibis sub furcam prudens, dominoque furenti
committes rem omnem et vitam et cum corpore famam.

  " Evasti : credo, metues doctusque cavebis ;
quaeres,[2] quando iterum paveas iterumque perire
possis, o totiens servus !   quae belua ruptis,   70
cum semel effugit, reddit se prava catenis ?
" non sum moechus," ais : neque ego, hercule, fur,
    ubi vasa[3]
praetereo sapiens argentea.   tolle periclum :
iam vaga prosiliet frenis Natura remotis.
tune mihi dominus, rerum imperiis hominumque   75
tot tantisque minor, quem ter vindicta quaterque
imposita haud umquam misera formidine privet ?
adde super[4] dictis quod non levius valeat : nam
sive vicarius est, qui servo paret, uti[5] mos
vester ait, seu conservus, tibi quid[6] sum ego ?   nempe
⁺u, mihi qui imperitas, alii[7] servis miser atque   81
duceris ut nervis alienis mobile lignum.

  "Quisnam igitur liber ? sapiens, sibi qui[8] imperiosus,
quem neque pauperies neque mors neque vincula
    terrent,
responsare cupidinibus, contemnere honores   85
fortis, et in se ipso totus,[9] teres atque rotundus,

----

  [1] peccatque, *II.*   [2] quaeres *El* : quaeris, *II.*
  [3] visa *V.*   [4] supra, *II.*   [5] uti] ut est, *II.*
    [6] quid *Goth.* : quod *MSS.*   [7] aliis, *II.*
      [8] sibi qui *l, Bentley* : sibique *V, MSS.*
        [9] *Bentley first punctuated after* totus.

----

  [a] As the man had done, ll. 53, 54.
  [b] *i.e.* like an unbridled horse.
  [c] The *vindicta* is the rod used in the formal manumission
of a slave in the presence of the praetor.

does not change either garb or position,[a] and she is not the chief sinner, since she is in dread of you and does not trust her lover. You with eyes open will pass under the yoke, and hand over to a furious master your fortune, your life, your person and repute.

[68] Suppose you have escaped: then, I take it, you will be afraid and cautious after your lesson. No, you will seek occasion so as again to be in terror, again to face ruin, O you slave many times over! But what beast, having once burst its bonds and escaped, perversely returns to them again? "I am no adulterer," you say. And, in faith, I am no thief either, when I wisely pass by your silver plate. Take away the risk, set aside restraint, and Nature will spring forward, to roam at will.[b] Are you my master, you, a slave to the dominion of so many men and things—you, whom the praetor's rod, though placed on your head three or four times over,[c] never frees from base terror? And over and above what I have said, add something of no less weight: whether one who obeys a slave is an underslave,[d] as the custom of your class names him, or a fellow-slave, what am I in respect of you? Why, you, who lord it over me, are the wretched slave of another master, and you are moved like a wooden puppet by wires that others pull.

[83] Who then is free? The wise man, who is lord over himself, whom neither poverty nor death nor bonds affright, who bravely defies his passions, and scorns ambition, who in himself is a whole, smoothed and rounded, so that nothing from outside can rest

[d] The *vicarius* was a slave bought by another out of his *peculium* to help him in his work.

externi ne quid valeat per leve morari,
in quem manca ruit semper Fortuna.
                                        Potesne[1]
ex his ut proprium quid noscere ? quinque talenta
poscit te mulier, vexat foribusque repulsum   90
perfundit gelida, rursus vocat : eripe turpi
colla iugi, ' liber, liber sum,' dic age ! non quis :
urget enim dominus mentem non lenis et acris
subiectat lasso stimulos versatque negantem.

Vel cum Pausiaca torpes, insane, tabella,   95
qui peccas minus atque ego, cum Fulvi Rutubaeque
aut Pacideiani contento poplite miror
proelia rubrica picta aut carbone, velut si
re vera pugnent, feriant vitentque moventes[2]
arma viri ? nequam et[3] cessator Davus ; at ipse 100
subtilis veterum iudex et callidus audis.

" Nil ego, si ducor libo fumante : tibi ingens
virtus atque animus cenis responsat opimis ?
obsequium ventris mihi perniciosius est cur ?
tergo plector enim. qui tu[4] impunitior illa,   105
quae parvo sumi nequeunt, obsonia captas ?
nempe inamarescunt epulae sine fine petitae,
illusique pedes vitiosum ferre recusant
corpus. an hic peccat, sub noctem qui puer uvam
furtiva mutat strigili ? qui praedia vendit,   110

---

[1] potestne, *II*.   [2] morientes, *II*.
[3] et *omitted, II*.   [4] qui dum φψl.

---

[a] The wise man of the Stoics is self-contained or in-
dependent of externals, αὐτάρκης, and is like the perfect
sphere of the κόσμος itself (*cf.* Plato, *Tim.* 33). In the
Protagoras 339 D, Plato also makes use of a figure of
Simonides, who calls the truly good man a square, τετρά-
γωνος. So too Aristotle, *Rhet.* iii. 11.

[b] These are names of gladiators. The last named is

on the polished surface, and against whom Fortune in her onset is ever maimed.[a]

88 Of these traits can you recognize any one as your own? A woman asks of you five talents, worries you, shuts her door in your face, drenches you in cold water, then—calls you back. Rescue your neck from the yoke of shame; come, say, "I am free, am free." You cannot; for you have a master, and no gentle one, plaguing your soul, pricking your weary side with the sharp spur, and driving you on against your will.

95 Or when, madman, you stand dazed before a picture of Pausias, how do you offend less than I, when I marvel at the contests of Fulvius, Rutuba, or Pacideianus,[b] with their straining legs, drawn in red chalk or charcoal, just as lifelike as if the heroes were really waving their weapons, and fighting, striking, and parrying? Davus is a "rascal and dawdler," but you are called a "fine and expert critic of antiques."

102 If I'm tempted by a smoking pasty, I'm a good-for-naught: but *you*—does your heroic virtue and spirit defy rich suppers? Why is it more ruinous for me to obey the stomach's call? My back, to be sure, pays for it. But how do you escape punishment more than I, when you hanker for those dainties which cannot be bought at small cost? Why, that feasting, endlessly indulged, turns to gall, and the feet you've duped refuse to bear up your sickly body. Is the slave guilty, who at fall of night swaps for grapes the flesh-brush he has stolen? Is there

borrowed from Lucilius; the other two may be contemporary with Horace. Pictures of gladiators were drawn on walls, and served the purpose of modern posters.

nil servile gulae parens habet ?   adde, quod idem
non horam tecum esse potes, non otia recte
ponere, teque ipsum vitas fugitivus et[1] erro,
iam vino quaerens, iam somno fallere Curam ;   114
frustra: nam comes atra premit sequiturque fugacem."

    Unde mihi lapidem ?

                " Quorsum est opus ? "

                            Unde sagittas ?

" Aut insanit homo aut versus facit."

                         Ocius hinc te
ni rapis, accedes opera agro nona Sabino.

         [1] ut.

nothing of the slave about one who sells his estates at his belly's bidding? And again, you cannot yourself bear to be in your own company, you cannot employ your leisure aright, you shun yourself, a runaway and vagabond, seeking now with wine, and now with sleep, to baffle Care.[a] In vain: that black consort dogs and follows your flight.

HOR. Where can I find a stone?

DAVUS. What's it for?

HOR. Or where arrows?

DAVUS. The man's raving, or else verse-making.

HOR. If you don't take yourself off in a jiffy, you'll make the ninth labourer on my Sabine farm.

[a] *Cf. Odes* iii. 1. 40.

A FIASCO OF A DINNER-PARTY

THE poet describes a dinner at which Maecenas was the guest of honour. Three men of letters were also in the company—Fundanius, Viscus, and Varius. The rest of the guests are undistinguished, and are probably imaginary characters who could not be identified. Porcius, for instance, true to his name, eats like a pig. Balatro is a buffoon, and Nomentanus is one of the traditional characters of satire. Moreover, the host, Nasidienus Rufus, is otherwise quite unknown.

These facts warrant us in acquitting Fundanius (and therefore the author who introduced him) of the charge of extremely bad taste in heaping ridicule on a host whose hospitality had been accepted. Horace, in fact, adopts a principle, which is illustrated in the previous Satire, of securing a certain amount of verisimilitude through the use of known facts and of drawing on his imagination for the rest of his material. The Satire is directed, partly against the ostentation and vulgarity sometimes displayed by wealth, and partly against the curious and affected erudition of pronounced epicures. In the latter respect it resembles the fourth Satire of the first book.

The party was arranged according to the following plan :

Medius Lectus

1. Fundanius ; 2. Viscus ; 3. Varius ; 4. Balatro ; 5. Vibidius ; 6. Maecenas ; 7. Nomentanus ; 8. Nasidienus ; 9. Porcius.

Fiske has shown that Lucilius was "the first to establish the traditions of the δεῖπνον in Latin Satire," and that in this Eighth Satire Horace keeps in fairly close touch with the twentieth book of Lucilius, where a banquet given by the *praeco* Granius was reported to the satirist by L. Licinius Crassus (*Lucilius and Horace*, pp. 408 ff.). But, as Lucilius wrote at least five satires on banquets, it is not surprising to find that Lejay (p. 580) regards his fifth book as the chief model followed here by Horace.

VIII.

Ut Nasidieni iuvit te cena beati ?
nam mihi quaerenti convivam dictus here illic
de medio potare die.
　　　　　　" Sic, ut mihi numquam
in vita fuerit melius."
　　　　　　　Da,[1] si grave non est,
quae prima iratum ventrem pacaverit[2] esca.　　　5
" In primis Lucanus aper ; leni fuit Austro
captus, ut aiebat cenae pater ; acria circum
rapula, lactucae, radices, qualia lassum
pervellunt stomachum, siser, allec, faecula Coa.
his ut[3] sublatis puer alte cinctus acernam　　　10
gausape purpureo mensam pertersit, et alter
sublegit quodcumque iaceret inutile quodque
posset cenantis offendere ; ut Attica virgo
cum sacris Cereris, procedit fuscus Hydaspes
Caecuba vina ferens, Alcon Chium maris expers.　15
hic erus : ' Albanum, Maecenas, sive Falernum
te magis appositis delectat, habemus utrumque.' "

　　[1] da φψ : dic *Bland.* (da *is the more unusual*).
　　[2] pacaverit *C* : peccaverit *E* : placaverit φψ.
　　　　　[3] ut *C Priscian* : ubi *E*.

---

[a] A dinner-party usually began at the ninth hour (about
3 P.M.), but an ultra-extravagant one might begin even earlier.

[b] The boar with relishes here formed the *gustatio*, and is
another sign of extravagant luxury ; *cf.* Pliny viii. 210, " in
principio (cenae) bini ternique mandantur apri." More
commonly it would appear as the *pièce de résistance.* See
note on *Sat.* ii. 4. 11.

Satire VIII

HORACE. How did you like your dinner with the rich Nasidienus? Yesterday, when I tried to get you as my own guest, I was told you had been dining there since midday.[a]

FUNDANIUS. So much so that never in my life did I have a better time.

HOR. Tell me, if you don't mind, what was the first dish to appease an angry appetite?

FUN. First there was a wild boar.[b] It was caught when a gentle south wind was blowing, as the father of the feast kept telling us. Around it were pungent turnips, lettuces, radishes—such things as whet a jaded appetite—skirret, fish-pickle, and Coan lees. When these were removed, a high-girt slave with purple napkin wiped well the maple-wood table, while a second swept up the scraps and anything that could offend the guests. Then, like an Attic maid[c] bearing Ceres' sacred emblems, there came forward dusky Hydaspes with Caecuban wine, and Alcon with Chian, unmixed with brine.[d] Then said our host: " If Alban is more to your taste, Maecenas, or Falernian, we have both."

[c] i.e. like a κανηφόρος in the rites of Demeter ; cf. Sat. i. 3. 9.

[d] The Caecuban was one of the finest Italian, as Chian was one of the best Greek, wines. The host's Chian being very good, he did not do what was often done—add sea-water to give it a tang. Columella (xii. 21. 37) gives directions as to the proportions to be used. The phrase maris expers corresponds to οὐ τεθαλαττωμένον in Athenaeus i. p. 32.

Divitias miseras ! sed quis cenantibus una,
Fundani, pulchre fuerit tibi, nosse laboro.
   "Summus ego et prope[1] me Viscus Thurinus et
     infra,   20
si memini, Varius ; cum Servilio Balatrone
Vibidius, quos[2] Maecenas adduxerat umbras.
Nomentanus erat super ipsum, Porcius infra,
ridiculus totas semel[3] absorbere placentas ;
Nomentanus ad hoc, qui, si quid forte lateret,   25
indice monstraret digito : nam cetera turba,
nos, inquam, cenamus avis, conchylia, piscis,
longe dissimilem noto celantia sucum ;
ut vel continuo patuit, cum passeris atque
ingustata mihi porrexerat ilia rhombi.   30
post hoc me docuit melimela rubere minorem
ad lunam delecta. quid hoc intersit ab ipso
audieris melius.
        "Tum Vibidius Balatroni :
' nos nisi damnose bibimus, moriemur inulti,'
et calices poscit maiores. vertere pallor   35
tum parochi faciem nil sic metuentis ut acris
potores, vel quod maledicunt liberius vel
fervida quod subtile exsurdant vina palatum.
invertunt Allifanis vinaria tota
Vibidius Balatroque, secutis omnibus ; imi[4]   40
convivae lecti nihilum nocuere lagoenis.

---

  [1] pro *V.*   [2] quas *Goth.*   [3] simul *E.*   [4] imis *C, II.*

---

  [a] The *umbrae* were uninvited guests who came with a man
of high station.
  [b] The *cetera turba* are the uninitiated guests as contrasted
with the knowing Nomentanus. The subject of *porrexerat*
is not the host, as commonly supposed, but Nomentanus,
who is doing the work assigned him. Palmer takes *ingustata*
to mean " untasted," implying that the odour was enough

HOR. O the misery of wealth! But who, Fundanius, were those at dinner, with whom you had so fine a time? I am eager to know.

FUN. Myself at the top, then next to me Viscus of Thurii, and below, if I remember, Varius. Then Vibidius and Servilius Balatro, the "shades" [a] that Maecenas had brought with him. Above our host was Nomentanus; below him, Porcius, who made us laugh by swallowing whole cheese-cakes at a mouthful. Nomentanus was there to see that if anything perchance escaped our notice, he might point it out with his forefinger; for the rest of the folk [b]—we, I mean—eat fowl, oysters, and fish, which had a flavour far different from any we knew, as, for instance, was made clear at once, after he had handed me the livers of a plaice and a turbot, a dish I had never tasted before. After this he informed me that the honey-apples were red because picked in the light of a waning moon. What difference that makes you would learn better from himself.

[23] Then said Vibidius to Balatro: "Unless we drink him bankrupt, we shall die unavenged," and he calls for larger cups. Then did paleness overspread the face of the host, who dreaded nothing so much as hard drinkers, either because they chaff one too freely or because fiery wines dull the delicate palate. Vibidius and Balatro tilt whole decanters of wine into Allifan goblets.[c] All followed suit, save the guests on the lowest couch, who did no harm to the flagons.[d]

to betray the nature of the food, but the point lies, not in the badness, but in the novelty, of the dishes.

[c] i.e. large cups made at Allifae in Samnium.

[d] Porcius and Nomentanus would, of course, do nothing to offend their host. They therefore "spared the bottle."

" Adfertur squillas inter murena natantis
in patina porrecta. sub hoc erus,' haec gravida,'
   inquit,
' capta est, deterior post partum carne futura.
his mixtum ius est : oleo, quod prima Venafri   45
pressit cella ; garo de sucis piscis Hiberi ;
vino quinquenni, verum citra mare nato,
dum coquitur (cocto Chium sic convenit, ut non
hoc magis ullum aliud) ; pipere albo, non sine aceto,
quod Methymnaeam vitio mutaverit[1] uvam.   50
erucas viridis, inulas ego primus amaras
monstravi incoquere ; illutos Curtillus echinos,
ut melius muria quod[2] testa marina remittat.'[3]
   " Interea suspensa gravis aulaea ruinas
in patinam fecere, trahentia pulveris atri   55
quantum non Aquilo Campanis excitat agris.
nos maius veriti, postquam nihil esse pericli
sensimus, erigimur.   Rufus posito capite, ut si
filius immaturus obisset, flere. quis esset
finis, ni sapiens sic Nomentanus amicum   60
tolleret : ' heu, Fortuna, quis est crudelior in nos
te deus ?   ut semper gaudes illudere rebus
humanis ! ' Varius mappa compescere risum
vix poterat. Balatro, suspendens omnia naso,
' haec est condicio vivendi,' aiebat, ' eoque   65
responsura tuo numquam est par fama labori.
tene, ut ego accipiar laute, torquerier omni
sollicitudine districtum, ne panis adustus,
ne male conditum ius apponatur, ut omnes

---

[1] motaverit, *I.*   [2] quod MSS.: quo *V*: quam *Bentley.*
   [3] remittas *E*: remittit *C.*

---

   [a] *i.e.* Italian, not Greek.

⁴² Then is brought in a lamprey, outstretched on a platter, with shrimps swimming all round it. Upon this the master: "This," said he, "was caught before spawning; if taken later, its flesh would have been poorer. The ingredients of the sauce are these: oil from Venafrum of the first pressing, roe from the juices of the Spanish mackerel, wine five years old, but produced this side of the sea,ᵃ poured in while it is on the boil—after boiling, Chian suits better than anything else—white pepper, and vinegar made from the fermenting of Lesbian vintage. I was the first to point out that one should boil in the sauce green rockets and bitter elecampane; Curtillus would use sea-urchins, unwashed, inasmuch as the yield of the sea-shellfish itself is better than a briny pickle."

⁵⁴ Meantime the canopy ᵇ spread above came down in mighty ruin upon the platter, trailing more black dust than the North-wind raises on Campanian plains. We feared a worse disaster, but finding there was no danger recover ourselves. Rufus drooped his head and wept as if his son had fallen by an untimely fate. What would have been the end, had not Nomentanus, the philosopher, thus rallied his friend: "Ah, Fortune, what god is more cruel toward us than thou! How thou dost ever delight to make sport of the life of man!" Varius could scarce smother a laugh with his napkin. Balatro, who sneers at everything, said: "These are the terms of life, and therefore the meed of fame will never equal your labour. To think that, in order that I may have lavish entertainment, you are to be racked and tortured with every anxiety, lest the bread be burned, lest sauce be served ill-seasoned, that all

ᵇ The *aulaea* were hangings used to decorate the walls.

praecincti recte pueri[1] comptique ministrent !　　70
adde hos praeterea casus, aulaea ruant si,
ut modo ;　si patinam pede lapsus frangat agaso.
sed convivatoris, uti ducis, ingenium res
adversae nudare solent, celare secundae.'
Nasidienus ad haec : ' tibi di quaecumque preceris[2]　75
commoda dent ! ita vir bonus es convivaque comis ; '
et soleas poscit.　tum in lecto quoque videres
stridere secreta divisos aure susurros."

　　Nullos his mallem ludos spectasse ; sed illa
redde, age, quae deinceps risisti.

　　　　　　　　　　" Vibidius dum　　80
quaerit de pueris num sit quoque fracta lagoena,
quod sibi poscenti non dentur[3] pocula, dumque
ridetur fictis rerum Balatrone secundo,
Nasidiene, redis mutatae frontis, ut arte
emendaturus fortunam.　deinde secuti　　85
mazonomo pueri magno discerpta ferentes
membra gruis sparsi sale multo non sine farre,
pinguibus et ficis pastum iecur anseris albae,[4]
et leporum avolsos, ut multo suavius, armos,
quam si cum lumbis quis edit.[5] tum[6] pectore adusto　90
vidimus et merulas poni et sine clune palumbes,
suavis res, si non causas narraret earum et
naturas dominus : quem nos sic fugimus ulti,
ut nihil omnino gustaremus, velut illis
Canidia adflasset peior serpentibus Afris.[7] "　　95

---

　　　[1] pueri recte *C Goth.*　　　　　[2] precaris *E Goth.*
　　　　　　[3] dentur *Cφ Bentley* : dantur *Eψ.*
　　[4] albae *V* : albi *mss.*　　[5] edat *Priscian.*　　[6] cum, *I.*
　　　　　[7] Afris *E Goth.* : atris *C, II, Bentley.*

---

　　[a] Their light slippers were removed when the guests took
their places ; to call for them was to indicate a wish to leave
the dining-room.

your slaves may be properly attired and neat for waiting ! Then, too, these risks besides—the canopy falling, as it did just now, or a numskull stumbling and breaking a dish ! But one who entertains is like a general : mishaps oft reveal his genius, smooth going hides it." To this replies Nasidienus : " Heaven grant you every blessing you crave, so kind a man are you, so civil a guest ! " and calls for his slippers.[a] Then on each couch you might note the buzz of whispers in secret ears exchanged.[b]

HOR. No play would I have rather seen ; but pray tell me, what did you find to laugh at next ?

FUN. While Vibidius is asking the servants whether the flagon also was broken, since cups were not brought him when called for, and while we were laughing at pretended jests, Balatro egging us on, back you come, Nasidienus, with altered brow, as if bent on mending misfortune by art. Then follow servants, bearing on a huge charger the limbs of a crane sprinkled with much salt and meal, and the liver of a white goose fattened on rich figs, and hares' limbs torn off, as being more dainty than if eaten with the loins. Then we saw blackbirds served with the breast burnt, and pigeons without the rumps— real dainties, did not our host unfold their laws and properties.[c] But off we ran, taking our revenge on him by tasting nothing at all, as though the things were blasted with Canidia's[d] breath, more deadly than African serpents.

---

[b] The remarkable accumulation of sibilants in l. 78 imitates the whispering.

[c] Nasidienus discourses upon the dishes with all the seriousness of a philosopher lecturing *de rerum natura*.

[d] For Canidia see *Sat.* i. 8. 24.

EPISTLES

I

TO MAECENAS

THE First Epistle, which serves as an introduction to the First Book, and is addressed to the poet's patron, Maecenas, professes to explain why Horace has given up the writing of lyric poetry. He is now too old for such folly, and his mind has turned to another field.

"Why," he asks, "should you wish the gladiator, who has earned his discharge, to return to his former training-school? A warning voice within bids me loose the old steed before he stumble at the end of his course. And so I give up my verses with other toys, and turn all my thoughts to philosophy, following no special school but letting myself be borne along as the breeze may set, now behaving as a true Stoic, being all for action, and now relapsing into the passiveness of a Cyrenaic (1-19).

"With impatience do I await the day when I may devote myself to the serious problems of life; meanwhile I must guide and comfort myself with what little knowledge I possess. A cure for all diseases of the soul may be found in the charms and spells of philosophy, if the patient will but submit to treatment (20-40).

"The first step in virtue and wisdom is to eschew

248

vice and folly. Men are anxious to avoid poverty and ought to be quite as eager to escape from evil desires, especially as the prize offered is so much greater (41-51).

" True, the world takes a different view, but the children who sing ' You'll be king, if you do right ' should teach us how much better than riches is the power to stand erect and free and to fling defiance at Fortune (52-69).

" If I were asked why I do not go along with the world and share its opinions, I should recall the fable of the fox declining the lion's invitation to enter his den, because the footprints point in only one direction. The man who once gives in to popular opinion becomes the victim of a hydra. Cutting off one head does no good. Men are capricious, and even the same man changes his views from hour to hour (70-93).

" I am as bad as others, but though you are quick to notice some carelessness in my dress or appearance, you fail to observe my graver inconsistencies of life and thought (94-105).

" In short, the Stoics are right : only the sage can be perfect, and even he may suffer from a cold ! "

EPISTULARUM

LIBER PRIMUS

I.

Prima dicte mihi, summa dicende Camena,
spectatum satis et donatum iam rude quaeris,
Maecenas, iterum antiquo me includere ludo.
non eadem est aetas, non mens. Veianius armis
Herculis ad postem fixis latet abditus agro,   5
ne populum extrema totiens exoret[1] harena.
est mihi purgatam crebro qui personet aurem :
" solve senescentem mature sanus equum, ne
peccet ad extremum ridendus et ilia ducat."
    Nunc itaque et versus et cetera ludicra pono ;   10
quid verum atque decens curo et rogo et omnis in hoc
    sum ;
condo et compono quae mox depromere possim.
ac ne forte roges, quo me duce, quo lare tuter :

[1] exornet $\phi\psi\delta$.

---

    a The first Satire, the first Epode, and the first Ode are
all addressed to Maecenas.
    b Horace compares himself to an old gladiator, who has
often won approval, and received the wooden foil which
was a symbol of discharge from the school of gladiators.
    c The defeated combatant would beg for his life. Veianius,
after his discharge, yielded to no inducements to return to
the arena.

250

EPISTLES

BOOK I

EPISTLE I

You, of whom my earliest Muse has told,[a] of whom my last shall tell—you Maecenas, seek to shut me up again in my old school, though well tested in the fray, and already presented with the foil.[b] My years, my mind, are not the same. Veianius hangs up his arms at Hercules' door, then lies hidden in the country, that he may not have to plead with the crowd again and again from the arena's edge.[c] Some one there is who is always dinning in my well-rinsed ear : "Be wise in time, and turn loose the ageing horse, lest at the last he stumble amid jeers and burst his wind."

[10] So now I lay aside my verses and all other toys. What is right and seemly is my study and pursuit, and to that am I wholly given. I am putting by and setting in order the stores on which I may some day draw. Do you ask, perchance, who is my chief, in what home I take shelter ? I am not bound over[d]

---

[d] Horace, still using terms applicable to a gladiator, who took an oath to the master of his training-school, is speaking of the acceptance of the formula of some school of philosophy.

nullius addictus[1] iurare in verba magistri,
quo me cumque rapit tempestas, deferor hospes.　15
nunc agilis fio et mersor civilibus undis,
virtutis verae custos rigidusque satelles ;
nunc in Aristippi furtim praecepta relabor
et[2] mihi res, non me rebus, subiungere conor.

　Ut nox longa quibus mentitur amica, diesque　20
longa videtur opus debentibus, ut piger annus
pupillis, quos dura premit custodia matrum ;
sic mihi tarda fluunt ingrataque tempora, quae spem
consiliumque morantur agendi naviter id quod
aeque pauperibus prodest, locupletibus aeque,　25
aeque neglectum pueris senibusque nocebit.
restat ut his ego me ipse regam solerque elementis.
non possis oculo[3] quantum contendere Lynceus,
non tamen idcirco contemnas lippus inungui ;
nec quia desperes invicti membra Glyconis,[4]　30
nodosa corpus nolis prohibere cheragra.
est quadam[5] prodire tenus, si non datur ultra.

　Fervet avaritia miseroque cupidine pectus :
sunt verba et voces, quibus hunc lenire dolorem
possis et magnam morbi deponere partem.　35
laudis amore tumes ; sunt certa piacula, quae te
ter pure lecto poterunt recreare libello.

---

[1] addictus, *II*: adductus *aEM, I, yet* addictus *is surely
correct.*
[2] ac.　　　　　　　　　　　　　[3] oculos.
[4] Milonis *known to Acron.*　　　　[5] quodam, *II.*

---

　[a] By *agilis* Horace translates πρακτικός, and *civilibus* =
πολιτικοῖς ; the Stoics approved of an active participation
in public life.
　[b] Aristippus founded the Cyrenaic school, which taught
that a man should control circumstances, not be controlled
by them.
　[c] As he has not yet been able to take up philosophy

to swear as any master dictates ; wherever the storm drives me, I turn in for comfort. Now I become all action,[a] and plunge into the tide of civil life, stern champion and follower of true Virtue ; now I slip back stealthily into the rules of Aristippus, and would bend the world to myself, not myself to the world.[b]

20 As the night seems long for one whose mistress proves false, and the day long for those who work for hire ; as the year lags for wards held in check by their mother's strict guardianship : so slow and thankless flow for me the hours which defer my hope and purpose of setting myself vigorously to that task which profits alike the poor, alike the rich, but, if neglected, will be harmful alike to young and to old. What remains is for me to guide and solace myself with these poor rudiments.[c] You may not be able, with your eyes, to see as far as Lynceus, yet you would not on that account scorn to anoint them, if sore. Nor, because you may not hope for unconquered Glycon's strength of limb, would you decline to keep your body free from the gnarls of gout. It is worth while to take some steps forward, though we may not go still further.

33 Is your bosom fevered with avarice and sordid covetousness? There are spells and sayings[d] whereby you may soothe the pain and cast much of the malady aside. Are you swelling with ambition? There are fixed charms which can fashion you anew, if with cleansing rites you read the booklet thrice. The

vigorously, his only comfort is to make the most of the little knowledge of it that he had.
[d] The lessons of philosophy are compared to the magic formulas which were used in the medical art of ancient days.

invidus, iracundus, iners, vinosus, amator,
nemo adeo ferus est, ut non mitescere possit,
si modo culturae patientem commodet aurem.　　40

　Virtus est vitium fugere et sapientia prima
stultitia caruisse.　vides, quae maxima credis
esse mala, exiguum censum turpemque repulsam,[1]
quanto devites animi capitisque labore ;
impiger extremos curris mercator ad Indos,　　45
per mare pauperiem fugiens, per saxa, per ignis :
ne cures ea, quae stulte miraris et optas,
discere[2] et audire et meliori credere non vis ?
quis circum pagos et circum compita pugnax
magna coronari contemnat Olympia, cui spes,　　50
cui sit condicio dulcis sine pulvere palmae ?

　Vilius argentum est auro, virtutibus aurum.
" o cives, cives, quaerenda pecunia primum est ;
virtus post nummos ! "　haec Ianus summus ab imo
prodocet, haec recinunt iuvenes dictata senesque,　　55
laevo suspensi loculos tabulamque lacerto.
est animus tibi, sunt mores, est lingua[3] fidesque,
sed[4] quadringentis sex septem milia desunt[5] ;[6]
plebs eris.　at pueri ludentes, " rex eris," aiunt,
" si recte facies."　hic murus aeneus esto,　　60
nil conscire sibi, nulla pallescere culpa.

　　　[1] laborem $R\delta\pi$.　　　　　　[2] dicere, II.
　　　[3] est lingua E : et lingua *other* MSS.
　　　[4] si.　　　　　　[5] desint $\phi\psi\lambda l$.
　　　[6] *The order of ll.* 57, 58 *thus in E, reversed in other* MSS.
Housman would place l. 56 *after l.* 59.

　　　[a] For the thought *cf. Sat.* i. 1. 30 ; i. 4. 29 ff.
　　　[b] *Cf. Sat.* ii. 3. 18.　The arch of Janus represents the
banking world of Rome.
　　　[c] Repeated from *Sat.* i. 6. 74.　In this respect the old
still behave as school-boys.
　　　[d] Enrolment in the *equites* implied a fortune of 400,000
sesterces.

254

slave to envy, anger, sloth, wine, lewdness—no one is so savage that he cannot be tamed, if only he lend to treatment a patient ear.

⁴¹ To flee vice is the beginning of virtue, and to have got rid of folly is the beginning of wisdom. You see with what anxious thought and peril of life you strive to avoid those ills you deem the greatest, a slender fortune and the shame of failure at the polls. Ardent trader that you are, you rush to the furthest Indies, fleeing poverty through sea, through rocks, through flame *ᵃ* : but that you may cease to care for the things which you foolishly admire and crave, will you not learn and listen and trust one wiser than yourself? What wrestler in the village games and at the cross-ways would scorn being crowned at the great Olympic games, who had the hope, who had the surety of victory's palm without the dust?

⁵² Of less worth than gold is silver, than virtue gold. " O citizens, citizens, money you first must seek ; virtue after pelf." This rule the Janus arcade proclaims from top to bottom *ᵇ* ; this is the lesson the old as well as the young are singing, " with slate and satchel slung over the left arm." *ᶜ* You have sense, you have morals, eloquence and honour, but there are six or seven thousands short of the four hundred *ᵈ* ; you will be in the crowd. Yet boys at play cry ; " You'll be king, if you do right." *ᵉ* Be this our wall of bronze, to have no guilt at heart, no wrongdoing to turn us pale.

ᵉ The Scholiast gives the verse, which children sang in their game, thus :

réx erit qui récte faciet ; quí non faciet, nón erit.

There is a pun in *rex* and *recte*.

Roscia, dic sodes, melior lex an puerorum est
nenia, quae regnum recte facientibus offert,
et maribus Curiis et decantata Camillis ?
isne tibi melius suadet, qui " rem facias, rem,   65
si possis, recte, si non, quocumque modo, rem,"
ut propius spectes lacrimosa poemata Pupi,
an qui Fortunae te responsare superbae
liberum et erectum praesens hortatur et aptat[1] ?

Quod si me populus Romanus forte roget, cur   70
non ut porticibus sic iudiciis fruar isdem,[2]
nec[3] sequar aut[4] fugiam quae[5] diligit ipse vel odit,
olim quod volpes aegroto cauta leoni
respondit, referam : " quia me vestigia terrent,
omnia te adversum spectantia, nulla retrorsum."   75
belua multorum es capitum. nam quid sequar aut
        quem ?
pars hominum gestit conducere publica ; sunt qui
frustis[6] et pomis viduas venentur avaras
excipiantque senes, quos in vivaria mittant ;
multis occulto crescit res faenore.
                            Verum   80
esto aliis alios rebus studiisque teneri :
idem eadem possunt horam durare probantes ?
" nullus in orbe[7] sinus Bais praelucet amoenis,"
si dixit dives, lacus et mare sentit amorem
festinantis eri ; cui si vitiosa libido   85

---

[1] optat *Goth.*   [2] idem *ERπ.*
[3] ne *E.*   [4] et *or* ac, *II.*   [5] quem *Rπ.*
[6] crustis.   [7] urbe φψδ.

---

[a] See *Sat.* i. 6. 40 and note.
[b] *Cf. Sat.* i. 4. 134, where see note.
[c] See the subject of *Sat.* ii. 5.
[d] For *excipiant cf. excipere aprum, Odes* iii. 12. 12.
animals were sometimes caught and turned into preserv
(Pliny viii. 52. 211). *Cf. Sat.* ii. 5. 44.

⁶² Tell me, pray, which is better, the Roscian law ^a or the children's jingle which offers a kingdom to those who " do right " — a jingle once trolled by the manly Curii and Camilli ? Does he advise you better, who bids you " make money, money by fair means if you can, if not, by any means money," and all that you may have a nearer view of the doleful plays of Pupius ; or he who, an ever present help, urges and fits you to stand free and erect, and defy scornful Fortune ?

⁷⁰ But if the people of Rome should ask me, perchance, why I do not use the same judgements even as I walk in the same colonnades ^b as they, why I do not follow or eschew what they love or hate, I should reply as once upon a time the prudent fox made answer to the sick lion : " Because those footprints frighten me ; they all lead toward your den, and none lead back." You are a many-headed monster-thing. For what am I to follow or whom ? Some men rejoice to farm state-revenues ; some with titbits and fruits hunt miserly widows,^c and net old men to stock their preserves ; ^d with many their money grows with interest unobserved.^e

But let it be that men are swayed by different aims and hobbies ; can the same persons persist for one hour in liking the same things ? " No bay in the world outshines lovely Baiae." If so the rich man has said, lake and sea suffer from the eager owner's fancy ; but if a morbid whim has given him the

---

^e Money grows by the " unobserved " accumulation of interest, just as a tree grows by the unobserved lapse of time, " crescit occulto velut arbor aevo," *Odes* i. 12. 45. The idea that *occulto* here means " secret, ' in the sense of " unlawful," is absurd.

fecerit auspicium, " cras ferramenta Teanum
tolletis, fabri ! " lectus genialis in aula est :
nil ait esse prius, melius nil caelibe vita ;
si non est, iurat bene solis esse maritis.
quo teneam voltus mutantem Protea nodo ?   90
quid pauper ? ride : mutat cenacula, lectos,
balnea, tonsores, conducto navigio aeque
nauseat ac locuples, quem ducit priva triremis.

   Si curatus inaequali tonsore capillos
occurri,[1] rides ; si forte subucula pexae   95
trita subest tunicae, vel si toga dissidet impar,
rides : quid, mea cum pugnat sententia secum,[2]
quod petiit spernit, repetit quod nuper omisit,
aestuat et vitae disconvenit ordine toto,
diruit, aedificat, mutat quadrata rotundis ?   100
insanire putas[3] sollemnia me neque rides,
nec medici credis nec curatoris egere
a praetore dati, rerum tutela mearum
cum sis et prave sectum stomacheris ob unguem
de te pendentis, te respicientis amici.   105

   Ad summam : sapiens uno minor est Iove, dives,
liber, honoratus, pulcher, rex denique regum,
praecipue sanus, nisi cum pituita molesta est.

----

[1] occurrit or occurro.   [2] mecum $R\delta\pi$ Goth.
              [3] putas, I Porph. : putat, II.

---

   [a] The usual way to consult the auspices would be to observe
the flight of birds and other means of augury, but the rich
man's own caprice is a sufficient guide for him.   Cf. " an sua
cuique deus fit dira cupido ? " (Virgil, Aen. ix. 185).   Teanum
was an inland town.

omen,[a] " My lads," he cries, " to-morrow you'll carry your tools to Teanum." Is the bed of his Genius [b] in his hall ? " Nothing," he says, " is finer or better than a single life." If it is not, he swears that only the married are well off. With what knot can I hold this face-changing Proteus ? What of the poor man ? Have your laugh ! He changes his garret, his bed, his baths, his barber. He hires a boat and gets just as sick as the rich man who sails in his private yacht.

94 If, when some uneven barber has cropped my hair, I come your way, you laugh ; if haply I have a tattered shirt beneath a new tunic, or if my gown sits badly and askew, you laugh. What, when my judgement is at strife with itself, scorns what it craved, asks again for what it lately cast aside ; when it shifts like a tide, and in the whole system of life is out of joint, pulling down, building up, and changing square to round ? You think my madness is the usual thing, and neither laugh at me nor deem that I need a physician or a guardian assigned by the court,[c] though you are keeper of my fortunes, and flare up at an ill-pared nail of the friend who hangs upon you and looks to you in all.

106 To sum up [d] : the wise man is less than Jove alone. He is rich, free, honoured, beautiful, nay a king of kings ; above all, sound [e] — save when troubled by the " flu " !

---

[b] The marriage-bed was dedicated to the Genius of the family.

[c] Cf. Sat. ii. 3. 217.

[d] Cf. Sat. i. 3. 124 and ff.

[e] Horace plays upon the double sense of *sanus*, " sound " and " sane."

II

TO LOLLIUS MAXIMUS

THE poem is addressed to a young man who is studying rhetoric in Rome, and who, if he is the same Lollius as is addressed in Epistle i. 18, had already served in the Cantabrian war of 25-24 B.C. Horace seeks to interest him in moral philosophy through Homer, whom the ancients perused, as we are told to read the *Apocrypha*, " for examples of life and instruction of manners."

The poet has been reading Homer afresh while in Praeneste, and pronounces him a wiser teacher than all the philosophers. The *Iliad* pictures for us the follies of princes and the sufferings of the people. The *Odyssey* shows us the value of courage and self-control. Ulysses is the truly wise man, in contrast with whom the worthless suitors of Penelope or the idle youth at the court of Alcinous are but ciphers, the undistinguished mass of mankind, mere consumers of earth's products (1-31).

And such ciphers are we. Surely it is time for us to wake up to the importance of right living and devote ourselves to study and virtue. To put off the day of reform is to be like the clown who waits for the stream to run dry (32-43).

Men are eager to become rich, but riches will not

bring health, either of body or of mind. We must clean the inside of the platter and make our hearts sound (44-54).

And so, in a Polonius strain, Horace gives a variety of moral maxims. In this quest of wisdom, the middle-aged poet must pursue his own quiet way, and the youthful Lollius must not expect him to be either too indifferent or too enthusiastic (55-71).

II.

Troiani belli scriptorem, Maxime Lolli,
dum tu declamas Romae, Praeneste relegi ;
qui quid sit pulchrum, quid turpe, quid utile, quid non,
planius[1] ac melius Chrysippo et Crantore dicit.
cur ita crediderim, nisi quid te distinet,[2] audi.   5

Fabula, qua Paridis propter narratur amorem
Graecia barbariae lento collisa duello,
stultorum regum et populorum continet aestus.[3]
Antenor censet belli[4] praecidere causam :
quid[5] Paris ? ut salvus regnet vivatque beatus   10
cogi posse negat.   Nestor componere litis
inter Peliden festinat et inter Atriden ;
hunc[6] amor, ira quidem communiter urit utrumque.
quidquid delirant reges, plectuntur Achivi.
seditione, dolis, scelere atque libidine et ira   15
Iliacos intra muros peccatur et extra.

Rursus, quid virtus et quid sapientia possit,
utile proposuit nobis exemplar Ulixen,

[1] plenius, *II*.
[2] distinet, *II E*[1] : destinet *a* : detinet *E*[2]*M*.
[3] aestum *V, II*.   [4] belli censet *E*.
[5] quod, *II*: *hence Bentley* quod Paris, ut.   [6] nunc.

---

[a] *i.e.* study rhetoric under a *rhetor*, or professor who
made his pupils prepare speeches on the themes given them
and often taken from history or literature ; *cf.* Juvenal vii.
150 ; x. 166.

EPISTLE II

While you, Lollius Maximus, declaim [a] at Rome,
I have been reading afresh at Praeneste the writer
of the Trojan War; who tells us what is fair, what
is foul, what is helpful, what not, more plainly and
better than Chrysippus or Crantor. Why I have
come to think so, let me tell you, unless there is
something else to take your attention.

[6] The story in which it is told how, because of
Paris's love Greece clashed in tedious war with a
foreign land, embraces the passions of foolish kings
and peoples. Antenor moves to cut away the cause
of the war.[b] What of Paris? To reign in safety
and to live in happiness—nothing, he says, can force
him.[c] Nestor is eager to settle the strife between
the sons of Peleus and of Atreus. Love fires one,
but anger both in common. Whatever folly the
kings commit, the Achaeans pay the penalty. With
faction, craft, crime, lust and wrath, within and
without the walls of Troy all goes wrong.

[17] Again, of the power of worth and wisdom he
has set before us an instructive pattern in Ulysses,

[b] Cf. *Iliad*, vii. 350, where Antenor urges that the Trojans
restore Helen to the Atridae.

[c] This is, of course, ironical. If we read *quod Paris, ut* with
Bentley, it would go with *cogi*, so that, without any irony,
Paris would say that he could not be forced into doing that,
viz. giving up Helen, in order to reign in safety.

263

qui domitor Troiae multorum providus urbes
et mores hominum inspexit, latumque per aequor,   20
dum sibi, dum sociis reditum parat, aspera multa
pertulit, adversis rerum immersabilis undis.
Sirenum voces et Circae pocula nosti ;
quae si cum sociis stultus cupidusque bibisset,
sub domina meretrice fuisset turpis et excors,   25
vixisset canis immundus vel amica luto sus.
nos numerus sumus et fruges consumere nati,
sponsi Penelopae nebulones, Alcinoique
in cute curanda plus aequo operata iuventus,
cui pulchrum fuit in medios dormire dies et   30
ad strepitum citharae cessatum ducere curam.[1]

  Ut iugulent hominem, surgunt de nocte latrones ;
ut te ipsum serves, non expergisceris ?   atqui[2]
si noles[3] sanus, curres[4] hydropicus ; et ni
posces ante diem librum cum lumine, si non   35
intendes animum studiis et rebus honestis,
invidia vel amore vigil torquebere.   nam cur
quae laedunt oculum[5] festinas demere ; si quid[6]
est animum, differs curandi tempus in annum ?
dimidium facti qui coepit habet ; sapere aude ;   40
incipe !   qui recte vivendi[7] prorogat horam,
rusticus exspectat dum defluat amnis ; at ille
labitur et labetur in omne volubilis aevum.

  Quaeritur argentum puerisque beata creandis
uxor, et incultae pacantur vomere silvae :   45

---

[1] curam, *I*: somnum *Eπ Goth. Bentley read* cessantem
ducere somnum. *W. R. Inge suggests* cessantem ducere
noctem (*C.R.* 1921, p. 103).
    [2] atque, *II, V.*   [3] nolis λ*l.*   [4] cures, *II*; *so Bentley.*
    [5] oculum *E, II* : oculos *aM Goth.*   [6] si quod *φψλl.*
    [7] qui recte vivendi *E Goth., Porph.* : vivendi qui recte
other MSS.

that tamer of Troy, who looked with discerning eyes upon the cities and manners of many men, and while for self and comrades he strove for a return across the broad seas, many hardships he endured, but could never be o'erwhelmed in the waves of adversity.[a] You know the Sirens' songs and Circe's cups; if, along with his comrades, he had drunk of these in folly and greed, he would have become the shapeless and witless vassal of a harlot mistress—would have lived as an unclean dog or a sow that loves the mire. We are but ciphers, born to consume earth's fruits, Penelope's good-for-naught suitors, young courtiers of Alcinous, unduly busy in keeping their skins sleek, whose pride it was to sleep till midday and to lull care to rest to the sound of the cithern.

[32] To cut men's throats, robbers rise up by night; to save your own life, won't you wake up? Nay, just as, if you won't take up running in health, you'll have to do it when dropsical; so, if you don't call for a book and a light before daybreak, if you don't devote your mind to honourable studies and pursuits, envy or passion will keep you awake in torment. Why indeed are you in a hurry to remove things which hurt the eye, while if aught is eating into your soul, you put off the time for cure till next year? Well begun is half done; dare to be wise; begin! He who puts off the hour of right living is like the bumpkin waiting for the river to run out: yet on it glides, and on it will glide, rolling its flood forever.

[44] We seek money and a rich wife to bear us children; the wild woods, too, are tamed by our

---

[a] This sentence gives a free rendering of the opening lines of the *Odyssey*.

quod satis est cui contingit,[1] nihil amplius optet.
non domus et fundus, non aeris acervus et auri
aegroto domini deduxit corpore febris,
non animo curas ; valeat possessor oportet,
si comportatis rebus bene cogitat uti.   50
qui cupit aut metuit, iuvat illum sic domus et res,
ut lippum pictae tabulae, fomenta[2] podagram,
auriculas citharae collecta sorde dolentis.
sincerum est nisi vas, quodcumque infundis acescit.

  Sperne voluptates ; nocet empta dolore voluptas.
semper avarus eget ; certum voto pete finem.   56
invidus alterius macrescit rebus opimis ;
invidia Siculi non invenere tyranni
maius tormentum. qui non moderabitur irae,[3]
infectum volet esse, dolor quod suaserit et mens,[4]   60
dum poenas odio per vim festinat inulto.
ira furor brevis est : animum rege ; qui nisi paret
imperat ; hunc frenis, hunc tu compesce catena.[5]

  Fingit equum tenera docilem cervice magister
ire viam qua[6] monstret eques ; venaticus, ex quo   65
tempore cervinam pellem latravit in aula,
militat in silvis catulus. nunc adbibe puro
pectore verba puer, nunc te melioribus offer.
quo semel est imbuta recens, servabit odorem
testa diu. quod si cessas aut strenuus anteis,   70
nec tardum opperior nec praecedentibus insto.

---

  [1] contigit is V^2.   [2] tomenta *Bouhier*.   [3] iram, *II*.
    [4] et mens] exmens *or* amens.
      [5] catenis *E Goth*.   [6] qua *E* : quam *a*.

---

  [a] Such as the cruel Dionysius or Phalaris.
  [b] *Cf.* "sapor, quo nova imbuas, durat" (Quintilian, i. 1. 5).
Unglazed ware, which Horace doubtless has in mind, is
more absorbent than glazed.

plough: but he, to whose lot sufficient falls, should covet nothing more. No house or land, no pile of bronze or gold, has ever freed the owner's sick body of fevers, or his sick mind of cares. The possessor must be sound in health, if he thinks of enjoying the stores he has gathered. To one with fears or cravings, house and fortune give as much pleasure as painted panels to sore eyes, warm wraps to the gout, or citherns to ears that suffer from secreted matter. Unless the vessel is clean, whatever you pour in turns sour.

[55] Scorn pleasures; pleasure bought with pain is harmful. The covetous is ever in want: aim at a fixed limit for your desires. The envious man grows lean when his neighbour waxes fat; than envy Sicilian tyrants [a] invented no worse torture. He who curbs not his anger will wish that undone which vexation and wrath prompted, as he made haste with violence to gratify his unsated hatred. Anger is short-lived madness. Rule your passion, for unless it obeys, it gives commands. Check it with bridle— check it, I pray you, with chains.

[64] While the colt has a tender neck and is able to learn, the groom trains him to go the way his rider directs. The hound that is to hunt does service in the woods from the time that it first barked at a deer-skin in the yard. Now, while still a boy, drink in my words with clean heart, now trust yourself to your betters. The jar will long keep the fragrance of what it was once steeped in when new.[b] But if you lag behind, or with vigour push on ahead, I neither wait for the slow nor press after those who hurry on before.

III

TO JULIUS FLORUS

THE Julius Florus, to whom this Epistle is addressed, and to whom Epistle ii. 2 is later dedicated, was one of a number of young literary men who accompanied Tiberius to the East in 20 B.C., when the prince was sent by Augustus to place Tigranes on the throne of Armenia after the murder of Artaxias. Horace, now forty-five years old, makes kindly inquiries about his younger literary friends, and urges Florus, whatever field of letters he is cultivating, not to neglect philosophy.

III.

Iuli Flore, quibus terrarum militet oris
Claudius Augusti privignus, scire laboro.
Thracane[1] vos Hebrusque nivali compede vinctus,
an freta vicinas inter currentia turris,[2]
an pingues Asiae campi collesque morantur ?   5
  Quid studiosa cohors operum struit ?   hoc quoque
    curo.
quis sibi res gestas Augusti scribere sumit ?
bella quis et paces longum diffundit in aevum ?
quid Titius, Romana brevi venturus in ora ?
Pindarici fontis qui non expalluit haustus,   10
fastidire lacus et rivos ausus apertos.
ut valet ?   ut meminit nostri ?   fidibusne Latinis
Thebanos aptare modos studet auspice Musa,
an tragica desaevit et ampullatur in arte ?
quid mihi Celsus agit ?   monitus multumque monen-
    dus,   15
privatas ut quaerat opes et tangere vitet

¹ Threcane *E*.
² terras *V*: terres δ^1: terris R^1.

  ᵃ *i.e.* Tiberius Claudius Nero, later the Emperor Tiberius.
  ᵇ The towers of Hero and Leander, at Sestos and Abydos,
on either side of the Hellespont.
  ᶜ In *lacos et rivos apertos* Horace refers to the artificial
pools and tanks from which anyone could draw water, as
contrasted with the natural springs in far distant hills, which

Epistle III

I long to know, Julius Florus, in what regions of
the earth Claudius,[a] step-son of Augustus, is now
campaigning.   Does Thrace stay your steps, and
Hebrus, bound in snowy fetters, or the straits that
run between neighbouring towers,[b] or Asia's fertile
plains and hills ?

[6] What works is the learned staff composing ?
This, too, I want to know.   Who takes upon him to
record the exploits of Augustus ?   Who adown dis-
tant ages makes known his deeds in war and peace ?
What of Titius, soon to be on the lips of Romans, who
quailed not at draughts of the Pindaric spring, but
dared to scorn the open [c] pools and streams ?   How
fares he ?   How mindful is he of me ?   Does he essay,
under favour of the Muse, to fit Theban measures to
the Latin lyre ?   Or does he storm and swell [d] in the
tragic art ?   What, pray, is Celsus doing ?   He was
warned, and must often be warned to search for
home treasures, and to shrink from touching the

one could reach only with difficulty.   Apart from the
metaphor, the contrast is between those Greek writers who
could easily be reproduced, and the inimitable Pindar.   For
the latter idea *cf. Odes*, iv. 2, " Pindarum quisquis studet
aemulari," etc.

[d] The word *ampullatur*, translating ληκυθίζει, is from
ampulla, a flask, the swelling body of which led to the use
of the word for *bombast*.   *Cf. Ars Poet.* 97.

271

scripta Palatinus quaecumque recepit Apollo,
ne, si forte suas repetitum venerit olim
grex avium plumas, moveat cornicula[1] risum
furtivis nudata coloribus. ipse quid audes ?   20
quae circumvolitas agilis thyma ?   non tibi parvum
ingenium, non incultum est et[2] turpiter hirtum.
seu linguam causis acuis seu civica iura
respondere[3] paras seu condis amabile carmen,
prima feres hederae victricis praemia.   quod si   25
frigida curarum fomenta relinquere posses,
quo te caelestis sapientia duceret, ires.[4]
hoc opus, hoc studium parvi properemus et ampli,
si patriae volumus, si nobis vivere cari.

Debes hoc etiam rescribere, sit[5] tibi curae   30
quantae conveniat Munatius ; an male sarta
gratia nequiquam coit et rescinditur ?   at[6] vos
seu calidus sanguis seu[7] rerum inscitia vexat
indomita cervice feros, ubicumque locorum
vivitis, indigni fraternum rumpere foedus,   35
pascitur in vestrum reditum votiva iuvenca.

---

[1] vulpecula *Servius on* Aen. xi. 522.

[2] nec φψλ.   [3] responsare *E.*

[4] *Hitzig would transpose ll.* 26, 27 *with each other, perhaps correctly.*

[5] si δ : *hence* si tibi curae est *Bentley, Orelli.*

[6] ac MSS.   [7] seu . . . seu *Acron :* heu . . . heu MSS.

---

a Celsus is urged to depend more upon himself, instead of drawing so freely upon earlier writers, whose works he consulted in the library of the temple of Apollo on the Palatine.

b Strictly speaking, the ivy applies only to the poet. For this *cf. Odes,* i. 1. 29.

writings which Apollo on the Palatine has admitted [a] : lest, if some day perchance the flock of birds come to reclaim their plumage, the poor crow, stripped of his stolen colours, awake laughter. And yourself— what do you venture on ? About what beds of thyme are you busily flitting ? No small gift is yours : not untilled is the field, or rough-grown and unsightly. Whether you sharpen your tongue for pleading, or essay to give advice on civil law, or build charming verse, you will win the first prize of the victor's ivy.[b] But could you but lay aside your cares—those cold compresses [c]—you would rise to where heavenly wisdom would lead. This task, this pursuit let us speed, small and great alike, if we would live dear to our country, and dear to ourselves.

[30] This, too, when you reply, you must tell me— whether you esteem Munatius as much as you should. Or does your friendship, like a wound ill-stitched, close vainly and tear open once more ? Yet, whether hot blood or ignorance of the world drives you both, wild steeds with untamed necks, wherever on earth you are living—you who are too good to break the bond of brotherhood—a votive heifer is fattening against your return.

[c] Horace seems to mean that the cares which weigh upon Florus are like the cold bandages which physicians in his day were prescribing for certain bodily ailments, cf. Suet. *Aug.* 81. The *curae* chilled the fire of inspiration, and were therefore far from beneficial, because Florus was continually wrapping himself up in his troubles. Some, however, prefer to take *curarum* as an objective genitive, so that *curarum fomenta* means " remedies against cares."

IV

TO ALBIUS TIBULLUS

Albius Tibullus, the elegiac poet, who died the same year as Virgil, 19 B.C., when still quite young, had returned from a campaign in Aquitania in 27 B.C., and then perhaps read for the first time the *Satires* of Horace. As the first verse of this Epistle refers only to the *Satires* and not to the *Odes*, this short letter seems to have been written before 23 B.C., when the *Odes* (Books i.-iii.) were published.

Tibullus seems to have been of a sensitive and somewhat melancholy disposition, like the English poet, Thomas Gray. Horace here tries to divert him, and concludes with an invitation to visit him, a prosperous Epicurean, at his Sabine farm.

The commonly accepted view that the Albius here addressed by Horace is the poet Tibullus has been rejected by Cruquius, Baehrens and, more recently, by Professor J. P. Postgate (*Selections from Tibullus*, 1903, p. 179). The identity of Albius and Tibullus is upheld by Professor B. L. Ullman in an article on "Horace and Tibullus" in the *American Journal of Philology*, xxxiii. (1912) pp. 149 ff., to which Professor Postgate replies briefly in the same volume, pp. 450 ff. Ullman also holds that Tibullus is the *Albi filius* of *Sat.* i. 4. 109, written when Tibullus was about sixteen years of age.

IV.

Albi, nostrorum sermonum candide iudex,
quid nunc te dicam facere in regione Pedana?
scribere quod Cassi Parmensis opuscula vincat,
an tacitum silvas inter reptare salubris,
curantem quidquid dignum sapiente bonoque[1] est? 5
non tu corpus eras sine pectore : di tibi formam,
di tibi divitias dederunt[2] artemque fruendi.
quid voveat dulci nutricula maius alumno,
qui[3] sapere et fari possit quae sentiat, et cui
gratia, fama, valetudo contingat abunde,   10
et mundus[4] victus non deficiente crumina?

    Inter spem curamque, timores inter et iras[5]
omnem crede diem tibi diluxisse supremum.
grata superveniet, quae non sperabitur hora.
me pinguem et nitidum bene curata cute vises,   15
cum ridere voles, Epicuri de[6] grege porcum.

[1] bonumque *Rπ*.   [2] dederant *EM*.
    [3] qui *EV Porph.* : quin *a, II* : qun *M*.
  [4] mundus, *I* : modus et, *II* : domus et *Bentley*.
 [5] tumores . . . iram *E*.   [6] cum *E*.

---

a i.e. the Satires. The word *Sermones* means " talks,"

Epistle IV

Albius, impartial critic of my " chats," [a] what shall I say you now are doing in your country at Pedum ? Writing something to outshine the pieces of Cassius of Parma[b] ?   Or strolling peacefully amid the healthful woods, and musing on all that is worthy of one wise and good ?   Never were you a body without soul.   The gods gave you beauty, the gods gave you wealth, and the art of enjoyment.[c]   For what more would a fond nurse pray for her sweet ward, if he could think aright and utter his thoughts—if favour, fame, and health fall to him richly, with a seemly living and a never failing purse ?

Amid hopes and cares, amid fears and passions, believe that every day that has dawned is your last. Welcome will come to you another hour unhoped for. As for me, when you want a laugh, you will find me in fine fettle, fat and sleek, a hog from Epicurus's herd.

" conversations," and was adopted by Horace for his *Satires*. See Introduction B, note *a*.

[b] The scholiasts identify him with Cassius Etruscus of *Sat*. i. 10. 61. So too Ullman, *loc. cit.* p. 164.

[c] If Ullman's view is correct, Horace is here contrasting the son Albius with the father of the same name.

V

TO TORQUATUS

HORACE here invites to a simple dinner, on the eve of the birthday of Augustus, a member of the wealthy family of the Manlii Torquati, probably the same as the one to whom the seventh ode of the Fourth Book is later addressed. Torquatus is asked to bring some guests.

As to the hour set for the dinner Porphyrio explains *supremo sole* (l. 3) as meaning *hora sexta*, *i.e.* midday, and Professor A. J. Bell favours this interpretation (*Classical Review*, xxix. (1915) p. 200. But Horace's simple dinner is quite unlike the extravagant one given by Nasidienus, which began *de medio die* (*Sat.* ii. 8. 3), and people who have spent a hot September in Rome will not think it likely that the sensitive poet would have invited his guests to come at high noon in that unpleasant month. As to the last two lines Torquatus is presumably a busy lawyer, and some of his clients might have to wait till late in the day in order to consult him. If so, this would be another reason why Horace would not expect his friend to come before evening. Maecenas, also a busy man, dined *sub lumina prima* (*Sat.* ii. 7. 33).

V.

Si potes Archiacis conviva recumbere lectis
nec modica cenare times holus omne patella,
supremo te sole domi, Torquate, manebo.
vina bibes iterum Tauro diffusa palustris
inter Minturnas Sinuessanumque Petrinum.   5
si melius quid habes, arcesse, vel imperium fer.
iamdudum splendet focus et tibi munda supellex.
mitte levis spes et certamina divitiarum
et Moschi causam : cras nato Caesare festus
dat veniam somnumque dies ; impune licebit   10
aestivam[1] sermone benigno tendere noctem.

Quo mihi fortunam,[2] si non conceditur uti ?
parcus ob heredis curam nimiumque severus
adsidet insano.   potare et spargere flores
incipiam, patiarque vel inconsultus haberi.   15
quid non ebrietas dissignat[3] ?   operta recludit,

[1] festivam.   [2] fortuna R : fortunas.   [3] designat $a\phi$ *Goth.*

a Archias was a maker of unpretentious furniture.
According to Porphyrio his couches were small ones.
See note on l. 29.

b 26 B.C.   At that time the wine had been poured from
the large *dolium* into the smaller *amphorae*.

c According to the Scholiasts, Moschus, a rhetorician
from Pergamum, was accused of poisoning, and defended
by Torquatus as well as by Asinius Pollio.

d September 23.   September is one of the warmest months
in Rome.

e In *dissignare* the original idea of *sealing* seems to be

280

EPISTLE V

If you can recline at my table on couches made
by Archias,[a] and are not afraid of " a dinner of
herbs " only, from a modest dish, I shall expect you,
Torquatus, at my house at sunset. You will drink
wine that was bottled in Taurus's second consulate [b]
between marshy Minturnae and Petrinum near
Sinuessa. If you have aught better, bid it be sent, or
submit to orders. Long has my hearth been bright,
and the furniture made neat for you. Dismiss airy
hopes and the struggle for wealth, and Moschus's
cause.[c] To-morrow, the festal day of Caesar's birth,[d]
gives excuse for sleeping late ; without penalty shall
we be free to prolong the summer night in genial
converse.

[12] Why is fortune mine, if I may not use it ? He
who, from regard to his heir, pinches and spares
vermuch is next door to a madman. I shall begin
the drinking and the scattering of flowers, and shall
suffer you, if you will, to think me reckless. What
miracle cannot the wine-cup work ! [e] It unlocks

egatived by the prefix *dis-*, and to "unseal" (a verb
appropriately used in the present connexion) signifies
according to Porphyrio) to "open," *i.e.* reveal something.
Hence it is used of any strange effect. *Cf.* Terence,
delphoe, 87, "modo quid dissignavit ? " " What out-of-
the-way thing has he now done ? " For the general thought
. Od. iii. 21. 13 ff.

spes iubet esse ratas, ad proelia trudit inertem,[1]
sollicitis animis onus eximit, addocet[2] artes.
fecundi[3] calices quem non fecere disertum ?
contracta quem non in paupertate solutum ?   20

    Haec ego procurare et idoneus imperor et non
invitus, ne turpe toral, ne sordida mappa
corruget naris, ne non et cantharus et lanx
ostendat tibi te, ne fidos inter amicos
sit qui dicta foras eliminet, ut[4] coeat par   25
iungaturque pari.

        Butram tibi Septiciumque,
et nisi cena prior potiorque puella Sabinum
detinet, adsumam.[5] locus est et pluribus umbris :
sed nimis arta premunt olidae convivia caprae.
tu quotus esse velis rescribe et rebus omissis   30
atria servantem postico falle clientem.

[1] inermem *aM*.

[2] et docet *E*.   [3] facundi *Eδπ Vollmer*.
[4] et φψλl.   [5] ad summam *a, II*.

[a] See note on *Sat.* ii. 8. 22.
[b] This unsavoury detail is meant to be jocular, but as i

secrets, bids hopes be fulfilled, thrusts the coward
into the field, takes the load from anxious hearts,
teaches new arts. The flowing bowl—whom has it
not made eloquent ? Whom has it not made free
even amid pinching poverty ?

²¹ Here is what I charge myself to provide—and
able and willing I am : that no untidy coverlet, no
soiled napkin wrinkle up your nose ; that tankard
and plate become for you a mirror ; that there be
none to carry abroad what is said among faithful
friends ; that like may meet and mate with like.

²⁶ Butra and Septicius I shall have to meet you,
and Sabinus, unless a better supper and a goodlier
girl detain him. There is room, too, for several
" shades " ᵃ ; but the reek of goats makes too
crowded feasts unpleasant.ᵇ Write back, pray, how
many you would like us to be ; then drop your
business, and by the back-door give the slip to the
client waiting in your hall.

was the warm season Horace does not want his small couches
to be too crowded.

VI

TO NUMICIUS

NOTHING is known about the person to whom this letter is addressed, but the ideas expressed in it have made it one of the most famous of Horace's epistles.

The key-note is struck in the opening phrase, *nil admirari*, a rendering of the τὸ μηδὲν θαυμάζειν of Pythagoras, or of ἡ ἀθαυμαστία of philosophers in general (Strabo, i. 3. 21). This ἀθαυμαστία, identical with the ἀθαμβία of Democritus (Cic. *De fin*. v. 29. 87), the ἀταραξία of the Epicureans, and the ἀπάθεια of the Stoics, is a philosophic calm, a composure of mind and feeling, a freedom from exciting emotions, which ancient philosophy often regarded as the *summum bonum* and which Tennyson defines so well in his *Lucretius* :

> O thou,
> Passionless bride, divine Tranquillity,
> Yearn'd after by the wisest of the wise,
> Who fail to find thee, being as thou art
> Without one pleasure and without one pain.

This " wise indifference," says Horace, is perhaps the only clue to happiness. If men can gaze unmoved on the wonders of the firmament, they can surely look calmly upon things of less moment, such

284

as wealth and honours, neither craving their rewards nor fearing their loss. " Nothing in excess " should be one's rule even in the pursuit of Virtue. And bear in mind that, however much you may long for treasures of art, for fame and wealth, death must be the end of all (1-27).

You think I am wrong ? If you are ill, you take medicine ; if you want to " live well," and know that Virtue alone can give you that boon, follow her at all costs. If, on the contrary, you think Virtue a mere name, then make haste to get rich. Be not like the Cappadocian king, who was so poor, but rather be like Lucullus, who didn't know how wealthy he was (28-48).

If you have set your heart on office and honours, stoop to all the tricks of the politicians (49-55). If " living well " means for you good eating (56-64) or love and pleasure (65, 66), then think of nothing else.

Such are my views. Have you anything better to offer ? (67, 68).

VI.

Nil admirari prope res est una, Numici,
solaque quae possit facere et servare beatum.
hunc solem et stellas et decedentia certis
tempora momentis sunt qui formidine nulla
imbuti spectent : quid censes munera terrae,   5
quid maris extremos Arabas ditantis et Indos,
ludicra quid, plausus et amici dona Quiritis,
quo spectanda modo, quo sensu credis et ore ?

Qui timet his adversa, fere miratur eodem
quo cupiens pacto : pavor est utrobique molestus,   10
improvisa simul species exterret utrumque.[1]
gaudeat an doleat, cupiat metuatne, quid ad rem,
si, quicquid vidit melius peiusve[2] sua spe,
defixis oculis animoque et corpore torpet ?
insani sapiens nomen ferat, aequus iniqui,   15
ultra quam satis est Virtutem si petat[3] ipsam.

I nunc, argentum et marmor vetus aeraque et artes
suspice,[4] cum gemmis Tyrios mirare colores ;
gaude quod spectant[5] oculi te mille loquentem ;
navus mane forum et vespertinus pete tectum,   20
ne plus frumenti dotalibus emetat agris
Mutus et (indignum, quod sit peioribus ortus)

---

[1] exterret (-it *R*) utrumque, *II*: *most editors* exterruit
utrum *aE*.
[2] peiusne *Rδ*.   [3] petet *aM*.
[4] suspice *Eλlπ*.   [5] spectent *E*.

286

Epistle VI

" Marvel at nothing "—that is perhaps the one
and only thing, Numicius, that can make a man
happy and keep him so. Yon sun, the stars and
seasons that pass in fixed courses—some can gaze
upon these with no strain of fear : what think you of
the gifts of earth, or what of the sea's, which makes
rich far distant Arabs and Indians—what of the shows,
the plaudits and the favours of the friendly Roman
—in what wise, with what feelings and eyes think
you they should be viewed ?

⁹ And he who fears their opposites " marvels " in
much the same way as the man who desires : in either
case 'tis the excitement that annoys, the moment some
unexpected appearance startles either. Whether
a man feel joy or grief, desire or fear, what matters
it if, when he has seen aught better or worse than
he expected, his eyes are fast riveted, and mind and
body are benumbed ? Let the wise man bear the
name of madman, the just of unjust, should he
pursue Virtue herself beyond due bounds.

¹⁷ Go now, gaze with rapture on silver plate,
antique marble, bronzes and works of art ; " marvel "
at gems and Tyrian dyes ; rejoice that a thousand
eyes survey you as you speak ; in your diligence get
you to the Forum early, to your home late, lest
Mutus reap more grain from the lands of his wife's
dower, and (oh the shame, for he sprang from meaner

hic tibi sit potius quam tu mirabilis illi.
quidquid sub terra est, in apricum proferet[1] aetas,
defodiet condetque nitentia. cum bene notum   25
porticus Agrippae, via te[2] conspexerit Appi,
ire tamen restat Numa quo devenit et Ancus.

   Si latus aut renes morbo temptantur acuto,
quaere fugam morbi. vis recte vivere : quis non ?
si Virtus hoc una potest dare, fortis omissis   30
hoc age deliciis.

          Virtutem verba putas[3] et
lucum ligna : cave ne portus occupet alter,
ne Cibyratica, ne Bithyna negotia perdas ;
mille talenta rotundentur, totidem altera, porro et[4]
tertia succedant et quae pars quadret[5] acervum.   35
scilicet uxorem cum dote fidemque et amicos
et genus et formam regina Pecunia donat,
ac bene nummatum decorat Suadela Venusque.
mancupiis locuples eget aeris Cappadocum rex :
ne[6] fueris hic tu. chlamydes Lucullus, ut aiunt,   40
si posset centum scaenae praebere rogatus,
" qui possum tot ? " ait ; " tamen et quaeram et quot
    habebo
mittam : " post paulo scribit sibi milia quinque
esse domi chlamydum ; partem vel tolleret omnis.
exilis domus est, ubi non et multa supersunt   45
et dominum fallunt et prosunt furibus. ergo

---

   [1] proferat *a M*.   [2] et via, *II*.
 [3] putes $A^2 \delta$ *Bentley*.   [4] et *omitted a M δ*.
   [5] quadrat *a M*.   [6] nec *E*.

---

   [a] Both were frequented by the fashionable world. The
portico of Agrippa, near the Pantheon, was opened in 25 B.C.
For the Appian Way *cf. Epode* iv. 14 and *Sat.* i. 5. 6.
   [b] This is a proverbial expression, applicable to the material-

stock !) lest you " marvel " at him rather than he at
you. Time will bring into the light whatever is
under the earth ; it will bury deep and hide what
now shines bright. When Agrippa's colonnade, when
Appius's way *a* has looked upon your well-known
form, still it remains for you to go where Numa and
Ancus have gone down before.

28 If your chest or reins are assailed by a sharp
disease, seek a remedy for the disease. You wish
to live aright (and who does not ?) ; if then Virtue
alone can confer this boon, boldly drop trifles and
set to work !

31 Do you think Virtue but words, and a forest *b* but
firewood ? Take care lest your rival make harbour
first, lest you lose your ventures from Cibyra and
Bithynia. Suppose you round off a thousand talents ;
as many in a second lot ; then add a third thousand,
and enough to square the heap. Of course a wife
and dowry, credit and friends, birth and beauty, are
the gift of Queen Cash, and the goddesses Persuasion
and Venus grace the man who is well-to-do. The
Cappadocian king *c* is rich in slaves, but lacks coin :
be not like him. Lucullus, 'tis said, was asked if he
could lend a hundred cloaks for the stage. " How
can I so many ? " he answers, " yet I'll look and send
as many as I have." A little later he writes : " I
have five thousand cloaks at home ; take some or
all." Poor is the house where there's not much to
spare, much that escapes the master and profits his

ists of the day, who were ready to cut down even sacred
groves.
c Viz. Ariobarzanes, of whom Cicero says, "erat rex
perpauper" (*Ad Att.* vi. 3). For Lucullus see Plutarch's
Lives. Lucullus. ch. 39. Horace expands the story somewhat.

si res sola potest facere et servare beatum,
hoc primus[1] repetas opus, hoc postremus omittas.

Si fortunatum species et gratia praestat,
mercemur servum, qui dictet nomina, laevum[2]   50
qui fodicet latus et cogat trans pondera[3] dextram
porrigere : " hic[4] multum in Fabia valet, ille Velina ;
cui libet hic fasces dabit eripietque curule
cui volet importunus ebur." " frater," " pater "adde :
ut cuique est aetas, ita quemque facetus adopta.[5]   55

Si bene qui cenat bene vivit, lucet, eamus
quo ducit gula ; piscemur, venemur, ut olim
Gargilius, qui mane plagas, venabula, servos
differtum transire[6] forum populumque[7] iubebat,
unus ut e multis populo spectante referret   60
emptum mulus aprum.   crudi tumidique lavemur,
quid deceat, quid non, obliti, Caerite cera
digni, remigium vitiosum Ithacensis Ulixei,
cui potior patria[8] fuit interdicta voluptas.
si, Mimnermus uti censet, sine amore iocisque   65
nil est iucundum, vivas in amore iocisque.

Vive, vale ! si quid novisti rectius istis,
candidus imperti ; si nil,[9] his utere mecum.

[1] primum, _II._
[2] laevum _E_ : saevum (_i.e._ scaevum) _aM, II_ ; _so Pithoeus._
[3] pondere, _II._   [4] his _or_ is $R\delta\pi$.
[5] adapta $\phi\psi\lambda l$.   [6] transferre _Goth._
[7] campum _Bentley._   patriae, _II._   [9] non, _II._

_a_ A slave, called _nomenclator_, had the duty of informing
his master of the names of people he did not know.
_b_ The scholiasts explain _pondera_ as the term applied to
the high stepping-stones used for crossing the streets as
may be seen in Pompeii.   Horace, therefore, is picturing
the ambitious politicians as hurrying over these to greet
a voter on the other side of the street.   Other interpretations,

knaves. So if wealth alone can make you happy and keep you so, be the first to go back to this task, the last to leave it off.

⁴⁹ If pomp and popularity make the fortunate man, let us buy a slave to call off names,ᵃ to nudge our left side, and make us stretch out the hand across the streets.ᵇ " This man has much influence in the Fabian tribe ; that in the Veline. This man will give the fasces to whom he will, or, if churlish, will snatch the curule ivory from whom he pleases." Throw in " Brother ! " " Father ! "—politely adopt each one according to his age.

⁵⁶ If he who dines well, lives well, then—'tis daybreak, let's be off, whither the palate guides us. Let us fish, let us hunt, like Gargilius in the story. At dawn of day he would bid his slaves with hunting-nets and spears pass through the throng in the crowded Forum, that in the sight of that same throng one mule of all the train might bring home a boar he had purchased. While gorged with undigested food, let us bathe, forgetful of what is or is not seemly, deserving to have our place in the Caere class,ᶜ like the wicked crew of Ulysses of Ithaca, to whom forbidden pleasure was dearer than fatherland. If, as Mimnermus holds, without love and jests there is no joy, live amid love and jests.

⁶⁷ Live long, farewell. If you know something better than these precepts, pass it on, my good fellow. If not, join me in following these.

such as that *pondera* means the weights on a shop-counter, are pure conjectures.

ᶜ As deserving to be disfranchised. The people of Caere were *municipes sine suffragii iure* (Gellius, xvi. 13). The word *cera* refers to the wax-covered tablets on which the lists of citizens were entered.

VII

TO MAECENAS

Maecenas has apparently reproached Horace for staying in the country longer than he had said he would, when he himself had to remain in Rome, and perhaps he had reminded the poet of his obligations to his patron.

Horace makes a manly and dignified reply. He assures his patron that he is not ungrateful for past benefits, but he must consider his health, and he refuses to surrender his personal independence. If that is demanded, he is willing to give up everything that Maecenas has conferred upon him.

The poet's attitude is illustrated by several stories, the last of which—the tale of Philippus and his client, Volteius Mena—takes up half of the poem. Of this Swift has made a very humorous use in his " Address to the Earl of Oxford."

VII.

Quinque dies tibi pollicitus me rure futurum,
Sextilem totum mendax desideror.   atque[1]
si me vivere vis sanum recteque valentem,
quam mihi das aegro, dabis aegrotare timenti,
Maecenas, veniam, dum ficus prima calorque[2]   5
dissignatorem decorat lictoribus atris,
dum pueris omnis pater et matercula pallet.
officiosaque sedulitas et opella forensis
adducit[3] febris et testamenta resignat.
quod si bruma nives Albanis illinet agris,   10
ad mare descendet vates tuus et sibi parcet
contractusque leget ; te, dulcis amice, reviset
cum Zephyris, si concedes,[4] et hirundine prima.
   Non quo more piris vesci Calaber iubet hospes,
tu me fecisti locupletem.   " vescere, sodes."   15
" iam satis est."   " at tu quantum vis tolle."   " be—
   nigne."
" non invisa feres pueris munuscula parvis."
" tam teneor dono, quam si dimittar onustus."
" ut libet ; haec porcis hodie comedenda relinques.[5] "

---

[1] atqui E, but cf. (e.g.) Terence, Andria 225.
[2] colorque Va.   [3] adducet Rδπ.
[4] concedis E.   [5] relinquis φψλl.

---

^a Quinque is a round number here.   Similarly, decem dies
may be used of " a long week."

294

Only a week [a] was I to stay in the country—such was my promise—but, false to my word, I am missed the whole of August. And yet, if you would have me live sound and in good health, the indulgence which you grant me when ill you will grant me when I fear to become ill, while the first figs and the heat adorn the undertaker with his black attendants, while every father and fond mother turns pale with fear for the children, and while diligence in courtesies [b] and the Forum's petty business bring on fevers and unseal wills. But if winter shall strew the Alban fields with snow, your poet will go down to the sea, will be careful of himself and, huddled up, will take to his reading: you, dear friend, he will—if you permit—revisit along with the zephyrs and the first swallow.

[14] 'Twas not in the way a Calabrian host invites you to eat his pears that you have made me rich. "Eat some, pray." "I've had enough." "Well, take away all you please." "No, thanks." "Your tiny tots will love the little gifts you take them." "I'm as much obliged for your offer as if you sent me away loaded down." "As you please; you'll be leaving them for the swine to gobble up to-day."

[b] The phrase refers to social duties, such as attendance upon the great.

prodigus et stultus donat quae spernit et odit ;   20
haec seges ingratos[1] tulit et feret omnibus annis.
vir bonus et sapiens dignis ait esse paratus,
nec tamen ignorat quid distent aera lupinis.
dignum praestabo me etiam pro laude merentis.
quod si me noles usquam discedere, reddes   25
forte latus, nigros angusta fronte capillos,
reddes dulce loqui, reddes ridere decorum et
inter vina fugam Cinarae maerere protervae.

  Forte per angustam tenuis volpecula[2] rimam
repserat in cumeram[3] frumenti, pastaque rursus   30
ire foras pleno tendebat corpore frustra ;
cui mustela procul, " si vis," ait, " effugere istinc,
macra cavum repetes artum, quem macra subisti."
hac ego si compellor imagine, cuncta resigno ;
nec somnum plebis laudo satur altilium nec   35
otia divitiis Arabum liberrima muto.
saepe verecundum laudasti, rexque paterque
audisti coram nec verbo parcius absens :
inspice si possum donata reponere laetus.
haud[4] male Telemachus, proles patientis[5] Ulixei :   40
" non est aptus equis Ithace locus, ut neque planis

---

[1] ingrato $E^2\delta^2$: ingratis $\phi\psi\lambda l$.
[2] nitedula *Bentley* : *accepted by Lachmann, Kiessling, Holder and others.*   [3] cameram π.
[4] at $\phi\psi\delta\lambda l$: aut $R\pi$.   [5] sapientis E.

---

[a] *i.e.* real money and the imitation lupine seeds, used for counters in playing games.
[b] For the beauty of a narrow brow *cf. Od.* i. 33. 5, " insignem tenui fronte Lycorida." Horace is becoming bald, and is *praecanus* (*Epist.* i. 20. 24).
[c] Bentley's conjecture *nitedula*, " shrew-mouse," has been

The foolish prodigal gives away what he despises and dislikes : the field thus sown has always yielded, and always will yield, a crop of ingratitude. Your good and wise man claims to be ready to help the worthy, and yet he knows well how coins and counters[a] differ. Worthy I, too, will show myself, as the glory of your good deed demands. But if you will never suffer me to leave you, you must give me back strength of lung, and black locks on a narrow brow[b] ; you must give back a pleasant prattle, give back graceful laughter and laments amid our cups o'er saucy Cinara's flight.

[29] Once it chanced that a pinched little fox[c] had crept through a narrow chink into a bin of corn, and when well fed was trying with stuffed stomach to get out again, but in vain. To him quoth a weasel hard by : " If you wish to escape from there, you must go back lean to the narrow gap which you entered when lean." If challenged by this fable, I give up all. I neither praise the poor man's sleep, when I am fed full on capons, nor would I barter my ease and my freedom for all the wealth of Araby. Often have you praised my modesty, and have been called " king "[d] and " father " to your face, nor do I stint my words behind your back. Try me, whether I can restore your gifts, and cheerfully too. 'Twas no poor answer of Telemachus, son of enduring Ulysses[e] : " Ithaca is no land meet for steeds, for

widely accepted, because in real life the fox does not eat grain. But the traditional text must be retained.

[d] The term *rex* was used of a patron ; *cf* " coram rege suo," *Epist.* i. 17. 43.

[e] In the *Odyssey* (iv. 601ff.). Telemachus, son of Odysseus, declines the horses and chariot offered him in friendship by Menelaus.

porrectus spatiis nec multae prodigus herbae :
Atride, magis apta tibi tua dona relinquam."
parvum parva decent : mihi iam non regia Roma,
sed vacuum Tibur placet aut imbelle Tarentum.   45
　Strenuus et fortis causisque Philippus agendis
clarus, ab officiis octavam circiter horam
dum redit atque Foro nimium distare Carinas
iam grandis natu queritur, conspexit, ut aiunt,
adrasum quendam vacua tonsoris in umbra   50
cultello proprios[1] purgantem[2] leniter unguis.
" Demetri," (puer hic non laeve iussa Philippi
accipiebat) " abi, quaere et refer, unde domo, quis,
cuius fortunae, quo sit patre quove patrono."
it,[3] redit et narrat, Volteium nomine Menam,   55
praeconem, tenui censu, sine crimine, notum
et properare loco[4] et cessare et quaerere et uti,
gaudentem parvisque sodalibus et lare certo[5]
et ludis et post decisa negotia Campo.
" scitari libet ex ipso quodcumque refers : dic   60
ad cenam veniat." non sane credere Mena,
mirari secum tacitus. quid multa ? " benigne,"
respondet.[6] " neget[7] ille mihi ? " " negat improbus
　　et te
neglegit aut horret."
　　　　　　Volteium mane Philippus
vilia vendentem tunicato scruta popello   65
occupat et salvere iubet prior. ille Philippo
excusare laborem et mercennaria vincla,

---

　　　[1] proprio.　　　　　　　[2] resecantem E Goth.
　　　　　[3] et, II.　　　　　　　　[4] locum, II.
　　[5] curto.　　[6] respondit δ Goth.　　[7] negat a Goth.

---

　[a] i.e. such games as those of the Circus and the athletic
contests in the Campus Martius.

it has no level courses outspread, nor is it lavish of much herbage. Son of Atreus, I will leave you your gifts, as being more meet for you." Small things befit small folk ; my own delight to-day is not queenly Rome, but quiet Tibur or peaceful Tarentum.

⁴⁶ Philippus, the famous pleader, a man of vigour and courage, was returning home from work about two o'clock. Being now somewhat on in years, he was grumbling at the Carinae being too far from the Forum, when (so the story goes) he caught sight of a man, close-shaven, sitting in a barber's empty booth, and with pocket-knife quietly cleaning his nails for himself. " Demetrius " (this lad was not slow to catch his master's orders), " go, ask, and bring me word, where that man's from, who he is, and what's his standing, who is his father, or who his patron." He goes, and comes back with the tale that his name is Volteius Mena, a crier at auctions, of modest fortune and blameless record, known to work hard and idle in season, to make money and spend it, taking pleasure in his humble friends and a home of his own and, when business is over, in the games and in the field of Mars.ᵃ " I'd like to hear from his own lips all you tell me. Bid him come to supper." Mena cannot really believe it ; he marvels in thoughtful silence. To be brief, " No, thank you," he answers. " Would he refuse me ? " " He does, the rascal, and either slights or dreads you."

⁶⁵ Next morning Philippus comes on Volteius selling cheap odds and ends to the common folk in tunics ᵇ and is first to give a greeting. The other makes work and the ties of his trade an excuse to

ᵇ The common people did not wear the toga in daily life.

quod non mane domum venisset, denique quod non
providisset[1] eum. " sic ignovisse putato   69
me tibi, si cenas hodie mecum." " ut libet." " ergo
post nonam venies : nunc i, rem strenuus auge."
ut ventum ad cenam est,[2] dicenda tacenda locutus
tandem dormitum dimittitur.

                Hic ubi saepe
occultum visus decurrere piscis ad hamum,
mane cliens et iam certus conviva, iubetur   75
rura suburbana indictis comes ire Latinis.
impositus mannis arvum caelumque Sabinum
non cessat laudare. videt ridetque Philippus,
et sibi dum requiem, dum risus undique quaerit,
dum septem donat sestertia, mutua septem   80
promittit, persuadet uti mercetur agellum.
mercatur. ne[3] te longis ambagibus[4] ultra
quam satis est morer, ex nitido fit rusticus atque
sulcos et vineta crepat mera, praeparat ulmos,
immoritur studiis et amore senescit habendi.   85
verum ubi oves furto, morbo periere capellae,
spem mentita seges, bos est enectus arando,
offensus damnis media de nocte caballum
arripit iratusque Philippi tendit ad aedis.   89
quem simul aspexit scabrum intonsumque Philippus,
" durus," ait, " Voltei, nimis attentusque videris
esse mihi." " pol, me miserum, patrone, vocares,
si velles," inquit, " verum mihi ponere[5] nomen.

     [1] praevidisset.   [2] est *omitted* π.
     [3] nec *Rl*π.   [4] ambiguus *R*π.
         [5] ponere *VaE* : dicere *R, II*.

---

   [a] *i.e.* to pay his respects, in view of the invitation sent him.
   [b] The *feriae Latinae* were held annually on a day appointed
and announced—usually at the end of April or the beginning
of May. All legal business was suspended for the time.

Philippus for not having come to his house that morning,[a] in fine for not seeing him first. "You're to take it that I've pardoned you only if you sup with me to-day." "As you please." "You will come then after three o'clock. Now go, set to and add to your wealth!" On coming to supper, he chatted about anything and everything, and then at last was sent off to bed.

73 When he had often been seen to run like a fish to the hidden hook, in the morning a client and now a constant guest, he was invited to come as companion, when the Latin games were proclaimed,[b] to a country estate near Rome. Mounted behind the ponies, he is ever praising the Sabine soil and climate. Philippus notes and smiles, and what with looking for his own relief and amusement from any source, and what with giving him seven thousand sesterces, and offering him a loan of seven thousand more, he persuades him to buy a little farm. He does so. Not to hold you too long with a rambling tale, our spruce cit becomes a rustic and chatters about nothing but furrows and vineyards, makes ready his elms, nearly kills himself over his hobbies, and grows old with his passion for getting. But when he has lost his sheep by theft and his goats by disease, when his crops have fooled his hopes and his ox is worn to death with ploughing, fretting over his losses, in the middle of the night he seizes his nag and in a rage makes straight for the house of Philippus. He, soon as he saw him, rough and unshorn, "Volteius," cries he, "you seem to me too hard-worked and over-strained." "Egad! my patron," said he, "you would call me miserable wretch, if you could give me my true name. But

quod te per Genium dextramque deosque Penatis
obsecro et obtestor, vitae me redde priori ! ” 95
  Qui semel[1] aspexit, quantum dimissa petitis
praestent, mature redeat repetatque relicta.
metiri se quemque suo modulo ac pede verum est.

  [1] semel *early editions* : simul *mss.* ; *taken from* l. 90.

by your genius, by your right hand and household gods, I implore and entreat you, put me back in my former life."

⁹⁶ Let him, who once has seen how far what he has given up excels what he has sought, go back in time and seek again the things he has left. 'Tis right that each should measure himself by his own rule and standard.

VIII

TO CELSUS ALBINOVANUS

This brief letter is addressed to the Celsus mentioned in the third epistle of this book as a member of the staff of Tiberius Claudius Nero.

The poet confesses that he himself is out of sorts and discontented, but the main point of his letter lies in the admonition to his friend not to be unduly elated by his good fortune.

VIII.

Celso gaudere et bene rem gerere Albinovano
Musa rogata refer, comiti scribaeque Neronis.
si quaeret[1] quid agam, dic multa et pulchra minantem
vivere nec recte nec suaviter ; haud[2] quia grando
contuderit vitis oleamque[3] momorderit aestus,   5
nec quia longinquis armentum aegrotet in agris ;
sed quia mente minus validus quam corpore toto
nil audire velim, nil discere, quod levet aegrum ;
fidis offendar medicis, irascar amicis,
cur me[4] funesto properent arcere[5] veterno ;   10
quae nocuere sequar, fugiam quae profore credam ;
Romae Tibur amem ventosus,[6] Tibure Romam.

Post haec, ut valeat, quo pacto rem gerat et se,
ut placeat iuveni percontare utque cohorti.
si dicet, " recte," primum gaudere, subinde   15
praeceptum auriculis hoc instillare memento :
" ut tu fortunam, sic nos te, Celse, feremus."

---

    [1] quaerit *a*.   [2] aut π'.   [3] oleamve *E*.
        [4] mihi *E*.   [5] urguere π.
    [6] venturus *V, II, Porph.* (*on* Serm. ii. 7. 28).

Epistle VIII

To Celsus Albinovanus greetings and good wishes !
This message bear, O Muse, at my request, to the
comrade and secretary of Nero. If he ask you how
I fare, tell him that despite many fine promises I
live a life neither wise nor pleasant ; not because
hail has beaten down my vines and heat blighted my
olives, nor because my herds are sickening on
distant pastures ; but because, less sound in mind
than in all my body, I will listen to nothing, will
learn nothing, to relieve my sickness ; quarrel with
my faithful physicians, and angrily ask my friends
why they are eager to rescue me from fatal
lethargy ; because I follow after what has hurt me,
avoid what I believe will help me, and am fickle as
the wind, at Rome loving Tibur, at Tibur Rome.

Then ask him how his own health is, how in estate
and person he is faring, how he stands in favour
with prince and staff. If he says " Well," first wish
him joy ; then by and by remember to drop this
warning in the dear fellow's ears : " As you bear
your fortune, Celsus, so we shall bear with you."

IX

TO TIBERIUS

THIS charming letter of introduction is addressed to the young prince Tiberius on behalf of one Septimius, probably the friend of *Carm*. ii. 6,

> Septimi, Gadis aditure mecum et
> Cantabrum indoctum iuga ferre nostra et
> barbaras Syrtis.

The delicate tact of the writer, who would seem selfish if he did not heed his friend's request, and might be guilty of effrontery if he did, has often been admired. The letter was probably written in 20 B.C., when Tiberius was preparing to set out for the East.

IX.

Septimius, Claudi, nimirum intellegit unus,
quanti me facias. nam cum rogat et prece cogit
scilicet ut tibi se laudare et tradere coner,
dignum mente domoque legentis honesta Neronis,
munere cum fungi propioris censet amici,   5
quid possim videt ac novit[1] me valdius ipso.
multa quidem dixi cur excusatus abirem ;
ֿed timui mea ne[2] finxisse minora putarer,
dֽ֗similator opis propriae, mihi commodus uni.
sic ego, maioris fugiens opprobria culpae,   10
frontis ad urbanae descendi praemia. quod si
depositum laudas ob amici iussa pudorem,
scribe tui gregis hunc et fortem crede bonumque.

[1] ac novit *aE Goth* : agnovit *A*², *II*.
[2] non *φψ*.

Epistle IX

Only Septimius of course understands how much, Claudius, you make of me. For when he begs and by prayer forces me—mark you !—to an endeavour to commend and present him to you, as one worthy of the mind and household of Nero, the lover of virtue—when he deems that I fill the place of a closer friend, he sees and knows what I can do more fully than myself. To be sure I gave him many reasons for letting me go excused ; but I feared that I might be thought to have made out my influence too small, falsely hiding my real power and seeking favour for myself alone. So to avoid the reproach of a graver fault, I have stooped to win the reward of town-bred impudence. But if you approve of my thus doffing modesty at the bidding of a friend, enrol him in your circle and believe him brave and good.

X

TO ARISTIUS FUSCUS

ACCORDING to the scholiasts, Aristius Fuscus, to whom this letter is addressed, was a dramatic writer and a scholar. He appears in the list of Horace's literary friends given in *Sat.* i. 10. 83, figures in an amusing rôle in *Sat.* i. 9. 61 ff., and is best known as the man to whom the famous *Integer vitae* ode (*Carm.* i. 22) is dedicated.

The Epistle is a rhapsody upon the simplicity and charm of country life addressed to a cultivated man of the town. In the country Horace is perfectly content, save for the fact that his friend is elsewhere.

X

Urbis amatorem Fuscum salvere iubemus
ruris amatores.   hac in re scilicet una
multum dissimiles, at[1] cetera paene gemelli
fraternis animis (quidquid[2] negat alter, et alter)
adnuimus pariter vetuli notique columbi.[3]   5

Tu nidum servas ; ego laudo ruris amoeni
rivos et musco circumlita saxa nemusque.
quid quaeris ?   vivo et regno, simul ista reliqui
quae vos ad caelum effertis[4] rumore secundo,
utque sacerdotis fugitivus liba recuso ;   10
pane egeo iam mellitis potiore placentis.

Vivere Naturae si[5] convenienter oportet,
ponendaeque[6] domo quaerenda est area primum,
novistine locum potiorem rure beato ?
est ubi plus tepeant hiemes, ubi gratior aura   15
leniat et rabiem Canis et momenta Leonis,
cum semel accepit Solem furibundus acutum ?
est ubi divellat[7] somnos minus invida Cura ?
deterius Libycis olet aut nitet herba lapillis ?

---

[1] at *VE* : ad *a, II.*   [2] si quid *E.*
[3] vetulis notisque columbis *V (corrected). Lambinus had
conjectured the same reading,* columbis *being governed by*
pariter.   [4] effertis *V* : fertis *MSS.*   [5] sic $\phi\psi$.
[6] ponendaque *one Bland.*   [7] depellat *a.*

---

[a] The slave in a priest's household was fed so much on
sacrificial cakes that he ran away to get plain fare.

314

Epistle X

To Fuscus, lover of the city, I, a lover of the country, send greetings. In this one point, to be sure, we differ much, but being in all else much like twins with the hearts of brothers—if one says " no," the other says " no " too—we nod a common assent like a couple of old familiar doves.

⁶ You keep the nest ; I praise the lovely country's brooks, its grove and moss-grown rocks. In short : I live and reign, as soon as I have left behind what you townsmen with shouts of applause extol to the skies. Like the priest's runaway slave, I loathe sweet wafers ; 'tis bread I want, and now prefer to honeyed cakes.ᵃ

¹² If " to live agreeably to Nature "ᵇ is our duty, and first we must choose a site for building our house, do you know any place to be preferred to the blissful country ? Is there any where winters are milder, where a more grateful breeze tempers the Dog-star's fury and the Lion's onset, when once in frenzy he has caught the sun's piercing shafts ?ᶜ Is there any where envious Care less distracts our slumber ? Is the grass poorer in fragrance or beauty than Libyan

ᵇ ὁμολογουμένως τῇ φύσει ζῆν : one of the Stoic rules of life.

ᶜ The Dog-star rises July 20, becoming visible on July 26. The sun enters Leo July 23. The constellation is compared to a lion roused to fury when wounded with arrows.

315

purior in vicis aqua tendit rumpere plumbum,   20
quam quae per pronum trepidat cum murmure rivum?
nempe inter varias nutritur silva columnas,
laudaturque domus longos quae prospicit agros.
Naturam expelles[1] furca, tamen usque recurret,
et mala perrumpet furtim fastidia[2] victrix.   25

Non, qui Sidonio contendere callidus ostro
nescit Aquinatem potantia vellera fucum,
certius accipiet damnum propiusve[3] medullis,
quam qui non poterit vero distinguere falsum.
quem res plus nimio delectavere secundae,   30
mutatae quatient. si quid mirabere, pones
invitus. fuge magna : licet sub paupere tecto
reges et regum vita praecurrere amicos.

Cervus equum pugna melior communibus herbis
pellebat, donec minor in certamine longo   35
imploravit opes hominis frenumque recepit ;
sed postquam victor violens[4] discessit ab hoste,
non equitem dorso, non frenum depulit ore.
sic qui pauperiem veritus potiore metallis
libertate caret, dominum vehet[5] improbus atque   40
serviet aeternum, quia parvo nesciet uti.
cui non conveniet sua res, ut[6] calceus olim,
si pede maior erit, subvertet, si minor, uret.

---

[1] expellas *early editions.*
[2] fastigia *a*, *II* : vestigia *V.*   [3] propiusque *a.*
[4] violens victor *E* : victo ridens *Haupt.*
[5] vehit *E.*   [6] et φψλl.

316

mosaics [a] ? Is the water purer which in city-streets struggles to burst its leaden pipes than that which dances and purls adown the sloping brook ? Why, amid your varied columns [b] you are nursing trees, and you praise the mansion which looks out on distant fields. You may drive out Nature with a pitchfork, yet she will ever hurry back, and, ere you know it, will burst through your foolish contempt in triumph.

²⁶ The man who has not the skill to match with Sidonian purple the fleeces that drink up Aquinum's dye,[c] will not suffer surer loss or one closer to his heart than he who shall fail to distinguish false from true. One whom Fortune's smiles have delighted overmuch, will reel under the shock of change. If you set your heart on aught, you will be loth to lay it down. Flee grandeur : though humble be your home, yet in life's race you may outstrip kings and the friends of kings.

³⁴ The stag could best the horse in fighting and used to drive him from their common pasture, until the loser in the long contest begged the help of man and took the bit. But after that, in overweening triumph, he parted from his foe, he did not dislodge the rider from his back or the bit from his mouth. So he who through fear of poverty forfeits liberty, which is better than mines of wealth, will in his avarice carry a master, and be a slave for ever, not knowing how to live on little. When a man's fortune will not fit him, 'tis as ofttimes with a shoe—if too big for the foot, it will trip him ; if too small, will chafe.

Roman house. In this court, trees as well as shrubs, were grown.

[c] A lichen found at Aquinum produced a colour like the famous Sidonian purple.

Laetus sorte tua vives sapienter, Aristi,
nec me dimittes[1] incastigatum, ubi plura   45
cogere quam satis est ac non cessare videbor.
imperat aut servit collecta pecunia cuique,
tortum digna sequi potius quam ducere funem.
  Haec tibi dictabam post fanum putre Vacunae,
excepto quod non simul esses, cetera laetus.   50

[1] dimittis $R\pi$.

[44] You will live wisely, Aristius, if cheerful in your lot, and you will not let me off unrebuked, when I seem to be gathering more than enough and never to rest. Money stored up is for each his lord or his slave, but ought to follow, not lead, the twisted rope.[a]

These lines I am dictating to you behind Vacuna's crumbling shrine, happy on all counts save that you are not with me.

---

[a] Probably a reference to some story of an animal being led by a rope and running away with its keeper.

XI

TO BULLATIUS

Bullatius, a friend of the poet's, has been travelling in the Province of Asia, and Horace, who seems to have had little of the *Wanderlust* himself, asks him whether, tired of journeying by land and sea, he would like to settle down at even so deserted a place as Lebedus. That lonely spot, with its outlook on the raging sea, appealed strongly to the poet, who would love to live there,

> The world forgetting, by the world forgot.

But after all a man's happiness depends, not on his place of abode, but on his state of mind.

XI.

Quid tibi visa Chios, Bullati, notaque Lesbos,
quid concinna Samos, quid Croesi regia Sardis,
Zmyrna quid et Colophon ?   maiora minorave[1] fama,
cunctane[2] prae Campo et Tiberino flumine sordent ?
an venit in votum Attalicis ex urbibus una,   5
an Lebedum laudas odio maris atque viarum ?
scis Lebedus quid sit : Gabiis desertior atque
Fidenis vicus ; tamen illic vivere vellem,
oblitusque meorum, obliviscendus et illis,
Neptunum procul e[3] terra spectare furentem.   10
. Sed neque qui Capua Romam petit, imbre lutoque
aspersus, volet in caupona vivere ; nec qui
frigus collegit, furnos et balnea laudat
ut[4] fortunatam plene praestantia vitam ;
nec si te validus iactaverit Auster in alto,   15
idcirco navem trans Aegaeum mare vendas.
  Incolumi Rhodos et Mytilene pulchra facit quod
paenula solstitio, campestre nivalibus auris,
per brumam Tiberis, Sextili mense caminus.

----

¹ minorave *MSS.* (-que *E*) : minorane *Bentley.*
² cunctaque *aRπ.*   ³ ex *aR* : et *E.*   ⁴ et, *ll.*

  ᵃ The most important were Pergamum, Apollonia, and
Thyatira.
  ᵇ According to some editors, ll. 7-10 are supposed to be
spoken by Bullatius, perhaps as a quotation from a letter,
but why may we not suppose that this lonely sea-side place,
which Horace had probably visited when he served with

Epistle XI

What did you think of Chios, my Bullatius, and of
famous Lesbos ? What of charming Samos ? What
of Sardis, royal home of Croesus ? What of Smyrna
and Colophon ? Whether above or below their
fame, do they all seem poor beside the Campus and
Tiber's stream ? Or is your heart set upon one of
the cities of Attalus ?[a] Or do you extol Lebedus,
because sick of sea and roads ? You know what
Lebedus is—a town more desolate than Gabii and
Fidenae : yet there would I love to live, and for-
getting my friends and by them forgotten, gaze
from the land on Neptune's distant rage.[b]

Yet he who travels from Capua to Rome, though
bespattered with rain and mud, will not want to
live on in an inn, nor does he who has caught a chill
cry up stoves and baths as fully furnishing a happy
life. And so you, though a stiff south wind has
tossed you on the deep, will not on that account sell
your ship on the far side of the Aegean Sea.

[17] To a sound man Rhodes or fair Mitylene is what
a heavy cloak is in summer, an athlete's garb when
snowy winds are blowing, the Tiber in winter, a
stove in the month of August. While one may, and

Brutus, appealed strongly to the poet? With l. 10 *cf.*
Lucretius, ii. 1 f. :

> suave, mari magno turbantibus aequora ventis,
> e terra magnum alterius spectare laborem.

dum licet ac voltum servat Fortuna benignum,   20
Romae laudetur Samos et Chios et Rhodos absens.
tu quamcumque deus tibi fortunaverit horam
grata sume manu, neu dulcia differ in annum ;
ut[1] quocumque loco fueris vixisse libenter
te dicas.   nam si ratio et prudentia curas,   25
non locus effusi late maris arbiter aufert,
caelum, non animum, mutant, qui trans mare currunt.
strenua nos exercet inertia : navibus atque
quadrigis petimus bene vivere.   quod petis hic est,
est Ulubris, animus si te non deficit aequus.   30

[1] tu *V, II.*

---

[a] *Cf.* "patriae quis exsul se quoque fugit ? " (*Odes* ii.
16. 19).

Fortune keeps a smiling face, at Rome let Samos be praised, and Chios and Rhodes—though far away ! And you—whatever hour God has given for your weal, take it with grateful hand, nor put off joys from year to year ; so that, in whatever place you have been, you may say that you have lived happily. For if 'tis reason and wisdom that take away cares, and not a site commanding a wide expanse of sea, they change their clime, not their mind, who rush across the sea.[a] 'Tis a busy idleness that is our bane; with yachts and cars we seek to make life happy. What you are seeking is here ; it is at Ulubrae,[b] if there fail you not a mind well balanced.

[b] Ulubrae, called *vacuae* by Juvenal (*Sat.* x. 101), was a decaying town in the Pomptine marshes, where the frogs were very clamorous (Cicero, *Ad fam.* vii. 81).

XII

TO ICCIUS

Horace introduces Grosphus to Iccius, and in doing so takes occasion to rally his friend on his discontent.

Iccius, whom in one of his *Odes* (i. 29) Horace rallies for deserting philosophy to take part in a military expedition to Arabia Felix, has now, some five years later, become the *procurator* or " agent," who had charge of Agrippa's estates in Sicily. Apparently he had written to Horace, grumbling because he was not an independent landowner, to which Horace replies that the agent of a large estate is able to live on the produce very comfortably, inasmuch as it is all at his disposal, though he is not the actual owner. Then in a somewhat ironical vein (12-20), Horace congratulates his friend on being able, amid all his business cares, to study the physics of Empedocles and the dialectic of the Stoics.

The letter closes with some bits of news, preceded by the request to show some courtesy to Pompeius Grosphus, whom we have also encountered in the *Odes* (ii. 16), where he is spoken of as a wealthy proprietor in Sicily.

XII.

Fructibus Agrippae Siculis, quos colligis, Icci,
si recte frueris, non est ut copia maior
ab Iove donari possit tibi.   tolle querellas :
pauper enim non est, cui rerum suppetit usus.
si ventri bene, si lateri est pedibusque tuis, nil   5
divitiae poterunt regales addere maius.
si forte in medio positorum abstemius herbis
vivis et urtica, sic vives protinus, ut te
confestim liquidus Fortunae rivus inauret,
vel quia naturam mutare pecunia nescit,   10
vel quia cuncta putas una virtute minora.
  Miramur, si Democriti pecus edit agellos
cultaque, dum peregre est animus sine corpore velox ;
cum tu inter scabiem tantam et contagia lucri
nil parvum sapias et adhuc sublimia cures :   15
quae mare compescant causae, quid temperet[1] annum,
stellae sponte sua iussaene vagentur et errent,
quid premat obscurum lunae, quid proferat orbem,
quid velit et possit rerum concordia discors,
Empedocles an Stertinium deliret acumen.   20
  Verum seu piscis seu porrum et caepe trucidas,

[1] temperat, *II.*

---

a A reference to the main principle of Empedocles'
philosophy that the life of the world is due to a perpetual
conflict of the two principles of Love and Strife.

Epistle XII

If, Iccius, you are enjoying as you should the Sicilian products which you collect for Agrippa, Jupiter himself could not give you greater abundance. Away with complaints ; for he is not poor, who has enough of things to use. If stomach, lungs, and feet are all in health, the wealth of kings can give you nothing more. If haply you hold aloof from what is within your reach, and live on nettles and other greens, you will go on living in the same way, though Fortune's stream suddenly flood you with gold : either because money cannot change your nature, or because you count all else below the one thing, virtue.

[12] We marvel that the herds of Democritus ate up his meadows and corn-fields, while his swift mind wandered abroad without his body ; though you, in the very midst of the contagious itch of gain, still have a taste far from mean, still set your thoughts on lofty themes : what causes hold the sea in check, what rules the year, whether stars roam at large of their own will or by law, what hides the moon's disk in darkness, what brings it into light, what is the meaning and what the effects of Nature's jarring harmony,[a] whether Empedocles is doting or subtle Stertinius.

[21] However, whether it is fish, or only leeks and

utere Pompeio Grospho et, si quid petet, ultro
defer ; nil Grosphus nisi verum orabit et aequum.
vilis amicorum est annona, bonis ubi quid deest.

Ne tamen ignores, quo sit Romana loco res,　　25
Cantaber Agrippae, Claudi virtute Neronis
Armenius cecidit ; ius imperiumque Phraates
Caesaris accepit genibus minor ; aurea fruges
Italiae pleno defudit[1] Copia cornu.

---

[1] defudit MSS. : defundit VA[2].

---

[a] According to the scholiast, fish are here mentioned as
costly fare in contrast to a simple diet.　In *trucidas*, however,
Horace makes a humorous allusion to the Pythagoreans,
whom Empedocles followed in regard to the doctrine of
transmigration of souls, for he asserted that he himself had
once been a fish (εἰν ἁλὶ ἔλλοπος ἰχθύς, Fr. 11 Müll.).　To
eat a fish, therefore, might mean murder.　This ban on
living things was extended even to vegetables, *cf. Sat.* ii. 6.
63 above, and Juvenal's well-known verse

onions that you butcher,[a] receive Pompeius Grosphus as a friend, and if he asks aught of you, give it freely: Grosphus will sue for nothing but what is right and fair. The market-price of friends is low, when good men are in need.

25 Yet, that you may not be ignorant how the world wags in Rome, the Cantabrian has fallen before the valour of Agrippa, the Armenian before that of Claudius Nero. Phraates, on humbled knees, has accepted Caesar's imperial sway.[b] Golden Plenty from full horn has poured her fruits upon Italy.

porrum et caepe nefas violare et frangere morsu

(15. 9), with Mayor's note.

[b] The Cantabrians were conquered by Agrippa in 19 B.C., shortly after Armenia had submitted to Tiberius. In connexion with the latter event, Phraates, the Parthian king, restored the Roman standards taken long before from Crassus at Carrhae.

XIII

TO VINIUS ASINA

HORACE is sending Augustus a copy of his poems,
probably the *Odes*, Books i., ii., iii., which were
published in 23 B.C. The volume is carried to court
by a messenger, one Vinius, whose cognomen is pre-
sumably Asina (l. 8), though the usual form of the
name is Asellus.

Instead of writing a formal note to the Emperor
to accompany the gift, Horace indulges in the fiction
of sending a letter of instructions to the messenger,
in which he humorously expresses his anxiety about
the reception of the poems.

XIII.

Ut proficiscentem docui te saepe diuque,
Augusto reddes signata volumina, Vini,[1]
si validus, si laetus erit, si denique poscet;
ne studio nostri pecces odiumque libellis
sedulus importes opera vehemente minister.   5
si te forte meae gravis uret[2] sarcina chartae,
abicito potius, quam quo perferre iuberis
clitellas ferus impingas, Asinaeque paternum
cognomen vertas in risum et fabula fias.

Viribus uteris per clivos, flumina, lamas.   10
victor propositi simul ac perveneris illuc,
sic positum servabis onus, ne forte sub ala
fasciculum portes librorum ut rusticus agnum,
ut vinosa glomus[3] furtivae Pyrria lanae,
ut cum pilleolo soleas conviva tribulis.   15
neu[4] volgo narres te sudavisse ferendo
carmina, quae possint oculos aurisque morari
Caesaris. oratus multa prece, nitere porro.
vade ; vale ; cave ne titubes mandataque frangas.

---

[1] vinni *or* venni MSS. (*but inscriptions favour the form*
Vinius).   [2] urit *E* : urat *Priscian*.
   [3] glomos φψλl.   [4] neu *a* : nec *E* : ne, *II*.

---

[a] *i.e.* the books. These, of course, could not be heavy in
themselves, though they might make "heavy reading."
   [b] This is said to be an allusion to a scene in one of the
plays of Titinius.
   [c] The *tribulis*, a humble man whom for political purposes
a richer member of the same tribe has invited to dinner, has

334

Epistle XIII

As I instructed you often and at length, when you set out, Vinius, you will deliver these close-sealed rolls to Augustus, *if* he's well, *if* he's in good spirits, *if*—in fine—he asks for them ; lest you blunder in your eagerness for me, and by officious service and excessive zeal bring resentment on my poor works. If haply my book's burden gall you with its weight, fling it from you, rather than savagely dash down your pack [a] where you are bidden to deliver it, and turn your father's name of Asina into a jest, and you become the talk of the town.

Put forth your strength over hills, streams, and fens ; when once you have achieved your purpose and reached your journey's end, you are to keep your burden so placed as not, for instance, to carry the little packet of books under your armpit, even as a bumpkin carries a lamb, as tipsy Pyrria a ball of stolen wool,[b] as a poor tribesman his slippers and felt cap, when asked out to dinner.[c] And mind you don't tell all the world that you have sweated in carrying verses that may win a hold on the eyes and ears of Caesar. Though besought by many a plea,[d] press on. Be off ; fare well ; take care you do not stumble and smash your precious charge.

no slave to take his cap and sandals, which he would need coming and going, though not in the dining-room.

[d] *i.e.* by inquisitive people.

XIV

TO THE BAILIFF OF HIS FARM

THIS epistle is professedly addressed to the slave, whom the poet had promoted from low rank in his town establishment to the position of bailiff or superintendent of his small country estate. The slave now hankers after city life, while the master, detained in Rome by a friend's bereavement, longs for the country, which he has always preferred. The difference between the two is due to their tastes. The slave still clings to his follies ; the master has learned wisdom with advancing years.

The theme is essentially the same as in Epistles viii. and x. of this book, while the setting of the letter is in marked contrast with *Sat.* ii. 7, where it is the slave who lectures the master.

XIV.

Vilice silvarum et mihi me reddentis agelli,
quem tu fastidis, habitatum quinque focis et
quinque bonos solitum Variam dimittere patres,[a]
certemus, spinas animone ego fortius an tu
evellas agro, et melior sit Horatius an res.   5

Me quamvis Lamiae pietas et cura moratur,
fratrem maerentis, rapto de fratre dolentis
insolabiliter, tamen istuc mens animusque
fert et amat spatiis obstantia rumpere claustra.
rure ego viventem, tu dicis in urbe beatum.   10
cui placet alterius, sua nimirum est odio sors.[1]
stultus uterque locum immeritum causatur inique :
in culpa est animus, qui se non effugit umquam.

Tu mediastinus tacita prece rura petebas,
nunc urbem et ludos et balnea vilicus optas :   15
me constare mihi scis et discedere tristem
quandocumque trahunt invisa negotia Romam.
non eadem miramur ; eo disconvenit inter
meque et te.   nam quae[2] deserta et inhospita tesqua[b]
credis, amoena vocat mecum qui sentit, et odit   20

----

¹ res *E*.   ² quae *E, II* : qua *Va*.

----

^a These were probably *coloni*, who held their land in
lease under Horace. They would go to Varia (now Vico-
varo) to market and for local elections.
   ^b *Cf. Epist.* i. ii. 27 and *Odes* ii. 16. 19.

Epistle XIV

Bailiff of my woods and of the little farm which makes me myself again — while you disdain it, though the home of five households and wont to send to Varia their five honest heads [a]—let us have a match to see whether I more stoutly root out thorns from the mind or you from the land, and whether Horace or his farm is in a better state.

[6] For me, though kept here by the love and grief of Lamia, who is sighing for his brother, grieving for his lost brother inconsolably, yet thither thought and feeling bear me longing to burst the barriers that block the track. I call him happy who lives in the country; you him who dwells in the city. One who likes another's lot, of course dislikes his own. Each is foolish and unfairly blames the undeserving place; what is at fault is the mind, which never escapes from itself.[b]

[14] You, as a common drudge, used to sigh in secret for the country; now as a bailiff you long for the town, its games and baths: as for me, you know that I'm consistent with myself, and depart in gloom, whenever hateful business drags me to Rome. Our tastes are not the same: therein lies the difference between you and me. What you hold to be desert and inhospitable wilds, he who shares my views calls

quae tu pulchra putas.   fornix tibi et uncta popina
incutiunt urbis desiderium, video, et quod
angulus iste feret piper et tus ocius uva,
nec vicina subest vinum praebere taberna
quae possit[1] tibi, nec meretrix tibicina, cuius   25
ad strepitum salias terrae gravis ; et tamen urges
iampridem non tacta ligonibus arva bovemque
disiunctum curas et strictis frondibus exples ;
addit opus pigro rivus, si decidit imber,
multa mole docendus aprico parcere prato.   30
    Nunc age, quid nostrum concentum[2] dividat audi.
quem tenues decuere togae nitidique capilli,
quem scis immunem Cinarae placuisse rapaci,
quem bibulum liquidi media de luce Falerni,
cena brevis iuvat et prope rivum somnus in herba ;   35
nec lusisse pudet, sed non incidere ludum.
non istic obliquo oculo mea commoda quisquam
limat, non odio obscuro morsuque venenat :
rident vicini glaebas et saxa moventem.
cum servis urbana diaria[3] rodere mavis ;   40
horum tu in numerum voto ruis ; invidet usum
lignorum et pecoris tibi calo argutus et horti.
optat ephippia bos, piger optat arare caballus.
quam scit uterque libens censebo exerceat artem.

---

          [1] possit *E, II* : posset *aR.*
    [2] consensum *E.*   [3] cibaria *R Goth.*

---

   [a] In the mouth of the bailiff, *angulus* is a term of contempt. The same expression, however, is used elsewhere by Horace of a place unique in his affections, " ille terrarum mihi praeter omnis angulus ridet " (*Odes* ii. 6. 13).
   [b] *i.e.* although you have no pleasures. From l. 22 to l. 30 Horace repeats some of the grumbling remarks of the bailiff.

340

lovely, and hates what you believe so beautiful. 'Tis the brothel, I see, and greasy cookshop that stir in you a longing for the city, and the fact that that poky spot[a] will grow pepper and spice as soon as grapes, and that there is no tavern hard by that can supply you with wine and no flute-playing courtesan, to whose strains you can dance and thump the ground. And yet[b] you toil over fields long untouched by the hoe, you care for the ox after he is unyoked, and you fill him up with fodder you have stripped ; when you are dead tired, the brook brings fresh work, for if rain has fallen, it must be taught by many a mounded dam to spare the sunny meadow.

31 Now come, hear what makes the discord in our common song. One whom fine-spun clothes became, and shining locks, one who, as you know, though empty-handed, found favour with greedy Cinara, and in midday hours would drink the clear Falernian, now takes pleasure in a simple meal, and a nap on the grass beside the stream : nor is it shameful to have once been foolish, but not to cut folly short. Where you live, no one with eye askance detracts from[c] my comforts, or poisons them with the bite of secret hate. As I move sods and stones the neighbours laugh. You would rather be munching rations with the slaves in town ; it is their number you fain would join : my sharp-witted groom envies you the use of fuel, flock, and garden. The ox longs for the horse's trappings : the horse, when lazy, longs to plough. What I shall advise is that each contentedly practise the trade he understands.

[c] The verb *limat* (lit. " files away "), as used with *obliquo oculo*, involves a play upon *limis oculis* (*cf. Sat.* ii. 5. 53).

XV

TO VALA

Ordered by his physician to take the cold-water cure, Horace writes to his friend Vala for information about two seaside places, Velia and Salernum, especially as to the climate, people, drinking water, game, and fish. As such an interest in personal luxuries may seem quite inconsistent with doctrines he has often preached, Horace humorously admits that he is like the well-known Maenius, who would loudly proclaim the blessings of a simple life, but, if he had the chance, would indulge his appetite to the full.

The opening paragraph (1-25) is loosely framed, with lengthy parentheses, giving an air of careless freedom of style, after the fashion of conversation in real life. Numonius Vala, who had a country house in southern Italy, belonged to a family of some distinction in Lucania, as is evidenced by coins and inscriptions.

XV.

Quae sit hiems Veliae, quod caelum, Vala, Salerni,
quorum hominum regio et qualis via (nam mihi Baias
Musa supervacuas Antonius, et tamen illis
me facit invisum, gelida cum perluor unda
per medium frigus.   sane murteta relinqui   5
dictaque cessantem nervis elidere morbum
sulfura contemni vicus gemit, invidus aegris,
qui caput et stomachum supponere fontibus audent
Clusinis[1] Gabiosque petunt et frigida rura.
mutandus locus est et deversoria[2] nota   10
praeteragendus equus. "quo tendis? non mihi Cumas
est iter aut Baias," laeva stomachosus habena
dicet[3] eques ; sed equi frenato[4] est auris in ore);
maior utrum populum frumenti copia pascat ;
collectosne bibant imbres puteosne perennis   15
iugis[5] aquae (nam vina nihil moror illius orae :
rure meo possum quidvis perferre patique ;
ad mare cum veni, generosum et lene requiro,
quod curas abigat, quod cum spe divite manet
in venas animumque meum, quod verba ministret,   20
quod me Lucanae iuvenem commendet[6] amicae) ;

[1] Clusinos *VE*.   [2] diversoria *ERφψ*.
    [3] dicit *E*.   [4] equis frenato π.
    [5] dulcis *VE*.   [6] commendat *aR*.

---

[a] Baiae was famous for its hot sulphur baths, but Musa
has prescribed the cold-water treatment, which is not to be
had there.

Epistle XV

What's the winter like, my Vala, at Velia, what's
the climate at Salernum, what sort of people live
there, what kind of road is it—for Antonius Musa
makes Baiae useless to me, and yet[a] puts me in ill
favour there, now that in midwinter I drench myself
in cold water. Of course the town murmurs at its
myrtle-groves being deserted, and its sulphur baths
despised, so famous for driving a lingering disorder
from the sinews, and takes offence at invalids who
dare to plunge head and stomach under the showers
from Clusium's springs, or who repair to Gabii and
its cold country-side. I must change my resort, and
drive my horse past the familiar lodgings. "Where
are you going? I'm not bound for Cumae or Baiae";
so will the rider say as he tugs in anger at the left
rein—but the horse's ear is in its bridled mouth[b]
—which town has the better supply of food, do they
drink rain-water from tanks, or have they spring-
water, welling forth all the year—(for that region's
wines I put out of court : in my country home I
can stand and suffer anything ; but when I go to
the seaside I need something generous and mellow,
to drive care away, to flow with rich hope into veins
and heart, to find me a flow of words, and to give me
the grace of youth with the ladies of Lucania)—

[b] The rider might have spared his words, for the horse
is guided only by the bit.

tractus uter pluris lepores, uter educet apros ;
utra magis piscis et echinos aequora celent,
pinguis ut inde domum possim Phaeaxque reverti,
scribere te nobis, tibi nos accredere par est.   25

  ¹Maenius, ut rebus maternis atque paternis
fortiter absumptis urbanus coepit haberi
scurra vagus, non qui certum praesepe teneret,
impransus non qui civem dinosceret hoste,
quaelibet in quemvis opprobria fingere saevus,²   30
pernicies et tempestas barathrumque macelli,
quidquid quaesierat, ventri donabat³ avaro.
hic ubi nequitiae fautoribus et timidis nil
aut paulum abstulerat, patinas cenabat omasi,
vilis et agninae,⁴ tribus ursis quod satis esset ;   35
scilicet ut ventres lamna candente nepotum
diceret urendos correctus⁵ Bestius. idem,
quidquid erat nactus praedae maioris, ubi omne
verterat⁶ in fumum et cinerem, " non hercule miror,"
aiebat, " si qui comedunt bona, cum sit obeso   40
nil melius turdo, nil vulva pulchrius ampla."

  Nimirum hic ego sum. nam tuta et parvola laudo,
cum res deficiunt, satis inter vilia fortis⁷ :
verum ubi quid melius contingit et unctius, idem
vos sapere et solos aio⁸ bene vivere, quorum   45
conspicitur nitidis fundata pecunia villis.⁹

---

  ¹ *Here a new Epistle begins in all important* MSS. *except* a.
              ² certus *two Bland.*
  ³ donarat *V, II :* donaret *Bentley.*   ⁴ agnini aλ.
  ⁵ correptus *ER :* corrector *Lambinus.*   ⁶ verteret *E.*
      ⁷ *In a ll.* 43-44 *follow* 39 ; *in* π *they follow* 38.
              ⁸ alio φψ.   ⁹ vallis φψ.

  ᵃ As if he were one of the *Alcinoi iuventus* of *Epist*
i. 2. 28.
  ᵇ The language is Plautine. Where food was concerned
he swept everything before him.

which country rears more hares, which, more boars, which one's seas give more hiding to fish and sea-urchins, so that I may return home from there a fat Phaeacian [a]—all this you must write us, and we must credit you in full.

26 Maenius gallantly used up all his mother and father had left him, then came into note as a city wit, a parasite at large, with no fixed fold, a man who when dinnerless knew not friend apart from foe, but would savagely trump up scandal against anybody, the market's ruin, a cyclone and abyss [b]—and so, whatever he gained, he gave to his greedy maw. This fellow, whenever he got little or nothing from those who applauded or feared his wicked wit, would sup on plates of tripe and cheap lamb, enough to satisfy three bears, so as actually to proclaim that prodigals should have their bellies branded with white-hot iron—he, a Bestius reformed! [c] Yet the same man, if he ever got hold of some larger booty, would turn it into smoke and ashes, and then, "In faith, I don't wonder," he would say, "if some devour their substance, since there is nothing better than a fat thrush, nothing finer than a large sow's paunch."

42 Such a man, in truth, am I. When means fail, I cry up a safe and lowly lot, resolute enough where all is paltry : but when something better and richer comes my way I, the same man, say that only men like you are wise and live well [d]—whose invested wealth is displayed in handsome villas.

[c] Nothing is known about Bestius, but he may well have been what Maenius was, a figure in Lucilius. According to Acron, he was severely frugal. Presumably he had been a spendthrift in earlier life. The *corrector* of Lambinus would give good sense, Bestius being an example of the rake in the pulpit. [d] For *bene vivere cf. Epist.* i. 6. 56 ; i. 11. 29.

XVI

TO QUINCTIUS

THE Quinctius addressed may be Quinctius Hirpinus of *Odes* ii. 11. He is evidently a prominent man (l. 18), who is perhaps in public office (ll. 33. 34), but nothing definite is known about him. The Epistle is the poet's commentary on the second Stoic paradox, ὅτι αὐτάρκης ἡ ἀρετὴ πρὸς εὐδαιμονίαν (Cic. *Parad.* 2).

To save you the trouble of asking about the products of my estate, my dear Quinctius, let me describe it to you. It lies in a valley among the hills, gets plenty of sun, has a good climate, grows an abundance of wild fruit and foliage, and possesses a copious spring of fresh water. In this charming retreat I enjoy good health even in the worst season of the year (1-16).

And now about yourself. Are you really the good and happy man that people think you are? Remember that popular applause is fickle, and often insincere, and that those who give titles can also take them away (17-40).

Well, who is the " good " man? The world will answer that it is he who keeps the laws, whose word is a bond and whose testimony is trusted, but those who live near him may know better. Such a man, eager to *seem* good, but not to *be* good, may be no better than the slave, who refrains from stealing merely from fear of being found out (40-62).

The man who has set his heart on money is a creature of desires and fears. He is a deserter from the cause of Virtue. You might treat him as a prisoner or put him to death, yet he may make a useful slave (63-72).

No, the truly good and wise man will be as fearless and independent as Dionysus in the play, for no misfortunes—not death itself—can daunt him (73-79).

XVI.

Ne perconteris, fundus meus, optime Quincti,
arvo pascat erum an bacis opulentet olivae,
pomisne an pratis[1] an amicta[2] vitibus ulmo,
scribetur tibi forma loquaciter et situs agri.

Continui montes, ni[3] dissocientur opaca   5
valle, sed ut veniens dextrum latus aspiciat sol,
laevum discedens[4] curru[5] fugiente vaporet.
temperiem laudes.   quid si[6] rubicunda benigni[7]
corna vepres et pruna ferant ? si[8] quercus et ilex
multa fruge pecus, multa dominum iuvet umbra ? 10
dicas adductum propius frondere Tarentum.
fons etiam rivo dare nomen idoneus, ut nec
frigidior Thracam nec purior ambiat Hebrus,
infirmo capiti fluit utilis, utilis[9] alvo.
hae latebrae dulces, etiam, si credis, amoenae,   15
incolumem tibi me praestant Septembribus horis.

[1] an pratis *E Goth.*: et pratis *most MSS.*
[2] amica *E.*
[3] si *aE* (sci *A²*). *The lemma of Porph. gives* si *but the note supports* ni.
[4] descendens *π*: decedens *Bentley.*   [5] cursu *V.*
[6] quod si *a.*   [7] benignae.
[8] si *omitted by a*; et (*for* si) *π.*
[9] aptus et utilis *A²Rπφ.*

---

[a] Ancient husbandry was chiefly concerned with five products, viz. grain, oil, fruit, cattle, and wine.
[b] *i.e.* the valley of the Digentia (see *Epist.* i. 18. 104),

Epistle XVI

Lest you, my good Quinctius, should have to ask me about my farm, whether it supports its master with plough-land, or makes him rich with olives, whether with apples or with meadows or with vine-clad elms,[a] I will describe for you in rambling style the nature and lie of the land.

[5] There are hills, quite unbroken, were they not cleft by one shady valley,[b] yet such that the rising sun looks on its right side, and when departing in his flying car warms the left. The climate would win your praise. What if you knew that the bushes bear a rich crop of ruddy cornels and plums, that oak and ilex gladden the cattle with plenteous fruitage, and their lord with plenteous shade? You would say that Tarentum with its verdure was brought nearer home. A spring, too, fit to give its name to a river, so that not cooler nor purer is Hebrus winding through Thrace, flows with healing for sickly heads and sickly stomachs. This retreat, so sweet —yes, believe me, so bewitching—keeps me, my friend, in sound health in September's heat.

now called Licenza. Kiessling prefers the rival reading *si dissocientur*, with *temperiem laudes* the main clause in a conditional sentence, meaning : " if you picture a mass of hills broken by a valley, you may imagine how pleasant the climate is."

Tu recte vivis, si curas esse quod audis.
iactamus iam pridem omnis te Roma beatum ;
sed vereor ne cui de te plus quam tibi credas,
neve putes alium sapiente bonoque beatum, 20
neu, si te populus sanum recteque valentem
dictitet, occultam febrem sub tempus[1] edendi
dissimules, donec manibus tremor incidat unctis.
stultorum incurata pudor malus ulcera celat.

Si quis bella tibi terra pugnata marique 25
dicat et his verbis vacuas permulceat auris :
" tene magis salvum populus velit an populum tu,
servet in ambiguo, qui consulit et tibi et urbi,
Iuppiter," Augusti laudes agnoscere possis :
cum pateris[2] sapiens emendatusque vocari, 30
respondesne tuo, dic sodes, nomine ? " nempe
vir bonus et prudens dici delector ego ac tu."
qui dedit hoc hodie, cras, si volet, auferet, ut[3] si
detulerit fasces indigno, detrahet[4] idem.
" pone, meum est " inquit : pono tristisque recedo. 35
idem si clamet furem, neget esse pudicum,
contendat laqueo collum pressisse paternum,
mordear opprobriis falsis mutemque colores ?
falsus honor iuvat et mendax infamia terret
quem nisi mendosum et medicandum[5] ?

---

[1] pectus *aR*π.
[2] pateris *Porph.* : poteris *aR* : cupias *E*.
[3] aut. [4] detrahat *R*.
[5] mendicandum *l*π : mendacem *Ma (corrected)*.

---

[a] The ancients ate with their fingers.
[b] According to the scholiasts the verses cited are from the " Panegyric on Augustus " by Varius, Virgil's great friend.

¹⁷ And you—you live the true life, if you take care to be what people call you. All we in Rome have long talked of you as happy ; but I fear, as touching yourself, that you may give more credit to others than to your own judgement, or that you may think someone other than the wise and good man can be happy ; or that, if over and over men say you are in sound and good health, you may, toward the dinner-hour, disguise the hidden fever, until a trembling falls upon your greasy hands.ᵃ Fools, through false shame, hide the unhealed sore.

²⁵ Suppose a man were to speak of wars fought by you on land and sea, and with words like these flatter your attentive ears :

> May He, to whom both thou and Rome are dear,
> Keep secret still, which is the fuller truth,
> The love of Rome for thee, or thine for her !

you would see in them the praises of Augustus.ᵇ When you suffer yourself to be called wise and flawless, do you answer, pray tell me, in your own name ? " To be sure, I like to be called a good man and wise, even as you do." But they who gave you this title to-day will, if they so please, take it away to-morrow ; even as, if they bestow the lictor's rods on one unworthy, they will likewise wrest them from him. " Put that down, 'tis ours," they say. I do so, and sadly withdraw. If the same people were to cry after me " Thief ! ", call me " Profligate," insist that I strangled my father, ought I to be stung by such lying charges, and change colour ? Whom does false honour delight, whom does lying calumny affright, save the man who is full of flaws and needs the doctor ?

2 A

353

Vir bonus est quis ?   40
" qui consulta patrum, qui leges iuraque servat,
quo multae magnaeque secantur iudice lites,
quo res sponsore[1] et quo causae teste tenentur."
sed videt hunc omnis domus et vicinia tota
introrsum[2] turpem, speciosum pelle decora.   45
" nec furtum feci nec fugi," si mihi dicat[3]
servus, " habes pretium, loris non ureris," aio.
"non hominem occidi" : "non pasces in cruce corvos."
"sum bonus et frugi" : renuit negitatque[4] Sabellus.
cautus enim metuit foveam lupus accipiterque   50
suspectos[5] laqueos et opertum miluus hamum.
oderunt peccare boni virtutis amore.
tu nihil admittes in te formidine poenae :
sit spes fallendi, miscebis sacra profanis.
nam de mille fabae modiis cum surripis unum,   55
damnum est, non facinus, mihi pacto lenius isto.
vir bonus, omne forum quem spectat et omne tribunal,
quandocumque deos vel porco vel bove placat,
" Iane pater ! " clare, clare cum dixit, " Apollo ! "
labra movet metuens audiri : " pulchra Laverna,   60
da mihi fallere, da iusto sanctoque[6] videri,
noctem peccatis et fraudibus obice nubem."
  Qui melior servo, qui[7] liberior sit avarus,
in triviis fixum cum se demittit[8] ob assem,

---

[1] res sponsore V : responsore MSS.
[2] introrsus π^2 : hunc prorsus, II.   [3] dicit.
[4] negitatque VE : negat atque a.
[5] suspectus M, II.
[6] iustum sanctumque $\phi\psi\lambda$.
[7] qui . . . qui V, I : quo . . . quo, II.
[8] demittit E : dimittit aM.

---

[a] Ll. 41-43 are the reply of the person addressed by the
poet. This ought to be Quinctius, but the poet is now

⁴⁰ Who is the " good man " ? " He who observes
the Senate's decrees, the statutes and laws ; whose
judgement settles many grave suits : whose surety
means safety for property ; whose testimony wins
suits at law." ᵃ Yet this very man all his household
and all his neighbours see to be foul within, though
fair without, under his comely skin. If a slave were
to say to me, " I never stole or ran away " : my
reply would be, " You have your reward ; you are
not flogged." " I never killed anyone." " You'll
hang on no cross to feed crows." " I am good and
honest." Our Sabine friend ᵇ shakes his head and
says, " No, no ! " For the wolf is wary and dreads
the pit, the hawk the suspected snare, the pike the
covered hook. The good hate vice because they
love virtue ; you ᶜ will commit no crime because
you dread punishment. Suppose there's a hope of
escaping detection ; you will make no difference
between sacred and profane. For when from a
thousand bushels of beans you steal one, my loss in
that case is less, but not your sin. This " good
man," for forum and tribunal the cynosure of every
eye, whenever with swine or ox he makes atonement
to the gods, cries with loud voice " Father Janus,"
with loud voice " Apollo," then moves his lips,
fearing to be heard : " Fair Laverna,ᵈ grant me to
escape detection ; grant me to pass as just and
upright, shroud my sins in night, my lies in clouds ! "

⁶³ How the miser is better than a slave, or is more
free, when he stoops at the cross-roads to pick up
carrying on a dialogue with an imaginary interlocutor.
So " tu " in l. 53.

ᵇ By *Sabellus* Horace means one of his honest Sabine
neighbours.

ᶜ *i.e.* the slave.   ᵈ The goddess of theft.

non video ; nam qui cupiet, metuet quoque ; porro, 65
qui metuens vivet, liber mihi non erit umquam.
perdidit arma, locum Virtutis deseruit, qui
semper in augenda festinat et obruitur re.
vendere cum possis captivum, occidere noli ;
serviet utiliter ; sine pascat durus aretque,   70
naviget ac mediis hiemet mercator in undis,
annonae prosit, portet frumenta penusque.

Vir bonus et sapiens audebit dicere : " Pentheu,
rector Thebarum, quid me perferre patique
indignum coges ? "
　　　　　　" Adimam bona."
　　　　　　　　　　" Nempe pecus, rem,   75
lectos, argentum : tollas licet."
　　　　　　　　　　　" In manicis et
compedibus saevo te sub custode tenebo."
" Ipse deus, simul atque volam, me solvet."   opinor,
hoc sentit " moriar."   mors ultima linea rerum est.[1]

---

[1] est *omitted by E.*

---

[a] We are told that Roman boys would solder a coin to
the pavement and then ridicule those who tried to pick it
up (so scholiast on Persius, v. 111).

[b] Such a man is really a slave, and should be treated as
such.

[c] As opposed to the man called *bonus* in ll. 32 and 57.

[d] The dialogue following is paraphrased from Euripides,
Bacchae, 492-8, a scene where the disguised Dionysus defies

the copper fastened there,[a] I do not see: for he who covets will also have fears; further, he who lives in fear, will never, to my mind, be free. A man has lost his weapons, has quitted his post with Virtue, who is ever busied and lost in making money. When you can sell a captive,[b] don't kill him: he will make a useful slave. If hardy, let him be shepherd or ploughman: let him go to sea, and winter as a trader in the midst of the waves: let him help the market: let him carry food and fodder.

[73] The truly good and wise man[c] will have courage to say:[d] " Pentheus, lord of Thebes, what shame will you compel me to stand and suffer ? "

" I will take away your goods."

" You mean my cattle, my substance, couches, plate ? You may take them."

" I will keep you in handcuffs and fetters, under a cruel jailer."

" God himself, the moment I choose, will set me free." This, I take it, is his meaning: " I will die."[e] Death is the line that marks the end of all.[f]

Pentheus, king of Thebes. The latter, intent on suppressing the Bacchic worship, has made a prisoner of the Lydian stranger, who, being really a god, sets the king's threats at nought.

[e] The *moriar* does not belong to the scene. The Stoics sanctioned suicide as an escape from life's evils.

[f] A chalk-line marked the goal in the race-course.

XVII

TO SCAEVA

THE subject of this and the following Epistle is
personal independence, as illustrated in the relations
of patron and *protégé*. Horace's own happy con-
nexion with Maecenas, which he sets forth so ad-
mirably in *Epist.* i. 7, furnished him with an experi-
ence which possibly led others to seek his advice as
to their conduct toward men of high station. As
to Scaeva, however, nothing is known about him,
and it is quite possible that there was no such person
in real life, but that the name was chosen to fit an
assumed character, it being the same as σκαιός,
" awkward " or " *gauche.*"

After disclaiming any peculiar right to give advice
on such a subject (1-5), and assuring Scaeva that if
he really wants to live a quiet, comfortable life, he
should retire from Rome altogether (6-10), Horace
proceeds in reality to defend himself against the
attacks made on him as a sycophant of the great.
He therefore contrasts the conduct of the Cyrenaic
Aristippus, who had plenty of *savoir faire* and
could adapt himself to any circumstances, with the
less sensible behaviour of Diogenes, the boorish
Cynic, who courted the common people and knew how
to live only amid sordid surroundings (13-32). To

gain distinction in life oneself is the highest ambition, but it is also no mean achievement to win favour with the great. He who succeeds in doing so is a true man and plays a manly part (33-42).

Here the tone abruptly changes, and in the last twenty lines (43-62) Horace lays down rules which the young aspirant for favour is supposed to follow. In this part the poet is far from serious, but, after his fashion, is indulging in good-natured irony.

XVII.

Quamvis, Scaeva, satis per te tibi consulis et scis,
quo tandem pacto deceat maioribus uti,
disce, docendus adhuc quae censet amiculus, ut si
caecus iter monstrare velit ; tamen aspice si quid
et nos, quod cures proprium fecisse, loquamur.   5
Si te grata quies et primam somnus in horam
delectat, si te pulvis strepitusque rotarum,
si laedit[1] caupona, Ferentinum ire iubebo.
nam neque divitibus contingunt gaudia solis,
nec vixit male, qui natus moriensque fefellit.   10
si prodesse tuis pauloque benignius ipsum
te tractare voles, accedes siccus ad unctum.[2]
" Si pranderet holus patienter, regibus uti
nollet Aristippus." " si sciret regibus uti,
fastidiret holus qui me notat." utrius horum   15
verba probes et facta doce, vel iunior audi
cur sit Aristippi potior sententia. namque
mordacem Cynicum sic eludebat, ut aiunt :

---

[1] laedet *a M, II.*
[2] ad unctum *Porph. MSS.* : inunctum *V* : adinunctum *E.*

---

[a] A quiet country town in the Alban region of Latium,
according to Professor W. B. M‘Daniel (*A.P.A.* xliii. pp. 67 ff.).
[b] According to the Epicurean precept, λάθε βιώσας.
[c] This remark is made by Diogenes the Cynic. The story
referred to is found in Diogenes Laertius, ii. 8. 68. The
Cynic was cleaning vegetables for dinner, when Aristippus
passed by. Said the former: " if you had learned to put up

EPISTLE XVII

Even though, Scaeva, you look after your own interests quite wisely by yourself, though you know on what terms, in fine, one should handle greater folk, yet learn the views of your humble friend, who still needs some teaching. It is as if a blind man sought to show the way; yet see whether even I have aught to say, which you may care to make your own.

[6] If pleasant ease and sleep till sunrise be your delight, if dust and noise of wheels, or if tavern offend you, I shall order you off to Ferentinum.[a] For joys fall not to the rich alone, and he has not lived amiss who from birth to death has passed unknown.[b] But if you wish to help your friends and to treat yourself a little more generously, you in your hunger will make for a rich table.

[13] "If Aristippus could be content to dine on greens, he would not want to live with princes."[c] "If he who censures me knew how to live with princes, he would sniff at greens." Of these two sages tell me whose words and deeds you approve; or, since you are the younger, hear why the view of Aristippus is the better. For this is the way, as the story goes, that he dodged the snapping cynic: "I

with this, you would not be courting princes." To this gibe Aristippus replied, "and you, if you knew how to consort with men, would not be cleaning greens."

" scurror ego ipse mihi, populo tu ; rectius[1] hoc et
splendidius multo est. equus ut me portet, alat rex,
officium facio ; tu poscis vilia, verum[2]   21
dante minor, quamvis fers te nullius egentem.''
omnis Aristippum decuit color et status et res,
temptantem maiora, fere praesentibus aequum.
contra, quem duplici panno patientia velat,   25
mirabor, vitae via si conversa decebit.
alter purpureum non exspectabit amictum,
quidlibet indutus celeberrima per loca[3] vadet,
personamque feret non inconcinnus utramque ;
alter Mileti textam cane peius et angui   30
vitabit[4] chlamydem, morietur frigore, si non
rettuleris pannum. refer et sine vivat ineptus.

Res gerere et captos ostendere civibus hostis
attingit solium Iovis et caelestia temptat :
principibus placuisse viris non ultima laus est.   35
non cuivis homini contingit adire Corinthum.
sedit qui timuit ne non succederet.

                                        " Esto.
quid, qui pervenit,[5] fecitne viriliter ? ''   atqui
hic est aut nusquam, quod quaerimus. hic onus horret,
ut parvis animis et parvo corpore maius ;   40

---

    [1] regibus φψ.
    [2] verum *or* verum es, *I, II* : rerum (*to be taken with* vilia)
only inferior MSS.
    [3] ioca, *II*.   [4] vitavit *a M*.   [5] pervenerit, *II*.

---

    [a] *Scurror* means " play the *scurra*." In effect, Diogenes
had taunted him with being a parasite.
    [b] The cloak worn by the Cynics is called *pannus* in
contempt. They wore no under-garment, but doubled the
cloak instead. Hence it was called διπλοΐς.
    [c] The poet refers in a general way to the triumphal career
of Augustus.

play the buffoon [a] for my own profit, you for the people's. My conduct is better and nobler by far. I do service that I may have a horse to ride and be fed by a prince : you sue for paltry doles ; but you become inferior to the giver, though you pose as needing no man." To Aristippus every form of life was fitting, every condition and circumstance ; he aimed at higher things, but as a rule was content with what he had. On the other hand, take the man whom endurance clothes with its double rags [b] : I shall marvel if a changed mode of life befit him. The one will not wait for a purple mantle ; he will put on anything and walk through the most crowded streets, and in no inelegant fashion will play either part. The other will shun a cloak woven at Miletus as worse than a dog or a snake, and will die of cold if you do not give him back his rags. Give them back and let him live his uncouth life.

[33] To achieve great deeds and to display captive foemen to one's fellow-citizens is to touch the throne of Jove and to scale the skies.[c] Yet to have won favour with the foremost men is not the lowest glory. It is not every man's lot to get to Corinth.[d] He who feared he might not win sat still.[e]

Be it so —what of him who reached the goal ? Did he play the man ? Nay, but here or nowhere is what we look for. One dreads the burden as too big for his small soul and small body : another lifts

[d] A rendering of the Greek proverb, Οὐ παντὸς ἀνδρὸς ἐς Κόρινθον ἔσθ' ὁ πλοῦς, which originally referred to the great expense of a self-indulgent life at Corinth. Here, however, the application is very different, viz. that not everyone can gain the prize of virtue.

[e] *i.e.* never entered the race.

hic subit et perfert.   aut virtus nomen inane est,
aut decus et pretium recte petit experiens vir.

    Coram rege sua[1] de paupertate tacentes
plus poscente ferent[2] : distat, sumasne pudenter
an rapias ; atqui rerum caput hoc erat, hic fons.   45
" indotata mihi soror est, paupercula mater,
et fundus nec vendibilis nec pascere firmus,"
qui dicit, clamat, " victum date ! " succinit alter,
" et mihi ! " dividuo findetur munere quadra.
sed tacitus pasci si posset corvus, haberet   50
plus dapis et rixae multo minus invidiaeque.

    Brundisium comes aut Surrentum ductus amoenum
qui queritur salebras et acerbum frigus et imbres,
aut cistam effractam et subducta viatica plorat,
nota refert meretricis acumina, saepe catellam,   55
saepe periscelidem raptam sibi flentis, uti mox
nulla fides damnis verisque doloribus adsit.
nec semel irrisus triviis attollere curat
fracto crure planum, licet illi plurima manet
lacrima, per sanctum iuratus dicat Osirim :   60
" credite, non ludo ; crudeles, tollite claudum ! "
" quaere peregrinum," vicinia rauca reclamat.

[1] sua *Bentley*: suo MSS.   [2] ferunt *E.*

---

    [a] In comedy the term *rex* is used by a parasite of his
patron ; *cf.* Plautus, *Capt.* 92 ; Terence, *Phormio* 338.
So βασιλεύς in Greek comedy ; *cf.* Meineke, fragm. p. 774
βασιλέως υἱὸν λέγεις ἀφῖχθαι.

    [b] Viz. getting as much as possible.

    [c] As a result of so much begging no one gets a whole loaf.

slander. A *protégé*, you see, must be ever watchful of his conduct. He must fall in with his patron's moods and at all times show a cheery face (67-95).

Above all, you must study the words of the wise and learn the secret of a tranquil life. That is what *I* have found in my peaceful country home, where I pray the gods for the blessings of life, for the means of living, and for a goodly supply of books. The *aequus animus* I will see to myself (96-112).

This Epistle is addressed to the Lollius whom we have already met in the second Epistle of this book. Yet the main theme of the letter is the same as that already treated in the seventeenth, viz. the manner in which a person should conduct himself in his intercourse with the great. Lollius, however, is not what Scaeva is conceived to have been, poor and of lowly station. He has an ancestral estate, large enough to be the scene of an historical pageant, and he was probably the son of the Lollius who was Consul in 21 B.C. (*cf. Epist.* i. 20. 28).

It is commonly supposed that the young Lollius is thinking of attaching himself to a man of great prominence in the state, with whom he would be on terms of confidential intimacy (ll. 37 f. ; 68 ff.), and that he has consulted Horace, who has himself been so successful with a patron. But most commentators take the letter too seriously. It is a satire and the poet is in a playful mood (see *e.g.* ll. 72 ff.). So, under the guise of a Professor of Social Philosophy, he gives his young friend a lecture in Stoic fashion on his favourite theme *bene vivere*, which here may be taken to mean " How to get on in the world."

XVIII.

Si bene te novi, metues, liberrime Lolli,
scurrantis speciem praebere, professus amicum
ut matrona meretrici dispar erit atque
discolor, infido scurrae distabit amicus.
est huic diversum vitio vitium prope maius,   5
asperitas agrestis et inconcinna gravisque,
quae se commendat tonsa cute, dentibus atris,
dum volt libertas dici mera veraque virtus.
virtus est medium vitiorum et utrimque[1] reductum.
alter in obsequium plus aequo pronus et imi   10
derisor lecti sic nutum divitis horret,
sic iterat voces et verba cadentia tollit,
ut puerum saevo credas dictata magistro
reddere vel partis mimum tractare secundas.
alter rixatur[2] de lana saepe caprina,[3]   15
propugnat nugis armatus : " scilicet, ut non
sit mihi prima fides, et vere quod placet ut non
acriter elatrem !   pretium aetas altera sordet."

[1] utrumque *aR*.
[2] rixatur *MSS.* : rixatus *V* : rixator *Muretus.*
[3] caprina et *Bentley.*

---

[a] *Cf. Epist.* i. 17. 19 and note.
[b] μεσότης δύο κακιῶν (Arist. *Nicomach. Eth.* ii. 6).
[c] *Cf. Sat.* ii. 8. 40 f., where the *scurrae* were with the host
on the lowest couch.

Epistle XVIII

If I know you well, my Lollius, most outspoken of men, you will shrink from appearing in the guise a parasite [a] when you have professed the friend. s matron and mistress will differ in temper and ne, so will the friend be distinct from the faithless arasite. There is a vice the opposite of this— erhaps a greater one—a clownish rudeness, awkward d offensive, which commends itself by shaggy skin and black teeth, while fain to pass for simple candour and pure virtue. Virtue is a mean between vices,[b] remote from both extremes. The one man, over-prone to servility, a jester of the lowest couch,[c] so reveres the rich man's nod, so echoes his speeches, and picks up his words as they fall, that you would think a schoolboy was repeating his lessons to a stern master or a mime-player acting a second part.[d] The other man wrangles often about goat's wool,[e] and donning his armour fights for trifles: " To think, forsooth, that I should not find credence first, or that I should not blurt out strongly what I really think ! A second life were poor at such a

---

[d] In the mimes the actor playing second part commonly imitated the chief actor in word and gesture.
[e] The question whether the hair of goats could be called *lana* or wool, was proverbial for a matter of no importance.

ambigitur quid enim? Castor sciat an Dolichos[1] plus
Brundisium Minuci melius via ducat an Appi.   2

  Quem damnosa Venus, quem praeceps alea nudat,
gloria quem supra vires et vestit et unguit,
quem tenet argenti sitis importuna famesque,
quem paupertatis pudor et fuga, dives amicus,
saepe decem vitiis instructior, odit et horret,   2
aut, si non odit, regit ac veluti pia mater
plus quam se sapere et virtutibus esse priorem
volt et ait prope vera : " meae (contendere noli)
stultitiam patiuntur opes ; tibi parvola res est.
arta decet sanum comitem toga ; desine mecum
certare." Eutrapelus, cuicumque nocere volebat,
vestimenta dabat pretiosa : " beatus enim iam
cum pulchris tunicis sumet[2] nova consilia et spes,
dormiet in lucem, scorto postponet honestum
officium, nummos alienos pascet, ad imum   3
Thraex erit aut holitoris aget[3] mercede caballum."

  Arcanum neque tu scrutaberis illius[4] umquam,
commissumque teges et vino tortus et ira.
nec tua laudabis studia aut aliena reprendes,[5]
nec, cum venari volet ille, poemata panges.[6]   4
gratia sic fratrum geminorum, Amphionis atque
Zethi, dissiluit, donec suspecta severo
conticuit lyra. fraternis cessisse putatur
moribus Amphion : tu cede potentis amici

---

[1] docilis *MSS.*   [2] sumit *E.*   [3] aget *E* : agit *a M.*
[4] ullius *MSS.*   [5] repedes *E.*   [6] pangas *E.*

---

[a] These were actors or gladiators.
[b] The story of how the brothers Zethus and Amphion
quarrelled about the rival merits of music and hunting was
set forth by Euripides in his *Antiope,* and was reproduced
in a play of the same name by Pacuvius.

370

price." Why, what's the question in dispute? Whether Castor or Dolichos [a] has more skill; which is the better road to Brundisium, that of Minucius or that of Appius!

21 The man whom ruinous passion or desperate gambling strips bare, whom vanity dresses up and perfumes beyond his means, who is possessed by an insatiate hunger and thirst for money, by the shame and dread of poverty, his rich friend, though often ten times as well equipped with vices, hates and abhors; or if he does not hate him schools him and like a fond mother would have him wiser and more virtuous than himself. He says to him what is pretty nearly true : " My wealth—don't try to rival me— fallows of folly : your means are but trifling. A narrow toga befits a client of sense; cease to vie with me." Eutrapelus, if he wished to injure someone, would give him costly clothes : " for now," said he, " the happy fellow will, together with his fine tunics, put on new plans and hopes, will sleep till dawn, will postpone honest business for a wanton, will swell his debts, and at last will become a gladiator, or the hired driver of a greengrocer's nag."

37 You will never pry into your patron's secrets, and if one is entrusted to you, you will keep it, though wine or anger puts you on the rack. Again, you will neither praise your own tastes, nor find fault with those of others, nor when your friend would go a-hunting, will you be penning poems. 'Twas so that the brotherly bond between the twins Amphion and Zethus parted asunder, till the lyre, on which the stern one looked askance, was hushed.[b] Amphion, 'tis thought, yielded to his brother's mood : do you yield to your great friend's gentle biddings;

371

lenibus imperiis, quotiensque educet[1] in agros   45
Aetolis[2] onerata plagis iumenta canesque,
surge et inhumanae senium depone Camenae,
cenes ut pariter pulmenta laboribus empta :
Romanis sollemne viris opus, utile famae
vitaeque et membris ; praesertim cum valeas et   50
vel cursu superare canem vel viribus aprum
possis.   adde virilia quod speciosius arma
non est qui tractet ; scis, quo clamore coronae
proelia sustineas campestria ; denique saevam
militiam puer et Cantabrica bella tulisti   55
sub duce qui templis Parthorum signa refigit
nunc et, si quid abest, Italis[3] adiudicat armis.[4]

Ac ne te retrahas et inexcusabilis absis,
quamvis nil extra numerum fecisse modumque
curas, interdum nugaris rure paterno :   60
partitur lintres exercitus, Actia pugna
te duce per pueros hostili more[5] refertur ;
adversarius est frater, lacus Hadria, donec
alterutrum velox Victoria fronde coronet.
consentire suis studiis qui crediderit te,   65
fautor utroque tuum laudabit pollice ludum.

        [1] educit *M* : ducit *or* ducet, *II*.
   [2] Aeoliis *van Vliet*.   [3] abest aliis π.
      [4] arvis *Bentley*.   [5] mole *E*.

---

[a] Probably a literary epithet, reminding the reader of
the mythical boar-hunt of Meleager in Calydon.   The con-
jectural *Aeoliis* is explained as equivalent to *Cumanis*, because
flax, which made strong nets (Pliny, *N.H.* xix. 1. 10), grew
near Cumae, a colony from Cyme in Aeolia.

[b] *Cf.* " tu pulmentaria quaere sudando," *Sat.* ii. 2. 20.

[c] *Cf. Sat.* ii. 2. 10 f., where hunting is called *Romana
militia*.

[d] *i.e.* the sports of the Campus Martius.

[e] In 20 b.c. Augustus recovered from the Parthians by

and when he takes out into the country his mules
laden with Aetolian [a] nets, and his dogs, up with you
and cast aside the glumness of your unsocial Muse,
that you may share his supper with a relish, whereof
toil has been the price [b]—'tis the wonted pastime
of the heroes of Rome,[c] is good for fame as well as
for life and limb—especially when you are in health,
and can outdo either the hound in speed or the boar
in strength. Add that there is none who more grace-
fully handles manly weapons : you know how loudly
the ring cheers when you uphold the combats of the
Campus.[d] In fine, while a mere youth, you served in
a hard campaign, and in the Cantabrian wars, under
a captain who even now is taking down our standards
from the Parthian temples [e] and, if aught is still
beyond our sway, is assigning it to the arms of Italy.

[58] Further, that you may not draw back and stand
aloof without excuse, bear in mind that, however
much you take care to do nothing out of time and
tune, you do sometimes amuse yourself at your
father's country-seat : your troops divide the skiffs [f];
with you as captain, the Actian fight is presented by
your slaves in true foemen's style ; opposing you is
your brother, the lake is the Adriatic ; till winged
Victory crowns with leafage one or the other chief-
tain. He who believes that you fall in with his
pursuits will with both thumbs [g] eagerly commend
your sport.

treaty the standards they had taken from Crassus ; *cf. Epist.*
i. 12. 28.

[f] In a sham fight on their father's estate, Lollius and his
brother have represented the famous battle of Actium.

[g] A reference to the way in which the audience in the
amphitheatre expressed approval. The precise form of the
gesture referred to is doubtful.

Protinus ut moneam (si quid monitoris eges tu)
quid de quoque viro et cui dicas, saepe videto.
percontatorem fugito : nam garrulus idem est,
nec retinent patulae commissa fideliter aures,   70
et semel emissum volat irrevocabile verbum.
non ancilla tuum iecur ulceret ulla puerve
intra marmoreum venerandi limen amici,
ne dominus pueri[1] pulchri caraeve puellae
munere te parvo beet aut incommodus angat.   75
qualem commendes, etiam atque etiam aspice, ne mox
incutiant aliena tibi peccata pudorem.
fallimur et quondam non dignum tradimus : ergo
quem sua culpa premet, deceptus omitte tueri,
ut penitus notum, si temptent crimina, serves   80
tuterisque tuo fidentem[2] praesidio : qui
dente Theonino cum circumroditur, ecquid[3]
ad te post paulo ventura pericula sentis ?
nam tua res agitur, paries cum proximus ardet,
et neglecta solent incendia sumere vires.   85

Dulcis inexpertis cultura potentis amici :
expertus metuit.[4] tu, dum tua navis in alto est,
hoc age, ne mutata retrorsum te ferat aura.
oderunt hilarem tristes tristemque iocosi,
sedatum celeres, agilem navumque remissi ;   90
potores [bibuli media de nocte Falerni[5]
oderunt] porrecta negantem pocula, quamvis
nocturnos iures te formidare tepores.

[1] pueri dominus *E, lemma in Porph.*
[2] fidens est φψλl: fidenter.   [3] et quid A^2ER.
[4] metuit *a M* : metuet *E, II.*
[5] *Line 91 does not occur in any good MS. unless inserted by a late hand. Meineke deleted* bibuli . . . oderunt *and retained* potores.

[a] Proverbial for calumny, though the origin of the expression is unknown.

⁶⁷ To continue my advice, if you need advice in aught—think often of what you say, and of whom, and to whom you say it. Avoid a questioner, for he is also a tattler. Open ears will not keep secrets loyally, and the word once let slip flies beyond recall. Let no maid or boy within your worshipful friend's marble threshold inflame your heart, lest the owner of the pretty boy or dear girl make you happy with a present so trifling or torment you if disobliging. What sort of a person you introduce, consider again and again, lest by and by the other's failings strike you with shame. At times we err and present some-one unworthy : therefore, if taken in, forbear to defend him whose own fault drags him down, in order that, if charges assail one you know thoroughly, you may watch over and protect the man who relies on your championship. For when he is nibbled at with Theon's tooth ᵃ of slander, don't you feel that a little later the peril will pass to yourself ? 'Tis your own safety that's at stake, when your neighbour's wall is in flames, and fires neglected are wont to gather strength.

⁸⁶ Those who have never tried think it pleasant to court a friend in power ; one who has tried dreads it. While your barque is on the deep, see to it lest the breeze shift and bear you back. The grave dislike the gay, the merry the grave, the quick the staid, the lazy the stirring man of action : drinkers [who quaff Falernian in midnight hours] ᵇ hate the man who declines the proffered cups, however much you swear that you dread fevers at night. Take the

ᵇ The words bracketed in the Latin were probably intro-duced as a gloss from *Epist.* i. 14. 34.

deme supercilio nubem : plerumque modestus
occupat obscuri speciem, taciturnus acerbi.   95

Inter cuncta leges et percontabere doctos,
qua ratione queas traducere leniter aevum,
num te semper inops agitet vexetque cupido,
num[1] pavor et rerum mediocriter utilium spes,
virtutem doctrina paret Naturane donet,   100
quid minuat curas, quid te tibi reddat amicum,
quid pure tranquillet, honos an dulce lucellum,
an secretum iter et fallentis semita vitae.

Me quotiens reficit gelidus Digentia rivus,
quem Mandela bibit, rugosus frigore pagus,   105
quid sentire putas ? quid credis, amice, precari ?
sit mihi quod nunc est, etiam minus, et[2] mihi vivam
quod superest aevi, si quid superesse volunt di ;
sit bona[3] librorum et provisae frugis in annum
copia, neu fluitem dubiae spe pendulus horae.[4]   110

Sed satis est orare Iovem, qui[5] ponit[6] et aufert,
det vitam, det opes ; aequum mi animum ipse
    parabo.''

> [1] num . . . num *all good* MSS., *V* : ne *or* non.
> [2] et *V, II* : ut *aEM Porph.*
> [3] spes bona *E.*   [4] aurae.
> [5] quae *a, II.*   [6] ponit *V, II* : donat, *I.*

---

[a] *i.e.* philosophers.
[b] These are things which may be contrasted with virtue,
the *summum bonum, e.g.* our possessions, classed by the
Stoics as ἀδιάφορα, indifferent things.
[c] Whether virtue can be taught (διδακτή, *cf. doctrina*) is
discussed in Plato's *Meno.*

cloud from your brow ; shyness oft gets the look of secrecy, silence of sour temper.

⁹⁶ Amid all this you must read and question the wise,ᵃ how you may be able to pass your days in tranquillity. Is greed, ever penniless, to drive and harass you, or fears and hopes about things that profit little ?ᵇ Does wisdom beget virtue,ᶜ or Nature bring her as a gift ? What will lessen care ? What will make you a friend to yourself ? What gives you unruffled calm—honour, or the sweets of dear gain, or a secluded journey along the pathway of a life unnoticed ᵈ ?

¹⁰⁴ For me, oft as Digentia ᵉ refreshes me, the icy brook of which Mandela drinks, that village wrinkled with cold, what deem you to be my feelings ? What, think you, my friend, are my prayers ? May I have my present store, or even less ; may I live to myself for what remains of life, if the gods will that aught remain. May I have a goodly supply of books and of food to last the year ; nor may I waver to and fro with the hopes of each uncertain hour.

¹¹¹ But 'tis enough to pray Jove, who gives and takes away, that he grant me life, and grant me means : a mind well balanced I will myself provide.ᶠ

ᵃ *Cf. Epist.* i. 17. 10.

ᵉ *Cf. Epist.* i. 16. 5, with its note *b*. Mandela, now Cantalupo Bardella, is a lofty village, whose people came down to the Digentia for their water.

ᶠ *i.e.* the gods may give me life, and the means of existence, but, as Henley says, " I am the captain of my soul."

XIX

TO MAECENAS

WRITING shortly before the publication of this book, in 20 B.C., Horace replies to the adverse criticism which had been levelled against his *Epodes* and *Odes* (Books i.-iii.). These, it was claimed, lacked originality and were mere imitations of Greek exemplars. Horace therefore contrasts the rude and servile imitation, to which he has himself been subjected, with his own generous use of noble models, according to rules followed by the great Greek poets themselves (1-34).

But the real reason why Horace has been assailed lies in the fact that the poet has not tried to please the general public or his offended critics. He refuses to resort to the usual methods of winning approval, and is therefore supposed to be arrogant. This is a charge which he declines to face (35-49).

XIX.

Prisco si credis, Maecenas docte, Cratino,
nulla placere diu nec vivere carmina possunt,
quae scribuntur aquae potoribus.[1] ut male sanos
adscripsit Liber Satyris Faunisque poetas,
vina fere dulces oluerunt mane Camenae.   5
laudibus arguitur vini vinosus Homerus ;
Ennius ipse pater numquam nisi potus ad arma
prosiluit dicenda. " Forum Putealque Libonis
mandabo siccis, adimam cantare severis " :
hoc simul edixi,[2] non cessavere poetae   10
nocturno certare mero, putere diurno.
quid ? si quis voltu torvo ferus et pede nudo
exiguaeque togae simulet textore[3] Catonem,
virtutemne repraesentet moresque Catonis ?
rupit Iarbitam Timagenis aemula lingua,[4]   15
dum studet urbanus tenditque disertus haberi.

---

[1] potioribus $ER\pi$.   [2] edixi E, *Porph.* : edixit a.
[3] ex ore $\phi\psi$: extore R.   [4] cena aE.

---

[a] On Cratinus see Index. In his Πυτίνη he jested upon
his own intemperance.

[b] *Cf. Iliad*, vi. 261 ἀνδρὶ δὲ κεκμηῶτι μένος μέγα οἶνος ἀέξει,
and the use of epithets applied to wine, such as εὐήνωρ, ἡδύποτος,
μελιηδής, μελίφρων.

[c] Ennius says of himself, "numquam poetor nisi si
podager."

Epistle XIX

If you follow old Cratinus,[a] my learned Maecenas,
no poems can please long, nor live, which are written
by water-drinkers. From the moment Liber en-
listed brain-sick poets among his Satyrs and Fauns,
the sweet Muses, as a rule, have had a scent of wine
about them in the morning. Homer, by his praises
of wine, is convicted as a winebibber.[b] Even Father
Ennius never sprang forth to tell of arms save after
much drinking.[c] "To the sober I shall assign the
Forum and Libo's Wall[d]; the stern I shall debar
from song." Ever since I put forth this edict,[e] poets
have never ceased to vie in wine-drinking by night,
to reek of it by day. What, if a man were to ape
Cato with grim and savage look, with bare feet and
the cut of a scanty gown, would he thus set before
us Cato's virtue and morals? In coping with Tima-
genes, his tongue brought ruin to Iarbitas[f]; so
keen was his aim and effort to be deemed a man of

---

[d] Cf. Sat. ii. 6. 35. The expression forum putealque
Libonis denotes a life of business.
[e] For the term used cf. Sat. ii. 2. 51.
[f] The precise meaning of rupit is uncertain. Porphyrio
takes it literally, as if the attempt to rival the eloquence
of Timagenes (a rhetorician of the day) made Iarbitas
"burst asunder." More probably the word has the general
sense of "ruined."

decipit exemplar vitiis imitabile : quod si
pallerem[1] casu, biberent exsangue cuminum.
o imitatores, servum pecus, ut mihi saepe
bilem, saepe iocum vestri movere tumultus !　　20

Libera per vacuum posui vestigia princeps,
non aliena meo pressi pede.　qui sibi fidet,[2]
dux reget[3] examen.　Parios[4] ego primus iambos
ostendi Latio, numeros animosque secutus
Archilochi, non res et agentia verba Lycamben.　25
ac ne me foliis ideo brevioribus ornes,
quod timui mutare modos et carminis artem,
temperat Archilochi Musam pede mascula Sappho,
temperat Alcaeus, sed rebus et ordine dispar,
nec socerum quaerit, quem versibus oblinat[5] atris,　30
nec sponsae laqueum famoso carmine nectit.
hunc ego, non alio dictum prius ore, Latinus[6]
volgavi fidicen.　iuvat immemorata ferentem
ingenuis[7] oculisque legi manibusque teneri.

Scire velis, mea cur ingratus opuscula lector　35
laudet ametque domi, premat extra limen iniquus :
non ego ventosae plebis suffragia venor
impensis cenarum et tritae munere vestis ;
non ego, nobilium scriptorum auditor[8] et ultor,

---

[1] pallerent $R\pi$.　　　　[2] fidit $\phi\psi\lambda l$.
[3] regit.　　[4] patrios, II.　　[5] obtinet II.
[6] Latinis λl.　　[7] ingeniis.　　[8] adiutor.

---

[a] A pale complexion was supposed to result from drinking cummin.

[b] *i.e.* in the *Epodes*.

[c] Sappho was worthy to rank with men. M. B. Ogle argues (against Bentley) in favour of construing *Musam* with *Archilochi*, and of interpreting *temperat* as "moderates" (*A.J.P.* xliii. (1922) pp. 55 ff.).

[d] A reference to Neobule and her father Lycambes, who were assailed by Archilochus ; *cf. Epod.* vi. 13.

wit and eloquence. A pattern with faults easy to copy leads astray. So if by chance I lost my colour, these poets would drink the bloodless cummin.*a* O you mimics, you slavish herd! How often your pother has stirred my spleen, how often my mirth!

²¹ I was the first to plant free footsteps on a virgin soil ; I walked not where others trod. Who trusts himself will lead and rule the swarm. I was the first to show to Latium the iambics *b* of Paros, following the rhythms and spirit of Archilochus, not the themes or the words that hounded Lycambes. And lest you should crown me with a scantier wreath because I feared to change the measures and form of verse, see how manlike *c* Sappho moulds her Muse by the rhythm of Archilochus ; how Alcaeus moulds his, though in his themes and arrangement he differs, looking for no father-in-law to besmear with deadly verses, and weaving no halter for his bride *d* with defaming rhyme. Him, never before sung by other lips, I, the lyrist of Latium, have made known.*e* It is my joy that I bring things untold before, and am read by the eyes and held in the hands of the gently born.

³⁵ Would you know why the ungrateful reader praises and loves my pieces at home, unjustly decries them abroad? I am not one to hunt for the votes of a fickle public at the cost of suppers and gifts of worn-out clothes.*f* I am not one who, listening to

---

e The poet referred to in *hunc* (l. 32) is Alcaeus, not Archilochus, and Horace is now boasting, not of his *Epodes*, but of his *Odes*.

f The poet here contrasts himself with the politician seeking votes. He does not invite people to come together to hear his poems, and then by unworthy means seek to win their approval.

grammaticas ambire tribus et pulpita dignor.   40
hinc illae lacrimae. " spissis indigna theatris
scripta pudet recitare et nugis addere pondus,"
si dixi, " rides," ait, " et Iovis auribus ista
servas : fidis enim manare poetica mella
te solum, tibi pulcher." ad haec ego naribus uti 45
formido et, luctantis acuto ne secer ungui,
" displicet iste¹ locus," clamo et diludia posco.
ludus enim genuit trepidum certamen et iram,
ira truces inimicitias et funebre bellum.

¹ ille, *II*.

ᵃ I take *nobiles* as used in irony, not in seriousness, for
the opening words of Juvenal " Semper ego auditor tantum ?
numquamne reponam . . . ? " show what l. 39 means as
a whole. *Ultor* is also ironical ; after listening to those
who called themselves *nobiles scriptores* the poet takes his
revenge by reciting. Others take *nobiles scriptores* to mean
Pollio, Virgil, Varius, etc., so that Horace says, " I hear
such good poets that I neglect and so offend the professors
of literature." In this case, *ultor* is added by way of jest.

ᵇ The *grammatici*, who lecture upon the poets from their
pulpita or platforms, are the professional teachers of litera-
ture. *Tribus* is said in contempt.

"noble writers" and taking my revenge,[a] deign to court the tribes of lecturing professors.[b] "Hence those tears."[c] If I say, "I am ashamed to recite my worthless writings in your crowded halls, and give undue weight to trifles," "You are in merry mood," says one, "and keep your lines for the ears of Jove.[d] Fair in your own eyes you are, and believe that you, and you alone, distil the honey of poesy." At this I am afraid to turn up a scornful nose, and lest, if he wrestle with me, I be torn by his sharp nails, "The place[e] you choose suits me not," I cry, and call for a truce in the sports. For such sport begets tumultuous strife and wrath, and wrath begets fierce quarrels, and war to the death.

[c] This expression, first used literally by Terence in his *Andria* (l. 125), where Pamphilus shed tears of sympathy at the funeral of Chrysis, became proverbial in Latin literature, and was used, as here, even when there were no actual tears; *cf.* Cic. *Pro Cael.* 25. 61.

[d] *i.e.* Augustus. *Cf. Sat.* ii. 6. 52.

[e] The battle of wits has become a gladiatorial contest. In this, a combatant, if he thought his opponent had an unfair advantage in position, might call for a pause in the struggle (*diludia*), and an adjustment of conditions.

XX

TO HIS BOOK

This is an Epilogue to the collection of Epistles, now ready for publication.

The poet addresses his Book, as if it were a young and handsome slave, who is eager to escape from his master's house and to see something of the great world. There are untold perils in the path. After a brief vogue, the book will be neglected or sent to the provinces, and finally its doom will be sealed when it becomes a school-book for lads to learn their letters from!

Yet, when the book finds an audience, the poet would have it impart some information about his own life and characteristics.

XX.

Vertumnum Ianumque, liber, spectare videris,
scilicet ut[1] prostes Sosiorum pumice mundus.[2]
odisti clavis et grata sigilla pudico ;
paucis ostendi gemis et communia laudas,
non ita nutritus. fuge quo descendere gestis.   5
non erit emisso reditus tibi. " quid miser egi ?
quid volui ? " dices, ubi quis[3] te laeserit, et scis
in breve te cogi, cum plenus languet amator.

Quod si non odio peccantis desipit augur,
carus eris Romae, donec te deserat[4] aetas ;   10
contrectatus ubi manibus sordescere volgi
coeperis, aut tineas pasces taciturnus inertis
aut fugies Uticam aut vinctus mitteris Ilerdam.
ridebit monitor non exauditus, ut ille
qui male parentem in rupes protrusit[5] asellum   15
iratus : quis enim invitum servare laboret ?
hoc quoque te manet, ut pueros elementa docentem
occupet extremis in vicis balba[6] senectus.

---

[1] ut *omitted by E.*   [2] nudus θψλl.
[3] quid MSS.   [4] deseret.   [5] protrudit *E.*   [6] bella *E.*

[a] *i.e.* the booksellers' quarters in Rome. There is a
double entendre in *prostes, pumice mundus* and in other
expressions in ll. 1-8.
[b] The pumice was used to smooth the ends of the roll.
For the Socii, well-known as booksellers, see *Ars Poet.* 345.
[c] Referring to the *scrinia* or cases, in which books were
kept under lock or seal.
[d] As applied to the book, *in breve cogi* means " rolled up

Epistle XX

You seem, my book, to be looking wistfully toward Vertumnus and Janus,[a] in order, forsooth, that you may go on sale, neatly polished with the pumice [b] of the Sosii. You hate the keys and seals,[c] so dear to the modest ; you grieve at being shown to few, and praise a life in public, though I did not rear you thus. Off with you, down to where you itch to go. When you are once let out, there will be no coming back. " What, alas ! have I done ? What did I want ? " you will say, when someone hurts you, and you find yourself packed into a corner,[d] whenever your sated lover grows languid.

[9] But unless hatred of your error makes the prophet lose his cunning, you will be loved in Rome till your youth leave you ; when you've been well thumbed by vulgar hands and begin to grow soiled, you will either in silence be food for vandal moths, or will run away to Utica, or be sent in bonds to Ilerda.[e] Your monitor, from whom you turned away your ear, will then have his laugh, like the man who in anger pushed his stubborn ass over the cliff : for who would care to save an ass against his will ? This fate, too, awaits you, that stammering age will come upon you as you teach boys their A B C in the city's outskirts.

small." With reference to the slave, it means " brought to poverty."   [e] *i.e.* sent to the provinces.

Cum tibi sol tepidus pluris admoverit auris,[1]
me libertino natum patre et in tenui re   20
maiores pinnas nido extendisse loqueris,
ut quantum generi demas virtutibus addas ;
me primis urbis belli placuisse domique,
corporis exigui, praecanum, solibus aptum,
irasci celerem, tamen ut placabilis essem.   25
forte meum si quis te percontabitur aevum,
me quater undenos sciat implevisse Decembris,
collegam Lepidum quo duxit[2] Lollius anno.

[1] annos.
[2] duxit *mss. Porph.* : dixit *urged by Keller, accepted by Wilkins, Rolfe.*

19 When the milder sun brings you a larger audience, you will tell them about me : that I was a freedman's son, and amid slender means spread wings too wide for my nest, thus adding to my merits what you take from my birth ; that I found favour, both in war and peace, with the foremost in the State ; of small stature, grey before my time, fond of the sun, quick in temper, yet so as to be easily appeased. If one chance to inquire my age, let him know that I completed my forty-fourth December in the year when Lollius drew Lepidus for colleague.[a]

[a] Lollius was consul in 21 B.C. The other consulship, first intended for Augustus himself, was later filled by the appointment of Lepidus.

BOOK II

I

TO AUGUSTUS

IN his *Life of Horace*, Suetonius tells us that the poet composed this Epistle for Augustus after the emperor, on reading certain of his *Sermones*, had complained because none of them were addressed to him : " Augustus scripta quidem eius usque adeo probavit . . . ut . . . post sermones vero quosdam lectos nullam sui mentionem habitam ita sit questus : ' irasci me tibi scito, quod non in plerisque eiusmodi scriptis mecum potissimum loquaris. An vereris ne apud posteros infame tibi sit, quod videaris familiaris nobis esse ? ' Expressitque eclogam ad se cuius initium est *cum tot sustines*," [a] etc. It is quite improbable that the *sermones* here referred to are either the *Satires*, which were published sixteen years earlier, or the First Book of *Epistles*, published some

---

[a] " Augustus appreciated his writings so highly that, after reading some of his *Sermones* and finding no mention therein of himself, he sent him this complaint: 'Know that I am angry with you, because in your several writings of this type you do not address me—me above all. Is it your fear that posterity may deem it to your discredit, that you seem to be intimate with me ?' And so he wrung from the poet the selection addressed to him, beginning *cum tot sustineas*."

392

six years before They must be the *Epistles* addressed
to Florus (ii. 2), and to the Pisones (*Ars Poetica*), the
present Epistle, therefore, being the latest of the
three in composition.

Burdened as you are, O Caesar, with cares of
State, you must not be approached by me in a long
discourse (1-4).

Unlike the demigods of story, whose benefits to
mankind were recognized only after death, your
great services to the world are acknowledged in
your lifetime (5-17), but this principle is not elsewhere
applied by the Romans to contemporary merit, for
they admire only what is ancient, and defend their
attitude on the ground that the best works of the
Greeks were their earliest (18-33). But how can a
line be drawn strictly between ancient and modern
(34-49) ?

Take a list of the older poets, and note how secure
they are in the reputation assigned them by the
critics. Ennius, for example, their " second Homer,"
cares little whether the promises of his Pythagorean
dreams are fulfilled. Naevius is as familiar to us as
if he were a recent writer. So with Pacuvius and
Accius in tragedy ; Afranius, Plautus, Caecilius, and
Terence in comedy (50-62).

This admiration should be more discriminating,
for these early writers are far from perfect and often
call for our indulgence rather than our approval.
It is really envy of contemporary merit that accounts
for this undue praise of the old writers and a
depreciation of the new (63-89).

How different was the attitude of the Greeks
toward novelty ! Once rid of war, they turned like
children from one amusement to another—athletics,

sculpture, painting, music, and tragedy, but in Rome we have been more serious, devoting ourselves to practical affairs, and only now, in these late days, turning to the writing of verses, as I am doing myself (90-117).

This craze is not without its advantages. Poets are free from many vices. They promote the education of the young and serve the cause of religion (118-138). Let us look at the history of dramatic poetry. Beginning with rude Fescennine verses, whose scurrility had to be checked by law, it came under the refining influence of Greek art, which led to the almost complete elimination of the earlier rusticity (139-160). For tragedy the Romans have a natural aptitude, but they lack the finishing touch. Comedy is supposed to involve less labour, but for that very reason failure can not be so easily excused. Plautus, for instance, is careless and slipshod, being more anxious to fill his purse than to write good plays (161-176). The dramatic writer depends for success upon his audience, and therefore I renounce the stage. The masses call for bears and boxers, and even the educated care more for what delights the restless eye than for good drama. If Democritus were alive to-day, he would laugh, not at the scene on the stage, but at the audience, who applaud the actor before he utters a word, simply because of his fine clothes (177-207)! Yet don't suppose that I undervalue an art which I cannot handle, for to me a great dramatic poet, who can move my soul with his airy creations, is a wondrous magician (208-213).

But I pray you, O Caesar, to bestow a share of your patronage on those who write, not for spectators, but for readers (214-218).

We poets, I know, often behave foolishly. We are tactless, over-sensitive to criticism, and expect too much consideration. But, after all, great merits call for great poets to celebrate them. Alexander was a good judge of painting and sculpture, but in poetry his taste was Boeotian, for he paid the wretched Choerilus for his poor verses. You, on the contrary, have chosen Virgil and Varius to sing your exploits, and you know that no sculptor reproduces the features of heroes more faithfully than the poet does their souls (219-250). If I could do so, I should much prefer to sing your exploits, but you are worthy of a greater poet, and I will not run the risk of bringing discredit upon you as well as upon myself. I should no more like to have a poor waxen portrait of myself offered for sale than to be sung in uncouth verses which sooner or later must come to an ignoble end, and provide wrapping material in a grocer's shop (250-270)!

LIBER SECUNDUS

I.

Cum tot sustineas et tanta negotia solus,
res Italas armis tuteris, moribus ornes,
legibus emendes, in publica commoda peccem,
si longo sermone morer tua tempora, Caesar.

Romulus et Liber pater et cum Castore Pollux, 5
post ingentia facta[1] deorum in templa recepti,
dum terras hominumque colunt genus, aspera bella
componunt, agros assignant, oppida condunt,
ploravere suis non respondere favorem
speratum meritis. diram qui contudit hydram 10
notaque[2] fatali portenta labore subegit,
comperit invidiam supremo fine domari.
urit enim fulgore suo, qui praegravat artis
infra se positas ; exstinctus amabitur idem.
praesenti tibi maturos largimur honores, 15
iurandasque tuum per numen[3] ponimus aras,
nil oriturum alias, nil ortum tale fatentes.

Sed tuus hic[4] populus sapiens et iustus in uno,
te nostris ducibus, te Grais anteferendo,

---

[1] fata *Bentley.*   [2] totaque *E.*
[3] numen *VE* : nomen *aM.*   [4] hoc *Bentley.*

---

[a] Augustus initiated many social reforms, in an effort to
improve the morals of the people, *cf. Odes* iii. 24. 35 ; iv.
5. 22 ; iv. 15. 9.   [b] Hercules.

396

BOOK II

Epistle I

Seeing that you alone carry the weight of so many great charges, guarding our Italian state with arms, gracing her with morals,[a] and reforming her with laws, I should sin against the public weal if with long talk, O Caesar, I were to delay your busy hours.

[5] Romulus, father Liber, Pollux and Castor, who, after mighty deeds, were welcomed into the temples of the gods, so long as they had care for earth and human kind, settling fierce wars, assigning lands, and founding towns, lamented that the goodwill hoped for matched not their deserts. He[b] who crushed the fell Hydra and laid low with fated toil the monsters of story found that Envy is quelled only by death that comes at last. For a man scorches with his brilliance who outweighs merits lowlier than his own, yet he, too, will win affection when his light is quenched. Upon you, however, while still among us, we bestow honours betimes, set up altars[c] to swear by in your name, and confess that nought like you will hereafter arise or has arisen ere now.

[18] Yet this people of yours, so wise and just in one respect, in ranking you above our own,

---

[c] According to Suetonius (*Claud.* ii.), an altar was first set up to Augustus at Lugdunum (Lyons) in 12 B.C., yet this Epistle must be a year or two earlier than that date.

cetera nequaquam simili ratione modoque   20
aestimat et, nisi quae terris semota suisque
temporibus defuncta videt, fastidit et odit ;
sic fautor veterum, ut tabulas peccare vetantis,
quas bis quinque viri sanxerunt, foedera regum
vel Gabiis vel cum rigidis aequata Sabinis,   25
pontificum libros, annosa volumina vatum
dictitet[1] Albano Musas in monte locutas.

Si, quia Graiorum[2] sunt antiquissima quaeque
scripta vel optima, Romani pensantur eadem
scriptores trutina, non est quod multa loquamur :   30
nil intra est olea,[3] nil extra est in nuce duri ;
venimus ad summum fortunae, pingimus atque
psallimus et luctamur Achivis doctius[4] unctis.

Si meliora dies, ut vina, poemata reddit,
scire velim, chartis pretium quotus arroget annus.   35
scriptor abhinc annos centum qui decidit, inter
perfectos veteresque[5] referri debet an inter
vilis atque novos ? excludat iurgia finis.
" est vetus atque probus, centum qui perficit annos."
quid, qui deperiit minor uno mense vel anno,   40
inter quos referendus erit ? veteresne poetas,
an quos et praesens et postera respuat[6] aetas ?

---

[1] dicat et $\phi\psi\lambda l$: dicit et $R\pi$.
[2] Graiorum VE: Graecorum aM, II.
[3] olea *Bentley after some inferior* MSS.: oleam MSS.
[4] scitius.   [5] veteresne, II.
[6] respuat V: respuit M: respuet $\phi\psi\lambda l$.

---

[a] The Twelve Tables, drawn up by the Decemvirs.
[b] A copy of a treaty made by Tarquinius Superbus with Gabii and written in archaic letters on bull's hide was still in existence in the time of Dionysius of Halicarnassus, *i.e.* the Augustan age (Dion. Hal. iv. 58).
[c] Books of ritual and religious law.

above Greek leaders, judges all other things by a wholly different rule and method, and scorns and detests all save what it sees has passed from earth and lived its days. So strong is its bias toward things ancient, that the Tables [a] forbidding transgression, which the ten men enacted, treaties in which our kings made equal terms with Gabii [b] or the sturdy Sabines, the Pontiffs' records,[c] the mouldy scrolls of seers [d]—these, it tells us over and over, were spoken by the Muses on the Alban mount.

[28] If, because among Greek writings the oldest are quite the best, we are to weigh Roman writers in the same balance, there is no need of many words. The olive has no hardness within, the nut has none without [e]; we have come to fortune's summit; we paint, we play and sing, we wrestle with more skill than the well-oiled Greeks.

[34] If poems are like wine which time improves, I should like to know what is the year that gives to writings fresh value. A writer who dropped off a hundred years ago, is he to be reckoned among the perfect and ancient, or among the worthless and modern? Let some limit banish disputes. "He is ancient," you say, "and good, who completes a hundred years." "What of one who passed away a month or a year short of that, in what class is he to be reckoned? The ancient poets, or those whom to-day and to-morrow must treat with scorn? "He

---

[d] Such as the Sibylline books.

[e] The Greeks and Romans may differ in the development of their genius just as much as olives and nuts, both of which are fruits, may differ in character from each other. Moreover, though we have conquered the world, it does not follow that we are superior to the Greeks in painting, in music, and in writing.

" iste quidem veteres inter ponetur honeste,
qui vel mense brevi vel toto est iunior anno."
utor permisso, caudaeque pilos ut equinae   45
paulatim vello et demo unum, demo etiam[1] unum,
dum cadat[2] elusus ratione ruentis acervi,
qui redit in[3] fastos[4] et virtutem aestimat annis
miraturque nihil nisi quod Libitina sacravit.

Ennius et sapiens et fortis et alter Homerus,   50
ut critici dicunt, leviter curare videtur,
quo promissa cadant et somnia Pythagorea.
Naevius in manibus non est et mentibus haeret
paene recens ? adeo sanctum est vetus omne poema.
ambigitur quotiens, uter utro sit prior, aufert   55
Pacuvius docti famam senis, Accius alti,
dicitur Afrani toga convenisse Menandro,
Plautus ad exemplar Siculi properare Epicharmi,
vincere Caecilius gravitate, Terentius arte.

[1] etiam, *I*: et item (*or* idem), *II*.
[2] cadet *M*.   [3] ad *E, Porph.*   [4] fastus *aMRπ*.

---

[a] Horace makes use of the logical puzzle known as *sorites* (σωρός, a heap). How many grains of sand make a heap or pile ? The addition of no one grain will make that a heap which was not a heap before. He also seems to have asked how many hairs make a tail. See Plutarch's story of the two horses in his *Sertorius*.

[b] Horace is giving a summary of the conventional literary opinions of his day as to the old writers. Ennius is called *sapiens* because of his philosophical poems, and *fortis*, because in his *Annales* he recounted the *fortia facta patrum*. As to *alter Homerus*, this exaggerated phrase was used of him by Lucilius (ed. Marx, frag. 1189).

[c] Ennius tells us that Homer, appearing to him in a dream, informed him that his soul now dwelt in Ennius's

surely will find a place of honour among the ancients, who is short by a brief month or even a whole year." I take what you allow, and like hairs in a horse's tail, first one and then another I pluck and pull away little by little, till, after the fashion of the falling heap,[a] he is baffled and thrown down, who looks back upon the annals, and values worth by years, and admires nothing but what the goddess of funerals has hallowed.

⁵⁰ Ennius,[b] the wise and valiant, the second Homer (as the critics style him), seems to care but little what becomes of his promises and Pythagorean dreams.[c] Is not Naevius in our hands, and clinging to our minds, almost as of yesterday?[d] So holy a thing is every ancient poem. As often as the question is raised, which is the better of the two, Pacuvius gains fame as the learned old writer, Accius as the lofty one. The gown[e] of Afranius, 'tis said, was of Menander's fit; Plautus hurries along[f] like his model, Epicharmus of Sicily. Caecilius wins the prize for dignity, Terence for art. These authors

body. This doctrine of transmigration of souls was taught by Pythagoras.

[d] Naevius died in 199 B.C. He wrote both tragedies and comedies, as well as an epic, the *Bellum Punicum* (this in Saturnian metre). Of the other writers named here, Pacuvius and Accius were tragic poets; the rest comic poets. For Livius see note *a* overleaf.

[e] Horace mentions the *toga* of Afranius, because that writer's plays were called *togatae*, being comedies based on Italic characters and customs, in contrast with the *palliatae*, which were Greek throughout.

[f] The verb *properare* implies rapidity of movement, which we are to associate with Epicharmus, the great writer of Sicilian comedy. This was " essentially burlesque " (Jevons, *Hist. of Greek Lit.* p. 240).

hos ediscit[1] et hos arto stipata theatro   60
spectat Roma potens ; habet hos numeratque poetas
ad nostrum tempus Livi scriptoris ab aevo.

   Interdum volgus rectum videt, est ubi peccat.
si veteres ita miratur laudatque poetas,
ut nihil anteferat, nihil illis comparet, errat.   65
si quaedam nimis antique, si pleraque dure
dicere credit eos, ignave multa fatetur,
et sapit et mecum facit et Iove iudicat aequo.
non equidem insector delendave[2] carmina Livi[3]
esse reor, memini quae plagosum mihi parvo   70
Orbilium dictare ; sed emendata videri
pulchraque et exactis minimum distantia miror.
inter quae verbum emicuit si forte decorum, et[4]
si versus paulo concinnior unus et alter,
iniuste totum ducit venditque poema.   75

   Indignor quicquam reprehendi, non quia crasse
compositum illepideve putetur, sed quia nuper,
nec veniam antiquis, sed honorem et[5] praemia posci.
recte necne[6] crocum floresque perambulet[7] Attae
fabula si dubitem, clament periisse pudorem   80
cuncti paene patres, ea cum reprehendere coner,
quae gravis Aesopus, quae doctus Roscius egit ;
vel quia nil rectum, nisi quod placuit sibi, ducunt,[8]

      [1] ediscet $R\pi$.   [2] -que, *II*.
    [3] Livii *M* : levi *aE* (*hence Bentley read* Laevi).
 [4] et *M, I*: *omitted in aE*.   [5] ac *E Goth*.   [6] necne] nec.
    [7] perambulat *aMRπ*.   [8] dicunt *Eπ*.

---

   [a] Livius Andronicus, earliest of Latin writers, brought
out two plays, a tragedy and a comedy, in 240 B.C. He
died in 204 B.C.

   [b] For *recte perambulat cf. recto stet fabula talo* (l. 176
below). The name *Atta* is said by Festus to have been a
nickname meaning " one with a light, tripping step."

   [c] The stage was perfumed with saffron-water. In *flores*

mighty Rome learns by heart; these she views, when packed in her narrow theatre; these she counts as her muster-roll of poets from the days of Livius [a] the writer to our own.

[63] At times the public see straight; sometimes they make mistakes. If they admire the ancient poets and cry them up so as to put nothing above them, nothing on their level, they are wrong. If they hold that sometimes their diction is too quaint, and ofttimes too harsh, if they admit that much of it is flat, then they have taste, they take my side, and give a verdict with Jove's assent. Mark you! I am not crying down the poems of Livius—I would not doom to destruction verses which I remember Orbilius of the rod dictated to me as a boy : but that they should be held faultless, and beautiful, and well-nigh perfect, amazes me. Among them, it may be a pleasing phrase shines forth, or one or two lines are somewhat better turned—then these unfairly carry off and sell the whole poem.

[76] I am impatient that any work is censured, not because it is thought to be coarse or inelegant in style, but because it is modern, and that what is claimed for the ancients should be, not indulgence, but honour and rewards. If I were to question whether a play of Atta's keeps its legs [b] or not amidst the saffron and flowers,[c] nearly all our elders would cry out that modesty is dead, when I attempt to blame what stately Aesopus and learned Roscius once acted ; either because they think nothing can be right save what has pleased themselves, or

Porphyrio finds a reference to a play of Atta's called *Matertera*, in which a great number of flowers were enumerated. Atta, a writer of *togatae*, died in 78 B.C. He was, therefore, not very ancient, though his fragments show many archaisms.

vel quia turpe putant parere minoribus, et quae
imberbes[1] didicere senes perdenda fateri.   85
iam Saliare Numae carmen qui laudat et illud,
quod mecum ignorat, solus volt scire videri,
ingeniis non ille favet plauditque sepultis,
nostra sed impugnat, nos nostraque lividus odit.

Quod si tam Graecis novitas invisa fuisset   90
quam nobis, quid nunc esset vetus ? aut quid haberet [2]
quod legeret tereretque viritim[3] publicus usus ?

Ut primum positis nugari Graecia bellis
coepit et in vitium fortuna labier aequa,
nunc athletarum studiis, nunc arsit equorum,   95
marmoris aut eboris fabros aut aeris amavit,
suspendit picta voltum mentemque tabella,
nunc tibicinibus, nunc[4] est gavisa tragoedis ;
sub nutrice puella velut si luderet infans,
quod cupide petiit, mature plena reliquit.   100
quid placet aut odio est, quod non mutabile credas ?[5]
hoc paces habuere bonae ventique secundi.

Romae dulce diu fuit et sollemne reclusa
mane domo vigilare, clienti promere iura,
cautos nominibus rectis expendere nummos,   105
maiores audire, minori dicere, per quae
crescere res posset, minui damnosa libido.

[1] imberbes *MSS.* : imberbi *Cruquius.*
[2] haberes, *II.*   [3] Quiritum *Ursinus.*   [4] tunc, *II.*
[5] *Line* 101 *gives a fair sense here. Lachmann, however,
transposed it so as to follow* 107 *and most editors accept his
verdict. Vollmer puts it after* 102.

---

[a] The hymns of the Salii, a priesthood of Mars instituted
by Numa, were almost unintelligible to the priests them-
selves in the days of Quintilian ; "Saliorum carmina vix
sacerdotibus suis satis intellecta " (Quint. i. 6. 40).

[b] Probably a reference to the Persian wars, which were

because they hold it a shame to yield to their juniors, and to confess in their old age that what they learned in beardless youth should be destroyed. Indeed, whoever cries up Numa's Salian hymn,[a] and would alone seem to understand what he knows as little of as I do, that man does not favour and applaud the genius of the dead, but assails ours to-day, spitefully hating us and everything of ours.

90 But if novelty had been as offensive to the Greeks as it is to us, what in these days would be ancient ? What would the public have to read and thumb, each according to his taste ?

93 From the day she dropped her wars,[b] Greece took to trifling, and amid fairer fortunes drifted into folly : she was all aglow with passion, now for athletes, now for horses ; she raved over workers in marble or ivory or bronze ; with eyes and soul she hung enraptured on the painted panel ; her joy was now in flautists, and now in actors of tragedy. Like a baby-girl playing at its nurse s feet, what she wanted in impatience, she soon, when satisfied, cast off. What likes and dislikes are there that you would not think easily changed ? Such was the effect of happy times of peace and prosperous gales.

103 At Rome it was long a pleasure and habit to be up at dawn with open doors, to set forth the law for clients, to pay out to sound debtors money under bonds, to give ear to one's elders and to tell one's juniors how an estate might be increased and ruinous

followed by a wonderful literary and artistic epoch in Athens. In what follows Horace speaks of the various arts and pursuits of peace from the old Roman point of view. When the Roman was not at war, he was at work (*cf.* ll. 103 ff.).

mutavit mentem populus levis et calet uno
scribendi studio ; pueri[1] patresque severi
fronde comas vincti cenant et carmina dictant.   110
ipse ego, qui nullos me adfirmo scribere versus,
invenior Parthis mendacior, et prius orto
sole vigil calamum et chartas et scrinia posco.
navem agere ignarus navis timet ; habrotonum aegro
non audet nisi qui didicit dare ; quod medicorum[2] est
promittunt medici[2] ; tractant fabrilia fabri :   116
scribimus indocti doctique poemata passim.

Hic error tamen et levis haec insania quantas
virtutes habeat, sic collige.   vatis avarus
non temere est animus ; versus amat, hoc studet unum ;
detrimenta, fugas servorum, incendia ridet ;   121
non fraudem socio puerove incogitat[3] ullam
pupillo ; vivit siliquis et pane secundo ;
militiae quamquam piger et malus, utilis urbi,
si das hoc, parvis quoque rebus magna iuvari.   125
os tenerum pueri balbumque poeta figurat,
torquet ab obscenis iam nunc sermonibus aurem,
mox etiam pectus praeceptis format amicis,
asperitatis et invidiae corrector et irae,
recte facta refert, orientia tempora notis   130
instruit exemplis, inopem solatur et aegrum.
castis cum pueris ignara puella mariti
disceret unde preces, vatem ni Musa dedisset ?
poscit opem chorus et praesentia numina sentit,
caelestis implorat aquas docta prece blandus,[4]   135
avertit morbos, metuenda pericula pellit,

---

[1] puerique *inferior* mss., *Bentley.*
[2] melicorum, melici *Bentley* : modicorum, modici *J. S. Phillimore.*   [3] puero vel cogitat *E.*   [4] blandos *a.*

---

[a] Even while dining, they have an amanuensis ready and they wear the ivy sacred to poets instead of the usual garland of flowers.

406

indulgence curbed. The fickle public has changed its taste and is fired throughout with a scribbling craze ; sons and grave sires sup crowned with leaves and dictate their lines.[a] I myself, who declare that I write no verses, prove to be more of a liar than the Parthians : before sunrise I wake, and call for pen, paper, and writing-case. A man who knows nothing of a ship fears to handle one ; no one dares to give southernwood to the sick unless he has learnt its use ; doctors undertake a doctor's work ; carpenters handle carpenters' tools : but, skilled or unskilled, we scribble poetry, all alike.

[108] And yet this craze, this mild madness, has its merits. How great these are, now consider. Seldom is the poet's heart set on gain : verses he loves ; this is his one passion. Money losses, runaway slaves, fires—he laughs at all. To cheat partner or youthful ward he never plans. His food is pulse and coarse bread. Though a poor soldier, and slow in the field, he serves the State, if you grant that even by small things are great ends helped. The poet fashions the tender, lisping lips of childhood ; even then he turns the ear from unseemly words ; presently, too, he moulds the heart by kindly precepts, correcting roughness and envy and anger. He tells of noble deeds, equips the rising age with famous examples, and to the helpless and sick at heart brings comfort. Whence, in company with chaste boys, would the unwedded maid learn the suppliant hymn, had the Muse not given them a bard ? Their chorus asks for aid and feels the presence of the gods, calls for showers from heaven, winning favour with the prayer he has taught, averts disease, drives away dreaded dangers, gains peace

impetrat et pacem et locupletem frugibus annum.
carmine di superi placantur, carmine Manes.

Agricolae prisci, fortes parvoque beati,
condita post frumenta levantes tempore festo   140
corpus et ipsum animum spe finis dura ferentem,
cum sociis operum et pueris[1] et coniuge fida,
Tellurem porco, Silvanum lacte piabant,
floribus et vino Genium memorem brevis aevi.
Fescennina per hunc inventa[2] licentia morem   145
versibus alternis opprobria rustica fudit,
libertasque recurrentis accepta per annos
lusit amabiliter, donec iam saevus apertam
in rabiem coepit verti iocus et per honestas
ire domos impune minax. doluere cruento   150
dente lacessiti ; fuit intactis quoque cura
condicione super communi ; quin etiam lex
poenaque lata,[3] malo quae nollet carmine quemquam
describi : vertere modum, formidine fustis
ad bene dicendum delectandumque redacti.   155

Graecia capta ferum victorem cepit et artis
intulit agresti Latio. sic horridus ille

---

[a] In ll. 131-132, Horace is thinking chiefly of the chorus of boys and girls who sang the *Carmen Saeculare* in 17 B.C.; in ll. 134-137, he sets forth the function of the chorus, especially in association with religious ceremonies.
[b] This account of the development of a Latin drama from a rustic origin may be compared with Virgil's sketch of the rise of the drama in *Georg.* ii. 385 ff., and with the outline given by Livy in Book vii. 2.
[c] Each man's guardian spirit ; *cf. Epist.* i. 7. 94.
[d] These Fescennine verses, the earliest form of Italian drama, survived in later times in the abusive songs sung at weddings and in triumphal processions. They were so

and a season rich in fruits. Song wins grace with the gods above, song wins it with the gods below.[a]

[139] The farmers [b] of old, a sturdy folk with simple wealth, when, after harvesting the grain, they sought relief at holiday time for the body, as well as for the soul, which bore its toils in hope of the end, together with slaves and faithful wife, partners of their labours, used to propitiate Earth with swine, Silvanus with milk, and with flowers and wine the Genius [c] who is ever mindful of the shortness of life. Through this custom came into use the Fescennine licence, which in alternate verse poured forth rustic taunts [d]; and the freedom, welcomed each returning year, was innocently gay, till jest, now growing cruel, turned to open frenzy, and stalked amid the homes of honest folk, fearless in its threatening. Stung to the quick were they who were bitten by a tooth that drew blood; even those untouched felt concern for the common cause, and at last a law [e] was carried with a penalty, forbidding the portrayal of any in abusive strain. Men changed their tune, and terror of the cudgel led them back to goodly and gracious forms of speech.

[156] Greece, the captive, made her savage victor captive, and brought the arts into rustic Latium.

named either from the town of Fescennium in Etruria, or from the fact that a symbol of life (*fascinum*) was often carried in procession in order to ward off the evil eye. Such a phallic symbol was in common use among the Greeks, and it is a well-known fact that the germ of Greek comedy is to be found in the phallic songs sung in the Dionysiac festivities.

[e] In the Twelve Tables, viz., as given by Cicero, *De rep.* iv. 10. 12, "si quis occentavisset sive carmen condidisset quod infamiam faceret flagitiumve alteri." *Cf. Sat.* ii. 1. 82.

defluxit numerus¹ Saturnius, et grave virus
munditiae pepulere² ; sed in longum tamen aevum
manserunt hodieque manent vestigia ruris.   160
serus enim Graecis admovit acumina chartis
et post Punica bella quietus quaerere coepit,
quid Sophocles et Thespis et Aeschylus utile ferrent.
temptavit quoque rem, si digne vertere posset,
et placuit sibi, natura sublimis et acer :   165
nam spirat tragicum satis et feliciter audet,
sed turpem putat inscite³ metuitque lituram.

Creditur, ex medio quia res accersit,⁴ habere
sudoris minimum, sed habet Comoedia tanto   169
plus oneris, quanto veniae minus.   adspice, Plautus
quo pacto partis tutetur amantis ephebi,
ut patris attenti, lenonis ut insidiosi,
quantus sit Dossennus edacibus in parasitis,
quam non adstricto percurrat pulpita socco.
gestit enim nummum in loculos demittere,⁵ post hoc
securus cadat an recto stet fabula talo.   176
Quem tulit ad scaenam ventoso Gloria curru,

¹ numeris $R\phi\psi$.   ² peperere $\phi\psi\lambda l$.
³ inscit(a)e a, II: inscriptis VE: inscitiae V^2a^2M.
⁴ accersit a, II, $Porph.$: accessit VE.
⁵ dimittere aM.

ᵃ This ancient Italian metre, now generally believed to
be based on accent instead of quantity, was used by Naevius
in his epic on the Punic War, and is illustrated by numerous
inscriptions.   With the introduction of Greek literature into
Rome, it gave way to the hexameter and other Greek
metrical forms.

ᵇ The word *vertere* means not merely to "translate,"
but rather to "transfer," *i.e.* from the Greek to the Roman
stage.

ᶜ *i.e.* as Pope says of Dryden, he lacks " the last and
greatest art, the art to blot."

ᵈ Dossennus, the sly villain, was one of the stock characters

Thus the stream of that rude Saturnian measure [a]
ran dry and good taste banished the offensive
poison; yet for many a year lived on, and still live
on, traces of our rustic past. For not till late did
the Roman turn his wit to Greek writings, and in
the peaceful days after the Punic wars he began to
ask what service Sophocles could render, and Thespis
and Aeschylus. He also made essay, whether he
could reproduce [b] in worthy style, and took pride in
his success, being gifted with spirit and vigour; for
he has some tragic inspiration, and is happy in his
ventures, but in ignorance, deeming it disgraceful,
hesitates to blot.[c]

[168] 'Tis thought that Comedy, drawing its themes
from daily life, calls for less labour; but in truth it
carries a heavier burden, as the indulgence allowed
is less. See how poorly Plautus maintains the part
of the youthful lover, how poorly that of the close
father, or of the tricky pander; what a Dossennus [d]
he is among his greedy parasites; with what a loose
sock [e] he scours the scene. Yes, he is eager to
drop a coin into his pocket and, that done, he cares
not whether his play fall or stand square on its feet.[f]

[177] The man whom Glory carries to the stage in

in the Atellan farce of the Oscans. The *nomen* of Plautus,
viz. *Maccius*, is plausibly derived from another of these
stock characters, *i.e.* Maccus, the buffoon.

[e] The *soccus*, or low slipper worn by the actors, represents
Comedy, as the *cothurnus*, or high buskin, stands for
Tragedy.

[f] Horace, wedded to classical standards, could not
appreciate Plautus fairly. Thus he here imputes to him a
sordid motive for characteristics which were probably due
to the influence of native forms of drama. See the trans-
lator's edition of the *Andria* of Terence (Introduction,
p. xxviii).

exanimat lentus spectator, sedulus inflat :
sic leve, sic parvum est, animum quod laudis avarum
subruit aut reficit.   valeat res ludicra, si me   180
palma negata macrum, donata reducit opimum.

Saepe etiam audacem fugat hoc terretque poetam,
quod numero plures, virtute et honore minores,
indocti stolidique et depugnare parati,
si discordet eques, media inter carmina poscunt   185
aut ursum aut pugiles : his nam plebecula gaudet.[1]
verum equitis quoque iam migravit ab aure voluptas
omnis ad incertos oculos et gaudia vana.
quattuor aut pluris premuntur in horas,
dum fugiunt equitum turmae peditumque catervae ;
mox trahitur manibus regum fortuna retortis,   191
esseda festinant, pilenta, petorrita, naves,
captivum portatur ebur, captiva Corinthus.
si foret in terris, rideret Democritus, seu
diversum confusa genus panthera camelo   195
sive elephans albus volgi converteret[2] ora ;
spectaret populum ludis attentius ipsis
ut sibi praebentem nimio[3] spectacula plura :
scriptores autem narrare putaret asello
fabellam surdo.   nam quae pervincere voces   200
evaluere sonum, referunt quem nostra theatra ?
Garganum mugire putes nemus aut mare Tuscum ;

[1] plaudet, *II.*
[2] converterit *Priscian, Bentley.*
[3] nimio *V, I*: mimo, *II Porph.; so Bentley, Orelli, Vollmer.*

[a] *i.e.* always looking for something fresh.   For the knights *cf. Sat.* i. 10. 76.   They occupied the first fourteen rows in the theatre, in accordance with the law of Roscius.

[b] *i.e.* the performance continues.   In the ancient theatre the curtain was lowered into the floor at the beginning and raised from it at the end of a play.

[c] *i.e.* the laughing philosopher.   See *Epist.* i. 12. 12.

[d] The camelopard or giraffe.

her windy car, the listless spectator leaves spiritless, the eager one exultant ; so light, so small is what casts down or upbuilds a soul that craves for praise. Farewell the comic stage, if denial of the palm sends me home lean, its bestowal plump !

182 Often even the bold poet is frightened and put to rout, when those who are stronger in number, but weaker in worth and rank, unlearned and stupid and ready to fight it out if the knights dispute with them, call in the middle of a play for a bear or for boxers: 'tis in such things the rabble delights. But now-adays all the pleasure even of the knights has passed from the ear to the vain delights of the wandering *a* eye. For four hours or more the curtains are kept down,*b* while troops of horse and files of foot sweep by : anon are dragged in kings, once fortune's favourites, their hands bound behind them : with hurry and scurry come chariots, carriages, wains, and ships ; and borne in triumph are spoils of ivory, spoils of Corinthian bronze. Were Democritus *c* still on earth, he would laugh ; whether it were some hybrid monster—a panther crossed with a camel *d* —or a white elephant, that drew the eyes of the crowd —he would gaze more intently on the people than on the play itself, as giving him more by far worth looking at. But for the authors—he would suppose that they were telling their tale to a deaf ass.*e* For what voices have ever prevailed to drown the din with which our theatres resound ? One might think it was the roaring of the Garganian forest or of the

---

e By introducing *asello*, Horace varies the old proverbial saying for wasted labour, *surdo fabellam narrare* (*cf.* Terence, *Heaut.* 222). There was a Greek saying, ὄνῳ τις ἔλεγε μῦθον · ὁ δὲ τὰ ὦτα ἐκίνει, "a man told a story to an ass; the ass only shook his ears."

tanto cum strepitu ludi spectantur et artes
divitiaeque peregrinae, quibus oblitus actor
cum stetit in scaena, concurrit dextera laevae.[1]   205
" dixit adhuc aliquid ? " " nil sane." " quid placet
    ergo ? "
" lana Tarentino violas imitata[2] veneno."
ac ne forte putes me, quae facere ipse recusem,
cum recte tractent alii, laudare maligne,
ille per extentum[3] funem mihi posse videtur   210
ire poeta, meum qui pectus inaniter angit,
irritat, mulcet, falsis terroribus implet,
ut magus, et modo me Thebis, modo ponit Athenis.

    Verum age et his, qui se lectori credere malunt
quam spectatoris fastidia ferre superbi,   215
curam redde brevem, si munus Apolline dignum
vis complere libris et vatibus addere calcar,
ut studio maiore petant Helicona virentem.

    Multa quidem nobis facimus mala saepe poetae
(ut vineta egomet caedam mea), cum tibi librum   220
sollicito damus aut fesso ; cum laedimur, unum
si quis amicorum est ausus reprehendere versum ;
cum loca iam recitata revolvimus irrevocati ;
cum lamentamur non apparere labores
nostros et tenui deducta poemata filo ;   225
cum speramus eo rem venturam[4] ut, simul atque
carmina rescieris nos fingere, commodus ultro
arcessas[5] et egere vetes et scribere cogas.

    [1] laeva, *II*.   [2] imitare, *II*.   [3] extensum *M*.
        [4] eo rem] forem *Rπ* : item fore venturum *φψλl*.
            [5] accersas *E*.

---

    [a] *i.e.* the actor's dress.
    [b] The library founded by Augustus in Apollo's temple on
the Palatine ; *cf. Epist.* i. 3. 17.

Tuscan Sea : amid such clamour is the entertain-
ment viewed, the works of art, and the foreign
finery, and when, overlaid with this, the actor
steps upon the stage, the right hand clashes with
the left. " Has he yet said anything ? " Not
a word. " Then what takes them so ? " 'Tis the
woollen robe ^a that vies with the violet in its Taren-
tine dye. And lest, perchance, you may think that
I begrudge praise when others are handling well
what I decline to try myself, methinks that poet is
able to walk a tight rope, who with airy nothings
wrings my heart, inflames, soothes, fills it with vain
alarms like a magician, and sets me down now at
Thebes, now at Athens.

²¹⁴ But come, upon those, too, who prefer to put
themselves in a reader's hands, rather than brook
the disdain of a scornful spectator, bestow a moment's
attention, if you wish to fill with volumes that gift
so worthy of Apollo,^b and to spur on our bards to
seek with greater zeal Helicon's verdant lawns.

²¹⁹ We poets doubtless often do much mischief to
our own cause—let me hack at my own vines ^c—
when you are anxious or weary and we offer you
our book ; when we are hurt if a friend has dared
to censure a single verse ; when, unasked, we turn
back to passages already read; when we complain
that men lose sight of our labours, and of our poems
so finely spun ; when we hope it will come to this,
that, as soon as you hear we are composing verses,
you will go so far as kindly to send for us, banish our
poverty, and compel us to write. None the less,

^c Proverbial of doing something to one's own injury.
Horace humorously includes himself among the poetasters
who are so annoying.

sed tamen est operae pretium cognoscere, qualis
aedituos habeat belli spectata domique   230
Virtus, indigno non committenda poetae.
gratus Alexandro regi magno fuit ille
Choerilus, incultis qui versibus et male natis
rettulit acceptos, regale nomisma, Philippos;
sed veluti tractata notam labemque remittunt   235
atramenta, fere scriptores carmine foedo
splendida facta linunt. idem rex ille, poema
qui tam ridiculum tam care prodigus emit,
edicto vetuit, ne quis se praeter Apellen
pingeret, aut alius Lysippo duceret aera   240
fortis Alexandri voltum simulantia. quod si
iudicium subtile videndis artibus illud
ad libros et ad haec Musarum dona vocares,
Boeotum in crasso iurares aere natum.

  At neque dedecorant tua de se iudicia atque   245
munera, quae multa dantis cum laude tulerunt
dilecti tibi[1] Vergilius Variusque[2] poetae,
nec magis expressi voltus per aenea signa,
quam per vatis opus mores animique virorum
clarorum apparent. nec sermones ego mallem   250
repentis per humum quam res componere gestas,
terrarumque situs et flumina dicere, et arces
montibus impositas et barbara regna, tuisque
auspiciis totum confecta duella per orbem,
claustraque custodem pacis cohibentia Ianum,   255

      [1] tui *E*.   [2] Varusque *V*.

   [a] *Virtus*, the sum total of a great man's merits, is here
personified, and poets are spoken of as the priests in her
temple.
   [b] The *Philippi* were gold coins which bore the image of
Philip of Macedon, and circulated freely throughout the
Greek world. Choerilus was an epic poet of Iasos in Caria,
mentioned again in *Ars Poetica*, 357.

'tis worth inquiring what manner of ministrants attend on Merit,[a] tried at home and in the field, and never to be entrusted to an unworthy poet. Well-pleasing to the great king Alexander was that poor Choerilus, who could thank his uncouth and misbegotten verses for the philips [b]—good royal coin —that he received; but as ink when handled leaves mark and stain, so ofttimes with unseemly verse poets put a blot on bright exploits. That same king who lavishly paid so dearly for a poem so foolish, by an edict forbade anyone save Apelles to paint him, or any other than Lysippus to model bronze in copying the features of brave Alexander. But call that judgement, so nice for viewing works of art, to books and to these gifts of the Muses, and you'd swear that he'd been born in Boeotia's heavy air.[c]

But Virgil and Varius, those poets whom you love, discredit not your judgement of them nor the gifts which, to the giver's great renown, they have received; and features are seen with no more truth, when moulded in statues of bronze, than are the manners and minds of famous heroes, when set forth in the poet's work. And for myself, I should not prefer my "chats," that crawl along the ground,[d] to the story of great exploits, the tale of distant lands and rivers, of forts on mountain tops, of barbaric realms, of the ending of wars under your auspices throughout the world, of bars that close on Janus,

[c] As the heavy air of the moist lowlands of Boeotia was contrasted with the clear atmosphere of Attica, so the Boeotians were proverbially dull, the Athenians sharp-witted; cf. Cicero, De fato, iv. 7.

[d] Under sermones Horace includes both his Satires and Epistles, which are inspired by a Musa pedestris (Sat. ii. 6. 17).

et formidatam Parthis te principe Romam,
si quantum cuperem possem quoque ; sed neque
    parvum
carmen maiestas recipit tua, nec meus audet
rem temptare pudor quam vires ferre recusent.
sedulitas autem stulte quem diligit urget,   260
praecipue cum se numeris commendat et arte ;
discit[1] enim citius meminitque libentius illud
quod quis deridet, quam quod probat et veneratur.
nil moror officium quod me gravat, ac neque ficto
in peius voltu proponi cereus usquam   265
nec prave factis decorari versibus opto,
ne rubeam pingui donatus munere, et una
cum scriptore meo, capsa porrectus[2] operta,[3]
deferar in vicum vendentem tus et odores
et piper et quidquid chartis amicitur ineptis.[4]   270

[1] discet *V*.   [2] porreptus *E*.
[3] aperta.   [4] inemptis.

---

[a] For the closing of the temple of Janus in peace *cf.*
Odes, iv. 15. 9, and with ll. 252, 253 *cf.* "arces Alpibus
impositas tremendis," in *Odes* iv. 14. 11.

[b] That Augustus was sensitive about being made the
subject of poor eulogies is stated by Suetonius (*Augustus*,
89).

[c] *i.e.* to have one's portrait in wax offered for sale.

[d] Horace means that sooner or later the work of a poor

guardian of peace,[a] and of that Rome who under your sway has become a terror to Parthians—if only I had power equal to my longing ; but neither does your majesty admit of a lowly strain,[b] nor does my modesty dare to essay a task beyond my strength to bear. Nay, officious zeal frets with its folly those it loves, above all when it commends itself by numbers and by art ; for men more quickly learn and more gladly recall what they deride than what they approve and esteem. Not for me attentions that are burdensome, and I want neither to be displayed anywhere in wax,[c] with my features misshaped, nor to be praised in verses ill-wrought, lest I have to blush at the stupid gift, and then, along with my poet, outstretched in a closed chest, be carried into the street where they sell frankincense and perfumes and pepper and everything else that is wrapped in sheets of useless paper.[d]

poet is found to be worthless, and his books can be used only for waste paper. Thus, under the figure of a funeral the poet is borne to his last resting-place—the grocer's shop ! *Cf.* Euphues' *Anatomy of Wit* : "We constantly see the booke that at Christmas lieth bound on the stacioner's stall, at Easter be broken in the haberdasher's shop." In l. 269 there is an amusing pun on *Vicus Tuscus*, the name of a street leading out of the Forum, along which were all kinds of shops ; *cf. Sat.* II. 3. 228.

II

TO FLORUS

If one were to offer a slave for sale, and declare his defects, the purchaser would have no right to complain of these later. So you, Florus, must not grumble at my not writing to you, for I warned you before you started that I never answer letters. And then, over and above this, you complain of my breaking my word, when you receive from me no poems (1-25).

Let me remind you of the story of a certain soldier of Lucullus. One night he had all his savings stolen. Upon this he rushed off furiously to storm a castle, and won thereby both glory and a rich reward. But later, when his general invited him to repeat the exploit, he declined, and advised the officer to send somebody who had lost his purse. I am like that soldier. I lost everything at Philippi, and took to poetry to make a living, but now that I have a competence I should be mad if I did not prefer ease to writing (26-54).

But there are other reasons why I do not write. Time is stealing from me my poetical power, as it has already taken from me my youth. After all, too, tastes vary, and while you are asking for Odes, others call for Epodes or Satires. Besides, how can you expect a man to write amid all the distractions of Rome ? The poet must live in seclusion, and then he becomes quite unfit for active life. If this is true of Athens, how much more so is it of noisy Rome ? How then can I deign to write poetry here ? (55-86).

"Deign," did I say ? Why, the only way to win success here as a poet is to join some mutual admiration club, and for my part I am no longer suing for favour—I am no longer writing, and I can decline to listen to the recitations of others (87-105).

Poor poets, however much derided, are well satisfied with themselves. But the writing of good poetry is a very serious matter, and demands a fine taste and careful discrimination in the choice of language. The result will seem easy, but that ease is the product of much labour. Perhaps it is better to be one of those self-complacent writers than to be ever finding fault with oneself. The man at Argos learned what a misfortune it is to be robbed of one's illusions (106-140).

The truth is, it is time for a man of my years to throw aside mere toys like poetry and take up the serious business of life, that of philosophy. So, beginning with the elements, I repeat to myself the wise precepts that I have picked up. Avarice, for example, is as much a disease as dropsy. For the latter you consult a doctor, and when the course prescribed brings no relief, you change the treatment or the doctor. Should not avarice be dealt with in like manner ? (141-154).

If wealth could make you wise, you ought to devote yourself wholly to it. And yet what comes from all this struggle to make money ? Ownership brings no more satisfaction than the right to use and enjoy, and even the law recognizes the fact that this *usucapio* is the same in the end as *dominium* or ownership. As a matter of fact, there is no such thing as out and out ownership, or ownership in perpetuity, for Death prevents that (155-179).

In any case, wealth takes many forms, and some care nothing for what others value so highly. Why this is so, I cannot say, but for my part I hold that life's pleasures are to be enjoyed in moderation. Let me but be free from squalor, and I shall be just as happy sailing on life's sea in a small as in a large ship (180-204).

But avarice is not the only evil that may assail the heart, and the wise man will free himself from all disturbing passions and fears. If one cannot live well, he should give way to those who can. When a man has had his share in the banquet of life, it is time to withdraw (205-216).

The Florus of this Epistle is the Julius Florus to whom *Epist.* i. 3 is also addressed. He is still in the suite of Tiberius, and as there is a great similarity of tone between this Epistle and the first of the First Book, it is likely that it was written shortly after the publication of that book in 20 B.C. At any rate, in view of the writer's renunciation of lyric poetry in this Epistle, it can hardly have been written in the years when the *Carmen Saeculare* and the Fourth Book of *Odes* came into being (17-13 B.C.).

II.

Flore, bono claroque fidelis amice Neroni,[a]
si quis forte velit puerum tibi vendere natum
Tibure vel Gabiis, et tecum sic agat : " hic et
candidus[b] et talos a vertice pulcher ad imos
fiet eritque tuus nummorum milibus octo,   5
verna ministeriis ad nutus aptus erilis,
litterulis Graecis imbutus, idoneus arti
cuilibet ; argilla quidvis[1] imitaberis[2] uda ;
quin etiam canet indoctum sed dulce bibenti.
multa fidem promissa levant, ubi plenius aequo   10
laudat venalis qui volt extrudere[3] merces.
res urget me nulla ; meo sum pauper in aere.
nemo hoc mangonum faceret tibi ; non temere a me
quivis ferret idem.   semel hic cessavit et, ut fit,
in scalis latuit metuens pendentis habenae :[c]   15
des nummos, excepta nihil te si fuga laedit[4] " :
ille ferat pretium poenae securus, opinor.
prudens emisti vitiosum ; dicta tibi est lex[5] :[d]

---

[1] quavis *E.*   [2] imitabimur, *II.*   [3] excludere *V, II.*
[4] laedit *V, Bentley* : laedat *MSS. Orelli.*   [5] est tibi lex, *I.*

---

[a] Tiberius Claudius Nero, the future Emperor Tiberius :
cf. *Epist.* i. 3. 2.   [b] *i.e.* home-born, not foreign.
   [c] *i.e.* the strap which was hanging up where all could
see it.
   [d] *i.e.* because he has not represented the slave as faultless,
but has expressly mentioned (*excepta*) a defect.   *Cf. Sat.*
ii. 3. 286.   Editors who (*e.g.* Orelli) read *laedat* (l. 16) make
424

Epistle II

My Florus, loyal friend of great and good Nero,[a]
suppose someone by chance should wish to sell you
a slave, born at Tibur or Gabii,[b] and should deal
with you thus : "Here's a handsome boy, comely
from top to toe ; you may take him, to have and to
hold, for eight thousand sesterces ; home-bred he is,
apt for service at his owner's beck, knows a bit of
Greek learning, and can master any art ; the clay
is soft—you will mould it to what you will ; more-
over, he will sing for you over your cups in a sweet
if artless fashion. Too many promises lessen con-
fidence, when a seller who wants to shove off his
wares praises them unduly. I am under no con-
straint ; I have slender means, but am not in debt.
None of the slave-dealers would give you such a
bargain ; not everyone would easily get the like
from me. Once he played truant, and hid himself,
as boys will do, under the stairs, fearing the hanging
strap.[c] Give me the sum asked, if his running off,
duly noted, does not trouble you " : the seller, I
take it, would get his price without fear of penalty.[d]
You bought him with your eyes open—fault and
all ; the condition was told you ; do you still pursue

the speech of the seller close with line 15, so that both *des* (l.
16), and *ferat* (l. 17) provide the apodosis or conclusion to
si quis forte velit (l. 2). We prefer to follow Bentley in
including l. 16 in the seller's speech.

insequeris tamen hunc et lite moraris iniqua ?
dixi me pigrum proficiscenti tibi, dixi   20
talibus officiis prope mancum, ne mea saevus
iurgares ad te quod epistula nulla rediret.[1]
quid tum profeci, mecum facientia iura
si tamen attemptas ?   quereris super hoc etiam, quod
exspectata tibi non mittam carmina mendax.   25

 Luculli miles collecta viatica multis
aerumnis, lassus dum noctu stertit, ad assem
perdiderat : post hoc vehemens lupus, et sibi et hosti
iratus pariter, ieiunis dentibus acer,
praesidium regale loco deiecit, ut aiunt,   30
summe munito et multarum divite rerum.
clarus ob id factum donis ornatur honestis,[2]
accipit et bis dena super sestertia nummum.
forte sub hoc tempus castellum evertere praetor
nescio quod cupiens hortari coepit eundem   35
verbis quae timido quoque possent addere mentem :
" i, bone, quo virtus tua te vocat, i pede fausto,
grandia laturus meritorum praemia.   quid stas ? "
post haec ille catus, quantumvis rusticus : " ibit,
ibit eo, quo vis, qui zonam perdidit," inquit.   40

 Romae nutriri mihi contigit atque doceri
iratus Grais quantum nocuisset Achilles.
adiecere bonae paulo plus artis Athenae,
scilicet ut vellem[3] curvo dinoscere rectum
atque inter silvas Academi quaerere verum.   45
dura sed emovere loco me tempora grato

---

[1] veniret φψλl.   [2] opimis *V*.
     [3] possim, *II* : possem.

---

 [a] Lucullus commanded the Roman forces in the war with
Mithridates, king of Pontus, from 74 B.C. to 67 B.C.
 [b] He studied Homer's *Iliad*.

the seller and annoy him with an unjust suit? I told you when you were leaving that I was lazy; I told you that for such duties I was well-nigh crippled, lest you should angrily scold, because no letter of mine reached you in reply. What good did I then do, if when right is on my side you still attack it? And then, over and above this, you complain that the verses you looked for I fail to send, false to my word.

26 A soldier of Lucullus,[a] by dint of many toils, had laid by savings, but one night, when weary and slumbering, had lost all down to the last penny. After this, furious as a wolf, angry with himself and his foe alike, and fiercely showing hungry teeth, he dislodged, they say, a royal garrison from a strongly fortified site, rich in vast treasure. Winning fame thereby, he was decorated with gifts of honour, and received, over and above, twenty thousand sesterces in coin. Soon after this it chanced that the commander, wishing to storm some fort, began to urge the man with words that might have given spirit even to a coward: " Go, sir, whither your valour calls you. Go, good luck to you!—to win big rewards for your merits. Why stand still? " On this the shrewd fellow, rustic though he was, replied: " Yes, he will go—go where you wish—he who has lost his wallet."

41 At Rome I had the luck to be bred, and taught how much Achilles' wrath had harmed the Greeks.[b] Kindly Athens added somewhat more training, so that, you know, I was eager to distinguish the straight from the crooked, and to hunt for truth in the groves of Academe. But troublous times tore me from that pleasant spot, and the tide of civil

427

civilisque rudem belli tulit aestus in arma
Caesaris Augusti non responsura lacertis.
unde simul primum me dimisere Philippi,[1]
decisis humilem pennis inopemque paterni   50
et laris et fundi, paupertas impulit audax
ut versus facerem : sed quod non desit[2] habentem
quae poterunt umquam satis expurgare cicutae,
ni melius dormire putem quam scribere versus ?

   Singula de nobis anni praedantur euntes ;   55
eripuere iocos, Venerem, convivia, ludum ;
tendunt extorquere poemata : quid faciam vis ?
denique non omnes eadem mirantur amantque :
carmine tu gaudes, hic delectatur iambis,
ille Bioneis sermonibus et sale nigro.   60
tres mihi convivae prope dissentire videntur,
poscentes vario multum diversa palato.
quid dem ? quid non dem ? renuis tu, quod[3] iubet
    alter ;
quod petis, id sane est invisum acidumque duobus.

   Praeter cetera me Romaene poemata censes   65
scribere posse inter tot curas totque labores ?
hic sponsum vocat, hic auditum scripta, relictis
omnibus officiis ; cubat hic in colle Quirini,
hic extremo in Aventino, visendus uterque ;
intervalla vides humane commoda. " verum   70
purae[4] sunt plateae, nihil ut meditantibus obstet."

---

[1] philippis φψλl.
[2] defit *G. W. Mooney in* Hermath. xv. *p.* 161 ; *cf. Tib.* iv. 1. 100.
[3] quod tu, *II (not* δ) ; *so Vollmer.*
[4] plures, *II* (plurae *R*).

---

   [a] After the defeat of Brutus at Philippi Horace withdrew
from the Republican cause, unlike Pompeius Varus and
other friends, who kept up the struggle under Sextus Pom-
peius. *Cf. Odes* ii. 7. 15. The poet's estate at Venusia was
doubtless confiscated.

   [b] *Cf. Sat.* ii. 1. 7.   [o] Such as Horace's *Epodes.*

strife flung me, a novice in war, amid weapons that
were to be no match for the strong arms of Caesar
Augustus. Soon as Philippi gave me discharge[a]
therefrom, brought low with wings clipped and
beggared of paternal home and estate, barefaced
poverty drove me to writing verses. But now that I
have sufficient store, what doses of hemlock could
ever suffice to cleanse my blood, if I were not to think
it better to slumber[b] than to scribble verses ?

⁵⁵ The years, as they pass, plunder us of all joys,
one by one. They have stripped me of mirth, love,
feasting, play ; they are striving to wrest from me
my poems. What would you have me do ? After
all, men have not all the same tastes and likes.
Lyric song is your delight, our neighbour here takes
pleasure in iambics,[c] the one yonder in Bion's satires,
with their caustic wit.[d] 'Tis, I fancy, much like
three guests who disagree ; their tastes vary, and
they call for widely different dishes. What am I to
put before them ? what not ? You refuse what
your neighbour orders : what you crave is, to be
sure, sour and distasteful to the other two.

⁶⁵ Besides all else, do you think I can write verses
at Rome amid all my cares and all my toils ? One
calls me to be surety, another, to leave all my duties
and listen to his writings. One lies sick on the
Quirinal hill, another on the Aventine's far side ; I
must visit both. The distances, you see, are com-
fortably convenient ! " Yes, but the streets are
clear, so that nothing need hinder you in conning

---

[d] Bion, an Athenian philosopher of the early third cent. B.C.,
was famous for his biting wit. His name represents Satire
in general, including Horace's own *Sermones* or *Satires*,
which contain but a minimum of the *sal niger* referred to.

festinat calidus mulis gerulisque redemptor,
torquet nunc lapidem, nunc ingens machina tignum,
tristia robustis luctantur funera plaustris,
hac rabiosa fugit canis, hac lutulenta ruit sus :   75
i nunc et versus tecum meditare canoros.
scriptorum chorus omnis amat nemus et fugit urbem,[1]
rite cliens Bacchi somno gaudentis et umbra :
tu me inter strepitus nocturnos atque diurnos
vis canere et contracta[2] sequi vestigia vatum ?   80
ingenium, sibi quod vacuas desumpsit Athenas
et studiis annos septem dedit insenuitque
libris et curis, statua taciturnius exit
plerumque et risu populum quatit : hic ego rerum
fluctibus in mediis et tempestatibus urbis   85
verba lyrae motura sonum conectere digner ?

　Frater erat Romae consulti rhetor, ut[3] alter
alterius sermone meros audiret honores,
Gracchus ut hic illi, foret huic ut Mucius ille.[4]
qui minus argutos vexat furor iste poetas ?   90
carmina compono, hic elegos.　mirabile visu
caelatumque novem Musis opus !　adspice primum,
quanto cum fastu, quanto molimine circum-
spectemus vacuam Romanis vatibus aedem !

---

　[1] urbes, *II.*
　[2] contracta *E, known to Porph.*: contacta *MSS., Porph.,
adopted by Orelli and others*: cantata *V*: non tacta *Bentley.*
　[3] et, *II* (*not* δ). *Bentley read* pactus (*for* frater) *and* consulto.
　[4] huic . . . ille *Lambinus, Bentley, all editors* : hic . . .
illi *MSS.*

---

　a *Hic, i.e.* in Rome, where it is even more difficult to
devote oneself to study than in Athens.
　b Under such conditions self-respect would prevent him
from writing.　This is further illustrated in the next
paragraph.　See p. 422.
　c Both the Gracchi, Tiberius and Gaius, were orators.
There were three well-known jurists named Mucius Scaevola.

verses." In hot haste rushes a contractor with mules
and porters; a huge crane is hoisting now a stone
and now a beam; mournful funerals jostle massive
wagons; this way runs a mad dog: that way rushes
a mud-bespattered sow. Now go, and thoughtfully
con melodious verses. The whole chorus of poets
loves the grove and flees the town, duly loyal to
Bacchus, who finds joy in sleep and shade. Would
you wish me, amid noises by night and noises by
day, to sing and pursue the minstrels' narrow path-
way? A gifted man, that has chosen for home
sequestered Athens, that has given seven years to his
studies and grown grey over his books and medi-
tations, when he walks abroad is often more mute
than a statue and makes the people shake with
laughter: and *here*,[a] amid the waves of life, amid
the tempests of the town, am I to deign [b] to weave
together words which shall awake the music of the
lyre?

87 Two brothers at Rome, a lawyer and a pleader,
were on such terms that nothing but compliments
would each hear from the other's lips: the one was
Gracchus to the other, the other Mucius to him.[c]
And our singer poets—how does this madness trouble
them any the less? I compose lyrics, my friend
elegiacs: " 'Tis wondrous to behold! A work of
art, engraven by the Muses nine!" Mark you
first, with what pride, with what importance, our
contemplative gaze wanders o'er the temple, now
open to Roman bards.[d] And by and by, if haply

[d] The temple of Apollo on the Palatine, with which was
associated a famous library in two sections, one for Greek,
the other for Latin books. On the walls were medallions
of famous authors. *Cf. Epist.* ii. 1. 216.

mox etiam, si forte vacas,[1] sequere et procul audi, 95
quid ferat et qua re sibi nectat uterque coronam.
caedimur et totidem plagis consumimus hostem
lento Samnites ad lumina prima duello.
discedo Alcaeus puncto illius ; ille meo quis ?
quis nisi Callimachus ? si plus adposcere visus, 100
fit Mimnermus et optivo cognomine crescit.
multa fero, ut placem genus irritabile vatum,
cum scribo et supplex populi suffragia capto ;
idem finitis studiis et mente recepta
obturem patulas impune legentibus auris. 105
  Ridentur mala qui componunt carmina ; verum
gaudent scribentes et se venerantur et ultro,
si taceas, laudant quidquid scripsere beati.
at qui legitimum cupiet fecisse poema,
cum tabulis animum censoris sumet honesti ; 110
audebit, quaecumque parum splendoris habebunt
et sine pondere erunt et honore indigna ferentur,[2]
verba movere loco, quamvis invita recedant
et versentur adhuc intra[3] penetralia Vestae ;

---

[1] vacat.   [2] feruntur, *I*, *δ*.   [3] inter *MSS*.

---

 [a] The two poets, indulging in mutual compliments, and
inflicting their compositions on each other, are humorously
compared to a pair of those heavy-armed gladiators known
as Samnites, who would engage in a wearisome, though
harmless fight, till night put an end to the contest.

 [b] It is commonly supposed that in this whole scene the
second poet referred to by Horace is Propertius, the elegiac
writer (*cf.* 1. 91) who called himself " the Roman Calli-
machus." Callimachus, an Alexandrian poet of the third
cent. B.C., was commonly held to be the greatest of Greek
elegists. For Mimnermus *cf. Epist.* i. 6. 65. He lived in
the latter half of the seventh cent. B.C., and was the first to
make elegy a vehicle for love-sentiment.

you have time, follow, and draw close to hear what each has to offer, and with what he weaves for himself a chaplet. We belabour each other, and with tit for tat use up our foe, like Samnites, in a long-drawn bout, till the first lamps are lighted.[a] By his vote I come off an Alcaeus. What is he by mine ? What, but a Callimachus ! If he seems to claim more, he becomes a Mimnermus, and is glorified with the title of his choice.[b] Much do I endure, to soothe the fretful tribe of bards, so long as I am scribbling, and humbly suing for public favour ; but now that my studies are ended and my wits recovered, I would, without fear of requital, stop up my open ears when they recite.[c]

[106] Those who write poor verses are a jest ; yet they rejoice in the writing and revere themselves ; and, should you say nothing, they themselves praise whatever they have produced—happy souls ! But the man whose aim is to have wrought a poem true to Art's rules, when he takes his tablets, will take also the spirit of an honest censor.[d] He will have the courage, if words fall short in dignity, lack weight, or be deemed unworthy of rank, to remove them from their place, albeit they are loth to withdraw, and still linger within Vesta's precincts.[e] Terms long

---

[c] Horace means that if he does not write, he need not listen. Others prefer to connect *impune* with *legentibus*. The others recite without fear of his retaliating.

[d] These lines were used by Dr. Johnson as the motto for his Dictionary.

[e] The allusion is obscure. Vesta perhaps stands for the most sacred traditions of Rome, so that the words rejected by the poet still remain in common use. Keller thinks that Horace uses a quotation from Ennius or some other early poet.

obscurata diu populo bonus eruet atque 115
proferet in lucem speciosa vocabula rerum,
quae priscis memorata Catonibus atque Cethegis
nunc situs informis premit et deserta vetustas ;
adsciscet nova, quae genitor produxerit usus.
vemens et liquidus[1] puroque simillimus amni 120
fundet opes Latiumque beabit divite lingua ;
luxuriantia compescet, nimis aspera sano
levabit cultu, virtute carentia[2] tollet,
ludentis speciem dabit et torquebitur, ut qui
nunc Satyrum, nunc agrestem Cyclopa movetur. 125
    Praetulerim scriptor delirus inersque videri,
dum mea delectent mala me vel denique fallant,
quam sapere et ringi.   fuit haud ignobilis Argis,[3]
qui se credebat miros audire tragoedos
in vacuo laetus sessor plausorque theatro ; 130
cetera qui vitae servaret munia recto
more, bonus sane vicinus, amabilis hospes,
comis in uxorem, posset qui ignoscere servis
et signo laeso non insanire lagoenae,
posset qui rupem et puteum vitare patentem.[4] 135
hic ubi cognatorum opibus curisque refectus
expulit elleboro morbum bilemque meraco,
et redit ad sese : " pol, me occidistis, amici,
non servastis," ait, " cui sic extorta voluptas
et demptus per vim mentis gratissimus error." 140

---

[1] vehemens *MSS.* : et vehemens liquidus *D.*
[2] carentia *DEM* : calentia *Va.*
[3] Argus.   [4] parentem, *II.*

---

[a] Cf. *Ars Poetica*, 50.   [b] Cf. *Ars Poetica*, 71, 72.
[c] Those who dance most easily do so as the result of hard
training ; cf. Pope :

    As those move easiest who have learn'd to dance.

[d] *Ringi* means literally " to show one's teeth like a snarling

lost in darkness the good poet will unearth for the
people's use and bring into the light—picturesque
terms which, though once spoken by a Cato and a
Cethegus of old,[a] now lie low through unseemly
neglect and dreary age. New ones he will adopt
which Use has fathered and brought forth.[b] Strong
and clear, and truly like a crystal river, he will pour
forth wealth and bless Latium with richness of
speech; he will prune down rankness of growth,
smooth with wholesome refinement what is rough,
sweep away what lacks force—wear the look of being
at play, and yet be on the rack, like a dancer who
plays now a Satyr, and now a clownish Cyclops.[c]

126 I should prefer to be thought a foolish and
clumsy scribbler, if only my failings please, or at
least escape me, rather than be wise and unhappy.[d]
Once at Argos there was a man of some rank, who
used to fancy that he was listening to wonderful
tragic actors, while he sat happy and applauded
in the empty theatre—a man who would correctly
perform all other duties of life, a most worthy
neighbour, an amiable host, kind to his wife, one
that could excuse his slaves, and not get frantic
if the seal of a flask were broken, one that could
avoid a precipice or an open well. This man was
cured by his kinsmen's help and care, but when with
strong hellebore he had driven out the malady and
its bile, and had come to himself again, he cried:
" Egad! you have killed me, my friends, not saved
me ; for thus you have robbed me of a pleasure and
taken away perforce the dearest illusion of my heart."

dog," and is used here of the unhappy, self-critical poet who
is never content with what he produces, in contrast with the
contented, self-complacent writer.

Nimirum sapere est abiectis utile nugis,
et tempestivum pueris concedere ludum,
ac non verba sequi fidibus modulanda Latinis,
sed verae numerosque modosque ediscere vitae.
quocirca mecum loquor haec tacitusque recordor : 145
   Si tibi nulla sitim finiret copia lymphae,
narrares medicis : quod, quanto plura parasti,
tanto plura cupis, nulline faterier audes ?
si volnus tibi monstrata radice vel herba
non fieret levius, fugeres radice vel herba   150
proficiente nihil curarier : audieras, cui
rem di donarent, illi decedere pravam
stultitiam ; et cum sis nihilo sapientior ex quo
plenior es, tamen uteris monitoribus isdem ?
   At si divitiae prudentem reddere possent, 155
si cupidum timidumque minus te, nempe ruberes,
viveret in terris te si quis avarior uno.
si proprium est, quod quis libra mercatus[1] et aere est,[1]
quaedam, si credis consultis, mancipat usus ;
qui te pascit ager tuus est, et vilicus Orbi,   160
cum segetes occat tibi mox frumenta daturas,[2]
te dominum sentit. das nummos, accipis uvam,
pullos, ova, cadum temeti : nempe modo isto
paulatim mercaris agrum, fortasse trecentis
aut etiam supra nummorum milibus emptum.   165
quid refert, vivas numerato nuper an olim ?

[1] mercatus, *I, π*: mercatur, *II*: est *omitted, II.*
[2] daturas *V, II*: daturus, *I.*

---

   a A reference to the common mode of conveying ownership
in property, viz. by a symbolic sale, in which a balance,
held by a third party, was struck by the purchaser with
a copper coin.
   b Usucapio, legal possession, uninterrupted and continued
for a certain time, resulted in ownership (*dominium*). But
perhaps Horace jocularly refers to matrimony, where in

¹⁴¹ In truth it is profitable to cast aside toys and to learn wisdom ; to leave to lads the sport that fits their age, and not to search out words that will fit the music of the Latin lyre, but to master the rhythms and measures of a genuine life. Therefore I talk thus to myself and silently recall these precepts :

If no amount of water could quench your thirst, you would tell your story to the doctor : seeing that the more you get, the more you want, do you not dare to make confession to any man ? If your wound were not relieved by the root or herb prescribed, you would give up being treated with the root or herb that did you no good : you had perhaps been told that perverse folly flees from him to whom the gods had given wealth ; but though you are no wiser since you became richer, do you still follow the same counsellors ?

¹⁵⁵ But surely if wealth could make you wise, if less wedded to desires and fears, you would blush if there lived upon earth a greater miser than you. If that is a man's own which he buys with bronze and balance,^a there are some things, if you trust the lawyers, which use ^b conveys ; the farm which gives you food is yours, and the bailiff of Orbius, when he harrows the corn-land which is shortly to give you grain, feels you to be his master. You give your coin ; you receive grapes, poultry, eggs, a jar of wine : in that way, mark you ! you are buying bit by bit the farm once purchased for three hundred thousand sesterces, or perhaps even more. What does it matter, whether you live on what was paid out lately or

certain cases *manus* might result from *usus*. So Polluck, *C.R.* xxxi. (1917).

emptor Aricini quondam[1] Veientis et arvi
emptum cenat holus, quamvis aliter putat ; emptis
sub noctem gelidam lignis calefactat aënum ;
sed vocat usque suum, qua[2] populus adsita certis   170
limitibus vicina refugit[3] iurgia ; tamquam
sit proprium quicquam, puncto quod mobilis horae
nunc prece, nunc pretio, nunc vi, nunc morte suprema
permutet dominos et cedat in altera iura.
sic[4] quia perpetuus nulli datur usus, et heres   175
heredem alterius[5] velut unda supervenit undam,
quid vici prosunt aut horrea ?   quidve Calabris
saltibus adiecti Lucani, si metit Orcus
grandia cum parvis, non exorabilis auro ?

Gemmas, marmor, ebur, Tyrrhena sigilla, tabellas,
argentum, vestes Gaetulo murice tinctas   181
sunt qui non habeant, est qui non curat habere.
cur alter fratrum cessare et ludere et ungui
praeferat Herodis palmetis pinguibus, alter
dives et importunus ad umbram lucis ab ortu   185
silvestrem flammis et ferro mitiget agrum,
scit Genius, natale comes qui temperat astrum,
naturae deus humanae, mortalis in unum
quodque caput, voltu mutabilis, albus et ater.
utar et ex modico, quantum res poscet, acervo   190
tollam, nec metuam quid de me iudicet heres,
quod non plura datis invenerit ; et tamen idem
scire volam, quantum simplex hilarisque nepoti

---

[1] quondam π[2]: quoniam *V, most MSS.*
[2] quia *ER*: quod π.   [3] refigit.
[4] sic *E*[2]*M*[2]: si *MSS., Porph.*   [5] alternis *Bentley.*

---

[a] Ownership may be transferred by donation in response
to an appeal (*prece*), and by confiscation (*vi*), as well as by
purchase and inheritance.

438

some time ago ? The man who once bought a farm
at Aricia or Veii bought the greens for his dinner,
though he thinks otherwise ; he bought the logs
with which he boils the kettle in the chill of nightfall.
Yet he calls it all his own, up to where the poplars,
planted beside fixed boundaries, prevent the wrangling
of neighbours : just as though anything were one's own,
which in a moment of flitting time, now by prayer,[a]
now by purchase, now by force, now—at the last—by
death, changes owners and passes under the power of
another. Thus since to none is granted lasting use,
and heir follows another's heir as wave follows wave,
what avail estates or granaries—what avail Lucanian
forests joined to Calabrian, if Death reaps great and
small —Death who never can be won over with gold ?

[180] Gems, marble, ivory, Tuscan vases, paintings,
plate, robes dyed in Gaetulian purple—there are
those who have not ; there is one who cares not to
have. Of two brothers one prefers, above Herod's
rich palm-groves,[b] idling and playing and the anoint-
ing of himself ; the other, wealthy and untiring, from
dawn to shady eve subdues his woodland farm with
flames and iron plough. Why so, the Genius alone
knows that companion who rules our star of birth,
the god of human nature, though mortal for each
single life, and changing in countenance, white or
black.[c] I shall use and from my modest heap take
what need requires, nor shall I fear what my heir
will think of me, because he does not find more than
I have given him. And yet, withal, I shall wish to
know how much the frank and cheerful giver is
distinct from the spendthrift, how much the frugal

---

[b] Herod the Great had famous groves of date palms near
Jericho.   [c] Cf. Epist. ii. 1. 144.

discrepet et quantum discordet parcus avaro.   194
distat enim, spargas tua prodigus, an neque sumptum
invitus facias neque plura parare labores,
ac potius, puer ut festis Quinquatribus olim,
exiguo gratoque fruaris tempore raptim.
pauperies immunda domus[1] procul absit[1]: ego, utrum
nave ferar magna an parva, ferar unus et idem.   200
non agimur tumidis velis Aquilone secundo :
non tamen adversis aetatem ducimus Austris,
viribus, ingenio, specie, virtute, loco, re[2]
extremi primorum, extremis usque priores.   204
    Non es avarus : abi. quid ? cetera iam simul isto
cum vitio fugere[3] ? caret tibi pectus inani
ambitione ? caret mortis formidine et ira ?
somnia, terrores magicos, miracula, sagas,
nocturnos lemures portentaque Thessala rides ?
natalis grate numeras ? ignoscis amicis ?   210
lenior et melior fis[4] accedente senecta ?
quid te exempta iuvat[5] spinis de pluribus una ?
vivere si recte nescis, decede peritis.
lusisti satis, edisti satis atque bibisti :
tempus abire tibi est, ne potum largius aequo   215
rideat et pulset lasciva decentius[6] aetas.

   [1] domus *and* absit *omitted, II (only* absit *omitted in R).*
Hence procul procul absit *Bentley.*
   [2] loco re, *I, R*: colore, *II.*
   [3] fugere *D, II*: fuge rite *aEM.*
   [4] sis *E.*   [5] iuvit *D*: levat.   [6] licentius π^2.

   [a] The *Quinquatrus,* or festival of Minerva, was a school-
vacation of five days, from March 19 to March 23.
   [b] For Thessalian witchcraft *cf. Epod.* v. 45 ; *Odes,* i. 27. 21.

is at variance with the miserly. For it does differ
whether you scatter your money lavishly, or whether,
while neither reluctant to spend, nor eager to add
to your store, you snatch enjoyment of the brief and
pleasant hour, like a schoolboy in the spring holidays.[a]
Far from me be squalid want at home : yet, be my
vessel large or small, I, the passenger aboard, shall
remain one and the same. Not with swelling sails
are we borne before a favouring north wind, yet we
drag not out our life struggling with southern gales ;
in strength, in wit, in person, in virtue, in station, in
fortune, behind the foremost, ever before the last.

[205] You are no miser. Good! What then? Have
all the other vices taken to flight with that? Is
your heart free from vain ambition? Is it free from
alarm and anger at death? Dreams, terrors of
magic, marvels, witches, ghosts of night, Thessalian
portents [b]—do you laugh at these? Do you count
your birthdays thankfully? Do you forgive your
friends? Do you grow gentler and better, as old
age draws near? What good does it do you to
pluck out a single one of many thorns? If you
know not how to live aright, make way for those
who do. You have played enough, have eaten and
drunk enough. 'Tis time to quit the feast,[c] lest,
when you have drunk too freely, youth mock and
jostle you, playing the wanton with better grace.

[c] *Cf. Sat.* i. 1. 118, where, as here, Horace has in mind
the famous passage in Lucretius, *De rerum nat.* iii. 938,

cur non ut plenus vitae conviva recedis ?

ARS POETICA

OR EPISTLE TO THE PISOS

THIS, the longest of Horace's poems, is found in nearly all MSS. under the title *Ars Poetica*, which is also the name assigned to it by Quintilian and used by the commentator Porphyrio. Yet the composition is a letter rather than a formal treatise, and it is hard to believe that Horace himself is responsible for the conventional title. It has the discursive and occasionally personal tone of an Epistle, whereas it lacks the completeness, precision, and logical order of a well-constructed treatise. It must therefore be judged by the same standards as the other *Epistles* and *Sermones*, and must be regarded as an expression of more or less random reflections, suggested by special circumstances, upon an art which peculiarly concerned one or more of the persons addressed. These are a father and two sons of the Piso family, but nobody knows with certainty what particular Pisos—and there are many on record—they are.

Though the writer touches upon various kinds of poetry, yet as fully one-third of the whole poem is concerned with the drama, it is a plausible inference that one at least of the Pisos — presumably the elder son (l. 366)—was about to write a play, perhaps one with an Homeric background (ll. 128, 129), and

possibly one conforming to the rules of the Greek
satyric drama (ll. 220 ff.). Thus the special interests
of the Pisos may have determined Horace's choice
of topics.

The following is a brief outline of the main subjects
handled in the letter :

(*a*) A poem demands unity, to be secured by
harmony and proportion, as well as a wise choice of
subject and good diction. Metre and style must be
appropriate to theme and to character. A good
model will always be found in Homer (ll. 1-152).

(*b*) Dramatic poetry calls for special care— as to
character drawing, propriety of representation, length
of a play, number of actors, use of the chorus and
its music, special features for the satyric type, verse-
forms, and employment of Greek models (ll. 153-
294).

(*c*) A poet's qualifications include common sense,
knowledge of character, adherence to high ideals,
combination of the *dulce* with the *utile*, intellectual
superiority, appreciation of the noble history and
lofty mission of poetry, and above all a willingness
to listen to and profit by impartial criticism (ll.
295-476).

The following is a more detailed analysis :

In poetry as in painting there must be unity and
simplicity (1-23). We poets must guard against
extremes, and while avoiding one error must not fall
into its opposite (24-31). A good sculptor pays careful
attention to details, but at the same time makes sure
that his work as a whole is successful (32-37).

A writer should confine himself to subjects within
his power. He will then be at no loss for words and
will follow a correct order, which will enable him to

say the right thing at the right moment (38-45). As to diction, he must be careful in his choice of language. He can, by means of a skilful combination, give a fresh tone to familiar terms, and he may even coin words in moderation as the old poets used to do. Like all other mortal things, words change and pass out of existence, for they are subject to the caprice of fashion (46-72).

The metres most fitting for the several types of verse were established by the great Greek poets, and we must follow them (73-85). So with the tone and style of the various kinds. In the drama, for example, the tragic and the comic are distinct, though occasionally they will overlap (86-98), for above all things a play must appeal to the feelings of an audience, and the language must be adapted to the characters impersonated. Where there is lack of such agreement, everybody will laugh in scorn (99-118).

Either follow tradition or invent a consistent story. Achilles, Medea, Orestes, and so on must be portrayed as they are known to us in Greek literature, while new characters must be handled with a consistency of their own (119-127). It is hard to deal with general notions, such as anger, greed, and cowardice, so as to individualize them for yourself and you, my friend Piso, are quite right to dramatize some Homeric theme, where the characters introduced have well-known traits, rather than attempt something distinctly original. And yet, even in such public property as the Homeric epics you may win private rights by handling your material in an original fashion. Make a simple beginning, like that of the *Odyssey*, where the sequel becomes clearer and increases in brilliancy. Homer indulges in no lengthy introduction, but hurries on with his narrative, omits what he cannot adorn, and never loses the thread of his story (128-152).

If you want your play to succeed, you must study the " strange, eventful history " of human life, and note the characteristics of the several ages of man, so that the different periods may not be confused (153-178). Events may be set forth in action or, less preferably, in narrative. The latter method, however, must be used in the case of revolting and incredible incidents (179-188).

A play should be in five acts. The *deus ex machina* should be employed only rarely, and there should never be more than three characters on the stage at one time (189-192). The Chorus should take a real part in the action ; it should not sing anything irrelevant, and should promote the cause of morality and religion (193-201). As to the music, the flute was once a simple instrument, which accompanied the chorus, and was not expected to fill large theatres as nowadays. With the growth of wealth and luxury in the state, and the consequent deterioration in the taste and character of the audience, the music became more florid and sensational, the diction more artificial, and the sentiments more obscure and oracular (202-219).

The satyric drama, with its chorus of goat-footed fauns, which was devised for spectators in their lighter moods, naturally assumed a gay and frolicsome tone as compared with the serious tragedy from which it sprang, but this does not warrant a writer in permitting his gods and heroes to use vulgar speech, or on the other hand in allowing them to indulge in ranting. There should be a happy mean between the language of tragedy and that of comedy. I would aim at a familiar style, so that anyone might think it easy to write in that fashion, but on trying would find out his mistake. The rustic fauns must not talk like city wits, nor yet use such coarse language that they will give offence to the better part of an audience (220-250).

As to metre, the iambic is strictly a rapid measure, so that a senarius is counted as a trimeter. But the older poets admitted the spondee so freely, that it obscured the rhythm and made it heavy. In fact, it is not every critic that can detect unmusical verses, and too much freedom has been allowed our native poets. Shall I presume on this or shall I write with caution? If I follow the latter course, I may avoid criticism, but I shall not win praise. The proper course is to study Greek models night and day. He who is conversant with them will see that our fathers' admiration for the rhythms, as well as the wit, of Plautus, was uncalled for (251-274).

Thespis, we are told, invented Tragedy, and Aeschylus perfected it. Old Attic Comedy, too, won no little renown until its licence had to be checked by law and its chorus was silenced (275-284). Our Roman poets, besides following the Greeks, were bold enough to invent forms of a national drama, and might have rivalled their masters, had they taken more pains. I beg you, my friends, to condemn every poem which has not been subjected to the finishing touch (285-294).

The idea that genius is allied to madness is carried so far that many would-be poets are slovenly in appearance and neglect their health. It is not worth

THE ART OF POETRY

while to compose poetry at the expense of your wits,
so, refraining from writing myself, I will teach the
art to others, even as a whetstone can sharpen
knives, though it cannot cut (295-308).

The first essential is wisdom. This you can
cultivate by study of the philosophers, and when
you have first learned from them valuable lessons of
life, you should apply yourself to life itself, and then
your personages will speak like real living beings.
Sometimes striking passages and characters properly
portrayed commend a mediocre play better than do
verses which lack substance, mere trifles, however
melodious (309-322).

The Greeks had genius, eloquence, and ambition ;
the Romans are too practical, even in their elementary
schooling. How can we expect a people thus trained
to develop poets ? Poetry aims at both instruction
and pleasure. In your didactic passages, be not
long-winded ; in your fiction, avoid extravagance.
Combine the *utile* with the *dulce*, for only thus will
you produce a book that will sell, and enjoy a wide
and lasting fame (323-346).

Absolute perfection, however, is not to be expected,
and we must allow for slight defects. When I come
across a good line in a poor poem, I am surprised
and amused ; I am merely grieved if Homer now
and then nods (347-360). The critic must bear in
mind that poetry is like painting. In each case the
aim in view is to be considered. A miniature should
bear close inspection ; a wall-painting is to be seen
from a distance. One thing which may be tolerated
in other fields, but which in the sphere of poetry,
whose aim is to give pleasure, is never allowed, is
mediocrity. Like the athlete, therefore, the poet

447

needs training—a truth overlooked by many. But you are too sensible to make a mistake here. You will write only when Minerva is auspicious, and what you write you will submit to a good critic. Even then you will be in no haste to publish (361-390).

Remember the glorious history of poetry, which—as the stories of Orpheus and Amphion show—has from the very infancy of the race promoted the cause of civilization. Then, from Homer on, it has inspired valour, has taught wisdom, has won the favour of princes, and has afforded relief after toil. Never need you be ashamed of the Muse (391-407).

The question has been asked whether it is natural ability or teaching that makes the poet. Both are necessary. However much people may boast of their gifts, ability without training will accomplish no more in writing than in running a race or in flute-playing (408-418).

It is easy for a rich poet to buy applause. Flatterers are like hired mourners at a funeral, who feel no grief, however much they may weep. So be not deceived, but take a lesson from those kings, who, acting on the adage *in vino veritas*, make men disclose the truth by plying them with wine (419-437).

Quintilius Varus was a frank and sincere critic, and if you would not take his advice he would leave you to your self-conceit. No honest man, for fear of giving offence, will conceal his friend's faults from him, for those faults may lead to serious consequences (438-452).

And think of the danger of a crazy poet roaming at large. First, there is danger for himself, for if, as he goes about with upturned gaze, he fall into a ditch, nobody will pull him out. Indeed, he may have gone in on purpose, like Empedocles, who, thinking himself divine, once leaped into burning Aetna. And secondly, there is danger for others, for if he is so stark, staring mad as to be ever making verses, he will become a public scourge, and if he catches some poor wretch he will fasten on him like a leech, and make him listen to his recitations until he has bored him to death (453-476)!

The sketch of a crazy poet with which the poem closes corresponds to that of the crazy painter with which it opens. Both painter and poet are used to impress upon readers the lesson that in poetry as in other arts the main principle to be followed is propriety. This idea of literary propriety, which runs through the whole epistle, is illustrated in many ways, and may be said to give the *Ars Poetica* an artistic unity. (So Roy Kenneth Hack, "The Doctrine of Literary Forms" in *Harvard Studies in Classical Philology*, vol. xxvii., 1916.)

DE ARTE POETICA[1]

Humano capiti[2] cervicem pictor equinam
iungere si velit, et varias inducere plumas
undique collatis membris, ut turpiter atrum
desinat in piscem mulier formosa superne,
spectatum admissi[3] risum teneatis, amici ?   5
credite, Pisones,[4] isti tabulae fore librum
persimilem, cuius, velut aegri[5] somnia, vanae
fingentur[6] species, ut nec pes nec caput uni
reddatur formae.   " pictoribus atque poetis
quidlibet[7] audendi[8] semper fuit aequa potestas."   10
scimus, et hanc veniam petimusque damusque
    vicissim ;
sed non ut placidis coeant immitia, non ut
serpentes avibus geminentur, tigribus agni.

Inceptis gravibus plerumque et magna professis
purpureus, late qui splendeat, unus et alter   15
adsuitur pannus, cum lucus et ara Dianae
et properantis aquae per amoenos ambitus agros
aut flumen Rhenum aut pluvius[9] describitur arcus.
sed nunc non erat his locus.   et fortasse cupressum
scis simulare : quid hoc, si fractis enatat exspes[10] 20

---

[1] For the Ars Poetica class I of the mss. includes aBCKM,
while class II includes Rφψδλlπ.
  [2] pectori B[1].   [3] missi BC.   [4] pisonis, II.   [5] aegris a[1]BR.
  [6] funguntur B: fingentur or finguntur.
  [7] quodlibet π.   [8] audiendi B.
  [9] fluvius, II.   [10] expers, II.

THE ART OF POETRY

IF a painter chose to join a human head to the neck
of a horse, and to spread feathers of many a hue over
limbs picked up now here now there, so that what at
the top is a lovely woman ends below in a black and
ugly fish, could you, my friends, if favoured with a
private view, refrain from laughing? Believe me,
dear Pisos, quite like such pictures would be a book,
whose idle fancies shall be shaped like a sick man's
dreams, so that neither head nor foot can be assigned
to a single shape. "Painters and poets," you say,
"have always had an equal right in hazarding any-
thing." We know it: this licence we poets claim
and in our turn we grant the like; but not so far
that savage should mate with tame, or serpents
couple with birds, lambs with tigers.

[14] Works with noble beginnings and grand promises
often have one or two purple patches so stitched on
as to glitter far and wide, when Diana's grove and
altar, and

> The winding stream a-speeding 'mid fair fields

or the river Rhine, or the rainbow is being described.[a]
For such things there is a place, but not just now.
Perhaps, too, you can draw a cypress. But what of
that, if you are paid to paint a sailor swimming from

---

[a] These examples are doubtless taken from poems current
in Horace's day.

navibus, aere dato qui pingitur ?   amphora coepit
institui : currente rota cur urceus exit ?
denique sit quod vis,[1] simplex dumtaxat et unum.

Maxima pars vatum, pater et iuvenes patre digni,
decipimur specie recti.   brevis esse laboro,   25
obscurus fio ; sectantem levia[2] nervi
deficiunt animique ; professus grandia turget ;
serpit humi tutus nimium timidusque procellae :
qui variare cupit rem prodigialiter unam,
delphinum silvis appingit, fluctibus aprum.   30
in vitium ducit culpae fuga, si caret arte.

Aemilium circa ludum faber imus[3] et unguis
exprimet et mollis imitabitur aere capillos,
infelix operis summa, quia ponere totum
nesciet.   hunc ego me,[4] si quid componere curem, 35
non magis esse velim, quam naso vivere pravo,[5]
spectandum nigris oculis nigroque[6] capillo.

Sumite materiam vestris, qui scribitis, aequam
viribus et versate diu, quid ferre recusent,
quid valeant umeri.   cui lecta potenter erit res,   40
nec facundia deseret hunc nec lucidus ordo.
ordinis haec virtus erit et venus, aut[7] ego fallor,
ut[8] iam nunc dicat iam nunc debentia dici,

---

[1] quidvis *K Bentley.*   [2] lenia *Bentley.*
[3] unus δ^1 *Bentley.*   [4] egomet $\delta\phi\psi.$
  [5] parvo $\delta\lambda\pi.$ [6] nigrove *BCK.*
[7] haut *or* haud *BCK, II* (except π).   [8] aut, *II.*

---

[a] One who has been saved from a shipwreck wants to
put a picture of the scene as a votive offering in a temple.

[b] So the scholiasts, *imus* being local amd meaning

his wrecked vessel in despair ? [a] That was a wine-jar, when the moulding began : why, as the wheel runs round, does it turn out a pitcher ? In short, be the work what you will, let it at least be simple and uniform.

24 Most of us poets, O father and ye sons worthy of the father, deceive ourselves by the semblance of truth. Striving to be brief, I become obscure. Aiming at smoothness, I fail in force and fire. One promising grandeur, is bombastic ; another, over-cautious and fearful of the gale, creeps along the ground. The man who tries to vary a single subject in monstrous fashion, is like a painter adding a dolphin to the woods, a boar to the waves. Shunning a fault may lead to error, if there be lack of art.

32 Near the Aemilian School, at the bottom of the row,[b] there is a craftsman who in bronze will mould nails and imitate waving locks, but is unhappy in the total result, because he cannot represent a whole figure. Now if I wanted to write something, I should no more wish to be like him, than to live with my nose turned askew, though admired for my black eyes and black hair.

38 Take a subject, ye writers, equal to your strength ; and ponder long what your shoulders refuse, and what they are able to bear. Whoever shall choose a theme within his range, neither speech will fail him, nor clearness of order. Of order, this, if I mistake not, will be the excellence and charm that the author of the long-promised poem shall say at the moment what at that moment should be said,

"the last" of a number of shops. Some, however, take it in the sense of "humblest." Bentley's *unus* is to be taken closely with *exprimet*, "mould better than any others."

pleraque differat et praesens in tempus omittat,
hoc amet, hoc spernat[1] promissi carminis auctor. 45
In verbis etiam tenuis cautusque serendis[2]
dixeris[3] egregie, notum si callida verbum
reddiderit iunctura novum. si forte necesse est
indiciis monstrare recentibus abdita rerum,[4]
fingere cinctutis non exaudita Cethegis 50
continget, dabiturque licentia sumpta pudenter :
et nova fictaque[5] nuper habebunt verba fidem, si
Graeco fonte cadent[6] parce detorta. quid autem
Caecilio Plautoque dabit Romanus ademptum
Vergilio Varioque[7] ? ego cur, adquirere pauca 55
si possum, invideor, cum lingua Catonis et Enni
sermonem patrium ditaverit et nova rerum
nomina protulerit ? licuit semperque licebit
signatum praesente nota producere[8] nomen.
ut silvae foliis[9] pronos mutantur in annos, 60
prima cadunt ; ita verborum vetus interit aetas,
et iuvenum ritu florent modo nata vigentque.
debemur morti nos nostraque : sive receptus
terra Neptunus classes Aquilonibus arcet,
regis opus, sterilisve[10] palus diu aptaque remis 65

[1] spernet *BC*.
[2] *Bentley transposed ll. 45 and 46, and has been followed by
most editors. The scholiasts, however, had l. 45 preceding l. 46.
Servius, too, though he cites l. 45 three times* (on Aeneid,
iv. 412, 415 ; Georgics, ii. 475) *nowhere applies it to diction.*
[3] dixerit *B*.   [4] rerum et, *II*.   [5] factaque.
[6] cadant *a*, *Servius on Virg.* Aen. vi. 34.
[7] Varoque φψδ.   [8] procudere *Bentley*.
[9] folia in silvis *Diomedes*.   [10] sterilisque, *I (except a)*.

---

[a] Bentley's transposition of lines 45 and 46, making
hoc . . . hoc refer to *verbis*, seems unnecessary. The tradi-
tional order is retained by Wickham and Rolfe. Horace
deals first with the arrangement of argumentative material,

reserving and omitting much for the present, loving
this point and scorning that.[a]

[46] Moreover, with a nice taste and care in
weaving words together, you will express yourself
most happily, if a skilful setting makes a familiar
word new. If haply one must betoken abstruse
things by novel terms, you will have a chance
to fashion words never heard of by the kilted[b]
Cethegi, and licence will be granted, if used with
modesty; while words, though new and of recent
make, will win acceptance, if they spring from a
Greek fount and are drawn therefrom but sparingly.[c]
Why indeed shall Romans grant this licence to
Caecilius and Plautus, and refuse it to Virgil and
Varius? And why should I be grudged the right of
adding, if I can, my little fund, when the tongue of
Cato and of Ennius has enriched our mother-speech
and brought to light new terms for things? It has
ever been, and ever will be, permitted to issue words
stamped with the mint-mark of the day. As forests
change their leaves with each year's decline, and the
earliest drop off[d]: so with words, the old race dies,
and, like the young of human kind, the new-born
bloom and thrive. We are doomed to death—we and
all things ours; whether Neptune, welcomed within
the land, protects our fleets from northern gales—a
truly royal work—or a marsh, long a waste where oars

and in l. 46 passes to diction (*cf.* Fiske, *Lucilius and Horace*,
p. 449 and note 50).

[b] The *cinctus* was a loin-cloth worn instead of the *tunica*
by the Romans in days of old.

[c] As Wickham has seen, the metaphor is taken from
irrigation; "the sluices must be opened sparingly."

[d] In Italian woods, as in Californian, leaves may stay on
the trees two or even three years. Only the oldest (*prima*)
drop off each autumn.

vicinas urbes alit et grave sentit aratrum,
seu cursum mutavit iniquum frugibus amnis
doctus iter melius : mortalia facta peribunt,
nedum sermonum stet honos et gratia vivax.
multa renascentur quae iam cecidere, cadentque   70
quae nunc sunt in honore vocabula, si volet usus,
quem penes arbitrium est et ius et norma loquendi.

  Res gestae regumque ducumque et tristia bella
quo scribi possent numero, monstravit Homerus.
versibus impariter iunctis querimonia primum,   75
post etiam inclusa est voti sententia compos ;
quis tamen exiguos elegos emiserit auctor,
grammatici certant et adhuc sub iudice lis est.
Archilochum proprio rabies armavit iambo :
hunc socci cepere pedem grandesque coturni   80
alternis aptum sermonibus et popularis
vincentem strepitus et natum rebus agendis.
musa dedit fidibus divos puerosque deorum
et pugilem victorem et equum certamine primum
et iuvenum curas et libera vina referre.   85
descriptas servare vices operumque colores

---

  a Horace finds three illustrations of human achievement
in certain engineering works planned by Julius Caesar or
Augustus. These were : (1) the building of the Julian
Harbour on the Campanian coast, where, under Agrippa,
Lakes Avernus and Lucrinus were connected by a deep
channel, and the sandy strip between the Lucrine Lake
and the sea was pierced so as to admit ships from the
Tuscan Sea ; *cf.* Virgil, *Georgics*, ii. 161 ff. ; (2) the draining
of the Pomptine marshes, planned by Julius Caesar and
perhaps executed by Augustus ; (3) the straightening of
the Tiber's course so as to protect Rome from floods.
  b Cf. Epistles ii. 2. 119.   *c* The dactylic hexameter.
  d The elegiac couplet, made up of a hexameter and a
pentameter (hence *impariter iunctis*), was commonly used
in inscriptions associated with votive offerings and expressed

were plied, feeds neighbouring towns and feels the weight of the plough ; or a river has changed the course which brought ruin to corn-fields and has learnt a better path [a] : all mortal things shall perish, much less shall the glory and glamour of speech endure and live. Many terms that have fallen out of use shall be born again, and those shall fall that are now in repute, if Usage so will it, in whose hands lies the judgement, the right and the rule of speech.[b]

[73] In what measure the exploits of kings and captains and the sorrows of war may be written, Homer has shown.[c] Verses yoked unequally first embraced lamentation, later also the sentiment of granted prayer [d] : yet who first put forth humble elegiacs, scholars dispute, and the case is still before the court. Rage armed Archilochus with his own *iambus* : this foot comic sock and high buskins alike adopted, as suited to alternate speech, able to drown the clamours of the pit, and by nature fit for action.[e] To the lyre the Muse granted tales of gods and children of gods, of the victor in boxing, of the horse first in the race, of the loves of swains, and of freedom over wine.[f] If I fail to keep and do not understand these well-marked shifts and shades of poetic forms,[g]

in the form of epigrams. The earliest elegiacs, however, were probably laments, such as those written by Archilochus on the loss of friends at sea.

[e] The iambic trimeter was the measure used in dialogue, both in comedies and tragedies. For Archilochus see *Epist.* i. 19. 23 ff.

[f] Greek lyric poetry embraced hymns to the gods and heroes, odes commemorating victories in the games, love poems, and drinking-songs. For Pindaric themes *cf. Odes*, iv. 2. 10-24.

[g] From here on Horace deals especially with dramatic poetry. Tone and style, diction and metre should all accord.

cur ego si nequeo ignoroque poeta salutor ?
cur nescire pudens prave quam discere malo ?
versibus exponi tragicis res comica non volt ;
indignatur item privatis ac prope socco   90
dignis carminibus narrari cena Thyestae.
singula quaeque locum teneant sortita decentem.[1]
interdum tamen et vocem Comoedia tollit,
iratusque Chremes tumido delitigat ore ;
et tragicus plerumque dolet sermone pedestri   95
Telephus et Peleus, cum pauper et exsul uterque
proicit ampullas et sesquipedalia verba,
si curat[2] cor spectantis tetigisse querella.
    Non satis est pulchra esse poemata ; dulcia sunto
et quocumque volent[3] animum auditoris agunto.   100
ut ridentibus arrident, ita flentibus adsunt[4]
humani voltus : si vis me flere, dolendum est
primum ipsi tibi : tunc[5] tua me infortunia laedent,
Telephe vel Peleu ; male si mandata loqueris,
aut dormitabo aut ridebo. tristia maestum   105
voltum verba decent, iratum plena minarum,
ludentem lasciva, severum seria dictu.
format enim Natura prius nos intus ad omnem
fortunarum habitum ; iuvat aut impellit ad iram,
aut ad humum maerore gravi deducit et angit ;   110
post effert animi motus interprete lingua.
si dicentis erunt fortunis absona dicta,
Romani tollent equites peditesque cachinnum.
intererit multum, divusne[6] loquatur an heros,
maturusne senex an adhuc florente iuventa   115

---

    [1] decentem *VBK*: decenter *aCM, II.*
     [2] curas.   [3] volunt, *II.*
     [4] adsunt *MSS.*: adflent *Bentley.*
   [5] tum *BCK.*   [6] Davusne *K.*

---

    [a] *Cf. Epist.* i. 3. 14.

why am I hailed as poet ? Why through false shame
do I prefer to be ignorant rather than to learn ? A
theme for Comedy refuses to be set forth in verses
of Tragedy ; likewise the feast of Thyestes scorns to
be told in strains of daily life that well nigh befit the
comic sock. Let each style keep the becoming
place allotted it. Yet at times even Comedy
raises her voice, and an angry Chremes storms in
swelling tones ; so, too, in Tragedy Telephus and
Peleus often grieve in the language of prose, when,
in poverty and exile, either hero throws aside his
bombast [a] and Brobdingnagian [b] words, should he
want his lament to touch the spectator's heart.

[99] Not enough is it for poems to have beauty :
they must have charm, and lead the hearer's soul
where they will. As men's faces smile on those
who smile, so they respond to those who weep. If
you would have me weep, you must first feel grief
yourself : then, O Telephus or Peleus, will your
misfortunes hurt me : if the words you utter are ill
suited, I shall laugh or fall asleep. Sad tones befit the
face of sorrow ; blustering accents that of anger ; jests
become the merry, solemn words the grave. For
Nature first shapes us within to meet every change
of fortune : she brings joy or impels to anger, or
bows us to the ground and tortures us under a load
of grief ; then, with the tongue for interpreter, she
proclaims the emotions of the soul. If the speaker's
words sound discordant with his fortunes, the
Romans, in boxes and pit alike, will raise a loud
guffaw. Vast difference will it make, whether a god
be speaking or a hero, a ripe old man or one still in

[b] *Sesquipedalia verba*, lit. " words a foot and a half in
length."

fervidus, et matrona potens an sedula nutrix,
mercatorne vagus cultorne virentis[1] agelli,
Colchus an Assyrius, Thebis nutritus an Argis.

Aut famam sequere aut sibi convenientia finge.
scriptor honoratum[2] si forte reponis Achillem,   120
impiger, iracundus, inexorabilis, acer,
iura neget sibi nata, nihil non arroget armis.
sit Medea ferox invictaque, flebilis Ino,
perfidus Ixion, Io vaga, tristis Orestes.
si quid inexpertum scaenae committis et audes   125
personam formare novam, servetur ad imum,
qualis ab incepto processerit, et sibi constet.

Difficile est proprie communia dicere ; tuque
rectius Iliacum carmen deducis in actus,
quam si proferres ignota indictaque primus.   130
publica materies privati iuris erit, si
non circa vilem patulumque moraberis orbem,
nec verbo verbum[3] curabis reddere fidus
interpres, nec desilies imitator in artum,
unde pedem proferre pudor vetet aut operis lex.   135

[1] vigentis *M, II.*   [2] Homereum *Bentley.*
[3] verbum verbo *C.*

---

[a] The Assyrian would be effeminate, as compared with
the Colchian, but both would be barbarians. The Theban
Creon is a headstrong tyrant, while the Argive Agamemnon
shows reserve and dignity.

[b] In the *Iliad* Achilles was first scorned by Agamemnon
but in the sequel (Book IX, the embassy) highly honoured.
Bentley conjectured that *honoratum* was a corruption of
Homereum, " the Achilles of Homer," but we are dealing
with a not uncommon use of the participle. So Elmore in
C.R. xxxiii. (1919) p. 102 ; *cf. Sat.* i. 6. 126.

[c] By *publica materies* Horace means Homer and the epic
field in general. A poet may make this his own by original-
ity in the handling. Commentators are divided as to
whether *communia* (l. 128) is identical with *publica materies*

the flower and fervour of youth, a dame of rank or a bustling nurse, a roaming trader or the tiller of a verdant field, a Colchian or an Assyrian, one bred at Thebes or at Argos.[a]

119 Either follow tradition or invent what is self-consistent. If haply, when you write, you bring back to the stage the honouring of Achilles,[b] let him be impatient, passionate, ruthless, fierce ; let him claim that laws are not for him, let him ever make appeal to the sword. Let Medea be fierce and unyielding, Ino tearful, Ixion forsworn, Io a wanderer, Orestes sorrowful. If it is an untried theme you entrust to the stage, and if you boldly fashion a fresh character, have it kept to the end even as it came forth at the first, and have it self-consistent.

128 It is hard to treat in your own way what is common : and you are doing better in spinning into acts a song of Troy than if, for the first time, you were giving the world a theme unknown and unsung. In ground open to all you will win private rights,[c] if you do not linger along the easy and open pathway, if you do not seek to render word for word as a slavish translator, and if in your copying you do not leap into the narrow well, out of which either shame or the laws of your task will keep you from stirring

or not. The language is in the domain of law and as *res communes*, things common to all mankind, as the air and sea, differ from *res publicae*, things which belong to all citizens of a state, as its roads and theatres, so here *communia* covers a larger field than *publica*, and denotes characteristics which are common among mankind. These may be compared to the general truths (τὰ καθόλου) of Aristotle (*Poet.* ix.), as distinguished from particular ones (τὰ καθ' ἕκαστον). In Horace it is obvious that *communia* does not apply to *Iliacum carmen*, which does, however, come under the *publica materies* of the poet.

461

nec sic incipies ut scriptor cyclicus olim :
" fortunam Priami cantabo et nobile[1] bellum."
quid dignum tanto feret hic promissor hiatu ?
parturient[2] montes, nascetur ridiculus mus.
quanto rectius hic, qui nil molitur inepte : 140
" dic mihi, Musa, virum, captae post tempora Troiae
qui[3] mores hominum multorum vidit et urbes."
non fumum ex fulgore, sed ex fumo dare lucem
cogitat, ut speciosa dehinc miracula promat,
Antiphaten Scyllamque et cum Cyclope Charybdin.
nec reditum Diomedis ab interitu Meleagri, 146
nec gemino bellum Troianum orditur ab ovo ;
semper ad eventum festinat et in medias res
non secus ac notas auditorem rapit, et quae
desperat tractata nitescere posse, relinquit, 150
atque ita mentitur, sic veris falsa remiscet,
primo ne medium, medio ne discrepet imum.

Tu quid ego et populus mecum desideret audi,
si plosoris[4] eges aulaea manentis et usque
sessuri,[5] donec cantor " vos plaudite " dicat, 155
aetatis cuiusque notandi sunt tibi mores,
mobilibusque[6] decor naturis dandus et annis.
reddere qui voces iam scit puer et pede certo
signat humum, gestit paribus colludere, et iram

¹ cantarat nobile *B*. ² parturiunt. ³ quis *B*.
 ⁴ plosoris *V, I*: plus oris, *II*: plausoris *B*².
 ⁵ sessori *B*. ⁶ nobilibusque *B*.

ᵃ Horace utilizes the fable of the goat that leapt into a well, but has nothing to say about the fox who persuaded him to do so.

ᵇ The opening of the *Odyssey*.

ᶜ Meleager was an uncle of Diomede, and therefore of an older generation.

ᵈ *i.e.* from the birth of Helen.

ᵉ The *cantor* was probably the young slave who stood

a step.[a] And you are not to begin as the Cyclic poet of old :

> Of Priam's fate and famous war I'll sing.

What will this boaster produce in keeping with such mouthing ? Mountains will labour, to birth will come a laughter-rousing mouse ! How much better he who makes no foolish effort :

> Sing, Muse, for me the man who on Troy's fall
> Saw the wide world, its ways and cities all.[b]

Not smoke after flame does he plan to give, but after smoke the light, that then he may set forth striking and wondrous tales—Antiphates, Scylla, Charybdis, and the Cyclops. Nor does he begin Diomede's return from the death of Meleager,[c] or the war of Troy from the twin eggs.[d] Ever he hastens to the issue, and hurries his hearer into the story's midst, as if already known, and what he fears he cannot make attractive with his touch he abandons ; and so skilfully does he invent, so closely does he blend facts and fiction, that the middle is not discordant with the beginning, nor the end with the middle.

[159] Now hear what I, and with me the public, expect. If you want an approving hearer, one who waits for the curtain, and will stay in his seat till the singer [e] cries " Give your applause," you must note the manners of each age, and give a befitting tone to shifting natures and their years. The child, who by now can utter words and set firm step upon the ground, delights to play with his mates, flies

near the flute-player and sang the *cantica* of a play, while the actor gesticulated. All the comedies of Plautus and Terence close with *plaudite* or an equivalent phrase.

colligit ac ponit temere et mutatur in horas.　　160
imberbis[1] iuvenis, tandem custode remoto,
gaudet equis canibusque et aprici gramine Campi,
cereus in vitium flecti, monitoribus asper,
utilium tardus provisor, prodigus aeris,
sublimis cupidusque et amata relinquere pernix.　165
conversis studiis aetas animusque virilis
quaerit opes et amicitias, inservit honori,
commisisse cavet quod mox mutare[2] laboret.
multa senem circumveniunt incommoda, vel quod
quaerit et inventis miser abstinet ac timet uti,　　170
vel quod res omnis timide gelideque ministrat,
dilator[3] spe longus, iners avidusque futuri,
difficilis, querulus, laudator temporis acti
se puero, castigator censorque minorum.
multa ferunt anni venientes commoda secum,　　175
multa recedentes adimunt.　ne forte seniles
mandentur iuveni partes pueroque viriles,
semper in adiunctis aevoque morabimur[4] aptis.[5]

　　Aut agitur res in scaenis aut acta refertur.
segnius irritant animos demissa per aurem　　180
quam quae sunt oculis subiecta fidelibus et quae
ipse sibi tradit spectator : non tamen intus
digna geri promes in scaenam, multaque tolles

---

　　[1] imberbis *aB*: imberbus *VCM*; *cf.* Epist. ii. 1. 85.
　　[2] mox mutare] permutare, *II*.　　　　[3] delator *B*.
　　　　[4] morabitur *B, II, Vollmer*.　　　[5] apti *B*.

---

　　[a] *i.e.* Campus Martius.
　　[b] *Spe longus* seems to be a translation of Aristotle's
δύσελπις (*Rhet.* ii. 12), hence Bentley conjectured *lentus* for
longus.　It is, however, in view of Horace's *spes longa*
(*Odes,* i. 4. 15 ; i. 11. 6) taken by some as " far-reaching
in hope," the hope requiring a long time for fulfilment.
Wickham suggests " patient in hope," but the quality is here
one of the *incommoda* of age, not one of its blessings.　The

into a passion and as lightly puts it aside, and
changes every hour. The beardless youth, freed at
last from his tutor, finds joy in horses and hounds
and the grass of the sunny Campus,[a] soft as wax for
moulding to evil, peevish with his counsellors, slow
to make needful provision, lavish of money, spirited,
of strong desires, but swift to change his fancies.
With altered aims, the age and spirit of the man
seeks wealth and friends, becomes a slave to am-
bition, and is fearful of having done what soon it
will be eager to change. Many ills encompass an
old man, whether because he seeks gain, and then
miserably holds aloof from his store and fears to use
it, or because, in all that he does, he lacks fire and
courage, is dilatory and slow to form hopes,[b] is
sluggish and greedy of a longer life, peevish, surly,
given to praising the days he spent as a boy, and to
reproving and condemning the young. Many bless-
ings do the advancing years bring with them ; many,
as they retire, they take away. So, lest haply we
assign a youth the part of age, or a boy that of man-
hood, we shall ever linger over traits that are joined
and fitted to the age.

[179] Either an event is acted on the stage, or the
action is narrated. Less vividly is the mind stirred
by what finds entrance through the ears than by
what is brought before the trusty eyes, and what
the spectator can see for himself. Yet you will not
bring upon the stage what should be performed
behind the scenes, and you will keep much from our

phrase is explanatory of *dilator*, even as *avidus futuri*
explains *iners*, for unlike the youth, who is absorbed in the
present, the old man fails to act promptly, because his heart
is in the future, however brief that is to be.

ex oculis, quae mox narret facundia praesens;
ne pueros coram populo Medea trucidet,   185
aut humana palam coquat exta nefarius Atreus,
aut in avem Procne vertatur, Cadmus in anguem.
quodcumque ostendis mihi sic, incredulus odi.

Neve minor neu sit quinto productior actu
fabula quae posci volt et spectata[1] reponi.   190
nec deus intersit, nisi dignus vindice nodus
inciderit, nec quarta loqui persona laboret.

Actoris partis chorus officiumque virile
defendat, neu quid medios intercinat actus
quod non proposito conducat et haereat apte.   195
ille bonis faveatque et consilietur amice,[2]
et regat iratos et amet peccare timentis[3];
ille dapes laudet mensae brevis, ille salubrem
iustitiam legesque et apertis otia portis;
ille tegat commissa deosque precetur et oret   200
ut redeat miseris, abeat fortuna superbis.

Tibia non, ut nunc, orichalco vincta[4] tubaeque
aemula, sed tenuis simplexque foramine pauco[5]
adspirare et adesse choris erat utilis atque
nondum spissa nimis complere sedilia flatu;   205
quo sane populus numerabilis, utpote parvus,
et frugi castusque[6] verecundusque coibat.
postquam coepit agros extendere victor et urbes
latior amplecti murus, vinoque diurno
placari Genius festis impune diebus,   210
accessit numerisque modisque licentia maior.

---

[1] spectata δλlπ: spectanda (exsp - BK) *other* MSS. *Both
known to scholiasts. The latter perhaps an early error,
due to* Sat. i. 10. 39.
   [2] amici(s), *II.*   [3] pacare tumentes.   [4] iuncta *CK.*
   [5] parvo, *II (except* π).   [6] cautusque *C*: catusque φψ.

---

[a] The *deus ex machina.* As *vindex*, he is to deliver men
from difficulties seemingly insoluble.

eyes, which an actor's ready tongue will narrate anon in our presence; so that Medea is not to butcher her boys before the people, nor impious Atreus cook human flesh upon the stage, nor Procne be turned into a bird, Cadmus into a snake. Whatever you thus show me, I discredit and abhor.

[189] Let no play be either shorter or longer than five acts, if when once seen it hopes to be called for and brought back to the stage. And let no god[a] intervene, unless a knot come worthy of such a deliverer, nor let a fourth actor essay to speak.[b]

[193] Let the Chorus sustain the part and strenuous duty of an actor, and sing nothing between acts which does not advance and fitly blend into the plot. It should side with the good and give friendly counsel; sway the angry and cherish the righteous. It should praise the fare of a modest board, praise wholesome justice, law, and peace with her open gates; should keep secrets, and pray and beseech the gods that fortune may return to the unhappy, and depart from the proud.

[202] The flute—not, as now, bound with brass and a rival of the trumpet, but slight and simple, with few stops—was once of use to lead and aid the chorus and to fill with its breath benches not yet too crowded, where, to be sure, folk gathered, easy to count, because few—sober folk, too, and chaste and modest. But when a conquering race began to widen its domain, and an ampler wall embraced its cities, and when, on festal days, appeasing the Genius[c] by daylight drinking brought no penalty, then both time and tune won greater licence. For what taste

[b] *i.e.* not more than three speaking characters are to be on the stage at once.   [c] *Cf. Epistles*, ii. 1. 144.

indoctus quid enim saperet liberque laborum
rusticus urbano confusus, turpis honesto ?
sic priscae motumque et luxuriem addidit arti
tibicen traxitque vagus per pulpita vestem ;   215
sic etiam fidibus voces crevere severis,
et tulit eloquium insolitum facundia praeceps,
utiliumque sagax rerum et divina futuri
sortilegis non discrepuit sententia Delphis.

Carmine qui tragico vilem certavit ob hircum, 220
mox etiam agrestis Satyros nudavit et asper
incolumi gravitate iocum[1] temptavit, eo quod
illecebris erat et grata novitate morandus
spectator, functusque sacris et potus et exlex.
verum ita risores, ita commendare dicaces   225
conveniet Satyros, ita vertere seria ludo,
ne quicumque deus, quicumque adhibebitur heros,
regali conspectus in auro nuper et ostro,
migret in obscuras humili sermone tabernas,
aut, dum vitat humum, nubes et inania captet.   230
effutire levis indigna Tragoedia versus,
ut festis matrona moveri iussa diebus,
intererit Satyris paulum pudibunda protervis.
non ego inornata et dominantia nomina solum

[1] locum *BKδπ*.

---

[a] Horace seems to speak flippantly of the style of choruses
in Greek tragedy. He assumes that as the music became
more florid, both speech and thought also lost their simplicity,
the former becoming dithyrambic, the latter oracular and
obscure. It is probable, however, that he has in view the
post-classical drama.

[b] Tragedy or " goat-song " was supposed to take its
name from the prize of a goat. It was so called, however,
because the singers were satyrs, dressed in goat-skins.
Satyric drama, the subject of this passage, is closely con-
nected with tragedy, and must not be handled as comedy.

could you expect of an unlettered throng just freed
from toil, rustic mixed up with city folk, vulgar with
nobly-born ? So to the early art the flute-player
added movement and display, and, strutting o'er the
stage, trailed a robe in train. So, too, to the sober
lyre new tones were given, and an impetuous style
brought in an unwonted diction ; and the thought,
full of wise saws and prophetic of the future, was
attuned to the oracles of Delphi.[a]

[220] The poet who in tragic song first competed for
a paltry goat [b] soon also brought on unclad the
woodland Satyrs, and with no loss of dignity roughly
essayed jesting, for only the lure and charm of novelty
could hold the spectator, who, after observance of
the rites,[c] was well drunken and in lawless mood.
But it will be fitting so to seek favour for your
laughing, bantering Satyrs, so to pass from grave to
gay, that no god, no hero, who shall be brought
upon the stage, and whom we have just beheld in
royal gold and purple, shall shift with vulgar speech
into dingy hovels, or, while shunning the ground,
catch at clouds and emptiness. Tragedy, scorning
to babble trivial verses, will, like a matron bidden
to dance on festal days, take her place in the
saucy Satyrs' circle with some little shame. Not
mine shall it be, ye Pisos, if writing Satyric plays, to

It came as a fourth play after a tragic trilogy. Horace
treats this form as if it had developed out of tragedy, whereas
in fact tragedy is an offshoot from it (see *e.g.* Barnett,
The Greek Drama, p. 11). As for a Satyric drama in Latin,
little is known about it, but Pomponius, according to
Porphyrio on l. 221, wrote three *Satyrica*, viz. *Atalanta*,
Sisyphus, and *Ariadne*.

[c] *i.e.* of Bacchus at the Dionysia, when plays were
performed.

verbaque, Pisones, Satyrorum scriptor amabo, 235
nec sic enitar tragico differre colori,
ut nihil intersit, Davusne loquatur et audax[1]
Pythias, emuncto lucrata Simone talentum,
an custos famulusque dei Silenus alumni.
ex noto fictum carmen sequar, ut sibi quivis 240
speret idem, sudet multum frustraque laboret
ausus idem : tantum series iuncturaque pollet,
tantum de medio sumptis accedit honoris.
silvis deducti caveant me iudice Fauni,
ne velut innati triviis ac paene forenses 245
aut nimium teneris iuvenentur versibus umquam,
aut immunda crepent ignominiosaque dicta :
offenduntur enim, quibus est equus et pater et res,
nec, si quid fricti[2] ciceris probat et nucis emptor,
aequis accipiunt animis donantve[3] corona. 250

Syllaba longa brevi subiecta vocatur iambus,
pes citus ; unde etiam trimetris accrescere iussit
nomen iambeis, cum senos redderet ictus
primus ad extremum similis sibi. non ita pridem,

---

[1] et audax *VBCK*: an audax *a, II.*
[2] fricti *aMφψ*: stricti *C*: fracti *BKδπ*.
[3] donantque π.

---

a For *nomina verbaque* cf. *Sat.* i. 3. 103. Plato (*Cratylus*, 431 B) uses ῥήματα and ὀνόματα to cover the whole of language. The epithet *dominantia* translates κύρια. Such words are the common, ordinary ones, which are contrasted with all that are in any way uncommon.

b Davus, Pythias and Simo are cited as names of typical characters in comedy (*cf. Sat.* i. 10. 40). On the other hand, Silenus, the jolly old philosopher, who was father of the Satyrs and guardian of the youthful Dionysus, appeared in Satyric dramas, *e.g.* the *Cyclops* of Euripides.

c By *carmen* Horace means poetic style, not plot, as some

affect only the plain nouns and verbs of established use [a] ; nor shall I strive so to part company with tragic tone, that it matters not whether Davus be speaking with shameless Pythias, who has won a talent by bamboozling Simo, or Silenus, who guards and serves his divine charge.[b] My aim shall be poetry,[c] so moulded from the familiar that anybody may hope for the same success, may sweat much and yet toil in vain when attempting the same : such is the power of order and connexion, such the beauty that may crown the commonplace. When the Fauns [d] are brought from the forest, they should, methinks, beware of behaving as though born at the crossways and almost as dwelling in the Forum, playing at times the young bloods with their mawkish verses, or cracking their bawdy and shameless jokes. For some take offence—knights, free-born, and men of substance—nor do they greet with kindly feelings or reward with a crown everything which the buyers of roasted beans and chestnuts [e] approve.

251 A long syllable following a short is called an *iambus*—a light foot ; hence it commanded that the name of trimeters should attach itself to iambic lines, though it yielded six beats, being from first to last the same throughout.[f] But not so long ago, that it

have taken it. Thus ll. 240-243 are in harmony with those that precede and those that follow. The word *fictum* suggests that this style will look like a new creation. This is to seem easy enough to tempt others to try it.

[d] *i.e.* Satyrs. These wild creatures of the woods must not speak as though they were natives of the city, whether vulgar and coarse or refined and sentimental.

[e] These are still cheap and popular articles of food in Italy.

[f] An iambic trimeter contains six feet, but it takes two feet to make one *metrum*.

tardior ut paulo graviorque veniret ad auris,　255
spondeos stabilis in iura paterna recepit
commodus et patiens, non ut de sede secunda
cederet aut quarta socialiter.　hic et in Acci
nobilibus trimetris apparet rarus, et Enni
in scaenam missos cum magno pondere versus　260
aut operae celeris nimium[1] curaque carentis
aut ignoratae premit artis crimine turpi.
non quivis videt immodulata poemata iudex,
et data Romanis venia est indigna poetis.
idcircone vager scribamque licenter ?　an omnis　265
visuros peccata putem mea, tutus et intra
spem veniae cautus ?　vitavi denique culpam,
non laudem merui.　vos exemplaria Graeca
nocturna versate manu, versate diurna.
at vestri proavi Plautinos et numeros et　270
laudavere sales, nimium patienter utrumque,
ne dicam stulte, mirati, si modo ego et vos
scimus inurbanum lepido seponere dicto
legitimumque sonum digitis callemus et aure.

Ignotum tragicae genus invenisse Camenae　275
dicitur et plaustris vexisse poemata Thespis,
quae canerent agerentque peruncti faecibus ora.[2]
post hunc personae pallaeque repertor honestae
Aeschylus et modicis instravit pulpita tignis
et docuit magnumque loqui nitique cothurno.　280

[1] nimium celeris *a*.　　　[2] ora *aKM, II*: atris *BC*.

---

[a] The admission of spondees to the odd places in the
trimeter, though mentioned by Horace as recent, is really
very old.　Pure iambic trimeters are occasionally used by
Catullus and by Horace (*Epode* xvi.).
[b] The epithet given by this poet's admirers.　*Cf. Epist.* i.
19. 39.　　　[c] See notes on *Epist.* ii. 1. 170-176.
[d] Jesting from wagons (τὰ ἐξ ἁμάξης σκώμματα), in the
processions which formed a feature of the vintage celebration,

might reach the ears with somewhat more slowness and weight, it admitted the steady spondees to its paternal rights,[a] being obliging and tolerant, but not so much so as to give up the second and fourth places in its friendly ranks. In the " noble " [b] trimeters of Accius this *iambus* appears but seldom ; and on the verses which Ennius hurled ponderously upon the stage it lays the shameful charge either of hasty and too careless work or of ignorance of the art. Not every critic discerns unmusical verses, and so undeserved indulgence has been granted our Roman poets. Am I therefore to run loose and write without restraint ? Or, supposing that all will see my faults, shall I seek safety and take care to keep within hope of pardon ? At the best I have escaped censure, I have earned no praise. For yourselves, handle Greek models by night, handle them by day. Yet your forefathers, you say, praised both the measures and the wit of Plautus. Too tolerant, not to say foolish, was their admiration of both, if you and I but know how to distinguish coarseness from wit, and with fingers and ear can catch the lawful rhythm.[c]

[275] Thespis is said to have discovered the Tragic Muse, a type unknown before, and to have carried his pieces in wagons to be sung and acted by players with faces smeared with wine-lees.[d] After him Aeschylus, inventor of the mask and comely robe, laid a stage of small planks, and taught a lofty speech and stately gait on the buskin. To these succeeded

is associated, not with Tragedy, but with Comedy. Horace seems to confuse the two. The words *peruncti faecibus ora* are an allusion to τρυγῳδία, a term used of comedy (*cf.* Aristophanes, *Acharnians*, 499, 500), and derived from τρύξ, " wine-lees."

successit vetus his comoedia, non sine multa
laude ; sed in vitium libertas excidit et vim
dignam lege regi : lex est accepta chorusque
turpiter obticuit sublato iure nocendi.

Nil intemptatum nostri liquere poetae,   285
nec minimum meruere decus vestigia Graeca
ausi deserere et celebrare domestica facta,
vel qui praetextas vel qui docuere togatas.
nec virtute foret clarisve[1] potentius armis
quam lingua Latium, si non offenderet unum   290
quemque poetarum limae labor et mora.   vos, o
Pompilius sanguis, carmen reprehendite quod non
multa dies et multa litura coercuit atque
praesectum[2] deciens non castigavit ad unguem.

Ingenium misera quia fortunatius arte   295
credit et excludit sanos Helicone poetas
Democritus, bona pars non unguis ponere curat,
non barbam,[3] secreta petit loca, balnea vitat.
nanciscetur enim pretium nomenque poetae,
si tribus Anticyris caput insanabile numquam   300
tonsori Licino commiserit.   o ego laevus,
qui purgor bilem sub verni temporis horam !
non alius faceret meliora poemata : verum
nil tanti est.   ergo fungar vice cotis, acutum
reddere quae ferrum valet, exsors ipsa[4] secandi ;   305

---

[1] clarisque *BCK*.
[2] praesectum *VBC* : perspectum π : perfectum *a, II.*
[3] barbas *B*.   [4] exsortita *aBCMRπ.*

---

[a] *Fabulae praetextae* (or *praetextatae*) were tragedies with
Roman themes, so called because of the *toga praetexta*
worn by the actors.   Similarly comedies, in which Roman
citizens appeared, were called *togatae*.   *Cf. Epist.* ii. 1. 57,
and note *e.*

Old Comedy, and won no little credit, but its freedom sank into excess and a violence deserving to be checked by law. The law was obeyed, and the chorus to its shame became mute, its right to injure being withdrawn.

[285] Our own poets have left no style untried, nor has least honour been earned when they have dared to leave the footsteps of the Greeks and sing of deeds at home, whether they have put native tragedies or native comedies upon the stage.[a] Nor would Latium be more supreme in valour and glory of arms than in letters, were it not that her poets, one and all, cannot brook the toil and tedium of the file. Do you, O sons of Pompilius,[b] condemn a poem which many a day and many a blot has not restrained and refined ten times over to the test of the close-cut nail.[c]

[295] Because Democritus believes that native talent is a greater boon than wretched art, and shuts out from Helicon poets in their sober senses, a goodly number take no pains to pare their nails or to shave their beards ; they haunt lonely places and shun the baths—for surely one will win the esteem and name of poet if he never entrusts to the barber Licinus a head that three Anticyras cannot cure.[d] Ah, fool that I am, who purge me of my bile as the season of spring comes on ! Not another man would compose better poems. Yet it's not worth while.[e] So I'll play a whetstone's part, which makes steel sharp, but of itself cannot cut. Though I write

[b] The Calpurnii are said to have been descended from Calpus, one of the sons of Numa Pompilius.

[c] A metaphor from sculpture ; cf. Sat. i. 5. 32.

[d] Cf. Sat. ii. 3. 82, 166.

[e] Viz. to write poetry and lose your wits.

munus et officium, nil scribens ipse, docebo,
unde parentur opes, quid alat formetque poetam,
quid deceat,[1] quid non, quo virtus, quo ferat error.
   Scribendi recte sapere est et principium et fons.
rem tibi Socraticae poterunt ostendere chartae,   310
verbaque provisam rem non invita sequentur.
qui didicit patriae quid debeat et quid amicis,
quo sit amore parens, quo frater amandus et hospes,
quod sit conscripti, quod iudicis officium, quae
partes in bellum missi ducis, ille profecto   315
reddere personae scit convenientia cuique.
respicere exemplar vitae morumque iubebo
doctum imitatorem et vivas hinc ducere voces.
interdum speciosa locis[2] morataque recte
fabula nullius veneris, sine pondere et arte,   320
valdius oblectat populum meliusque moratur
quam versus inopes rerum nugaeque canorae.
   Grais ingenium, Grais dedit ore rotundo
Musa loqui, praeter laudem nullius avaris.
Romani pueri longis rationibus assem   325
discunt in partis centum diducere. "dicat
filius Albani[3] : si de quincunce remota est
uncia, quid superat? poteras[4] dixisse." "triens."
   "eu !
rem poteris servare tuam. redit uncia, quid fit ?"
"semis." an,[5] haec animos aerugo et cura peculi   330

[1] doceat *aRδ*.   [2] iocis *K, II*.
[3] Albini, *II*.   [4] poterat *a, II*.
        [5] an *VB*: ad *aCMK, II*.

---

   [a] I take *doctum* as a repetition of *qui didicit* (l. 312).
The drama is an imitation of life, and the would-be dramatist
who has first learned about life from his studies should next
turn to real life and make his own observations.

   [b] Some take *locis* as equivalent to *sententiis*, moral reflec-
tions or commonplaces, which may be used anywhere.

naught myself, I will teach the poet's office and duty; whence he draws his stores; what nurtures and fashions him; what befits him and what not; whither the right course leads and whither the wrong.

309 Of good writing the source and fount is wisdom. Your matter the Socratic pages can set forth, and when matter is in hand words will not be loath to follow. He who has learned what he owes his country and his friends, what love is due a parent, a brother, and a guest, what is imposed on senator and judge, what is the function of a general sent to war, he surely knows how to give each character his fitting part. I would advise one who has learned the imitative art to look to life and manners for a model, and draw from thence living words.[a] At times a play marked by attractive passages [b] and characters fitly sketched, though lacking in charm, though without force and art, gives the people more delight and holds them better than verses void of thought, and sonorous trifles.

323 To the Greeks the Muse gave native wit, to the Greeks she gave speech in well-rounded phrase [c]; they craved naught but glory. Our Romans, by many a long sum, learn in childhood to divide the *as* into a hundred parts. " Let the son of Albinus answer.[d] If from five-twelfths one ounce be taken, what remains? You might have told me by now." " A third." " Good! you will be able to look after your means. An ounce is added; what's the result?" " A half." When once this canker, this lust of petty

[c] *Ore rotundo* is here used of style, not utterance.
[d] This is a school-lesson in arithmetic. The Romans used a duodecimal system (their *as* being divided into twelve ounces), and the children learn to reduce figures to decimals (*in partes centum*).

cum semel imbuerit, speramus[1] carmina fingi
posse linenda cedro et levi servanda cupresso ?

   Aut prodesse volunt aut delectare poetae
aut simul et iucunda et idonea dicere vitae.
quidquid praecipies, esto brevis, ut cito dicta   335
percipiant animi dociles teneantque fideles :
omne supervacuum pleno de pectore manat.
ficta voluptatis causa sint proxima veris,
ne[2] quodcumque velit[3] poscat sibi fabula credi,
neu pransae Lamiae vivum puerum extrahat alvo. 340
centuriae seniorum agitant expertia frugis,
celsi praetereunt austera poemata Ramnes :
omne tulit punctum qui miscuit utile dulci,
lectorem delectando pariterque monendo.
hic meret aera[4] liber Sosiis, hic et mare transit   345
et longum noto scriptori prorogat aevum.

   Sunt delicta tamen quibus ignovisse velimus :
nam neque chorda sonum reddit, quem volt manus
    et mens,
poscentique gravem persaepe remittit acutum ;
nec semper feriet quodcumque minabitur arcus.   350
verum ubi plura nitent in carmine, non ego paucis
offendar maculis, quas aut incuria fudit
aut humana parum cavit natura. quid ergo est ?
ut scriptor si peccat idem librarius usque,
quamvis est monitus, venia caret, et[5] citharoedus 355
ridetur, chorda qui semper oberrat[6] eadem :

---

   [1] speramus, *II.*   [2] nec *BC.*   [3] volet, *II.*
  [4] aere *C, II (but not π).*   [5] ut.   [6] oberret *aM.*

---

   [a] Lamia was " a bugbear of the Greek nursery."
   [b] An ancient classification of the citizens into *seniores*
and *iuniores* is here referred to. The former were between
the ages of forty-six and sixty. The terms Ramnes, Tities,
and Luceres were applied to the three centuries of *equites*

gain has stained the soul, can we hope for poems to
be fashioned, worthy to be smeared with cedar-oil,
and kept in polished cypress ?

333 Poets aim either to benefit, or to amuse, or to
utter words at once both pleasing and helpful to life.
Whenever you instruct, be brief, so that what is
quickly said the mind may readily grasp and faith-
fully hold : every word in excess flows away from
the full mind. Fictions meant to please should be
close to the real, so that your play must not ask for
belief in anything it chooses, nor from the Ogress's [a]
belly, after dinner, draw forth a living child. The
centuries of the elders chase from the stage what
is profitless ; the proud Ramnes disdain poems [b]
devoid of charms. He has won every vote who has
blended profit and pleasure, at once delighting and
instructing the reader. That is the book to make
money for the Sosii [c] ; this the one to cross the sea
and extend to a distant day its author's fame.

347 Yet faults there are which we can gladly
pardon ; for the string does not always yield the
sound which hand and heart intend, but when you
call for a flat often returns you a sharp ; nor will
the bow always hit whatever mark it threatens.
But when the beauties in a poem are more in number,
I shall not take offence at a few blots which a careless
hand has let drop, or human frailty has failed to
avert. What, then, is the truth ? As a copying
clerk is without excuse if, however much warned, he
always makes the same mistake, and a harper is
laughed at who always blunders on the same string :

formed by Romulus, so that " Ramnes " is here used for
the young aristocrats.

   [c] For the Sosii, famous booksellers, cf. Epist. i. 20. 2.

HORACE

sic mihi, qui multum cessat, fit Choerilus ille,
quem bis terve[1] bonum cum risu miror ; et idem
indignor quandoque bonus dormitat Homerus,
verum operi[2] longo fas est obrepere somnum.   360
   Ut pictura poesis : erit quae, si propius stes,
te capiat magis, et quaedam, si longius abstes.
haec amat obscurum, volet haec sub luce videri,
iudicis argutum quae non formidat acumen ;
haec placuit semel, haec deciens repetita placebit. 365
   O maior iuvenum, quamvis et voce paterna
fingeris ad rectum et per te sapis, hoc tibi dictum
tolle memor, certis medium et tolerabile rebus
recte concedi.   consultus iuris et actor
causarum mediocris abest virtute diserti   370
Messallae, nec scit[3] quantum Cascellius Aulus,
sed tamen in pretio est : mediocribus esse poetis
non homines, non di, non concessere columnae.
ut gratas inter mensas symphonia discors   374
et crassum unguentum et Sardo cum melle papaver
offendunt, poterat duci quia cena sine istis :
sic animis natum inventumque poema iuvandis,
si paulum summo decessit, vergit[4] ad imum.
ludere qui nescit, campestribus abstinet armis,
indoctusque pilae discive trochive quiescit,   380
ne spissae risum tollant impune coronae :
qui nescit versus tamen audet fingere.   quidni ?
liber et ingenuus, praesertim census equestrem
summam nummorum vitioque remotus ab omni.

---

  [1] terque *aCM*.   [2] opere δ: opere in *aM*.
  [3] nec scit *VB*: nescit *aCM*.   [4] pergit *BC*.

---

  [a] *Dormitat* = ἀπονυστάξει. *Cf.* ἐν ἐπιστολῇ γράψας . . .
ἀπονυστάξειν τὸν Δημοσθένην (Plutarch, *Cicero*, 24).
  [b] Poppy-seeds, when roasted and served with honey, were
considered a delicacy, but were spoilt if the honey had a
bitter flavour.

so the poet who often defaults, becomes, methinks, another Choerilus, whose one or two good lines cause laughter and surprise; and yet I also feel aggrieved, whenever good Homer "nods," [a] but when a work is long, a drowsy mood may well creep over it.

361 A poem is like a picture: one strikes your fancy more, the nearer you stand; another, the farther away. This courts the shade, that will wish to be seen in the light, and dreads not the critic insight of the judge. This pleased but once; that, though ten times called for, will always please.

366 O you elder youth, though wise yourself and trained to right judgement by a father's voice, take to heart and remember this saying, that only some things rightly brook the medium and the bearable. A lawyer and pleader of middling rank falls short of the merit of eloquent Messalla, and knows not as much as Aulus Cascellius, yet he has a value. But that poets be of middling rank, neither men nor gods nor booksellers ever brooked. As at pleasant banquets an orchestra out of tune, an unguent that is thick, and poppy-seeds served with Sardinian honey, [b] give offence, because the feast might have gone on without them: so a poem, whose birth and creation are for the soul's delight, if in aught it falls short of the top, sinks to the bottom. He who cannot play a game, shuns the weapons of the Campus, [c] and, if unskilled in ball or quoit or hoop, remains aloof, lest the crowded circle break out in righteous laughter. Yet the man who knows not how dares to frame verses. Why not? He is free, even free-born, nay, is rated at the fortune of a knight, and stands clear from every blemish.

[a] The Campus Martius in Rome.

Tu nihil invita dices faciesve[1] Minerva ; 385
id tibi iudicium est, ea mens. si quid tamen olim
scripseris, in Maeci descendat iudicis auris
et patris et nostras, nonumque prematur in annum,
membranis intus positis : delere licebit
quod non edideris ; nescit vox missa reverti. 390
   Silvestris homines sacer interpresque deorum
caedibus et victu foedo deterruit Orpheus,
dictus ob hoc lenire tigris rabidosque[2] leones.
dictus et Amphion, Thebanae conditor urbis,[3]
saxa movere sono testudinis et prece blanda 395
ducere quo vellet. fuit haec sapientia quondam,
publica privatis secernere, sacra profanis,
concubitu prohibere vago, dare iura maritis,
oppida moliri, leges incidere ligno.
sic honor et nomen divinis vatibus atque 400
carminibus venit. post hos insignis Homerus
Tyrtaeusque mares animos in Martia bella
versibus exacuit ; dictae per carmina sortes,
et vitae monstrata via est, et gratia regum
Pieriis temptata modis, ludusque repertus 405
et longorum operum finis : ne forte pudori
sit tibi Musa lyrae sollers et cantor Apollo.

----

[1] faciesque *aM*.   [2] rapidos *aCM, II.*   [3] arcis *aM*.

----

[a] The phrase *invita Minerva* is explained by Cicero,
De off. i. 31. 10, as meaning *adversante et repugnante
natura* ; *cf.* "crassa Minerva," *Sat.* ii. 2. 3.
  [b] *Cf. Sat.* i. 10. 38.   [c] *Cf. Epist.* i. 20. 6.
  [d] The laws of Solon were published thus.
  [e] The first poets were inspired teachers.
  [f] Tyrtaeus, who according to tradition was a lame Attic
schoolmaster, composed marching-songs and martial elegies
for the Spartans in the seventh century B.C.

385 But *you* will say nothing and do nothing against Minerva's will [a]; such is your judgement, such your good sense. Yet if ever you do write anything, let it enter the ears of some critical Maecius,[b] and your father's, and my own ; then put your parchment in the closet and keep it back till the ninth year. What you have not published you can destroy ; the word once sent forth can never come back.[c]

391 While men still roamed the woods, Orpheus, the holy prophet of the gods, made them shrink from bloodshed and brutal living; hence the fable that he tamed tigers and ravening lions ; hence too the fable that Amphion, builder of Thebes's citadel, moved stones by the sound of his lyre, and led them whither he would by his supplicating spell. In days of yore, this was wisdom, to draw a line between public and private rights, between things sacred and things common, to check vagrant union, to give rules for wedded life, to build towns, and grave laws on tables of wood[d] ; and so honour and fame fell to bards and their songs, as divine.[e] After these Homer won his renown, and Tyrtaeus[f] with his verses fired manly hearts for battles of Mars. In song oracles were given, and the way of life was shown[g] ; the favour of kings was sought in Pierian strains,[h] and mirth was found to close toil's long spell.[i] So you need not blush for the Muse skilled in the lyre, and for Apollo, god of song.

[g] In didactic poetry such as Hesiod's, and gnomic poetry such as Solon's.

[h] A reference to Pindar, Simonides, and Bacchylides.

[i] The *ludus* is such festal mirth as was exhibited in the dramatic performances of the Dionysia. *Cf. Epist.* ii. 1. 139 ff.

483

Natura fieret laudabile carmen an arte,
quaesitum est : ego nec studium sine divite vena,
nec rude quid prosit[1] video ingenium : alterius sic 410
altera poscit opem res et coniurat amice.
qui studet optatam cursu contingere metam,
multa tulit fecitque puer, sudavit et alsit,
abstinuit Venere et vino ; qui Pythia cantat
tibicen, didicit prius extimuitque magistrum.   415
nunc[2] satis est[3] dixisse : "ego mira poemata pango ;
occupet extremum scabies ; mihi turpe relinqui est
et quod non didici sane nescire fateri."

Ut praeco, ad merces turbam qui cogit emendas,
adsentatores iubet ad lucrum ire poeta   420
dives agris,[4] dives positis in faenore nummis.
si[5] vero est, unctum qui recte ponere possit
et spondere levi pro paupere et eripere atris[6]
litibus implicitum, mirabor, si sciet inter-
noscere mendacem verumque beatus amicum.   425
tu seu donaris seu quid donare voles cui,[7]
nolito ad versus tibi factos ducere plenum
laetitiae : clamabit enim " pulchre ! bene ! recte ! "
pallescet super his, etiam stillabit amicis
ex oculis rorem, saliet, tundet pede terram.   430
ut qui conducti plorant in funere dicunt
et faciunt prope plura dolentibus ex animo, sic
derisor vero plus laudatore movetur.
reges dicuntur multis urgere cullullis

---

[1] possit.   [2] nec.   [3] et *BC*.   [4] agri *BC*.
[5] sin λπ.   [6] artis: *so Bentley.*   [7] qui *B* : quoi *V*.

---

[a] An allusion to a game of tag, in which the children cried:
  hábeat scabiem quísquis ad me vénerit novíssimus.

Horace means that people play at poetry like children. *Cf.*
Ep. i. 1. 59.

⁴⁰⁸ Often it is asked whether a praiseworthy poem be due to Nature or to art. For my part, I do not see of what avail is either study, when not enriched by Nature's vein, or native wit, if untrained; so truly does each claim the other's aid, and make with it a friendly league. He who in the race-course craves to reach the longed-for goal, has borne much and done much as a boy, has sweated and shivered, has kept aloof from wine and women. The flautist who plays at the Pythian games, has first learned his lessons and been in awe of a master. To-day 'tis enough to say: " I fashion wondrous poems: the devil take the hindmost! ᵃ 'Tis unseemly for me to be left behind, and to confess that I really do not know what I have never learned."

⁴¹⁹ Like the crier, who gathers a crowd to the auction of his wares, so the poet bids flatterers flock to the call of gain, if he is rich in lands, and rich in moneys put out at interest. But if he be one who can fitly serve a dainty dinner, and be surety for a poor man of little credit, or can rescue one entangled in gloomy suits-at-law, I shall wonder if the happy fellow will be able to distinguish between a false and a true friend. And you, if you have given or mean to give a present to anyone, do not bring him, in the fulness of his joy, to hear verses you have written. For he will call out " Fine! good! perfect! " He will change colour over them; he will even distil the dew from his friendly eyes, he will dance and thump the ground with his foot. As hired mourners at a funeral say and do almost more than those who grieve at heart, so the man who mocks is more moved than the true admirer. Kings, we are told, ply with many a bumper and test with

et torquere mero, quem perspexisse laborent,[1]   435
an sit amicitia dignus : si carmina condes,
numquam te fallent[2] animi sub volpe latentes.

Quintilio si quid recitares, " corrige, sodes,
hoc," aiebat, " et hoc."   melius te posse negares
bis terque expertum frustra, delere iubebat   440
et male tornatos[3] incudi reddere versus.
si defendere delictum quam vertere malles,
nullum ultra verbum aut operam insumebat inanem,
quin sine rivali teque et tua solus amares.

vir bonus et prudens versus reprehendet inertis,   445
culpabit duros, incomptis allinet atrum
transverso calamo signum, ambitiosa recidet
ornamenta, parum claris lucem dare coget,
arguet ambigue dictum, mutanda notabit,
fiet Aristarchus ; nec[4] dicet: "cur ego amicum   450
offendam in nugis ? "   hae nugae seria ducent
in mala derisum semel exceptumque sinistre.

Ut mala quem scabies aut morbus regius urget
aut fanaticus error et iracunda Diana,
vesanum tetigisse timent fugientque[5] poëtam   455
qui sapiunt ; agitant pueri incautique sequuntur.
hic, dum sublimis versus ructatur et errat,

---

[1] laborant, *II (not φ)*.   [2] fallant *φψδ*.
[3] torquatos *E* : ter natos *Bentley*.   [4] non, *II*.
[5] fugientque *aE* : fugentque *M* : fugiuntque *K*.

---

[a] In one of Aesop's fables, the crow, yielding to the fox's flattery, drops the cheese he has found.
[b] *i.e.* Quintilius Varus, whose death is lamented in *Odes*, i. 24.
[c] The name of Aristarchus, famous as an Homeric scholar of Alexandria in the second century B.C., had become proverbial as that of a keen critic.

wine the man they are anxious to see through, whether he be worthy of their friendship. If you mean to fashion verses, never let the intent that lurks beneath the fox ensnare you.[a]

435 If you ever read aught to Quintilius,[b] he would say : " Pray correct this and this." If, after two or three vain trials, you said you could not do better, he would bid you blot it out, and return the ill-shaped verses to the anvil. If you preferred defending your mistake to amending it, he would waste not a word more, would spend no fruitless toil, to prevent your loving yourself and your work alone without a rival. An honest and sensible man will censure lifeless lines, he will find fault with harsh ones ; if they are graceless, he will draw his pen across and smear them with a black stroke ; he will cut away pretentious ornament ; he will force you to flood the obscure with light, will convict the doubtful phrase, will mark what should be changed, will prove an Aristarchus.[c] He will not say, " Why should I give offence to a friend about trifles ? " These trifles will bring that friend into serious trouble, if once he has been laughed down and given an unlucky reception.

453 As when the accursed itch plagues a man, or the disease of kings,[d] or a fit of frenzy and Diana's wrath,[e] so men of sense fear to touch a crazy poet and run away ; children tease and pursue him rashly. He, with head upraised, splutters verses and off he strays ;

[d] The *morbus regius*, said to be so called because the patient was treated with costly remedies, which only the rich (*reges*) could afford, was our jaundice and was supposed to be contagious.

[e] " Lunacy " was supposed to be caused by the moon, and the moon-goddess was Diana.

si[1] veluti merulis intentus decidit auceps
in puteum foveamve, licet " succurrite " longum
clamet " io cives ! " non sit qui tollere curet.   460
si curet quis opem ferre et demittere[2] funem,
" qui scis, an prudens huc se deiecerit[3] atque
servari nolit ? " dicam, Siculique poetae
narrabo interitum.   deus immortalis haberi
dum cupit Empedocles, ardentem frigidus Aetnam
insiluit.   sit ius liceatque perire poetis :   466
invitum qui servat, idem facit occidenti.
nec semel hoc fecit, nec, si retractus erit, iam
fiet homo et ponet famosae mortis amorem.
nec satis apparet, cur versus factitet, utrum   470
minxerit in patrios cineres, an triste bidental
moverit incestus : certe furit, ac velut ursus,
obiectos[4] caveae valuit si frangere clatros,
indoctum doctumque fugat recitator acerbus ;
quem vero arripuit, tenet occiditque legendo,   475
non missura cutem, nisi plena cruoris, hirudo.

[1] si <i>Kδ</i>: sic <i>aEM</i>.   [2] dimittere <i>most MSS.</i>
[3] proiecerit, <i>II.</i>   [4] obiectas <i>E.</i>

---

   [a] So Thales is said to have fallen into a well while studying
the stars (Plato, <i>Theaetetus</i>, 174 A).

then if, like a fowler with his eyes upon blackbirds, he fall into a well [a] or pit, despite his far-reaching cry, " Help, O fellow-citizens ! " not a soul will care to pull him out. And if one should care to lend aid and let down a rope, " How do you know," I'll say, " but that he threw himself in on purpose, and does not wish to be saved ? " and I'll tell the tale of the Sicilian poet's end. Empedocles, eager to be thought a god immortal, coolly leapt into burning Aetna. Let poets have the right and power to destroy themselves. Who saves a man against his will does the same as murder him. Not for the first time has he done this, nor if he is pulled out will he at once become a human being and lay aside his craving for a notable death. Nor is it very clear how he comes to be a verse-monger. Has he defiled ancestral ashes or in sacrilege disturbed a hallowed plot [b] ? At any rate he is mad, and, like a bear, if he has had strength to break the confining bars of his cage, he puts learned and unlearned alike to flight by the scourge of his recitals. If he catches a man, he holds him fast and reads him to death—a leech that will not let go the skin, till gorged with blood.

[b] The *bidental* was a spot struck by lightning, which was consecrated by a sacrifice of sheep (*bidentes*).

INDEX OF PROPER NAMES

The references are to books and lines in the Latin text. Abbreviations:
A.P. = *Ars Poetica*; *E.* = *Epistles*; *S.* = *Satires* or *Sermones*; also *adj.* =
adjective; *al.* = alius; *fem.* = feminine; *plur.* = plural; *sing.* = singular;
subst. = substantive.

ACADEMUS, an old Athenian hero. In a garden dedicated to him and called Academia, Plato and his successors taught. *E.* ii. 2. 45

Accius, Roman tragic poet, born 170 B.C., *S.* i. 10. 53; *E.* ii. 1. 56; *A.P.* 258

Achilles, hero of the *Iliad*, *S.* i. 7. 12; ii. 3. 193; *E.* ii. 2. 42; *A.P.* 120. See Pelides

Achivi, the Greeks, *S.* ii. 3. 194; *E.* i. 2. 14; ii. 1. 33

Actius, *adj.*, of Actium, promontory and town of Greece on the Ambracian Gulf, where Octavius defeated Antony in 31 B.C., *E.* i. 18. 61

Aegaeus, *adj.*, Aegean, applied to the sea between Greece and Asia Minor, *E.* i. 11. 16

Aemilius, *adj.*, of Aemilius (Lepidus), who, according to Porphyrio, set up a gladiatorial school, *A.P.* 32

Aeneas, the Trojan hero, son of Anchises and Venus, *S.* ii. 5. 63

Aeschylus, Greek tragic poet, *E.* ii. 1. 163; *A.P.* 279

Aesopus, Roman tragic actor, *S.* ii. 3. 239; *E.* ii. 1. 82

Aetna, the famous Mt. Etna in Sicily, *A.P.* 465

Aetolus, *adj.*, of Aetolia, in central Greece, *E.* i. 18. 46

Afer, *adj.*, African, *S.* ii. 4. 58; ii. 8. 95

Afranius, a writer of comedies with a Roman setting, known as *togatae*, *E.* ii. 1. 57

Africa, *i.e.* Africa Provincia, the Roman province of Africa, *S.* ii. 3. 87

Agave, daughter of Cadmus, wife of Echion, king of Thebes, who in the madness of Bacchic rites tore her son Pentheus to pieces, *S.* ii. 3. 203

Agrippa, *i.e.* M. Vipsanius Agrippa, son-in-law of Augustus, aedile in 33 B.C., *S.* ii. 3. 185; erected the Portico of Neptune in 27 B.C., *E.* i. 6. 26; had estates in Sicily, *E.* 1. 12. 1; conquered the Cantabri in 20-19 B.C., *E.* i. 12. 26

Aiax, Greek hero, son of Telamon, and brother of Teucer. In his tragedy, the *Ajax*, Sophocles represents Menelaus as forbidding Teucer to bury the dead hero, *S.* ii. 3. 187, 193, 201, 211

Albanus, *adj.*, Alban, associated with the Alban hills, or the Alban Mount (now Monte Cavo) near Rome, *S.* ii. 4. 72; *E.* i. 7. 10; ii. 1. 27

Albinovanus, *i.e.* Celsus Albinovanus, *E.* i. 8. 1. See Celsus

Albinus, probably a usurer, *A.P.* 327

Albius, (1) a man of expensive tastes, *S.* i. 4. 28, 109; (2) the poet, Albius Tibullus, *E.* i. 4. 1, possibly son of (1)

Albucius, a name from Lucilius, *S.* ii. 1. 48; ii. 2. 67

491

INDEX OF PROPER NAMES

Alcaeus, Lesbian poet, *E.* i. 19. 29; ii. 2. 99

Alcinous, king of Phaeacia and host of Ulysses, *E.* i. 2. 28

Alcon, a Greek slave, *S.* ii. 8. 15

Alexander, *i.e.* Alexander the Great, king of Macedon, *E.* ii. 1. 232, 241

Alfenus, a barber, who is said to have become eminent in the law, *S.* i. 3. 130

Allifanus, *adj.*, of Allifae, a town of Samnium, known for its pottery, *S.* ii. 8. 39

Alpes, the Alps, *S.* ii. 5. 41

Alpinus, properly an *adj.*, of the Alps, a nickname given to M. Furius Bibaculus, who wrote an *Aethiopis* and a poem on Gaul, *S.* i. 10. 36. See also Furius

Amphion, son of Jupiter and Antiope, mother of Zethus, and famous player on the lyre. The citadel of Thebes was built to the accompaniment of his music. *E.* i. 18. 41, 44; *A.P.* 394. See Zethus

Ancus, Ancus Marcius, fourth king of Rome, *E.* i. 6. 27

Antenor, a Trojan chief, who proposed to restore Helen to the Greeks, *E.* i. 2. 9

Anticyra, a town in Phocis on the Corinthian gulf, famous for its hellebore, *S.* ii. 3. 83, 166, *A.P.* 300

Antiphates, king of the Laestrygones (Homer, *Od.* x. 100 f.), *A.P.* 145

Antonius, (1) Marcus Antonius, the triumvir, *S.* i. 5. 33; (2) Antonius Musa, a freedman and physician, who cured Augustus by cold-water treatment, *E.* i. 15. 3

Anxur, the old name of Terracina, originally built at the top of a hill, but later rebuilt on the plain below, *S.* i. 5. 26

Anytus, one of the accusers of Socrates, *S.* ii. 4. 3

Apella, a Jewish freedman, *S.* i. 5. 100

Apelles, a famous Greek painter, *E.* ii. 1. 239

Apollo, the god, *S.* i. 9. 78; ii. 5.

60; *E.* i. 3. 17; i. 16. 59; ii. 1. 216; *A.P.* 407

Appia (Via), Appian Way, *S.* i. 5. 6

Appius, *i.e.* Appius Claudius Caecus, who in 312 B.C. built the Appian Way and Aqueduct, *E.* i. 6. 26; i. 18. 20. The Forum Appi, 43 miles south of Rome, was also named from him, *S.* i. 53. The Appius mentioned in *S.* i. 6. 21 is perhaps Appius Claudius Pulcher, who was censor in 50 B.C.

Apulia, a district of Italy, *S.* i. 5. 77

Apulus, *adj.*, of Apulia, *S.* ii. 1. 34, 38

Aquarius, the water-bearer, a sign of the Zodiac, *S.* i. 1. 36

Aquilo, the north wind, or the North, *S.* ii. 6. 25; ii. 8. 56; *A.P.* 64

Aquinas, *adj.*, of Aquinum, a town of Latium, *E.* i. 10. 27

Arabs, an Arab, *E.* i. 6. 6; i. 7. 36

Arbuscula, an actress or *mima*, celebrated in Cicero's time (*Ad Att.* iv. 15), *S.* i. 10. 77

Archiacus, *adj.*, of Archias, a maker of furniture, *E.* i. 5. 1

Archilochus, Greek iambic poet, flourished about 650 B.C., *S.* ii. 3. 12; *E.* i. 19. 25, 28; *A.P.* 79

Arellius, a rich neighbour of Horace, *S.* ii. 6. 78

Argi, city of Argos, in the Peloponnesus, often representative of Greece in general, *S.* ii. 3. 132; *E.* ii. 2. 128; *A.P.* 118

Aricia, a town sixteen miles south of Rome, *S.* i. 5. 1

Aricinus, *adj.*, of Aricia, *E.* ii. 2. 167

Aristarchus, a great Homeric critic, flourished at Alexandria about 180 B.C.; *A.P.* 450

Aristippus, founder of the Cyrenaic school of philosophy, *S.* ii. 3. 100; *E.* i. 1. 18; i. 17. 14, 23

Aristius Fuscus, a friend of Horace, *S.* i. 9. 61; i. 10. 83; *E.* i. 10. 1

Aristophanes, the most famous of Attic writers of comedy, *S.* i. 4. 1

Armenius, *adj.*, Armenian, *E.* i. 12. 27

Arrius, whose praenomen was Quintus, and who gave a great funeral

492

INDEX OF PROPER NAMES

493

INDEX OF PROPER NAMES

INDEX OF PROPER NAMES

INDEX OF PROPER NAMES

INDEX OF PROPER NAMES

a human head, but the body of a bird, *S.* ii. 2. 40

Hebrus, a river of Thrace, now Maritza, *E.* i. 3. 3 ; i. 16. 13

Hecate, a goddess of the lower world, and sister of Latona, identified with Diana on earth and Luna in heaven, and therefore represented with three heads, *S.* i. 8. 33

Hector, eldest son of Priam, chief hero of Troy, slain by Achilles, *S.* i. 7. 12

Helena, wife of Menelaus, carried off by Paris to Troy, *S.* i. 3. 107

Helicon, famous mountain in Boeotia, abode of the Muses, *E.* ii. 1. 118 ; *A.P.* 296

Heliodorus, a rhetorician, known only from *S.* i. 5. 2. See p. 63

Hellas, a girl murdered by her lover Marius, *S.* ii. 3. 277

Hercules, son of Jupiter and Alcmena, renowned for his "Labours," *E.* i. 1. 5 ; sometimes, like Mercury, regarded as a god of gain, *S.* ii. 6. 13

Hermogenes Tigellius, a singer and poet despised by Horace, *S.* i. 3. 129 ; i. 4. 72 ; i. 9. 25 ; i. 10. 18, 80, 90. See Tigellius and p. 54, note *b*

Herodes, *i.e.* Herod the Great, who derived a large revenue from the palm-groves of Judaea, especially about Jericho, *E.* ii. 2. 184

Hiberus, *adj.*, Iberian, Spanish, The *piscis Hiberus* was the scomber or mackerel, *S.* ii. 8. 46

Homerus, the Greek epic poet ; *S.* i. 10. 52 ; *E.* i. 19. 6 ; ii. 1. 50 ; *A.P.* 74, 359, 401 (*cf. E.* i. 2. 1)

Horatius, *i.e.* Quintus Horatius Flaccus, the poet, *E.* i. 14. 5. See Flaccus and Quintus

Hydaspes, an Indian slave, named from the river Hydaspes, now Djelun, *S.* ii. 8. 14

Hydra, a seven-headed snake, killed by Hercules, *E.* ii. 1. 10

Hymettius, *adj.*, of Hymettus, a mountain of Attica, *S.* ii. 2. 15

Hypsaea, a blind woman, who is said to have also had the name Plotia or Plautia, *S.* i. 2. 91

Ianus, a two-faced Italian deity, god of beginnings, entrances, and undertakings, whose temple, said to have been built originally by Numa, stood in the Argiletum, north of the Roman Forum. It was opened on the declaration of war, but kept closed in time of peace. *S.* ii. 6. 20 ; *E.* i. 16. 59 ; i. 20. 1 ; ii. 1. 255. Certain arches in the Forum itself also went by the name of *Ianus*, and were the centre of the banking business of Rome, *S.* ii. 3. 18 ; *E.* i. 1. 54

Iarbita, a Moor, *E.* i. 19. 15

Iccius, a friend of Horace, procurator of Agrippa's estates in Sicily, *E.* i. 12. 1 (*cf. Odes* i. 29)

Idus, the Ides, the middle of the Roman month, the fifteenth day in March, May, July, October ; the thirteenth in the other months, *S.* i. 6. 75

Ilerda, a town in Spain, now Lerida, *E.* i. 20. 13

Ilia, mother of Romulus and Remus, *S.* i. 2. 126

Iliacus, *adj.*, of Ilion, Trojan ; *E.* i. 2. 16 ; *A.P.* 129

Iliona or Ilione, eldest daughter of Priam, wife of Polymnestor, king of Thrace, whose son Deiphilus was killed by his father. This furnished the subject of the tragedy *Ilione* by Pacuvius. *S.* ii. 3. 61

Indi, inhabitants of India, *E.* i. 1. 45 ; i. 6. 6

Ino, daughter of Cadmus and wife of Athamas, who, after her husband went mad and tore one of her children to pieces, was changed into a sea-goddess, *A.P.* 123

Io, daughter of Inachus, loved by Jupiter and changed by Juno into a heifer, *A.P.* 124

Italia, Italy, *S.* i. 6. 35 ; *E.* i. 12. 29

Italus, *adj.*, Italian, *S.* i. 7. 32 ; ii. 6. 56 ; *E.* i. 18. 57 ; ii. 1. 2

Ithaca, Ithaca, an island off the west coast of Greece, *S.* ii. 5. 4 ; *E.* i. 7. 41

498

INDEX OF PROPER NAMES

499

INDEX OF PROPER NAMES

INDEX OF PROPER NAMES

was a freedman, and took the Roman gentile name *Volteius* from his patron. *E.* i. 7. 55, 61. See Volteius

Menander, famous writer of the New Attic Comedy, lived from 342 to 290 B.C., *S.* ii. 3. 11; *E.* ii. 1. 57

Menelaus, son of Atreus, brother of Agamemnon, and husband of Helen, *S.* ii. 3. 198. See Atrides

Menenius, a madman, *S.* ii. 3. 287

Mercurialis, *adj.*, of Mercury, the god of gain, *S.* ii. 3. 25

Mercurius, Mercury, son of Jupiter and Maia, and messenger of the gods, god of gain and good luck, *S.* ii. 3. 68 (*cf.* ii. 6. 5)

Messalla, a name associated with the aristocratic Valerian gens. M. Valerius Messalla Corvinus, orator and historian, was consul in 31 B.C., and triumphed over the Aquitani in 27 B.C. He had a brother, L. Gellius Publicola, who was consul in 36 B.C. *S.* i. 6. 42; i. 10. 85; *A.P.* 371

Messius, *S.* i. 5. 52, 54. See Cicirrhus

Metella, perhaps Caecilia Metella, divorced wife of P. Cornelius Lentulus Spinther, *S.* ii. 3. 239

Metellus, *i.e.* Q. Caecilius Metellus Macedonicus, consul 143 B.C., political opponent of Scipio, *S.* ii. 1. 67

Methymnaeus, *adj.*, of Methymna, a town in Lesbos, *S.* ii. 8. 50

Miletus, a city of Ionia in Asia Minor, *E.* i. 17. 30

Milonius, according to Porphyrio, a *scurra* or parasite, *S.* ii. 1. 24

Mimnermus, an elegiac poet of Colophon, of the sixth century B.C., *E.* i. 6. 65; ii. 2. 101

Minerva, goddess of wisdom, patroness of arts and science, *S.* ii. 2. 3; *A.P.* 385

Minturnae, a town on the borders of Latium and Campania, at the mouth of the Liris, *E.* i. 5. 5

Minucius, who gave his name to the *Via Minucia*, which ran from Brundisium to Beneventum, *E.* i. 18. 20

Misenum, a promontory of Campania, north of the bay of Naples, *S.* ii. 4. 33

Mitylene, capital of Lesbos, *E.* i. 11. 17

Molossus, *adj.*, of the Molossians, who lived in Eastern Epirus, *S.* ii. 6. 114

Moschus, a rhetorician from Pergamum, who was tried for poisoning, *E.* i. 5. 9

Mucius, a famous lawyer, probably P. Mucius Scaevola, consul in 133 B.C., or his son Q. Mucius Scaevola, consul in 95 B.C., *E.* ii. 2. 89

Mulvius, a parasite, *S.* ii. 7. 36

Munatius, son of L. Munatius Plancus, the consul of 42 B.C. (see *Odes* i. 7. 19; iii. 14. 28); *E.* i. 3. 31

Murena, *i.e.* L. Licinius Murena, brother-in-law of Maecenas, *S.* i. 5. 38

Musa, (1) a Muse, *S.* i. 5. 53; ii. 3. 105; ii. 6. 17; *E.* i. 3. 13; i. 8. 2; i. 19. 28; ii. 1. 27, 133, 243; ii. 2. 92; *A.P.* 83, 141, 324, 407; (2) Musa Antonius. See Antonius

Mutus, unknown elsewhere, *E.* i. 6. 22

Naevius, (1) a spendthrift, *S.* i. 1. 101; *S.* ii. 2. 68 (perhaps not the same); (2) a poet from Campania of the third century B.C. (he wrote dramas and also an epic, the *Bellum Punicum*, this last in Saturnian verse), *E.* ii. 1. 53

Nasica, a man who, being in debt to Coranus, gave him his daughter in marriage, *S.* ii. 5. 57, 65, 67

Nasidienus, Rufus (probably a fictitious name), a wealthy upstart, *S.* ii. 8. 1, 58, 75, 84

Natta, a stingy person, *S.* i. 6. 124

Neptunus, Neptune, god of the sea, *E.* i. 11. 10; *A.P.* 64

Nero, *i.e.* Tiberius Claudius Nero, *E.* i. 8. 2; i. 9. 4; i. 12. 26; ii. 2. 1. See Claudius

Nestor, son of Neleus, king of Pylus, oldest of the Greeks before Troy, *E.* i. 2. 11

501

INDEX OF PROPER NAMES

INDEX OF PROPER NAMES

INDEX OF PROPER NAMES

INDEX OF PROPER NAMES

INDEX OF PROPER NAMES

507

INDEX OF PROPER NAMES

INDEX OF PROPER NAMES

Printed in Great Britain by R. & R. Clark, Limited, *Edinburgh.*

THE LOEB CLASSICAL LIBRARY

VOLUMES ALREADY PUBLISHED

LATIN AUTHORS

APULEIUS. THE GOLDEN ASS (METAMORPHO-SES). Trans. by W. Adlington (1566). Revised by S. Gaselee. (*4th Impression.*)

AULUS GELLIUS. Trans. by J. C. Rolfe. 3 Vols.

AUSONIUS. Trans. by H. G. Evelyn White. 2 Vols.

BOETHIUS: TRACTS AND DE CONSOLATIONE PHILOSOPHIAE. Trans. by the Rev. H. F. Stewart and E. K. Rand. (*2nd Impression.*)

CAESAR: CIVIL WARS. Trans. by A. G. Peskett. (*3rd Impression.*)

CAESAR: GALLIC WAR. Trans. by H. J. Edwards. (*4th Impression.*)

CATULLUS. Trans. by F. W. Cornish; TIBULLUS. Trans. by J. P. Postgate; PERVIGILIUM VENERIS. Trans. by J. W. Mackail. (*8th Impression.*)

CICERO: DE FINIBUS. Trans. by H. Rackham. (*2nd Impression.*)

CICERO: DE OFFICIIS. Trans. by Walter Miller. (*3rd Impression.*)

CICERO: DE REPUBLICA AND DE LEGIBUS. Trans. by Clinton Keyes.

CICERO: DE SENECTUTE, DE AMICITIA, DE DIVINATIONE. Trans. by W. A. Falconer. (*2nd Impression.*)

CICERO: LETTERS TO ATTICUS. Trans. by E. O. Winstedt. 3 Vols. (Vol. I. *4th*, II. *3rd*, and III. *2nd Impression.*)

CICERO: LETTERS TO HIS FRIENDS. Trans. by W. Glynn Williams. 3 Vols.

CICERO: PHILIPPICS. Trans. by W. C. A. Ker.

CICERO: PRO ARCHIA POETA, POST REDITUM IN SENATU, POST REDITUM AD QUIRITES, DE DOMO SUA, DE HARUSPICUM RESPONSIS, PRO PLANCIO. Trans. by N. H. Watts.

CICERO: PRO CAECINA, PRO LEGE MANILIA, PRO CLUENTIO, PRO RABIRIO. Trans. by H. Grose Hodge.

1

CICERO: TUSCULAN DISPUTATIONS. Trans. by J. E. King.

CICERO: VERRINE ORATIONS. Trans. by L. H. G. Greenwood. 2 Vols. Vol. I.

CLAUDIAN. Trans. by M. Platnauer. 2 Vols.

CONFESSIONS OF ST. AUGUSTINE. Trans. by W. Watts (1631). 2 Vols. (Vol. I. *4th*, Vol. II. *3rd. Imp.*)

FRONTINUS: STRATAGEMS AND AQUEDUCTS. Trans. by C. E. Bennett.

FRONTO: CORRESPONDENCE. Trans. by C. R. Haines. 2 Vols.

HORACE: ODES AND EPODES. Trans. by C. E. Bennett. (*8th Impression revised.*)

HORACE: SATIRES, EPISTLES, ARS POETICA. Trans. by H. R. Fairclough. (*2nd Impression revised.*)

JUVENAL AND PERSIUS. Trans. by G. G. Ramsay. (*4th Impression.*)

LIVY. Trans. by B. O. Foster. 13 Vols. Vols. I.-IV. (Vol. I. *2nd Impression revised.*)

LUCAN. Trans. by J. D. Duff.

LUCRETIUS. Trans. by W. H. D. Rouse. (*2nd Edition.*)

MARTIAL. Trans. by W. C. A. Ker. 2 Vols. (*2nd Impression revised.*)

OVID: HEROIDES, AMORES. Trans. by Grant Showerman. (*2nd Impression.*)

OVID: METAMORPHOSES. Trans. by F. J. Miller. 2 Vols. (Vol. I. *4th Impression.* II. *3rd Impression.*)

OVID: TRISTIA AND EX PONTO. Trans. by A. L. Wheeler.

PETRONIUS. Trans. by M. Heseltine; SENECA: APO-COLOCYNTOSIS. Trans. by W. H. D. Rouse. (*4th Imp.*)

PLAUTUS. Trans. by Paul Nixon. 5 Vols. Vols. I.-III. (Vol. I. *3rd Impression.*)

PLINY: LETTERS. Melmoth's translation revised by W. M. L. Hutchinson. 2 Vols. (*3rd Impression.*)

PROPERTIUS. Trans. by H. E. Butler. (*3rd Impression.*)

QUINTILIAN. Trans. by H. E. Butler. 4 Vols.

SALLUST. Trans. by J. C. Rolfe.

SCRIPTORES HISTORIAE AUGUSTAE. Trans. by D. Magie. 3 Vols. Vols. I. and II.

SENECA: EPISTULAE MORALES. Trans. by R. M. Gummere. 3 Vols. (Vol. I. *2nd Impression.*)

THE LOEB CLASSICAL LIBRARY

SENECA : MORAL ESSAYS. Trans. by J. W. Basore.
3 Vols. Vol. I.
SENECA : TRAGEDIES. Trans. by F. J. Miller.
2 Vols. (2nd Impression revised.)
STATIUS. Trans. by J. H. Mozley. 2 Vols.
SUETONIUS. Trans. by J. C. Rolfe. 2 Vols. (Vol. I. 4th
Impression revised, Vol. II. 3rd Impression.)
TACITUS : DIALOGUS. Trans. by Sir Wm. Peterson ;
and AGRICOLA AND GERMANIA. Trans. by Maurice
Hutton. (3rd Impression.)
TACITUS : HISTORIES. Trans. by C. H. Moore. 2 Vols.
Vol. I.
TERENCE. Trans. by John Sargeaunt. 2 Vols. (5th
Impression.)
VELLEIUS PATERCULUS AND RES GESTAE DIVI
AUGUSTI. Trans. by F. W. Shipley.
VIRGIL. Trans. by H. R. Fairclough. 2 Vols. (Vol. I.
7th Impression, II. 5th Impression.)

GREEK AUTHORS

ACHILLES TATIUS. Trans. by S. Gaselee.
AENEAS TACTICUS, ASCLEPIODOTUS AND ONA-
SANDER. Trans. by The Illinois Greek Club.
AESCHINES. Trans. by C. D. Adams.
AESCHYLUS. Trans. by H. Weir Smyth. 2 Vols.
(Vol. I. 2nd Impression.)
APOLLODORUS. Trans. by Sir James G. Frazer. 2 Vols.
APOLLONIUS RHODIUS. Trans. by R. C. Seaton.
(3rd Impression.)
THE APOSTOLIC FATHERS. Trans. by Kirsopp Lake.
2 Vols. (Vol. I. 4th Impression, II. 3rd Impression.)
APPIAN'S ROMAN HISTORY. Trans. by Horace
White. 4 Vols. (Vols. I. and IV. 2nd Impression.)
ARISTOPHANES. Trans. by Benjamin Bickley Rogers.
3 Vols. (Verse translation.) (2nd Impression.)
ARISTOTLE : THE "ART" OF RHETORIC. Trans.
by J. H. Freese.
ARISTOTLE : THE NICOMACHEAN ETHICS. Trans.
by H. Rackham.

3

THE LOEB CLASSICAL LIBRARY

ARISTOTLE: THE PHYSICS. Trans. by the Rev. P. Wicksteed. 2 Vols. Vol. I.

ARISTOTLE: POETICS: "LONGINUS": ON THE SUBLIME. Trans. by W. Hamilton Fyfe, AND DEMETRIUS: ON STYLE. Trans. by W. Rhys Roberts.

ATHENAEUS: THE DEIPNOSOPHISTS. Trans. by C. B. Gulick. 7 Vols. Vols. I.–III.

CALLIMACHUS AND LYCOPHRON. Trans. by A. W. Mair, AND ARATUS, trans. by G. R. Mair.

CLEMENT OF ALEXANDRIA. Trans. by the Rev. G. W. Butterworth.

DAPHNIS AND CHLOE. Thornley's translation revised by J. M. Edmonds: AND PARTHENIUS. Trans. by S. Gaselee. (2nd Impression.)

DEMOSTHENES: DE CORONA AND DE FALSA LEGATIONE. Trans. by C. A. Vince and J. H. Vince.

DIO CASSIUS: ROMAN HISTORY. Trans. by E. Cary. 9 Vols.

DIOGENES LAERTIUS. Trans. by R. D. Hicks. 2 Vols.

EPICTETUS. Trans. by W. A. Oldfather. 2 Vols.

EURIPIDES. Trans. by A. S. Way. 4 Vols. (Verse trans.) (Vols. I. and IV. 3rd, II. 4th, III. 2nd Imp.)

EUSEBIUS: ECCLESIASTICAL HISTORY. Trans. by Kirsopp Lake. 2 Vols. Vol. I.

GALEN: ON THE NATURAL FACULTIES. Trans. by A. J. Brock. (2nd Impression.)

THE GREEK ANTHOLOGY. Trans. by W. R. Paton. 5 Vols. (Vol. I. 3rd, II. 2nd Impression.)

THE GREEK BUCOLIC POETS (THEOCRITUS, BION, MOSCHUS). Trans. by J. M. Edmonds. (5th Imp.)

HERODOTUS. Trans. by A. D. Godley. 4 Vols. (Vols. I.–III. 2nd Impression.)

HESIOD AND THE HOMERIC HYMNS. Trans. by H. G. Evelyn White. (3rd Impression.)

HIPPOCRATES. Trans. by W. H. S. Jones and E. T. Withington. 4 Vols. Vols. I.-III.

HOMER: ILIAD. Trans. by A. T. Murray. 2 Vols. (Vol. I. 2nd Impression.)

HOMER: ODYSSEY. Trans. by A. T. Murray. 2 Vols. (3rd Impression.)

ISAEUS. Trans. by E. S. Forster.

ISOCRATES. Trans. by G. Norlin. 3 Vols. Vols. I. and II.

THE LOEB CLASSICAL LIBRARY

JOSEPHUS. Trans. by H. St. J. Thackeray. 8 Vols. Vols. I.-III.

JULIAN. Trans. by Wilmer Cave Wright. 3 Vols.

LUCIAN. Trans. by A. M. Harmon. 8 Vols. Vols. I.-IV. (Vol. I. 3rd, II. 2nd Impression.)

LYRA GRAECA. Trans. by J. M. Edmonds. 3 Vols. (Vol. I. 2nd Edition revised and enlarged.)

MARCUS AURELIUS. Trans. by C. R. Haines. (2nd Impression.)

MENANDER. Trans. by F. G. Allinson.

OPPIAN, COLLUTHUS AND TRYPHIODORUS. Trans. by A. W. Mair.

PAUSANIAS: DESCRIPTION OF GREECE. Trans. by W. H. S. Jones. 5 Vols. and Companion Vol. Vols. I. and II.

PHILO. Trans. by F. M. Colson and the Rev. G. H. Whitaker. 10 Vols. Vols. I. and II.

PHILOSTRATUS: THE LIFE OF APOLLONIUS OF TYANA. Trans. by F. C. Conybeare. 2 Vols. (Vol. I. 3rd, II. 2nd Impression.)

PHILOSTRATUS AND EUNAPIUS: LIVES OF THE SOPHISTS. Trans. by Wilmer Cave Wright.

PINDAR. Trans. by Sir J. E. Sandys. (4th Impression.)

PLATO: CHARMIDES, ALCIBIADES I. and II., HIPPARCHUS, THE LOVERS, THEAGES, MINOS, EPINOMIS. Trans. by W. R. M. Lamb.

PLATO: CRATYLUS, PARMENIDES, GREATER AND LESSER HIPPIAS. Trans. by H. N. Fowler.

PLATO: EUTHYPHRO, APOLOGY, CRITO, PHAEDO, PHAEDRUS. Trans. by H. N. Fowler. (6th Impression.)

PLATO: LACHES, PROTAGORAS, MENO, EUTHY-DEMUS. Trans. by W. R. M. Lamb.

PLATO: LAWS. Trans. by Rev. R. G. Bury. 2 Vols.

PLATO: LYSIS, SYMPOSIUM, GORGIAS. Trans. by W. R. M. Lamb.

PLATO: STATESMAN, PHILEBUS. Trans. by H. N. Fowler; ION. Trans. by W. R. M. Lamb.

PLATO: THEAETETUS, SOPHIST. Trans. by H. N. Fowler. (2nd Impression.)

PLUTARCH: THE PARALLEL LIVES. Trans. by B. Perrin. 11 Vols. (Vols. I., II. and VII. 2nd Impression.)

THE LOEB CLASSICAL LIBRARY

PLUTARCH: MORALIA. Trans. by F. C. Babbitt. 14 Vols. Vols. I. and II.

POLYBIUS. Trans. by W. R. Paton. 6 Vols.

PROCOPIUS; HISTORY OF THE WARS. Trans. by H. B. Dewing. 7 Vols. Vols. I.-V.

QUINTUS SMYRNAEUS. Trans. by A. S. Way. (Verse translation.)

ST. BASIL: THE LETTERS. Trans. by R. Deferrari. 4 Vols. Vols. I. and II.

ST. JOHN DAMASCENE: BARLAAM AND IOASAPH. Trans. by the Rev. G. R. Woodward and Harold Mattingly.

SOPHOCLES. Trans. by F. Storr. 2 Vols. (Verse translation.) (Vol. I. *5th Impression*, II. *3rd Impression*.)

STRABO: GEOGRAPHY. Trans. by Horace L. Jones. 8 Vols. Vols. I.-VI.

THEOPHRASTUS: THE CHARACTERS. Trans. by J. M. Edmonds; HERODES, CERCIDAS AND THE GREEK CHOLIAMBIC POETS. Trans. by A. D. Knox.

THEOPHRASTUS: ENQUIRY INTO PLANTS. Trans. by Sir Arthur Hort, Bart. 2 Vols.

THUCYDIDES. Trans. by C. F. Smith. 4 Vols. (Vol. I. *2nd Impression revised*.)

XENOPHON: CYROPAEDIA. Trans. by Walter Miller. 2 Vols. (Vol. I. *2nd Impression*.)

XENOPHON: HELLENICA, ANABASIS, APOLOGY, AND SYMPOSIUM. Trans. by C. L. Brownson and O. J. Todd. 3 Vols.

XENOPHON: MEMORABILIA AND OECONOMICUS. Trans. by E. C. Marchant.

XENOPHON: SCRIPTA MINORA. Trans. by E. C. Marchant.

THE LOEB CLASSICAL LIBRARY

VOLUMES IN PREPARATION

THE LOEB CLASSICAL LIBRARY

LATIN AUTHORS

AMMIANUS MARCELLINUS, J. C. Rolfe.

BEDE: ECCLESIASTICAL HISTORY, J. E. King.

CICERO: CATILINE ORATIONS, B. L. Ullman.

CICERO: DE NATURA DEORUM, H. Rackham.

CICERO: DE ORATORE, ORATOR, BRUTUS, Charles Stuttaford.

CICERO: IN PISONEM, PRO SCAURO, PRO FONTEIO, PRO MILONE, PRO RABIRIO POSTUMO, PRO MARCELLO, PRO LIGARIO, PRO REGE DEIOTARO, N. H. Watts.

CICERO: PRO QUINCTIO, PRO ROSCIO AMERINO, PRO ROSCIO COMOEDO, CONTRA RULLUM, J. H. Freese.

CICERO: PRO SEXTIO, IN VATINIUM, PRO CAELIO, PRO PROVINCIIS CONSULARIBUS, PRO BALBO, D. Morrah.

CORNELIUS NEPOS, J. C. Rolfe.

ENNIUS, LUCILIUS, AND OTHER SPECIMENS OF OLD LATIN, E. H. Warmington.

FLORUS, E. S. Forster.

MINUCIUS FELIX, W. C. A. Ker.

OVID: ARS AMATORIA, REMEDIA AMORIS, ETC., J. H. Mozley.

OVID: FASTI, Sir J. G. Frazer.

PLINY: NATURAL HISTORY, W. H. S. Jones and L. F. Newman.

ST. AUGUSTINE: MINOR WORKS.

ST. JEROME'S LETTERS: F. A. Wright.

SIDONIUS, E. V. Arnold and W. B. Anderson.

TACITUS: ANNALS, John Jackson.

TERTULLIAN: APOLOGY, T. R. Glover.

VALERIUS FLACCUS, A. F. Scholfield.

VITRUVIUS: DE ARCHITECTURA, F. Granger.

DESCRIPTIVE PROSPECTUS ON APPLICATION

London   . .   WILLIAM HEINEMANN LTD

New York   . .   G. P. PUTNAM'S SONS